RENEGADE

RENEGADE

MARJORIE QUARTON

ANDRE DEUTSCH

First published 1991 by
André Deutsch Limited
105–106 Great Russell Street, London WC1B 3LJ

ISBN 0 233 98722 3

Printed in Great Britain by
St Edmundsbury Press, Bury St Edmunds, Suffolk

For Claire

Author's Note

Henry Fulton, born in 1765, was an Irish clergyman who became committed to the United Irish movement. His activities were discovered, and he was transported to Botany Bay in 1799. Because he was once Vicar of Monsea in Tipperary – a living which belonged to the Crannagh estate which has always been my home – a descendant of his, Clive Fulton, visited me in the summer of 1985, seeking information about his ancestor. I could give him none; but I was so intrigued by what he told me of Henry's story that I began to do research on it.

Little can be found about Henry Fulton's life before he was arrested; indeed, it seems that someone has been at pains to remove information from the records. It would not be surprising if his family was instrumental in such suppression, since they would have felt his conduct to be deeply disgraceful. Because information was so sparse I decided to abandon my first idea, which was to write Henry's biography, and instead to use the scraps I had discovered by weaving them into a work of fiction. There is a note at the end of the book for those who wish to know how much of the story is based on documents.

Renegade is a novel, so although I did much reading and consultation while writing it, I feel that a bibliography and a list of acknowledgements – which would be enormously long it if included everyone who helped and encouraged me in so many ways – would be out of place. I am profoundly grateful to all those who helped me, and hope that they will accept my thanks collectively.

For the part of Henry's story that took place in Australia there is much more documentation. I was not able to visit Australia. The research was undertaken by Keith Barrie, whose efficiency and enthusiasm helped to keep me writing. To him, and to Clive Fulton who introduced me to my subject, I owe a special word of thanks.

MQ

PART ONE

Chapter One

Henry Fulton had been at Trinity College only two days when Joscelyn Darcy flung a glass of wine in his face and told him to name his friends.

Henry sprang at Darcy, putting up his fists, but several pairs of hands pulled him back. He struggled violently, half blinded by the wine in his eyes, but he was held fast. A babble of voices offered conflicting advice – he hardly heard them. There were roars of laughter as his arms tangled in the folds of his voluminous black gown. He couldn't see the men who held him; he couldn't see who had bent his right arm behind his back and was pressing it agonisingly upward.

'Let me go,' he yelled. 'If this man wants to fight, by God, he shall.' He lunged forward, his foot skidded in the puddle of wine, and he dropped heavily on one knee. There were fresh shouts of mirth from the shadows behind him, and Darcy, his hands on his hips, bellowed with laughter. 'Why, it's not an insolent dog after all,' he said. 'It's a mad dog. In the interest of public safety, it should be shot.'

'Let me get at him – I'll break his neck.' But as the wine dried on his face, Henry's quick temper was already subsiding. He began to be amused at the ridiculous figure he cut, all six feet two inches of him, slithering about helplessly while this stranger insulted him.

He wondered what he had said to provoke such an extreme reaction from Joscelyn Darcy. They had been discussing the Paris riots, and Henry had suggested that the aristocracy there might be even more idle and uncaring than in Ireland. The word 'even' had been tactless. Darcy's silver-laced gown showed that he was the son of a baronet (gold-laced gowns were worn by the sons of peers). Perhaps Darcy had been given grounds for a mild protest, but hardly for a challenge. And there was no excuse for the second insult.

Henry had entered the University of Dublin a fortnight into the

3

New Year, 1788, as a pensioner, and had been the only new scholar. He knew hardly any of the faces crowding round him, even in daylight. Now, with the candlelight glinting on eyes and shoebuckles, while black gowns merged into black shadows and powdered hair gleamed in the flickering light, the scene was dreamlike, unreal.

The cruel hold on his right arm was relaxed, and he became aware of a stocky young man at his other side. 'Steady, Fulton. Take it easy, man.' A familiar accent. The Northern Irish burr reminded Henry of home. He scarcely knew Donald Cuffe, a stolid character destined for the Church, but he had heard that Donald was a native of his own home town, Lisburn in Co Antrim. The Cuffes milled flour half a mile from the place where the Fulton damask factory stood, but Donald had been educated in Belfast.

'You mustn't let Darcy fight you here,' Donald said urgently. 'You'll be expelled.'

'I don't for the life of me know why he wants to fight me anywhere.'

'He enjoys fighting.' Donald seemed to think this sufficient excuse. 'Mind you choose pistols – he'll fillet you if you settle for swords.'

Darcy said, 'There's a second for you, Fulton. What more suitable than that the corn merchant should act for the linen draper? Honest Ulster burghers both, if somewhat thick-headed. As to weapons, let it be pistols by all means – or would you be more at home with cudgels?'

Henry's wrists were firmly seized before he could plunge forward again – fortunately, as he would have looked foolish. Darcy was making no attempt to defend himself. Instead, he yawned offensively. 'You may as well act for me, Ned,' he said, looking past Henry's right shoulder.

'No, Joss, you go too far.' The voice was at Henry's side, and belonged to the man who had been restraining him most harshly. 'Get somebody else to do your dirty work.' Henry could just see a swarthy face close to his own. The voice was rough and hard like its owner's grasp. 'I thought better of you. Call it off.'

'Call it off? Not I.'

'Why pick a quarrel with a student new to Dublin? Shame on you, Joss. Fulton, you are entitled to refuse to fight without loss of face.'

'I have no choice. He has insulted my family as well as myself.' Henry's anger had returned with the reference to cudgels. He turned to Donald Cuffe. 'We are hardly acquainted, but I have need of a second. Will you – '

'Forgive me, but I must beg to be excused,' said Donald. 'A student of Divinity, one, moreover, soon to be ordained, must not condone duelling.'

'I need a second, not a sermon,' Henry retorted.

'It's murder,' said Donald, in a more normal voice. 'Sheer bloody murder. I want no part in it.'

The man who had refused to act for Darcy gave Henry's arm a hard shake. 'No fighting here. Understood?' he said.

Henry nodded unwillingly, and the painful grip was released. The man came forward, and Henry saw that he was tall and heavily built, at least thirty years old. His dark, ugly, somehow attractive face was concerned as he looked Henry up and down appraisingly. 'Can you shoot straight?' he asked.

'No,' said Henry.

'A pity. It would serve Joss right if you beat him at his own game. No matter. I'll coach you and I'll act for you.'

'I'm much obliged – I don't even know your name.'

'Ned Fitzmaurice, at your service.'

'Are you a student?' Ned looked more like a soldier.

'A perpetual one,' said Ned, laughing. 'My uncle has obtained a commission for me, otherwise I might be reading history at ninety. Come, Fulton, leave these sots to their own devices. The sooner you start practising the better. I'll lend you a pair of pistols.'

Henry felt more than ever as if he had strayed on to a stage without having learned his part. He said to Joscelyn Darcy, 'I'll deal with you later,' and it sounded like the idle threat of a child. Burning with resentment, he followed Ned out of the room.

Henry's forty-eight hours at Trinity had been punctuated by the banging of pistols, as the scholars lost no opportunity to practise the manly art. They fired at targets, at stray cats and, occasionally, at one another; but, for the most part, out of doors. He had assumed that target practice was a local sport, like cock-fighting or curricle racing. When these hot-headed young men graduated, they would, he supposed, settle down and take up chess or billiards instead.

Duels were fought in his native Co Antrim. Men were killed, and their killers left the country until the fuss died down. Duelling was a regrettable fact of life, but not a sport.

Following Ned Fitzmaurice along the high-vaulted corridors and up the ill-lit stairs, Henry could have wept with vexation. His urgent need was to use his fists now – not a gun tomorrow or the day after. He wanted to knock Darcy down, breaking his teeth if possible, and make him apologise. By tomorrow, he knew he would have no stomach for a fight. His hot temper was short-lived and he never bore a grudge.

'They'll call out the Watch if we shoot at night,' Ned was saying, 'but we can decide on a plan of action. Are you familiar with the Galway rule book? It's almost always used here – the Tipperary rules are considered sadly out of date . . . You are not familiar with *any* rules? Impossible. How am I to save you?'

'There was no real quarrel,' said Henry. 'Surely I'm not in mortal danger? I thought it was a tasteless joke which should have been punished then and there.'

'It was no joke,' said Ned. His face set into even grimmer lines as he watched Henry dubiously handling a long-barrelled duelling pistol. 'Have you no knowledge of guns at all?'

'None, but I intend to learn.'

'I hope you may learn in time.' He smiled reluctantly as a thought struck him. 'Henry,' he said. 'Henry. What a plodding, respectable name. How could Henry win a duel? I shall call you Harry. Henry is destined to push a quill or measure yards of cloth – Harry might astonish us. Attend to what I say, Harry, and by my soul, you may have a chance.'

Henry listened to Ned's advice and obediently read the Galway rule book. He got used to the weight of a pistol in his hand and learned the correct stance. He tried to believe that he might soon be dead, but instinct told him he would be spared. Blind optimism? He didn't think so.

He had not had time to settle at Trinity. He hadn't even met his tutor, Dr Ross, who was ill in bed. He found it hard to adapt to a timetable in which three o'clock dinner and Chapel were the only fixed points. He had expected his time to be mapped out for him as it was at Dr Mawhinney's school at Lisburn. He hadn't expected to find little boys of eleven or twelve years old at University, nor yet mature students like Ned. He had thought most would be near his own age – twenty-two.

Henry's father and uncles had graduated from Trinity before him. He had asked his father about his experiences, and John Fulton had responded with tales of low life in the 'sixties; of taverns, music halls and gaming hells, of horse races, women and crude practical jokes. His uncles, both clergymen, had nothing to say about their years in Dublin. He wondered if any of his relations had been involved in a duel. He tried to imagine stout Uncle Joseph or pious Uncle Richard issuing a challenge, but failed. He felt a pang of home-sickness as he returned to the common room.

The smoky, crowded room had taken on a nightmarish aspect. The gowned figures, now singing tunelessly; the smells of smoke, wine and sweat; the heat of an enormous turf fire – they all combined to make Henry feel strange, almost light-headed. Or perhaps it was the leaden pastry on the beef pie he'd eaten for dinner. He had drunk little, but at home he never drank at all. It was easier to desist than to endure his parents' lectures on the perils of imbibing spirituous liquors, as they termed them.

Joscelyn Darcy had found a second, Jonathan Barry from Cork; they were the centre of an uproarious group near the door. Ned strolled across to a party of friends, beckoning Henry to follow but he did not. A feeling of detachment prevented him. He watched Darcy from a shadowed corner, disliking him, yet with a kind of envy. Darcy's handsome face was flushed scarlet with excitement and claret. It was a face lacking in character, expressing only the most basic emotions, but he looked as if life held no uncertainties for him. He knew what he wanted to do, and he meant to do it.

Were they really going to try to kill one another? Darcy looked as if he was discussing a horse race. Henry, in his uncertain, restless frame of mind, half welcomed the duel as a positive event. Did he really want to study mathematics for three years? He wasn't sure. But he knew he wasn't ready to die and didn't believe he would. He took a candle from the stand and went to bed.

As a boy, Henry had no doubts about his future. He wanted to be a sailor. He wanted to use his aptitude for figures to study navigation. Then, he thought, he would be able to travel to the ends of the earth like Captain Cook, and to chart unknown seas. His father had not approved. He knew of the privations and degradation of the navy, except for the privileged few. However, his business involved trading with India, and he thought Henry's appetite for travel could be appeased by a few useful trips to Bombay. Then he could be eased into an office job there. A junior assistant bearing the firm's name would be a definite asset.

Henry suspected his father's plans for him, and meant to deal with the situation when it arose. In the meantime, he was full of half-formed ideals and beliefs. He wondered, as he climbed into bed, if he would ever outgrow his feeling of not belonging, and if he did indeed belong anywhere.

In the small hours, he lay awake, listening to the distant noises of the city, and the nearer whoops and yells of some scholars returning from an evening of revelry. Down on the quays, dogs barked and sheep bleated as a flock was driven in from the country for slaughter. He could hear the watchman with his bill and lantern, calling the hour.

Henry began to wish that he had stayed downstairs and smothered his loneliness with drink. He fought the sensation that he was an outsider looking in; an observer rather than a partaker, belonging nowhere. As the slow night passed, the sounds he heard hardened into images. He saw the cheerful faces and brightly coloured clothes of a party of students staggering past the porter's lodge. He saw a late coach and four trundling down Nassau Street. Then the picture faded, and he seemed to see the pale faces of the myriads of Dubliners who lived on familiar terms with starvation, unlike the prosperous weavers of Lisburn. Filthy children scattered like chaff ahead of the rumbling coach, diving into stinking alleys, their faces old with street cunning and want. He could see and even smell the collapsing hovels which clung around the cathedrals and offices of handsome new Georgian Dublin.

On the edge of sleep, he saw the tall buildings sway like grass, tilting towards him. Then the faces in his mind became grotesque, mouthing and goggling, while bony fingers pointed at him mockingly. An old woman's face came nearer and nearer, toothless mouth agape, it wasn't a human mouth but the mouth of a pistol. And he tried to run and could not, heaving up each foot in turn uselessly, until he screamed silently in nightmare panic and woke himself up.

Henry sat up sweating, the dream receding slowly. He had experienced it before, many times, but the pointing gun was new. As before, the terror left him with an urgency of work not done, a vocation not followed, not even understood. He felt caged in the cold room, and wondered for the first time if travelling the seas was really what he wanted. A ship would imprison him as surely as a classroom or an office.

The careers suggested by his father – commerce, law, the Church, politics – sounded bleak and impersonal. His father, a free-thinker who associated with Catholic liberals and took a 'patriotic' newspaper, refused to discuss his views with his son. He warned Henry against joining any of the progressive groups at Trinity, saying that only a rich man could afford to have unorthodox ideas.

Henry agreed. He had little interest in politics. He sometimes thought he would enjoy manual work in the factory, although he would never be allowed to do it. Just now, he wanted to roll up his sleeves and attack some daunting problem. His lips twitched as he thought how much he had wanted to roll up his sleeves and attack Joscelyn Darcy.

'I ought to be a soldier,' he muttered, and fell asleep. He dreamed no more that night.

Chapter Two

The next day, Ned Fitzmaurice was in a foul mood. First, he made a final attempt to dissuade Joscelyn Darcy. When reason failed, he lost his hard-held temper, and swore at the younger man for several minutes. Joscelyn balanced idly on the corner of a table swinging one foot to and fro.

'That's enough,' he said, when Ned paused for breath. 'Don't oblige me to shoot you as well. One corpse will suffice. You should talk to my second, not to me. What about your famous book of rules? You know that you are forbidden to influence a principal.'

Jonathan Barry, the second, also refused to budge. The fight was arranged for Phoenix Park the following morning.

Ned then searched for Henry and was told that he was attending a lecture. When he emerged with his books and a bundle of notes, Ned hustled him away to a secluded corner of the grounds, gave him a pistol and instructed him to fire at a large tree growing in front of the wall. Most of Henry's bullets missed the tree altogether. Ned steadied his aim, narrowly escaping death when Henry fumbled the hair trigger, and tried cajolery and oaths to no avail. Two hours later the ground was littered with chips of stone and bits of bark, and Henry had run out of bullets. A bell rang and he said, 'Well, Ned, you'll never make a marksman of me, but I've worked up a rare appetite for dinner.'

'You might live to dine tomorrow if you would help yourself,' snapped Ned. 'I doubt if anyone else can.' He wondered for the hundredth time what lunacy had prompted him to help this odd, dreamy young man, whose temper flared and died like a torch. He spent the evening losing at cards.

Henry was still cheerful the following morning when he rose at daybreak. He felt excited but not afraid. Ned was waiting with two cases of pistols. 'Best be going,' he said shortly. 'I have seen some poor marksmen, but I never dreamed it possible to be as bad a shot as you. You're so bad that it's downright interesting.'

It was a freezing morning, and Henry did cabman's exercises to keep warm. 'I told you I couldn't hit a pig in a passage,' he said. 'With luck, the early hour and the brandy Darcy drank last night will spoil his aim. You tell me he is a dead shot, but how many has he killed? None I think.'

'You aren't even slightly apprehensive, are you?' said Ned. 'If I can't teach you self-preservation, perhaps I can terrify you into taking this matter seriously.'

'I doubt it.'

'If by any chance Joss misses you,' said Ned, with slow emphasis, 'you will both advance one pace and fire again as I have already explained. You fire your first shots at ten paces. Even if Joss doesn't disable you at ten paces, he will certainly kill you at eight.'

'Whose paces?' asked Henry. 'If mine, I swear I could stride clean out of range.'

Ned jammed his hands deeper into his pockets. The young fool was bent on suicide. 'Jonathan Barry and I will pace the ground. Why the devil didn't you study the rules? Haven't you any regard for your life? You will hit nothing, unless a bystander – Barry perhaps. I shall be hiding behind a tree. You will drop with a bullet clean through your heart. Farewell Harry.'

'Not much loss perhaps.'

'Perhaps not, but I am responsible for you today. If you hit Darcy, it will be an accident.'

'I had better not aim at him in that case,' said Henry, smiling. It was an infectious smile. He had a long, mobile mouth which turned up sharply at the corners. His nose was long too; narrow bridged, between wideset hazel eyes. An odd face, thought Ned sourly. It was hard to dislike Henry. Ned usually liked only what he could understand, but he respected courage, and the thought of the one-sided conflict revolted him.

'Hurry up,' he said roughly. 'Get it over.'

'By all means. The walk will warm us up. And don't fret – I won't die today, I know it.'

A new bridge was being built across the Liffey, near the Houses of Parliament. The workmen were huddled round a brazier, wrapped in ragged cloaks, waiting for their foreman to arrive.

Henry paused to marvel at the size of the chunks of granite which had been lugged to the spot by teams of eight horses. The stone, quarried in the Dublin Mountains, was the hardest imaginable, with scraps of mica sparkling on its cold grey surface. Henry warmed his hands at a brazier and exchanged greetings with the labourers. The quay was unpaved, the ruts frozen hard. The tide was out and the supports for the bridge projected a couple of feet above the water. A dead sheep had been washed up against the nearest, and the scummy depths stank.

Ned found himself alone. He looked back, shouted at Henry as if he were a disobedient child. 'Don't dawdle, man.' He pulled his cloak round his shoulders and set his hat more firmly on his dark brown wig. Henry, catching up with long strides, was bare-headed and wore his own hair long, tied back at the nape.

The air was diamond clear; piercingly cold. The dawn sky was duck-egg blue, traced with scraps of pink cloud. Here and there a column of brown turf smoke rose, perfectly straight, from a factory chimney. Tall spires, domes and towers were dark above the horizon. Henry thought that nothing could be more peaceful. Then the silence was shattered by a herd of cattle, coming in from Co Meath. The two men flattened themselves against a housefront as the beasts shouldered past, blowing and bellowing, snarling dogs at their heels. The ragged barefooted drovers yelled and cursed and swung their ashplants.

'Pah,' said Ned, as a wave of warm air and the pungent stink of frightened cattle seemed to strike them bodily. Henry was silent. The sheer vitality of the scene had shaken him. He stood still and wondered about dying.

They had passed the new Courts of Justice when Henry asked, 'Why did Darcy challenge me? I thought it was for sport, but you are serious when you say he means to kill me, are you not?'

Ned stepped over a frozen puddle and skirted a pile of refuse before he answered. 'Joss needs to kill somebody – anybody,' he said. 'Old Sir Matthew hasn't a brass farthing, and Joss has set his heart on the Grand Tour.'

'Why should I be sacrificed for the whim of a spoiled child? I had rather kill him.'

'You couldn't. Not with a gun anyway – perhaps cudgels would have been a better idea. No, I have given the matter much thought since I heard of his plan. You must drop as he fires and play dead. It's your only chance. Against the rules of course, but I shall be behind a tree and will not see.'

'Never!'

'Die then – I wash my hands of you.'

Henry didn't mention the duel again. Instead, he asked Ned all manner of questions about the places they were passing, getting negative answers or none. 'How little you know about this city,' he said at last.

'Possibly, but I know something about a gun. I might live long enough to discover the answers – if I were interested.' Ned hunched his shoulders and blew into the palms of his cold hands.

'What does interest you?' Henry persisted.

'Horses. Women, provided they are pretty and don't chatter, but mainly horses. Here are the Park gates at last.'

Joscelyn Darcy and Jonathan Barry arrived by coach. They drove up to the chosen spot, a clump of sycamores, where the postilions dismounted and ran to their horses' heads. Clouds of steam rose from the sweating animals, which stamped and snorted restively, their harness jingling. Disturbed rooks flew up from the trees with a great cawing and clatter.

It was evident that Jonathan Barry was much the worse for wear. He climbed down from the coach, and stood holding a wheel for support, swaying glassy-eyed, his cloak clutched crookedly, his hat askew. Darcy appeared to be sober but in a poor temper, swearing at Barry, at the postilions and, as soon as he was in earshot, at Ned.

The dreamlike detachment of two nights earlier had returned to Henry. He leaned casually against a tree, feeling invulnerable. Darcy's bullets, he thought, would swerve away from him, deflected by destiny.

Ned caught Barry roughly by the shoulder, saving him from falling as the horses fidgeted and the wheel turned. 'A fine second,' he said. 'And what about the doctor? Have you forgotten him?'

'No, rot his carcase. He's here somewhere.' Darcy stirred an object in the straw on the bottom of the coach with his foot. 'Drunk.'

'Much good he'll be.'

'Calm yourself, Ned. I shan't need him for myself, and even the cleverest sawbones cannot raise the dead.'

Ned said in a furious undertone, 'For two pins, I'd take Fulton's place and teach you a lesson, Joss.'

Darcy laughed. 'I've no doubt you would, but, whatever the linen-draper's shortcomings, he would never allow it. Poor devil, I almost pity him myself. You should have brought him with a garland round his neck.'

Ned glared at him. 'Whatever the outcome of today, you have lost one friend,' he said. 'If you kill Harry Fulton, I promise I'll make you suffer for it some day.' He offered the pistols for Barry's inspection, and received a vague assurance that they were probably much the same.

Henry told himself sternly that he would soon be fighting for his life. He watched with detached interest as Ned and Barry paced the ground. Darcy discarded his long blue cloak, his coat with buttons as big as saucers, and his embroidered waistcoat. He emerged, dashing if chilly, in a frilled cambric shirt with ruffles of Limerick lace. He secured his long, rather dirty fair hair with a broad black satin ribbon, shook the ruffles back from his wrist and kissed the pistol with a flourish. 'I cut a pretty figure, do I not?' he said.

'You do not.' Henry's anger flared. 'You look like a posturing fool.' Stripped to his plain Ulster linen shirt and drab breeches, he couldn't match the other man's raffish elegance. He accepted his loaded and primed gun from Ned, and suggested that everyone within range had better take cover.

The level sun of early morning had looked like being a problem. Now it had disappeared behind a cloud which, at first gold-edged, then purplish-black, rushed up the pale sky, darkening it. A sharp breeze sprang up, rattling the frozen twigs. As the two men took aim, there was a sudden hard scud of frozen rain. Driven straight into Darcy's face, it was like a handful of thrown grit.

Joscelyn Darcy had too much sense to come drunk to a duel, but he disregarded any threat from Henry. He had swallowed a fair amount of cognac to keep the cold out, and was not quite at his ice-cold best. He fired and, as Henry's bullet buried itself in a tree a yard to the right, his passed between Henry's left arm and his ribs, making two holes in his shirt and peeling three inches of skin off his side.

'Reload!' shouted Darcy. 'My aim was spoiled by the hail.'

Henry at once stepped forward, signing to Ned that he wished to reload, although blood was already soaking his shirt and breeches. Ned ignored him.

'Enough!' he roared. And, as Barry fumblingly reloaded Joscelyn's pistol, he advanced and snatched it away.

Ned cursed and kicked the snoring doctor in vain. Plainly, Henry was not going to get any help there. He unwound his neck-cloth and mopped the now streaming blood. There was no pain yet. 'Do you believe in fate?' Henry asked.

'No. I believe in the devil's own luck. Get into the coach, man.'

Henry had been told that the Provost of Trinity was himself a keen duellist, so he felt aggrieved when he was severely reprimanded and confined to his room for his part in the affair; especially as Joscelyn received only the mildest rebuke of the 'boys will be boys' variety and no punishment at all. Henry, studying in his room, bothered by the pain of his wound, smarted at the injustice.

It was a week before he was released from detention. His tutor, Dr Ross, summoned him to his study, greeting him with none of the frosty sarcasm he was learning to expect.

A message had arrived for Henry from the Misses Leland. He was instructed to wait upon them at 18 Clare Street that very afternoon.

'Were you acquainted with the late Dr Leland?' asked Dr Ross. He was a tiny dried-up man, who looked more like a jockey fallen on evil days than a college don.

'No sir, he was my father's tutor and friend. I had intended to wait on his widow and sisters as soon as possible.'

'Mrs Leland keeps her bed nowadays. Miss Eliza and Miss Mary are formidable classical scholars; it is an unusual honour for a student to be invited to their house. Miss Eliza informs me that you intend to take Holy Orders.'

'No sir, that is not my intention.'

Dr Ross chuckled, a sound like the rustling of dry leaves. He said, 'Your intentions may not be a match for Eliza Leland's.' As Henry turned to go, the doctor added, 'You will wonder why you have seen nothing of Fitzmaurice since your foolish prank. He has obtained his commission and has gone to join his regiment at short notice.'

'Indeed sir? What is his regiment?'

'I cannot say. The man is a philistine and a fool. Too many like him waste the time and patience of their tutors. I am not interested in his military career. You may go.'

Back in his room, Henry changed into his Sunday best, feeling nervous. He was not looking forward to meeting the two bluestockings in Clare Street. He was relieved to hear that he wouldn't be meeting Dr Leland's widow, only his unmarried sisters. Dr Leland, who had died three years earlier, had helped Henry's two clergyman uncles to their comfortable livings and had impressed his father with his liberal ideas.

Henry comforted himself with the thought that he had fought Joscelyn Darcy and survived. Surely a dish of tea with two old ladies was a less frightening ordeal.

Chapter Three

Clare Street lay between Nassau Street and Merrion Square. The coaches and carriages of the rich and fashionable often passed that way, and Henry kept close to the iron railings which fronted the houses on the right hand side, to avoid being splashed with mud. The houses were neat, square, not large, with balconied windows. Number 18 was the dingiest in the row, its cream paint peeling, its railings spotted with rust. Henry scraped the mire from his shoes on the wrought iron scraper before knocking.

The hall on the ground floor was sparsely furnished and extremely cold. Henry reluctantly handed over his coat to the ancient bow-legged man who had opened the door. The old man had shrunk until his tattered livery hung loose from his shoulders, and his stockings were wrinkled from knee to ankle. He scuttled up the stairs ahead of Henry to the landing on the first floor, threw open a pair of doors and announced in a loud, cracked voice, 'Mr Henry Fulton'.

Henry had expected the ladies to be alone. He heard the sound of chattering voices in the drawing-room with consternation. There was a sudden silence as he cautiously entered the room, scarlet-faced and feeling nine feet tall. He tried not to stare at a remarkably pretty girl who was seated near the fire, narrowly avoided taking a header over a carved footstool, and crossed what seemed like acres of Chinese carpet to where his hostesses sat watching him, he thought, like vultures.

Miss Eliza and Miss Mary Leland could have passed for twins, although there were five years between them. The two ladies had shared their brother's house for thirty-five years, and had grown more and more alike. Both had their hair dressed high, in the fashion of a decade earlier, while their décolletages displayed scrawny necks and bony chests. Each wore a black ribbon with an oval cameo round her throat; each wore layers of petticoats. They were seated side by side on a gilt settee, and each extended her right hand, palm down. Henry, not knowing which was Miss Eliza, but well aware that he would give mortal offence if he greeted the younger sister first, had nothing to guide him, as neither spoke.

There were about a dozen people in the room, and one of them, noticing Henry's plight, addressed one of the ladies pointedly as 'Miss Mary'. Henry threw him a grateful glance as he approached the other sister. He saw a slightly built man whose linen bands showed that he was a clergyman. His plum-coloured velvet coat and black breeches were of the latest cut and the richest materials. He wore a heavy signet ring and silver shoebuckles, moved with ease and assurance, and his voice was decided. Henry was surprised to note that the man looked only a few years older than he was himself – perhaps twenty-five or six.

Miss Leland acknowledged Henry's greeting, and indicated the clergyman by pointing her fan. 'Mr Knox is Chaplain of the House of Commons,' she said. 'He is ambitious – are you not, William?' Her voice had an unpleasant edge, and Mr Knox coloured in annoyance.

'How you intend to reconcile these advanced ideas of yours with your progress towards a bishopric, I cannot imagine,' continued Miss Leland.

'How fortunate that you need not concern yourself on my behalf,' said Mr Knox smoothly.

Henry might have been invisible. He edged away, towards the fireplace where a turf fire sulked in a basket grate, and where the extremely pretty girl was warming her hands. To his annoyance, he was waylaid by another clergyman, who introduced himself as James Walker, rector of Roscrea in County Tipperary. The rector's personaltiy was unremarkable, and he conversed, rather than talked (about tithes, and the difficulty of collecting them). Henry, rigid with boredom, wondered how soon he could decently leave the gathering. Out of the corner of his eye he saw the dark-haired girl watching him.

'Allow me to present my daughter,' said Mr Walker. The girl held out her hand, smiling shyly. Henry took it, looked into her eyes – and suddenly realised that she was pulling her hand away, though gently: he had forgotten to release it. He was thinking: 'I am going to know this face better than any other face in the world.' The slant of those finely pencilled eyebrows, the way her dark eyelashes were thick rather than long ('eyes put in with an inky finger' his granny used to say); the delicious fullness of her lower lip and her mouth's deep corners: was it that they were going to be a part of his life, or had they always been part of it? Had she been his in a former existence? Heresy, said his conditioned conscience; but whatever he made himself think, nothing changed the feeling. This girl was his. This girl would be his wife.

Her name was Anne. Had someone said so? He didn't think so. But he knew it, and loved the name because it was hers.

'Have you been long in Dublin, sir?' asked Anne Walker.

Henry recovered himself with an effort and made a more or less intelligible reply. 'And you?' he asked. 'Are you staying here?'

Anne looked up, met his burning gaze and looked down quickly. 'Yes, but I return to Tipperary shortly,' she said. Her voice was a polite murmur, but she made room for him to sit beside her on the narrow sofa by the fire.

Henry's delight was short-lived, as he had to rise again at once to greet a lady who immediately took his place and sat there firmly. Plainly she was Anne's mother, youngest of the Leland sisters. Sarah Walker had Anne's deep blue eyes, black hair and fair skin, but not her delicacy of feature or her lively expression, nor yet her trim figure. She settled on the green brocade like a broody hen on a clutch of eggs, and began to lecture Henry about the music of Handel.

Henry didn't take in a word, although he listened attentively. He watched Anne's bent head and decided she was fighting a desire to giggle. He noticed that her gown with its plain white fichu was unfashionable, as was her little velvet hat. None of the ladies present followed the current style of high-crowned beavers with nodding ostrich plumes which Henry had noticed in modish Capel Street.

He answered Mrs Walker mechanically, still in a state of shock. There had never been a woman in his life. He had been waiting, he thought, for Anne. He stood, facing the ladies on the sofa, and wondered if he was trembling visibly.

William Knox was leaving, and paused to speak to him, moving a chair in his direction. 'Do sit down, Mr Fulton. Do you feel unwell?'

Henry gratefully accepted the spindle-legged gilt chair. 'My side troubles me a little. I was involved in a duel.'

Mrs Walker gave a shocked gasp. Anne looked up quickly, with interest, but said nothing.

'I think I was saved by a miracle,' said Henry, speaking lightly and meaning every word. He glanced from Mrs Walker's bulk to the vague black-clad presence of the Reverend James. Another miracle would be needed, he thought, if he was to win this adorable girl.

Henry could think of no way short of force to remove Mrs Walker from her daughter's side. Now she was verbally describing an aria, quoting the lyric and indicating the accompaniment by humming, and going 'la la' and 'deedle deedle', and 'pom pom'.

Inspiration struck. 'Will you not sing it for us?' asked Henry, rising as Mrs Walker, nothing loath, got up and made for the harpsichord.

'An excellent idea,' she said. 'You shall turn the pages for me.' This time, there was no mistaking Anne's smothered giggle. Mrs Walker sang well. She continued to sing until Miss Eliza ordered her to stop, when she flushed crimson and flounced back to the sofa.

'My sister tells me you are going into the Church,' she said to Henry.

'No, ma'am, I am studying mathematics.' Even as he spoke, Henry knew that whatever career he chose, he was destined to be a misfit – unless . . . He came out of his reverie. Everyone not of the family had left. When he took his leave, Miss Eliza invited him to call again. Mindful of Anne, he agreed eagerly.

'My sister and I are translating some manuscripts from the Greek. I daresay you can help. I had hoped that Mr Knox might do so, but unfortunately he is, as I said, ambitious.'

'I can try,' said Henry doubtfully. 'I am not very conversant with Greek.'

'Of course you can help. Greek is one of the principal languages of the scriptures.'

'But I am studying mathematics, not Divinity,' said Henry.

'Fiddlesticks,' said Miss Leland.

Henry presented himself hopefully at Clare Street two days later. He was astonished by the amount of free time that his studies allowed. This time, Dan, the major domo, showed him into a study which opened off the drawing-room. The ladies were seated at a walnut writing table, side by side as before.

Henry was again struck by their extraordinary likeness. They looked a couple of withered old beldames, but he knew that neither had reached sixty. He had judged Mrs Walker to be at least ten years younger than either. As soon as he could politely do so, he asked after Mrs Walker and Miss Anne – how they were, whether they were at home.

'They returned to Roscrea yesterday,' snapped Miss Eliza. She laid aside the book she had been studying and fixed Henry with a hard stare. 'Did you come here to see me or my niece?' she demanded, with alarming directness.

'I had hoped to meet both.'

'Hah! I don't believe a word of it.'

The writing table was heaped with rolls of parchment, tattered books and odd sheets of paper. Some loose pages had blown on to the floor. Bitterly disappointed, Henry bent to pick them up, As he stooped, the healing skin on his side hurt him badly, making him catch his breath. When he straightened, Miss Eliza, tapping the hilt of a paper knife against her teeth, was watching him so sharply that he felt himself blush. A schoolboy trick, he thought he had out-grown it.

'My late brother,' she said, 'as I assume you know, was the author of a life of Philip of Macedon. *The* life, I should say. It is unlikely ever to be surpassed. After completing this work, he turned to his immortal translation of Demosthenes. However, it had long been his intention to write a life of Alexander, Philip's son. Sadly, he did not live to do it. My sister and I have assembled the notes he made. We expect the research to take two years and the writing a further two. The first volume should be ready early in 1792.'

Henry tried to speak, but Miss Eliza talked on, over and round him. At last she paused, and he said, rather lamely, 'A laudable ambition.'

So far, except to greet him, Miss Mary had been silent. But now she suddenly cried out, 'Oh, you mustn't speak like that – you sound like a Methodist!'

Annoyed, Henry asked, 'What would you have me sound like, Miss Mary?'

'A man about town. If you do not, you will never be accepted in Dublin, and you will be of no use to us. If you can obtain the entrée into the houses of scholarly men, you may borrow books for us.'

God forbid, thought Henry. Aloud, he said, 'So a Methodist would say, "a laudable ambition"? How would a man about town have responded?'

To his amazement, Miss Mary sprang to her feet, struck an attitude, looked down her nose and said, in a strange falsetto, 'Why, rot me and sink me, ma'am, but upon my soul that is a most laudable ambition.'

Henry burst out laughing, but quickly composed his features when he realised that both ladies were in deadly earnest.

Miss Eliza glared. 'I detest frivolity,' she pronounced. 'The late Doctor Leland despised levity. He would have been grieved and angry.'

Henry stifled his laughter. The late doctor's portrait by Sir Joshua Reynolds, which hung above the fireplace, showed a round-cheeked, curly-haired old man with a benevolent smile. Grief and anger would be foreign to such a countenance, thought Henry.

Miss Eliza pushed a pile of documents in his direction. 'Make yourself useful,' she commanded. 'Arrange these manuscripts in chronological order. When you have finished, you may sharpen some quills for me. Simple tasks, but necessary.'

Henry did as he was told. If he did not, he would never be invited to number 18 again and would lose his link with Anne Walker. It was a high price to pay.

After an hour or so, Old Dan tottered into the room with a tray bearing a bottle, glasses and a plate of sugared biscuits. Henry accepted a glass of claret with some surprise; he had never seen ladies drink it before. It was excellent, and in due course the bottle was replaced by another. He nibbled biscuits, wondering if he dared ask any more questions about the Walkers – in particular when they might return. He decided not to risk it.

Henry made himself so useful that he was invited to Clare Street again and again. Each time, he hoped to find Anne Walker there; each time he was disappointed. Miss Eliza continued to treat him like a dunce; he couldn't like her but respected her scholarship. Miss Mary, although continually put down by her sister, was friendly enough, especially when mellowed by several glasses of claret. At every visit, vast amounts of claret were drunk by all three. Henry was never offered an ordinary meal or a dish of tea.

Old Mrs Leland was a presence felt but not seen, bedbound overhead. Now and then her handbell would ring, and Kate, her maid, would come dashing up from the basement. Usually she would return with a request for Miss Mary to go to her sister-in-law with the day's work. Miss Mary was well read and good at research, but not nearly as dedicated as Miss Eliza. She confessed to Henry that she would prefer to be writing a romantic novel.

In February, the weather grew unseasonably warm. Trees budded and birds sang. Fever broke out in Dublin, and the ill-housed, half-starved people died by the dozen. The most helpless died first – the infants. These included many put out to nurse by their rich parents.

A ball was given at Dublin Castle to raise money for the sick. Those who were not sick or poor avoided the narrow streets of the city centre and carried bottles of vinegar or bunches of sweet herbs to sniff. Others moved to the country until the nuisance had abated.

One day as Henry was walking along Nassau Street he had to stand aside to allow a funeral to pass. He removed his hat as two men, haggard-faced and dressed in ragged black, went by carrying on their shoulders a small coffin made of rough, splintered planks. Behind, two older men and a group of wailing women shuffled through the mud. One of them, a girl of fourteen or so, staggered as she walked, her face as flushed as the others were pale.

Henry couldn't get the incident out of his mind. True, dead and dying people were plentiful just then – it was the look of dull acceptance on the mourners' faces that had struck him. How could they be so resigned to the death of their children? He told Miss Eliza about it.

She said impatiently, 'You are not an ill young man, Henry, I beg you will not dabble in good works and start to mope and whine.'

'Good God, ma'am, can I not try to better the lot of a few unfortunates and still remain cheerful?'

'Not in my experience, no.' Miss Eliza drew the manuscript towards her.

★

At Easter, Henry was obliged to go home. He had no money left, or he might have devised an urgent reason for visiting Roscrea. He had still heard nothing of Anne.

The day that he was to catch the Belfast Mail, he called to say goodbye to the sisters. Claret flowed, and so did Miss Mary's tears. 'I shall miss you so, dear Henry,' she wept.

'Control yourself, Mary. He will return.'

Miss Mary gulped and wiped her eyes. 'My dear, dear boy,' she said, 'You have lightened our task and brought youth and gaiety into our lives. We have agreed, my sister and I, that you should be rewarded for all the work you have done. We have decided to give you a memento, something which belonged to our brother.'

'*You* have decided,' corrected Miss Eliza. 'I will leave you to bestow it yourself. These romantical vapourings sicken me.' She swept out of the room with an angry rustle of skirts.

There was a linen-bag lying on a side table, and Henry had wondered why it was there. Miss Mary took a folded garment out of it, handling it reverently. 'I want you to have my brother's cartouche cape,' she said. 'I hate to see you dressed in drab colours. If you are to be a man about town, you must dress the part.' She shook out the garment and held it up – a cloak of the best superfine cloth, bright blue in colour. 'Put it on if you please.'

'You are far too kind. I will be the envy of everyone at home.' Henry swung the cape round his shoulders, and was startled by his reflection, tall and debonair, in the oval mirror on the wall. He looked like a different person.

'It is hardly suitable for a clergyman perhaps – '

'I'm not going to be a clergyman,' said Henry automatically.

' – but as you see it is completely reversible. The lining is black, so you may be as funereal as you choose. Take it off – turn it – so. There! Oh, Henry, how handsome you look. You can have no idea.'

She stood gazing up into his face. Her own was thickly painted, with a bright spot of rouge on either cheek. She looked like an elderly doll. She gave him a flirtatious glance from under wrinkled lids, and he wondered with alarm whether she expected him to kiss her. To his profound relief, Miss Eliza reappeared at that moment, and Miss Mary turned away with a self-conscious titter.

'Observe our Henry, sister. He looks a dashing beau, does he not?'

'He looks like a highwayman's apprentice.' Miss Eliza looked him up and down critically. 'Take this. You need something to fasten that ridiculous garment.' She put a large, square gold brooch in his hand. 'Hold your tongue, man. I can't abide thanks. And you'd best be going – I can't abide farewells either.'

At home once more, Henry found that his father had changed. News of the duel had reached him of course, but he seemed too occupied to be much concerned. Henry had kept out of politics and University societies at his father's express wish, but now he was encouraged to attend meetings where democracy was spoken of as something to be desired. A broadsheet was passed from hand to hand, which openly advocated this perilous philosophy.

Compared to Dublin, Lisburn seemed like a paradise for the less fortunate. It was clean and prosperous, and there was employment for the able-bodied. Hundreds worked at John Fulton's damask factory, where designs of extraordinary complexity were turned out. A tablecloth for the Viceroy, decorated with scenes from the classics, had taken two years to complete.

Henry had taken for granted that his home town, so bustling and well-to-do, must be a contented place, but Dublin had sharpened his senses, and he noticed an undercurrent of grumbling resentment. In Dublin, violence was always bubbling just below the surface. This had been the way of it for so long that an eruption no longer seemed likely. The city had seemed to Henry menacing only in its hopeless-ness. The very merriment of its poor had drawn his attention to their needs. Dublin was alive with cripples and beggars. The old and infirm, unless their families could support them, were obliged to beg. In Dublin, people sang, danced, fought, drank themselves senseless, wept, blasphemed, yelled abuse, laughed and suffered. In Lisburn, they were quiet as a rule. When angry, they muttered. After three months at Trinity, Henry had learned to understand Dublin better.

One of his boyhood companions, Tom Warren, had recently been ordained, and was now a busy, threadbare curate. He told Henry stories of intrigue, plot and counterplot, and of secret societies. 'How do you know all this?' Henry asked.

'A curate has the entry into every house. If he is young, poor, and appears to hold no strong views, he will be confided in. I have little interest in politics – except for that horror of disaffection which we all must feel.'

Henry thought about it. He had no vocation in the accepted sense, but had the oddest feeling that he was being called to the Church. There was something of fear in it, something of temptation, and part of him wanted to dismiss it. Surely it would be a great bore to be a parson? But he was becoming discontented with his own lack of purpose, and continued to be nagged by a need which he had not yet identified; the need to be taken beyond himself by something more important than everyday considerations. Was Miss Eliza's fixed idea entirely coincidence? He began to listen to his uncles' sermons with more attention, but they were mostly arid discussions on obscure points of doctrine. Trying to keep awake during one of them, his mind went back to the New Testament reading for the day. Simple parables – a lost sheep, a missing coin – told to simple people originally and remembered by everyone.

He dragged his mind back to the sermon, now winding its dreary way down to its end. He wondered if there was anything in the gospels quite so boring.

A few days later, he attended a performance of *Judas Maccabeus*. He wondered whether Anne Walker shared her mother's passion for Handel. In his mind's eye, he saw Anne all of a sudden, with blinding clarity, seated at the forte piano in a large gloomy drawing-room. He had considered writing to her several times. Handel would provide an excuse to do so. A little melody tinkled in his head. He wondered where he had heard it before.

Chapter Four

———————◆<·●·>◆———————

The Dublin Mail jolted its cumbersome way southward through an innocent countryside, gently steaming after a fall of thundery rain. The fertile pastures of Meath stretched in every direction as far as the horizon, where lilac hills shimmered through the mist. Cattle grazed, birds sang. If there had been a poet in the coach, he might have been inspired.

Henry, who had no poetry in him, sat crouched in the cramped space, his long legs painfully jack-knifed. The road was vile. Rain and frost had channelled deep ruts which had set like cement in the recent drought. A cloudburst had muddied the surface and laid the dust, leaving the road as slippery as glass. An extra vicious bump almost landed Henry in the lap of the paunchy man sitting beside him. The windows were shut; he felt stifled by the foul air. Passionately, he wished he had a horse. As if to mock his thoughts, a gentleman on a dappled grey cantered by, easily overtaking them and going on his way with a wave of his whip towards the coach. He was not obliged to travel on the churned up thoroughfare, but could ride on soft grass. Even a parson, shallow black hat crammed well down on his wig, overtook them, although his hack was a mere pony. If only, thought Henry, he could afford a horse of his own . . . it was an idle dream, he never had any money.

They paused to deliver a packet in an ugly village; a place of sagging thatch and scratching hens. When they moved on, a couple of rough-haired boys ran beside them, tattered shirts flapping, keeping pace with the team, shouting and laughing. They carelessly dodged the coachman's whip, aimed at bare shins, and mimicked the guard's curses.

Henry would have liked to have run with them, for the sheer pleasure of running and of getting some clean air into his lungs. Still, in spite of his discomfort, he was in high spirits. The silent, pot-bellied man beside him gave him a suspicious look, and Henry realised that he was smiling. He made an effort to straighten his face, and his neighbour turned away, reassured.

The fat man sweltered in a calf-length coat, probably because he carried a pistol in its pocket. Henry was the only unarmed passenger on the coach. Two outriders with guns had accompanied the Mail through the dangerous area near Dundalk, while the guard, perched up behind, had charge of a case full of blunder-busses. He carried two horse-pistols and a cutlass in his belt, and his nervous eyes searched the hedges. A guard was a sitting duck if there was an ambush.

The night before, the Belfast Stage had been set upon at Derri-aghy. Guard and driver had been shot, passengers robbed. The traces had been cut and the horses turned loose so that nobody could fetch help. This was the latest in a series of attacks carried out by Whiteboys, highwaymen, or traitors to the Crown, according to the politics of the teller. Henry had joined the Mail at Derriaghy, near his father's home, to a tense atmosphere, but now the travellers relaxed – or seemed to. When a large dog rushed barking at the wheels, every man's hand went to the butt of his gun. Then came the shamefaced pretending have been searching for a handkerchief or a letter.

Late in the afternoon they stopped at the village of Balbriggan and changed horses. Henry got out to stretch his legs, and heard a distant horn and the thud of many hoofs. A moment later, a travelling coach swept into view, heading north. Swaying high on its leather slings, drawn by six strong horses, it hurtled through the village without pausing. Flanking it were armed outriders and an escort of heavy dragoons; inside, Henry glimpsed a scarlet uniform, gold braid, white whiskers. The coach and its retinue thundered out of sight, while the fresh horses being harnessed to the Mail threw up their heads and stared after it.

Henry helped the fat man who had been sitting beside him to mount the steps of the coach. 'I wonder who that was,' he said.

The fat man puffed and panted for a minute before he could reply. 'Some bloody general, off to stir up trouble,' he said. He was a well-to-do squireen, with the flat accent of the north midlands. 'There's plenty of fighting among ordinary folk without the army lending a hand.' He settled himself in his seat gasping, and mopped his brow. 'Brigands – faction fights – duels . . .' he muttered.

Henry had been penned between this man and the window in stuffy silence for the best part of two days. Glad of any conversation, he introduced himself, and his neighbour looked sharply at him, with small, bulging grey eyes set under untidy gingerish brows. 'Fulton, eh? And at Trinity? Were you by any chance challenged and wounded by a bloodthirsty cub called Darcy? One of the Drogheda Darcys?'

'I was. Indeed I was lucky to survive. I can't aim straight and Darcy can shoot a candle flame out. I had no wish to fight him.'

The fat man looked as if he might explode. His bloodshot eyes bulged more than ever; the horseshoe of flesh around his jowls wobbled as he spoke. 'Duels! Never accept a challenge, young man. Better a living coward than a dead hero. There are plenty of barbarians only too happy to shoot you or skewer you for fun. My own son lies mortally ill in Dublin after a vulgar fracas with that same Darcy, may he rot in hell. A meaningless brawl in a gaming saloon.'

'I hope he may recover, sir.' Henry tried to inch away from the furious, sweaty face so unpleasantly close to his own.

'My son, Sebastian Bertram, is in employment at Mr La Touche's bank. Banking is a gentleman's profession, as you know. While drinking, Darcy called my son a tradesman, and offered other insults of the same kind. Tradesman, by God! I must tell you that I am Augustus Bertram from Navan – I daresay the name is familiar to you. Sebastian received a ball through the lung and will be lucky to survive. Darcy will face a murder charge if he dies.'

'What about Darcy?' asked Henry. 'I suppose he escaped without a scratch as usual.'

'Far from it. His knee was shattered, but his miserable life is in no danger, other than the normal risk of gangrene. If the affair comes to a murder trial, you should bear witness to Darcy's bad character. I am on my way to meet my son's barrister-at-law, Sir Jonah Barrington.'

When the coach arrived at Dawson Street, after dark, Sir Jonah was there to meet it. He was a plump man with a humorous face, and Henry recognised him at once. He had often met him walking between Clare Street and the Houses of Parliament; his home was only a few doors away from the Lelands'. Henry was easily persuaded to sup at the Mailcoach Inn with the two men. As usual, he was short of cash, and the cheaper eating houses looked and smelt disgusting.

Sir Jonah refused to discuss the case over supper. He was a talkative man who laughed merrily at his own jokes and seemed to know everyone in the dining-room. Friends crowded round their table. Sir Jonah called for wine and launched into a series of anecdotes about duels, most of them amusing, some of them highly improbable. Mr Bertram worried his way through a large steak in silence, and silently paid the bill.

At the close of the evening, Sir Jonah gave Henry his card with his address – 28 Clare Street. 'Call on me when next you visit those two old harpies,' he suggested.

'I would like to call on your socially, sir. I would prefer not to give evidence unless I must. I don't bear Darcy any malice.'

'We'll see, we'll see. Bertram may yet recover.'

Darcy was no longer at Trinity, but lodging in Fleet Street within sight of the college. Henry saw him a few days later, a shuffling white-faced stranger with a crutch under his arm. He couldn't dredge up any bitterness against Darcy, whose devil-may-care character had its charm. Henry reminded himself of Sebastian Bertram, who had almost bled to death, who would have only one lung for the rest of his life. But Sebastian was a stranger. His father's puffy, petulant face intervened.

To Henry's relief, Sebastian gradually recovered and, although large sums of money reputedly changed hands, the case never came to court. Darcy had fought one duel too many, and was obliged to leave the country for a time, so he got his wish – the Grand Tour.

He set off on the first part of his journey by sea, being carried aboard from his father's coach. There, he was assisted to his cabin by his two companions. These were his personal servant, a silent, bovine man, and a scholarly out-of-work clergyman, the Reverend Horace Purefoy. This gentleman was an aspiring poet in the throes of composing an epic, and was fond of reading his work aloud. Henry, hearing of this, decided that Darcy was being sufficiently punished.

Shortly after his return to Trinity, Henry walked down to Clare Street after Commons. He called briefly on Sir Jonah Barrington, then retraced his steps to number 18. He had missed Miss Eliza's acid tongue, and knew that both women were fond of him in their different ways. As for Anne Walker, he had received no replies to three letters, but wasn't discouraged. He knew he would see her again, and her aunts' house seemed the most likely place. Although they had met only once, her features were as clear in his mind as those of his own sister. He imagined her working around the house, cutting roses in a garden he had never seen, twirling through the movements of a country dance in some ornate ballroom. But try as he might, he couldn't summon up a picture of her reading his letters.

He found the two ladies hard at work at their desk – they might not have stirred since he left them. Seated opposite, in what Henry thought of as his own chair, was an old man wearing an enormous wig, and clothes as outdated as theirs. Between them stood two empty claret bottles and a platter of biscuit crumbs.

Miss Mary jumped to her feet and threw her arms round Henry, while her sister watched her scornfully. 'When you have finished mauling Henry, sister,' she said, 'I will present him.' Then, addressing the old man: 'Sir Timothy, may I introduce Mr Fulton. He has been helping us with our research.'

Sir Timothy rose creakily, clutching the edge of the desk with knobbed fingers stiff with rings and rheumatism. 'Your servant, sir,' he muttered, giving Henry a jealous scowl. 'I was about to take my leave.' He kissed the ladies' hands with a foppish toss of his powdered curls, and nodded curtly in Henry's direction. Instead of leaving the room, he waited expectantly, gripping the back of a chair.

Miss Eliza handed him a list. 'When you return on Thursday, you may bring me Cosgrove's *History of Macedonia* and Hayward's *Heroes of Antiquity* from the library,' she said briskly. 'For Maunsell's *Transcripts from the Greek* you will need to go to the Depôt of Classical Manuscripts in Church Street. A little more claret before you go? Biscuits?'

Sir Timothy declined, accepted the list and hobbled out. Henry could hear Dan bawling for a chair in the street below.

'Is my place usurped?' Henry asked. Miss Mary simpered girlishly, but Miss Eliza ignored the flippancy.

'Sit down, Henry, and make yourself useful – if you have not forgot how. Let us not waste time on idle banter.'

'Your pardon, ma'am,' said Henry penitently. Theirs was a game with as many moves as chess. Sometimes he was expected to be defiant and to argue – just now, meekness was required.

Miss Eliza spoke a little – not much – more kindly. 'I am glad to see you again. You run errands better than Sir Timothy, who goes everywhere by chair at our expense. As for William Knox, he thinks himself too fine a thing to assist us.' She rang the bell. 'Dan, another bottle of claret and some more biscuits.'

Henry asked for news of the Walkers. He had been worried, he said, to hear of the violence everywhere in Tipperary, often directed against the clergy.

Miss Eliza shrugged impatiently. 'Parsons are attacked because they collect the tithes which are their just dues, by force if necessary. They have trouble with those who can't or won't pay. My late brother used to make excuses for the peasants – illiterate savages. He didn't know what he was talking about, of course.'

Henry managed not to ask what she knew of the Tipperary peasantry. 'Hardly savages,' he began angrily.

'No? I suppose you consider the cropping of a tithe-proctor's ears a civilised act?'

'No, of course not. But – '

'Exactly. And if you are about to suggest that the womenfolk would be safer in Dublin, you may save your breath.'

Henry breathed deeply, trying to control his temper. He daren't risk losing his one link with Anne. When he could trust his voice, he said, 'I have been speaking with a Mr Teeling, a friend of my father's, whilst at home. He is a Papist gentleman, and has suffered for his beliefs. I have been taking religious inequality for granted – there is more injustice than I thought. Our clergy, who are in the best position to put things to rights, show up in a poor light. In fact,' he went on, oblivious of the bad impression he was making, 'I am beginning to think of entering the Church myself after all. It would be a fine thing if I could . . .' He became aware of Miss Eliza's icy glare and faltered.

'Dear me,' she said. 'I see that your unfortunate tendency towards good works persists. I trust that you are not turning into an enlightened young man. Enlightenment is tedious in the young and dangerous in the mature. Emancipation is an ideal of the misinformed.'

'But ma'am, is not your own way of life emancipated?'

'Nothing of the sort! The very idea! And the people of this country go on very well as they are, each in his appointed sphere. You would be well advised not to meddle.'

Henry wondered how it was possible to have absorbed so much education and to have remained so ignorant. 'I beg pardon if I vex you,' he persisted, 'but I cannot see the perils of enlightenment.'

'Can you not? It leads to banishment and death. From the time that Adam was banished from Eden and Socrates drank the hemlock, enlightenment has been attended by danger. You may copy these notes in a fair hand, if you do not feel the task to be beneath you.'

Henry copied them. He didn't trust himself to say more. Miss Mary patted his arm and said she vowed he would make an elegant curate.

Miss Eliza's derision was intended to nip Henry's tepid and half formed liberalism in the bud. Instead, it acted like water in the desert. He sprouted ideals – impractical, visionary, quixotic. At the University there was no shortage of young men with avant garde ideas, and they gravitated into one another's company, having little in common besides unorthodoxy. They held meetings, argued and declaimed, and were laughed at by their fellows. Henry could see that many of them were unrealistic, and did not want to become one of their set, but he began to do a good deal of listening.

Henry's visits to Clare Street almost ceased. Sir Timothy was a jealous rival with the advantage of having no other occupation. Perversely, Miss Eliza tried to woo Henry back, sending messages by Dan. He might have abandoned her completely had not old Mrs Leland died, obliging him to attend the funeral. Afterwards, he joined the gathering at number 18, where ratafia and sugar cakes were served.

He set off for the funeral in a mood more associated with weddings. Anne's mother was Mrs Leland's daughter. The whole family was bound to attend. He was disappointed. There was an outbreak of agrarian violence within a mile of Roscrea, and Mr Walker refused to allow his wife and daughter to attempt the journey.

That night, in his room, Henry again wrote to Anne. She had never replied, but at least she didn't ask him to stop. She was more and more a necessary part of his life.

Chapter Five

◆—<·●·>—◆

Anne Walker slapped the butter to and fro in the wooden tub. She poured away the last rinse, added a fistful of salt and worked it into the yellow mound with the butter-hands. Every deft stroke was a little harder than necessary; she frowned, her mouth set.

It was hard for Anne to look put out, her eyes were too gentle, and her mouth, with its 'bee-stung' lower lip and deep corners, seemed always to be smiling.

Anne enjoyed churning, and making butter and cheese. She was fond of gardening too, and of looking after her ducks and hens. But it was unreasonable of her mother to expect her to keep house and organise meals as well. Her parents had private means, in addition to her father's stipend and share of the tithes, but they were stingy about paying wages, and gave Anne no allowance.

She smacked the butter crossly from side to side, her mind occupied with food. Six – possibly seven – extra people to feed at short notice. It was too much. She would have to move into Hetty's room, because horrid old Sir Timothy was coming and was sure to bring his valet. The sucking pig was killed and dressed of course . . . The side of beef – dear God, let's hope it doesn't go bad before it's finished, but the pork must be eaten first. The cockerels weren't plucked yet – Bridie must do that . . . The jellies had set, but more would be needed.

Bridie, the dairy maid, idled in the doorway, a basin balanced on her hip, talking to Mick, the yardman. She spoke in Irish, the preferred language of both, for they came from the Cloncannon hills where English was rarely heard. Anne, who could understand every word they said, tried not to listen. The time for admitting that she knew Irish was long past, but she often felt she was eavesdropping.

Anne had been reared at Bonmahon, a seaside village in County Waterford where her father had been curate. His wife's influence and money had speedily moved him to a more central area, but it had

34

taken all Dr Leland's influence and that of a bishop or two, to make a rector of him. He was entirely without ambition.

Anne's childhood had been a lonely one, her Irish-speaking nurse being her closest companion. When the family moved, Anne was twelve and Hetty a baby. Thomas, the youngest, was born two years later. Between Anne and Hetty, five infants had been born and failed to survive. Mrs Walker, who could shed tears over the death of a child in a novel, was philosophical about losing her own. 'It's foolish to cry,' she told Anne. 'Babies die; they always have and they always will.'

James and Sarah Walker lived in chilly isolation, caring little for one another. It was hard to believe that they had been married for twenty-two years and had produced eight children. Sarah had once been a lively girl with a fine singing voice and an inflated idea of her own importance. She had grown into a fat little woman, all of whose emotions were reserved for music and for trashy novels. She preferred books about death, unrequited love, ruined castles and ruined lives, involving herself in the stories until they were more real than her own life. Her handsome face often bore an expression of anguish, puzzling to anyone who didn't know her.

Anne, packing the last of the butter into boxes, wondered if her mother would be happier if she helped in the house and garden. Her settled gloom was harder to endure than Aunt Eliza's waspish tongue, any day.

Bridie and Mick were talking about Anne. They called her, 'the Young One' so that she wouldn't overhear her name. 'Twenty-one if she's a day. High time she was off the carpet.' Bridie giggled, a hand to her mouth. They would be exchanging coarse jokes about her next, and serve her right for listening. Anne cooled her hands on the dairy shelf, a broad slab of slate, ten feet long. She took down the cream cheeses in their muslin bags, covered them with folded cloths and set weights on them. Then she took off the long pinafore that covered her grey cotton dress from neck to ankle, hung it on the back of the door, rinsed her hands and went outside.

She was still out of temper. All this extra work because her aunts were coming to stay, and Aunt Eliza was impossible to please anyway. They had visited the Glebe House two years ago and stayed six weeks. Aunt Eliza had nagged, Aunt Mary had stayed in bed with a migraine, and Sir Timothy, Eliza's shrivelled old beau, had pinched the maids' bottoms and tried to flirt with Anne. The aunts had brought three servants, two personal maids and a cowed Divinity student. Poor young man, he was dreadfully teased by the children and was terrified of Miss Eliza. They were bringing him again, or another like him . . . 'Our protégé'. Still, any young man was better than none.

The Glebe House stood on a hill, surrounded by lime trees, and she went to lean against a smooth grey trunk, enjoying the honey-scented shade while bees buzzed furiously in the branches overhead.

It was a hot afternoon in August – a typical peaceful summer's day. Hard to believe that the June riots had happened, that shops had been looted and houses burned. Hard to believe that they had had to barricade the windows against Whiteboys, while the Militia patrolled the streets after curfew and the Yeomanry galloped about, looking for trouble. James Walker had received a letter with a crude drawing of a coffin and a smeared cross, drawn in brownish blood.

Even more frightening were things which were never explained; the sound of a horse galloping full tilt in the darkness, pursued by another; a sudden shrill scream, choked off just as suddenly; a trail of drops of blood across a meadow. Anne shuddered.

From the high ground, she looked down on the market town of Roscrea, snug in its hollow. Away on the Dublin road, she heard the sound of the post-horn at the turnpike. She thought how pleasant it would be if anyone were to write to her.

Dinner was at three o'clock and Anne was late. Sarah Walker raised her eyebrows in surprise. Anne was never late. Sarah often said, 'Anne has never been any trouble'. This was high praise from Mrs Walker, who regarded daughters more as useful possessions than as people in their own right. Some daughters, she knew, demanded and spent money, others pursued or were pursued by unsuitable men; some refused to attend Divine Service. Anne had never caused her parents a moment's anxiety. Vaguely, Mrs Walker supposed she would marry some day – not too soon though – an extra servant would have to be engaged in her place.

Certainly she had given no sign of expecting the letters addressed to her from a student at Trinity College (that tall, clumsy man, with the wild-eyed look) – which her mother had intercepted. True, he appreciated music, but he was a nobody and, worse, an excitable nobody. Anne's father had been right to destroy the letters at his wife's bidding. Most of the Reverend James's actions were done at his wife's bidding.

When they were alone, Mrs Walker said to him, 'I wonder who this protégé of Eliza's can be. I trust not that Mr Higgins again – a dead bore.'

'Far worse,' said James Walker, handing her a letter. 'This came by today's mail. No doubt you will know what to do.'

His wife studied the single sheet, its jagged handwriting crossed. 'Henry Fulton. The wretched youth is persistent. You should write to him.'

'Read it.'

Mrs Walker read the letter, which started, 'My dear Miss Anne', incredulously. First, the young man said that Miss Leland had asked him to join the party visiting Roscrea. He hoped that, although she hadn't acknowledged his earlier letters, she would be pleased to see him; if not, he would stay elsewhere. Then there was a lively description of a race meeting at Phoenix Park, and one of Sir Timothy, powdered and primped, fresh from the barber. 'I cannot tell you,' Henry wrote, 'how much I look forward to meeting you again. You are always in my thoughts, and have become a part of my life . . .'

Mrs Walker scrunched the paper in her hand. Had she read it to the end, Henry would never have set foot in her house.

> Your aunt Eliza continues as alarming as ever. How she and Miss Mary contrive to find so much energy, I cannot tell, for their veins must surely by now be filled with claret rather than blood – all the rest is biscuit. Miss Mary has a *tendre* for me, almost as terrifying as Miss Eliza's tongue-lashings. I doubt if they will allow me out of their sight. Will you come and deliver me?

The letter was signed, 'Henry Fulton'.

Mrs Walker hurled the crumpled paper into the grate. 'Is it possible that my sisters are bringing that puppy here?'

James Walker nodded sombrely. 'He is even now on the road,' he said. 'I will leave you to deal with him.'

'It is your place, not mine. What can *I* say to him?'

'You are the best judge of that. Now, if you will excuse me . . .' He hurried out of the room.

James Walker was an idle man, doing the minimum required to draw his stipend. He spent much of each day at Castle Craig, playing endless hands of bezique with old Colonel Craig, and going through the motions of tutoring Ambrose Craig in Latin. He and his wife had met at the first performance of Handel's *Messiah*, and now, owing to her efforts, the *Messiah* was to be performed in Roscrea. It had been a huge success in Cashel. Choir, soloists and orchestra had been gathered together from various parishes and vigorously schooled, while six trumpeters had been borrowed from the garrison.

Mrs Walker was still in mourning for her mother. If the music had been secular, she could have taken no part. She had been amazed when her sisters accepted her half-hearted invitation to attend, and horrified when they announced a date of arrival three weeks before the performance. She wished they were not bringing Sir Timothy. She suspected that, after thirty years, he was still Misss Eliza's lover – disgusting! As for this Fulton man, she would decide what was to be done with him all in good time. Eliza and Mary would arrive in a few hours, and who knew how many hangers-on they might decide to bring with them.

It was late evening when the visitors arrived. Anne had been unable to settle to anything. Usually methodical, she had almost missed her dinner as she was still in the garden, picking raspberries to make a fool, when the bell rang. After dinner, she sat down to sew. Hetty's India muslin was outgrown, and Anne lengthened the skirt and widened the waist skilfully with ribbon insertions. Sarah neglected her younger daughter, a cheerful tomboy, inseparable from her brother Thomas.

Anne finished the dress. She played a hand of piquet with her father, then another. The sun set and she walked out in the twilight and stood under the limes. Her parents were out of temper, her mother especially. When she asked who the aunts were bringing with them, Mrs Walker had snapped 'You'll discover that soon enough.'

When the coach with the Leland arms on the panels came into view, she couldn't tell how many were inside, but there appeared to be somebody sitting *vis-à-vis* the other passengers – three occupants at least. The coach was followed by a chaise containing four people

38

– servants, presumably. A tall man on a small horse rode alongside, his feet dangling beneath its belly. Anne strained her eyes, but it was too dark to see if it was anyone she knew. Then she saw that two more horsemen were riding behind, one plump, one slim and dressed in black.

She counted. Here were six supper guests and eight who would eat in the kitchen, for there were postilions and drivers to be catered for. Fourteen. She picked up her skirts and ran into the house.

The Leland ladies owned a travelling coach, an ancient thing, riddled with woodworm, its cushions stuffed with straw and smelling of mice. Six hired horses drew the coach; slow, clumsy beasts, driven by an elderly, slow-witted coachman. With the postilions and horses, he would return to Dublin the following day, leaving the coach behind.

Miss Eliza and Miss Mary sat, as erect as ever, side by side, and Sir Timothy perched opposite. His old bones felt as if they might be shaken apart. He had run out of gallantries hours before.

Henry Fulton had found the ride from Dublin almost as maddening as the coach trip from Lisburn. He was mounted on a smart little cob which could trot twelve miles in an hour, but the speed of the two vehicles was barely six. The cob bounced along, shaking its head and snatching at the bit mile after mile. It was extraordinarily tiring. His two mounted companions, Sir Jonah Barrington and William Knox, had a great deal to say to each other and very little to say to him. Sir Jonah, who had lent Henry the cob, had also forced a pistol into his hand. Now it was in his belt, and he was thankful that he had not been obliged to fire it.

When they reined in at the turnpike, Sir Jonah, who knew the road, had pointed with his whip towards a clump of large trees on rising ground to the left. A sizeable house was just visible among them, its chimneys dark against the evening sky. 'That's the Glebe House. Ready for supper, are you? I declare I could eat a whole goose.'

Henry wasn't thinking about food. Ever since they left Dublin the previous morning, his joy in his good fortune had put everything else out of his head. He looked towards the house, and knew that Anne was there – not indoors, but waiting under the trees. Now that the time had come, he delayed the meeting. Instead of riding up the drive with the rest of the party, he put up his cob at the Castle Inn, and followed on foot. His idea was to arrive unobtrusively, while his hostess was busy with the other guests.

The plan misfired. Instead of being one of a group of six, he arrived alone as the horses were being led away, and had to find Mrs Walker and remind her of their meeting at Clare Street. She was barely civil, and her husband took his line from her. Anne must have showed them my letters, thought Henry.

At supper, he sat half way along the table, between Miss Mary and Hetty. Hetty had been allowed to attend in order to even the numbers. Anne and William Knox sat opposite. Between Anne and Henry stood a huge and hideous silver epergne, which hid her from him completely.

'What is your name, sir?' asked Hetty. She was small and slight, with big eyes and a button nose.

'My name is Henry, and I hope you will call me by it. And yours?'

'Why, it's the same as yours – Henrietta. But everybody calls me Hetty, and so must you. Are you in love with Anne? You look as though you were.'

'Good heavens, do I? How can you tell?'

'Because you keep staring at that silver ornament, and it is so ugly: and you must be hungry but have barely touched your pork. I thought you were trying to see my sister across the table.'

'Hetty, you are far too observant.' Henry laughed, and speared a piece of pork.

'Two years ago,' said Hetty, 'my aunts stayed all summer. They brought a man called Gabriel Higgins with them – Thomas and I called him Gaby. We didn't like him, so we put a hedgehog in his bed. You are much nicer. Are you going to be a curate?'

'Perhaps, some day. And I assure you, I am very nice, so you may spare me the hedgehog.'

'Gaby was going to be a curate. Thomas put treacle in his riding boots. Of course, we were only children then.'

'And now you are full grown. How old are you, Hetty?'

'Eleven, and Thomas is nine. Don't worry, he is quite reformed. Mr Jones beats him hard and often, he is the Parish Clerk and is teaching him arithmetic and Latin. *Are* you in love with Anne, Henry?'

'How could I be? I have met her only once. I look forward to knowing her better.'

'You will,' promised Hetty. 'Once the aunts come, it would take gunpowder to move them, Anne says.'

After supper, Anne slipped away. Miss Eliza ordered Henry to play backgammon with Sir Timothy. He hoped the old man would decline, but he did not.

The next day, Sir Jonah and William Knox, who were travelling to Limerick, resumed their journey. Sir Timothy stayed in bed. Anne appeared briefly at breakfast and was immediately dispatched to the kitchen by her mother.

After the meal, Miss Eliza instructed Henry to fetch her portable writing desk and her small portmanteau. He deciphered an account of a battle, printed in Greek on paper foxed by damp. At dinner, he ate roast beef, galantine, raspberry fool and junket, while Mrs Walker and Miss Eliza argued heatedly across him. He had no opportunity to talk to Anne, and wondered how long Mrs Walker would contrive to keep them apart. He didn't see her again until supper, and the expectation of a long visit promised by Hetty began to lose its calming effect.

The next morning, early, he saw her from his bedroom window, cutting cabbages in the kitchen garden. He watched her stooping and straightening as he tied his neckcloth and fastened back his hair, taking pleasure in her gracefulness. He couldn't see her face, as she wore a wide straw hat. He wished that he dared call out and attract her attention. She glanced up at that moment and looked straight at him. He left the window and bounded downstairs, three at a time. He joined her in the garden, breathless.

Henry wasn't wanting in manners, but when he found himself face to face with Anne at last, he was suddenly tongue-tied. The small talk he had ready seemed trite and irrelevant. 'Good morning,' was all he could produce.

'Take care,' said Anne, 'you're standing on the onions. Good morning, Mr Fulton.' She looked mischievous. With that deeply indented mouth, you couldn't tell if she was smiling, thought Henry. He caught a glimpse of Mrs Walker through the parlour window, standing with her back turned. She was small like Anne, but was built like a ship's figurehead. Henry thought she moved as if propelled by a gale. She was sure to come surging along if she saw them alone. 'Did you not receive my letters?' he asked urgently.

Anne sliced off the outside leaves of a cabbage. 'No, I did not,' she said. 'I heard of them only last evening from my Aunt Eliza. My father intercepted and burned them – I am so very sorry. How rude you must have thought me when I didn't reply.'

'I thought you were indifferent.' Henry looked down on the top of the straw hat. He could see nothing of Anne except a tanned arm supporting the basket which rested on her hip. He remembered the Dublin beauties, whose skin never saw the sun.

She glanced up, under the brim of the intrusive hat. 'Why are you staring at my arm? Is there a spider on it?'

'No. I was thinking how well the sun has treated you. Your arm is like a fresh egg – brown and pearly.'

'And hard and shiny?' she teased. 'I didn't know you were poetical, Mr Fulton.'

'I'm not. I spoke the truth. Why should I dissemble?'

'If you don't learn to dissemble, your ears will be boxed one of these days.'

'Box them then. Shall I fetch you a stool to stand on?'

She took an angry step towards him, then burst out laughing. 'Oh, you are impossible.' She hurried away to the kitchen. As Henry went in through the front door, he met Mrs Walker coming out. She wished him good morning without a frown, so she could not have seen them together. And at breakfast, to his amazement, she smiled at him.

If Henry thought that Sarah had warmed to him personally, he was wrong. She had been talking to her sister. 'Eliza, who is this young man? Why have you taken him up? There is a strangeness about him – and besides, his clothes are shabby.'

'Rubbish, Sarah. You imagine things. He is most able – quite a master of Latin and Greek. His father has just purchased a fine mansion where he entertains freely. He is a wealthy merchant with interests in India. His brother is a patron of the arts.'

'That's all very well, but he is making sheep's eyes at Anne. I don't want her carried off by a penniless student.'

Eliza snorted. 'Nor I. But William Knox thinks well of Henry. By the time he is ordained, William will have attained his bishopric and will find him a living hereabouts. As for being penniless – we shall see.'

'I cannot wait to see our Henry in his cassock and bands,' cried Miss Mary. 'He will make a famous parson, I know he will.'

'One curate is much like another,' said Miss Eliza, crushingly.

Chapter Six

By the time Henry had been at Roscrea for a week the power of Anne's charm had ceased to seem mysterious. It was no longer a matter of speculating about former lives or feeling that the future cast its light backwards. Instead it was an intoxicatingly real blend of longing to make love to her and seeing that she was the most likeable person he had ever met. Talking to her was so easy, laughing with her was so delightful – as well as being an enchantress she was, he now realised, a friend: his best friend. As their easy companionship developed he became sure in his head as well as his heart that they belonged together, and felt so happy that he even managed not to propose to her until the end of their second week together.

One fine afternoon they set off for a picnic with the younger children and the governess. Henry and Anne walked together, the children skirmishing round them like puppies. Behind rode Miss Harding in a pony trap containing picnic baskets. They turned off the road at Mount Heaton, and followed a dirt track by the river, shaded by beech trees.

The day was sultry – clouds of midges whirred above the water. Anne and Hetty had dabbed camphor on necks and wrists to keep them off. Henry refused an offer of camphor from Hetty, and walked in his own private cloud of midges until he swallowed one, whereupon he allowed her to dab the oil on his hands and forehead.

Round the next bend, they heard chattering voices, laughter and someone singing. Then a dozen young men and women appeared, walking towards the town. As soon as they saw the picnic party, they stopped talking and sidled past. They were ragged and barefoot, but nothing like the starving scarecrows of the Dublin slums. Henry and Anne wished them good day, and they murmured shyly in return.

'Those are peasants from Shinrone way,' said Anne. 'I almost envy them the freedom of bare feet and no staylaces. I expect they are looking for work in the harvest. In the winter, when there is no work, their lot is very hard.'

Henry turned and looked after the little group, now humbly standing aside to allow the trap to pass. Miss Harding looked straight ahead, her mouth set. The road might have been deserted. 'Your governess won't teach manners by example,' Henry said.

'No, but you should disregard her sour expression. She can't help having a mouth like a steel trap.'

The children came tearing back, saying they had found a splendid place for a picnic. Then they raced off again, shouting to Anne to hurry. Henry remarked, 'Yours is a lovely name, Miss Anne. It is a favourite of mine.'

She looked surprised. 'Truly? It is plain and old-fashioned. My mother wished to call me Cecilia, after the patron saint of music, but Aunt Eliza thought it had a Papish ring and forbade it.'

'Your aunt usually succeeds in making others do as she wishes,' said Henry. 'She did not invite me to accompany her here – she informed me of my destination and the date of our departure. I have learned more Greek from her than from my tutor, and more about Alexander the Great than anyone could wish to know.'

'She forced you to come here against your will?' Anne gave him a sidelong glance.

'Absolutely. I resisted every inch of the way.' He took her hand in his, and swung it to and fro as they walked, but she moved away when they arrived at the clearing where the children were waiting.

Later, the meal eaten, they sat under the trees, watching Miss Harding slowly fall asleep. Her head nodded, then jerked up as the pony stamped at the flies. Her eyes flew open, sent a searching glance in Anne's direction, then slowly shut. At last, her chin sank on her breast and she began to snore gently.

Henry stood up and silently held out his hand to Anne. She looked up at him, hesitating, then she accepted it and they strolled away down the path.

'Here we are. Sitting side by side, for all the world like my two aunts,' said Anne. She was sharing Henry's coat, so was obliged to sit close to him.

Henry was feeling a little breathless, but not seriously nervous.

45

He said, 'I love you, Anne. I think you know already. Will you marry me?'

She said quietly, 'I knew – I guessed. But are you sure? So soon?'

'I have always been sure. Answer me, Anne, will you marry me?'

She watched a beetle scurrying across her skirt, her head bent. 'Perhaps . . . some day. But how can you talk about marriage? It will be years before you attain your degree.'

'Dearest Anne,' he said, 'I knew you wouldn't play the coquette and affect astonishment. Yes, my degree is far ahead, but I don't believe I can wait for you for years. Why should I not seek a position as a tutor? Thanks to your aunts, I have an exhaustive knowledge of dead languages and ancient history. I could teach mathematics too.'

The beetle spread wings like crinkled green paper and flew away. She watched it go. 'You should be a clergyman, if that is what you want.'

'I want you.' Henry swivelled round so that he was sitting on his heels in front of her. 'I want you for my wife. Why should we have to wait? Life is short, after all.'

'Because we *cannot* marry and you know it. You would have to leave Trinity and exist on whatever pocket money your father decides to give you. If you defy his wishes, he might not give you anything. Wait until you are ordained. Aunt Eliza tells me you want to help the poor and needy; you can't do that if you are poor yourself.'

'True. But I want, not so much to help them as to create a society in which help would be unnecessary.'

'Utopia? No, Henry, that won't come in our time. Perhaps it never will.'

'Would you help me build such a society?'

'You might as well ask me to help you to learn how to fly. I would support you in anything, but I think you are unrealistic. Should we not walk back?'

'No, we should not. You sidetrack me deliberately. We were discussing our marriage and you made me talk about the poor who are always with us. Tell me, will you wait for me, then?'

There was a short silence. He took the signet ring off his little finger and fitted it on to Anne's fourth finger. 'You haven't answered me,' he said.

She looked at his bent head with the thin nose and the wide

mouth, the eyes downcast. His expression told her nothing. 'You must give me time to reflect,' she said, removing the ring and giving it back. 'I have become fond of you, as you know, but you are not an easy person to fathom and you frighten me a little. Could we talk about it again in a week or two? I suppose you haven't spoken to Mama?'

'No, nor yet to Papa, which would be more seemly if less productive. I suppose you are right. A nasty habit of yours, being right. You should strive to overcome it.' There was a smile in his voice, and he helped her to her feet, keeping hold of both her hands. She looked up at him, expecting a kiss, but he pulled her against him roughly, snatched off her hat and buried his face in her hair. Holding her tightly, he said indistinctly, 'Oh God, why must we wait? I wish I could persuade you to run away with me.'

He was trembling. Anne, who was trying not to tremble, spoke as if to an unreasonable child. 'Run away? Where? To the Antipodes? Anywhere closer, and we would be fetched home in disgrace. I had rather wait ten years. People who elope and get married by roving couple-beggars always return of themselves, begging forgiveness. How would you like that?'

He loosened his hold on her. 'Practical, down-to-earth little Anne. Will you be able to tether me and my dreams to the ground when we are married?'

'When, rather than if?'

'When.' More seriously, he added, 'I think you have the most beautiful mouth I have ever seen.' He touched it with the tip of a finger.

'I'm afraid you are a flatterer,' Anne replied, although she knew he was not. She wondered if he could hear her heart beating. Inhibited by convention and innocence, she stood quite still, fearing her own feelings and knowing nothing about his.

'Boo.' Thomas bounced out from behind a tree. Henry let Anne go, grabbed at him and missed. Thomas fled, and swarmed up a tree with a sound of rending pantaloons. Henry caught him by the ankle, slung him over his shoulder and fetched him down. Then he cuffed the boy hard.

'Never do that again,' he said, in a voice that Anne hadn't heard before. 'Of all things, I detest spying and eavesdropping. Get away to your nurse.'

47

More stung by the word 'nurse' than by the rest, Thomas made off as fast as he could.

That evening at supper, Anne was quieter than usual. Henry sat between Hetty and Miss Eliza, whose sharp black eyes darted from him to Anne and back. Mrs Walker discoursed about the latest rehearsal to Sir Timothy, who picked at his food and ogled the maid. The Reverend James listened patiently, while Miss Mary told him some hitherto unpublished titbits about Alexander the Great. Hetty wriggled with boredom, and Henry gave her a conspiratorial wink. She grinned at him. 'You denied it when I said you were in love with Anne, but I was right, wasn't I?'

'Yes, you were right,' said Henry absently. He had just seen Sir Timothy leaning towards Anne with a leer which showed all of his few remaining teeth. Anne drew back sharply.

Hetty prattled on. 'Anne is a great beauty, I think, though I know one is not supposed to say so of one's sister. I wish *I* had dark blue eyes and raven hair and an eighteen-inch waist, then a handsome young man might fall in love with *me*.'

Henry laid down his fork. 'Listen to me,' he said. 'You insult your sister with your glib talk. There is more to Anne than a beautiful face. If she had ginger hair and gooseberry green eyes, she would still be the same person. I would still have fallen in love with her.'

'Wouldn't it have taken longer?' enquired Hetty.

Henry laughed. 'I suppose it might,' he said.

The corn ripened, and the reapers moved into the Glebe House barley field. The wives and families of the outdoor staff joined in the saving of the harvest, so Anne walked out to the field at mid-day with bread, beer and apples in a basket.

Henry overtook her before she had gone far. They followed the meadow path where willow-herb and purple spikes of loosestrife grew waist high and creamy meadow-sweet shed pollen on their clothes. He walked a yard away from Anne, knowing they could be seen from the windows. Looking back to see if Mrs Walker's face was visible behind the panes, he saw Miss Harding panting after them, red faced and disagreeable as ever. 'Miss Anne, you must return at once. The choristers from Dunkerrin will soon be here, and your mother wishes you to prepare a cold collation.'

'Oh, that can wait, I shan't be long,' said Anne.

'You are to return immediately,' persisted Miss Harding.

Henry was carrying Anne's basket. 'You had better go,' he told her, wondering how much Thomas had seen and understood. He watched her striding back, vexation in every step, Miss Harding left far behind. Then he walked the rest of the way to the harvest field.

The day was dull, with a promise of thunder. There had been reports of disastrous storms on the Continent; hailstones which could kill cattle, and floods which inundated crops. France was suffering its third spoiled harvest in succession.

Henry watched as the men cut the corn with reaping-hooks. Behind them, the women gathered it into sheaves, tying each one with a girdle of straw, cunningly twisted and knotted. They stooked the sheaves in clumps of six or eight. Older children gleaned fallen straws, younger ones played, and a baby, wrapped in a shawl, slept beside a stook, thumb in mouth.

Henry set down the basket and began to stook. Instantly, all work ceased. The women and children gaped at him; the men straightened their backs and stared. Embarrassed, Henry stopped working. 'There's bread and porter there when you want it,' he said.

'Thank you, your honour.' The man who spoke raised a finger to his hat in salute and made for the basket, followed by the others. They walked round, rather than past Henry, and he noticed that, while he had been led to the place by chattering voices, the party sat down to eat and drink in silence. Puzzled, he went away.

That night, the weather broke; it grew suddenly colder, and a gusty wind blew in from the north-west. The freshly made stooks blew over within minutes. By morning, they would have settled into position, their bearded heads firmly entangled. The patient women restooked the sheaves, and saw them blow over again, until a cloudburst sent them running for home.

For a week the rain poured down night and day, and more than half the grain was lost, mouldy and sprouting in the fields. Those who could read got a sort of gloomy satisfaction from the accounts of worse devastation abroad. Those who could not, sullenly dragged their stooks to higher ground, turned them to face the south, and watched the corn shed its grain before it could be drawn in out of the fields.

The tithe-proctors who had failed to collect cash on May the first, now sent wagons into the fields, escorted by yeomen, to exact payment in kind. Henry, who hadn't seen this sort of thing before, was greatly concerned. James Walker was a good-natured man, and wouldn't allow tithes to be collected by force, but it seemed wrong that they should be collected at all. Most of the country people were Catholic, paying to support a Church not theirs. James Walker was a well-off man, although many curates preached a charity they could have done with themselves.

Henry knew better than to mention his doubts to Miss Eliza, but he told her about his encounter with the harvesters. 'I do not understand them,' he finished.

Miss Eliza sipped a glass of inferior Madeira (James was stingy with claret). 'If you, who are an educated man, do not understand them, how can you expect ignorant peasants to understand you? They, not having had lessons in deportment, gape open-mouthed at what they do not understand. Whether it is a poor wretch in Bedlam, a dancing bear, or a foolish young man who strays from his appointed place.'

Henry, perceiving a kind of crazy logic in this, said no more.

The production of the *Messiah* was now only days away. Mrs Walker talked about it at every meal, until Miss Eliza's scanty patience deserted her and they quarrelled. Sides were taken, Sir Timothy backing Miss Eliza and Miss Mary backing Mrs Walker. That evening, the whole party was to visit Boula Rectory for supper, cards and music, but in the end, only Mrs Walker, Miss Mary, Henry and Anne set off.

The Walkers' coach was comfortable, and their horses the best to be had. Nothing could disguise the vileness of the roads, but the party travelled in reasonable comfort. The last quarter of a mile was uphill, and the coachman walked his team. On either side lay fields of stubble with rows of blackened stooks still waiting to be drawn in. 'The loss of so much grain must cause great hardship,' Henry remarked.

Mrs Walker, who was humming to herself, looked out at the

depressing scene as if she had not noticed it before. 'I confess, I take little interest in agriculture,' she said.

The coach drew up at the hall door, and Henry thankfully uncoiled his legs and jumped out. 'You were not designed by nature for riding in coaches, Mr Fulton,' said Anne, dimpling at him as he handed her down the steps.

'Nor yet for riding most horses,' said Miss Mary. 'Do you remember that little scampering hack of Sir Jonah's, Henry dear? I declare I thought every moment it would tread on your toe.'

Henry laughed and agreed, but Mrs Walker gave her sister a stony look. 'You exaggerate, Mary,' she said.

Canon Morrisson was a magistrate, and brother of the Lieutenant of the county. A swarthy, thick-lipped man, he was fashionably dressed in a crimped wig, broad, braided lapels, and buttons as big as crown pieces. He was absent from his parish for all but the obligatory three months of the year, leaving the work to his curate. A reluctant parson, who had inherited his living, he had recently arrived from his mansion near Parsonstown with his wife and nine children. The two eldest were young men in their late teens, the remaining seven were in the schoolroom or the nursery.

After a light meal, the Morrissons and their guests settled down to a musical evening. The Canon played the flute, his sons the violin and guitar, his wife the harpsichord. His seventeen-year-old daughter had a pure soprano voice like a boy's, which blended well with Mrs Walker's rich contralto. 'And He shall feed His flock like a shepherd,' they sang.

'A most touching rendering, sister,' said Miss Mary, wiping away a tear. All were involved in the forthcoming performance except Henry, who had managed to conceal the fact that he could sing. An audience of one, he sat on a narrow couch by the window.

Hearing a great clatter down below, he looked out and saw a number of wagons, heavily loaded with corn and drawn by teams of two horses. Workmen were leading them past the windows, armed with heavy thorn sticks, while scarlet-coated yeomen rode alongside. The procession rumbled under the archway into the stable-yard, where a sergeant shouted orders to his men, who presently reappeared and trotted away.

'What's all that to-do?' cried Mrs Morrisson, and her daughter answered, 'It's nothing, Mama, just the tithe grain arriving.'

The servant girl who had just brought in a branch of lighted candles, set them down clumsily, so that their grease spattered the satin-wood side table. Seeing that only Henry had noticed, she withdrew quickly. He could hear her running.

When the singing was over, Anne and Miss Mary joined Henry on the window seat. Some of the servants had been brought in to join in the choruses and Anne was glad when they had gone. She had sensed tension among them, and an eagerness to leave. She looked uneasily at the metal grilles which were fitted to the insides of the window frames; she had seen such things many times before, but this was the first time she had felt glad they were there. When the light faded, a footman appeared, closed the heavy shutters and slid the bolts home.

Some of the younger children had come downstairs and were clamouring for a game of blind man's buff. Henry, Anne and the older Morrissons joined in, while Mrs Walker watched disapprovingly. Then Mrs Morrisson, who had changed into a red petticoat, black shawl, green stockings and brogues, danced a jig, accompanied by the flute, fiddle and bones.

Anne was unhappy. There was something false and patronising in Mrs Morrisson's capering; the children had started a noisy game of kiss-in-the-ring. The room was dreadfully stuffy; smells of candle-grease, eau de Cologne and sweat vied with each other. Henry had not sought out her company – she wondered what he was thinking and how to deal with him. She liked him and knew she could love him, but her practical nature told her to be cautious. The back of her neck prickled – he was looking at her.

The door flew open and a dozen people crowded through. Servants, children, an apprentice boy, all talking at once, some in English, some in Irish. One word was common to both – 'White-boys! Whiteboys!' The governess shrieked 'Murder!' and burst into tears, all the children started crying at once, Miss Mary screamed hysterically. The Canon bawled out, 'Silence!'

In the sudden hush, he asked the housekeeper, a stout woman with grey hair escaping from a mob cap, 'What nonsense is this? Is there any truth in it?'

'Indeed there is, sir. The Whiteboys are taking away the tithe wagons, and they say if they are stopped they will torch the house. Seamus Duff is half killed and some of our men have run away.'

The Canon turned to the roomful of people. 'Women and children stay here,' he said. 'The men come with me. You too, Fulton.'

Henry, who had hesitated, his eyes on Anne, as the Morrisson boys went to join their father, asked, 'Should the ladies be left without any protection? Suppose the house is attacked while we are outside?'

'Cowards may remain behind, with the babes and the infirm,' shouted the Canon. Flushing crimson, Henry followed him into the hall.

Anne went as far as the door and watched the men arming themselves with blunderbusses, pistols and swords. She didn't believe Henry was a coward. He didn't look back as he left the house.

For more than an hour, the party remained in the sitting room. Mrs Morrisson, who, like her husband, was more furious than frightened, went upstairs and fetched down her two youngest and their nurse, in case the house was fired. The baby yelled, and the atmosphere grew positively thick. There were confused sounds outside – shouts, running feet, a number of shots, then silence.

The silence stretched into what seemed like a long time. Anne sat near the door, the whimpering baby on her lap, straining her ears. Then there was a scuffling noise, followed by a loud banging on the front door and a voice bellowing., 'Open up!' Miss Mary began to squeak and shiver again, but the housekeeper recognised the voice and unbolted the door. Young Nick Morrisson came in backwards, carrying a body, while his brother followed, supporting its feet.

The victim was a farm labourer, a grizzled man in tail coat and frieze breeches. He lay on the flagstones, his face and head covered with blood which trickled into the cracks in the floor. 'God save us all, he's killed!' screamed the housekeeper, crossing herself, while others behind her did the same.

'Dead men don't bleed,' said Nick. 'He's one of ours – somebody help him.'

Mrs Morrisson backed away, saying that she felt faint. The

servants retreated into the shadows. It was Anne who asked for water and bandages; Anne who, handing the baby to his nurse, knelt on the floor and wiped away the blood. 'He's been cruelly beaten about the head,' she said. 'I need a sponge, lint, gauze and linen bandages.' A maid ran to fetch them, and soon the man began to groan and shake his head, then to try to sit up.

Canon Morrisson came in at that point. 'Only one man injured,' he said, 'And the horses and wagons are safe. The scoundrels have fled into the hills, except for one, who fell to Nick's pistol.'

'Where is Mr Fulton?' asked Anne.

'Mr Fulton? I thought he had returned ahead of us. He never fired a shot that I saw.' The Canon's voice was full of contempt.

The workman was carried away to the servants' quarters, and Mrs Walker wondered if it was safe to drive home. 'Not without your supper,' said Mrs Morrisson.

'Not without Henry,' said Anne.

'Poor Henry,' said Miss Mary. 'Even now he may be weltering –'

'Pray hush, aunt,' snapped Anne.

Gradually, the excitement died down, the adults at last had their supper, and still there was no sign of Henry. Neither did anyone seem inclined to go and look for him. Anne slipped away on the pretext of saying goodnight to the children. She went to the side door and quietly let herself out.

The night was close and still, with a smell of wet ashes. The raiders had tried to burn a load of damp corn, having failed to capture it. There was no sound at all. She stepped outside cautiously in her light shoes with the little heels and silver buckles. When Henry appeared, crashing through the shrubbery, quite close to her, she ran to him and put her arms round him without a word.

She noticed that his shirt was open and his neckcloth gone.

The party from Roscrea stayed overnight, returning home in daylight. Asked where he had been after the wounded workman had been brought indoors, Henry said, 'There was also a wounded peasant. He might easily have bled to death.'

'No great loss,' said Nick, who had fired the shot.

'You fired into a crowd in the dark. You could have killed anybody.'

'I wish I had. Teach them a lesson.' The two men glared at each other.

Mrs Walker interrupted with farewells and reminders about the time of the concert. Henry climbed into the coach, seething with temper. He wondered whose was the borrowed neckcloth the footman had brought him. Not Nick's he hoped. He had woken in high spirits, remembering Anne's unguarded remarks – 'I thought you'd been killed. I couldn't have borne it – I love you.' Now his happiness was dimmed. His thoughts kept returning to the bare-footed lad howling like an animal with a bullet through his shoulder. He had little to say on the way home.

There had been disturbances in Roscrea too. As the coach arrived in the town, they were stopped and questioned by a militia officer; there were soldiers everywhere. Some shops had been broken into and looted, and a farmer, said to be an informer, had been murdered in the street. Curfew was imposed and an extra company of the Prince of Wales's Fencibles drafted in from Limerick.

Mrs Walker was near tears as she sat down to dinner. At a meeting that morning, the committee had decided to postpone the performance of the *Messiah* until the curfew should be lifted.

Chapter Seven

Miss Eliza had intended to remain in Roscrea until September, when Henry's term started. She was driven out by her sister's sulks and complainings as the choir and orchestra went back to their parishes and refused to take any further interest in Handel. She was undisturbed by the continuing outbreaks of violence, saying merely, 'If my sister insists on living in the wilds of Tipperary, she must expect trouble with the natives.' She hired a team of horses and a riding animal for Henry, and all returned to Dublin.

Henry was thoughtful as he jogged along beside the coach. The Whiteboys' attack on the tithe wagons was forgotten; replaced in most minds by the fresh horror of murder. But Henry couldn't forget that night at Boula Rectory. He had felt he must not attack without knowing whom or what he was shooting at, so he had remained to defend the wagons while the Morrisson boys dashed hallooing into the dark. Nick had fired his pistol and, when the shot was followed by a terrified howl, he had rushed forward with drawn sword. Then a figure had appeared out of the darkness, wide-mouthed, screaming. The lad, running blindly past Nick, who swiped and missed, had tripped, falling heavily. Henry yelled, 'Keep off!' to Nick, with such fury that he had disappeared hastily. Seeing that blood was pouring from the boy's shoulder, Henry had yanked off his neckcloth and dropped on his knees. But the boy, as soon as he felt a touch, had rolled over and on to his feet in one desperate movement and raced crying into the dark. He was about fourteen years old.

Before he left, Henry persuaded Anne to accept his ring. Neither had spoken to her father. Now that they had agreed to marry, a long wait seemed endurable. The ring was set with a bloodstone engraved with the Fulton crest, in a heavy gold setting. Henry threaded it on a hair ribbon and hung it round Anne's neck where it was hidden by her gown. She had no ring to offer him, so gave him an old gold cross, paper thin, with scratched initials and a date – 1603. It had come down to her from some forgotten ancestor. A cross was considered to be a sign of Popish tendencies, and she was not allowed to wear it.

Henry returned to Trinity determined to get through his course faster by attending every lecture, but his interest soon flagged. He could not forget that night at Boula and found that Dublin's poverty and squalor had become more disturbing than ever. When a slight acquaintance invited him to join something called The Society for Promoting the Rights of Man, he did so and soon began to be fully engaged in its activities.

The Society's debates, held openly, advocated religious tolerance and a basic education for all. They were held to be harmless if rather fanciful. When one of the members suggested that Ireland might fare better as a republic with an elected president, he was rebuked and asked to leave the meeting. Henry, amazed by this strange notion, waylaid the young man afterwards to discuss it further. He was disappointed to find that the other man had been propounding a theory rather than making a practical suggestion.

Henry missed Anne sorely. They exchanged weekly letters, but he had to be careful how he wrote, knowing that her parents wouldn't hesitate to read them. He stayed in Dublin for Christmas with one of his new friends, rather than travel north again.

It was a cruelly hard winter, with weeks of frost. Food became scarce; the turf barges were locked in ice on the canal, and unable to deliver fuel to the city. Poor people stole floorboards, skirtings and even doors from empty buildings to make fires. Ironically, the gross overcrowding which caused so much disease saved many children and old people from freezing to death.

Eliza Leland, the turf being damp, revived her fire with a pile of Henry's discarded notes. The sudden blaze set the chimney on fire, but mercifully the house itself didn't catch. Sir Timothy, unable to travel each day from the house in Church Street which he shared with his much tried wife, moved unobtrusively into number 18 and took over old Mrs Leland's room. Once settled there, his jealous dislike of Henry waned and he welcomed him genially, playing host, although Miss Eliza constantly put him in his place with a variety of blistering snubs.

The life of Alexander stagnated – Henry suspected that the sisters were bored with it. Although the book was still supposed to be the reason for his visit, they had changed imperceptibly to social calls. There were other callers – always male – William Knox and Sir Jonah Barrington among them.

One day Sir Jonah arrived as Henry was leaving and found himself alone with Miss Eliza. 'Mark my words,' he said, 'there will be trouble in France. People are freezing to death in the streets of Paris, and there will be famine in the spring. Natural disasters play into the hands of political agitators – especially if the upper classes are unsympathetic. Don't you agree?'

'Sympathy for a discontented majority is dangerous folly,' pronounced Miss Eliza. 'It is possible to browbeat the mob with impunity provided such actions are carried out with panache, and treated as correct and normal. Once chinks appear in the armour of the rulers, sharp-eyed rabble-rousers will be there to explore them.'

Sir Jonah laughed. 'There are no chinks in your armour, ma'am,' he said.

'I should hope not indeed. Henry has some of these deluded ideas about reform. He is moonstruck, and will ruin himself with his reckless philanthropy.'

'Fulton is an excellent young man,' said Sir Jonah. 'I deplore his liking for democracy, but he is sound and genuine, and has an honest, open manner which I cannot help admiring.'

'I daresay,' said Miss Eliza scornfully. 'Such a head-in-the-clouds idealism might do very well for a rich bachelor, but Henry plans to marry my niece and live with her in penury. I expect they will fill their house with babies and be inordinately happy, until Henry's unbridled charity lands him in the debtors' prison. I have no patience with such lack of sense. Altruism is praiseworthy no doubt, but it is a devilish bad provider.'

Sir Jonah went home chuckling to himself. Miss Eliza kept him supplied with anecdotes to amuse his friends, and he had taken a fancy to Henry which surprised himself. Oddness, a lack of worldliness and a firm belief in fate were not qualities that he usually admired. A pity, thought Sir Jonah, that Henry is so much in the company of his elders. That young attorney, Mr Tone, has much in common with Fulton: a heedless attitude to everyday life, a romantic vision of the future – poor material indeed for a barrister, not a grain of cynicism in him. Sir Jonah had briefly taken Tone under his wing, but despaired of making him work at his new career. He and Henry Fulton would be soul mates. He resolved to introduce them.

In early summer, Henry was invited to the wedding of Lieutenant Fitzmaurice of the 7th Dragoons, and the Hon Rachael Manton of Merrion Square.

Henry had often wondered how Ned, his reluctant second, was faring in the army, having had no news of him since the duel with Joscelyn Darcy. Delighted, because he had felt they could be friends, Henry read the scrawled note on the back of the formal card. '. . . Our acquaintance was of the shortest, but I was deeply impressed by your courage and have often wished to renew our friendship . . .'

The wedding took place at the bride's house on a Saturday. Henry walked there in his best bottle green velvet with lace ruffles, silver shoebuckles and powdered hair. It was a warm sunny evening; as he strolled along, he wished passionately that Anne was by his side. Then his happiness would be complete.

The entrance was crowded with smart carriages, lined up, each setting down its load of fashionable ladies and gentlemen and passing on. Ned, looking more at home in uniform, with clanking sabre and jingling spurs, than he had in his college gown, shook Henry's hand warmly. 'I told you I'd marry an out-and-outer,' he said.

'I trust she doesn't chatter,' Henry said laughing, as he remembered another conversation.

'Let me tell you something, Harry. All women have faults, but it is easier to overlook them in a beauty. Since you ask, yes, I fear she does chatter.'

Rachael was slim, fair-skinned and exquisite. She wore white satin with a shawl of gold lace. On her piled silver-blonde hair, she wore an astonishing white satin bonnet trimmed with veiling and ostrich plumes, and decorated with a diamond aigrette; a copy of one worn by Queen Marie Antoinette. Rachael was just seventeen years old.

After the ceremony there was a supper with venison, dressed crab, salmon, sucking pig and a vast array of side dishes. Ned ate moderately but drank steadily. Henry thought he had aged. Afterwards, there was a ball which lasted until dawn. Any good-looking, unattached young man who was not roaring drunk and preferred dancing to cards or backgammon, was bound to be in tremendous demand. Henry partnered pretty girls in every dance, and never the same one twice. He flirted mildly with half a dozen, but as he did so he compared each mentally with Anne. None, he decided, could hold a candle to her.

He partnered the bride in a country dance, and looked into huge, grey-blue eyes, as she gazed up at him, chattering artlessly. The sticky little paw clutched in his hand was soft, white, ringed with emeralds and diamonds. He recalled the clasp of Anne's hand – firm and cool – and missed Rachael's next remark.

Henry, awkward when he was feeling shy, was a graceful and tireless dancer. Whenever there was an interval, Ned plied him with punch. He reeled back to the college in time for breakfast.

A week before the end of term, Henry was buying a book in a Nassau Street store when he saw Sir Jonah Barrington sorting through a pile of secondhand volumes. He greeted Henry, saying, 'Just the man I hoped to meet. I would like to introduce you to somebody with whom you have much in common. May I present Mr Theobald Wolfe Tone? Theo, this is Mr Henry Fulton. I have mentioned him to you more than once.'

Henry bowed to the slight, insignificant man beside Sir Jonah, thinking that he must be recovering from an illness. His face was pockmarked and narrow, with a prominent bony nose. His skin was sallow. He looked straight at Henry with brilliant dark eyes and said, 'Your servant, sir. You look concerned. Is my appearance so sickly? I assure you it is misleading.' His laughter helped to cover Henry's confusion, but he had no chance to reply as Tone immediately went on to talk amusingly on half a dozen topics, hardly pausing to draw breath.

When Henry looked away, he saw that Sir Jonah had gone. Tone broke off in order to pay for the book he had bought. His slight, narrow-shouldered figure in its barrister's gown was unremarkable from behind – the spell of the intense eyes and harsh compelling voice was broken.

Oddly, he wore no wig, his fine, dark brown hair was unpowdered, in a queue. More oddly, his full-bottomed court wig was visible in a shopping basket he was carrying.

Tone swung round. 'You are wondering why I don't wear my wig,' he said, disconcerting Henry again. 'Of course you are. Sir Jonah will tell you that a barrister without a wig is like a house without a roof. You will see why I wear none if you attend the court. When I clap a wig on my head, all sausage curls and powder, I look like a rat peeping out of a truss of straw.' He stowed the book in the basket with the wig and made for the door, saying over his shoulder, 'I lodge in Clarendon Street and am going there now. Would you care to accompany me?'

Bemused, Henry walked up the street beside Tone. He was glad that his new friend gave him no chance to talk, because he needed to analyse his feelings. When he had first met Anne, he had thought *She is mine – this is the one*, with utter certainty. Now he thought, *This is the man I have been waiting for*. What could it mean? He had unconsciously been seeking a man who shared his views, who would be worthy of respect and who would advise him – he knew this now. But Theobald Wolfe Tone's talk had so far been easy, light, facetious; the facile chat of someone trying to put a shy man at his ease. There was nothing arresting about Tone except his glowing eyes, yet Henry knew that Tone belonged to his future, just as surely as he knew that Jonah Barrington did not.

As they walked to Clarendon Street, he said to Tone, 'With your gift for persuasive speech, you will make a fine advocate.'

'Not I. I have no taste for the profession. I could not make a case for a man whom I suspected to be guilty, and I am a champion of lost causes. I back losers at Phoenix Park and the Temple alike.'

'Do you not intend to continue in Law then?'

'No,' said Tone. 'I will not long grace this profession. I am idle by nature and should have been a soldier. Law is a curst illiberal business – not half as harmless as soldiering.'

'Might I ask why you took up your present career then?'

'Of course. Improvident fool that I am, I fell in love with a girl of fifteen while I was at Trinity, carried her off and married her, incurring the fury of her parents as well as my own. They are only now beginning to come about. As for me, I am a married man of twenty-four with a wife and infant to support, and a father who is close to ruin. I used to fancy a life of high adventure, but am in no position to choose a career.' As he unlocked the door of his lodgings, he asked, 'And you, Fulton? What do you intend to do with your life? I shall never regret running away with my dearest Matty, but I would not advise you to do likewise.'

'I went to University to study mathematics, but am now attending

Divinity lectures,' said Henry. 'I am courting a beautiful girl down in Tipperary and would willingly cut short my studies to marry her, but she won't allow it.'

Tone pulled off his gown and threw it on a chair. He filled two glasses from a decanter, and handed one to Henry. 'Sensible as well as beautiful. You do not sound like a man whose vocation rules his life.'

'It doesn't. I am not sure that I have one. Other considerations draw me to the Church.'

Tone drained his glass, filled it again and tilted the decanter in Henry's direction. 'A vocation is the only excuse for joining that tribe of blood-sucking hypocrites,' he said. 'The Clergy who have inherited or bought their livings are the curse of this benighted country. And they grow rich.'

Henry wondered why Tone's words didn't make him angry, and decided that, with reservations, he agreed with them. 'I don't expect to grow rich,' he said. 'The young lady I hope to marry is the daughter of a clergyman who is tolerably content and in no way grasping, but I have seen so much injustice caused by bigotry and greed that I would like to help.'

Tone threw himself into an easy chair. 'You would do better to be like me and attend court in a foolish wig and gown,' he said. 'I have nothing against an honest curate, but don't imagine you will better anyone's lot. You will be too busy and too poor. I might call on you in your humble lodgings.'

'Thank you, sir. You are too good.'

'I will not, however, visit you in your palace when you are a bloated bishop.'

Henry burst out laughing. 'When I am a bloated bishop, you will be Lord Chief Justice,' he said.

When he left an hour later, he felt as if he had known Tone all his life. They spoke the same language and laughed at each other's jokes. Tone's obvious devotion to his young wife and little girl irritated Sir Jonah, but Henry understood it and looked forward to meeting them. He thought that if Anne had been a flighty fifteen year old rather than an unusually mature and responsible twenty-two, he might well have lost his head and persuaded her to elope with him.

He and Tone arranged to meet again.

★

About this time, Henry wrote a formal letter to James Walker, requesting his daughter's hand in marriage. He asked if they might be officially betrothed, adding that he feared that the wedding would probably not take place for a further two years, by which time he hoped to have gained his degree.

The reply to the letter was written in Mrs Walker's hand and contained a flat refusal. She accused Henry of open sympathy with thieves and murderers and – what appeared to be worse in her eyes – rudeness to Nick Morrisson. She went on to say that she was arranging a more suitable match for Anne. Soon afterwards, a letter arrived from Anne herself.

> . . . you must not mind Mama – she is Cast Down because *The Messiah* is still Postponed, probably until Winter – the Music is so Beautiful and so well suited to the Noble Words that I had Thought I would Never Tire of it – Now I know every Word and Every Note, and I feel that One More Rehearsal will see me Carried Out in Strong Hysterics – I believe that Mama has heard that your Father has some Dealings with Catholic Emancipists and holds Radical Views – I do not think she Dislikes you Personally – If only you could contrive to Come Here again – Do you know Nobody who might ask you to Visit? A Mr Fetherstonhaugh has Offered for me – a most Obliging sort of Man but I dislike him Extremely – do not Fret on my Account, I shall not be married Against my Will – there is but One Man for me – I am determined to be Patient . . .

Henry didn't go home to Lisburn that summer of 1789. Home was too far from Anne, and who knew, he might miss a chance of seeing her. It seemed like a lifetime since they had parted. Miss Eliza and Miss Mary didn't intend to visit their sister that year. 'Sarah has not yet staged that concert of hers,' said Miss Eliza. 'Until she does, I refuse to go near her. Why do you not spend some time with your new friend Mr Tone? I declare he is as strange as you are yourself. You should deal famously.'

They did deal famously. Henry visited Tone's lodgings again, and met his wife, Matty, a gentle, serious girl who looked too young to be the mother of a three-year-old daughter. She was pregnant and far from well. Tone fussed over her, made pretty speeches, half serious, half not; and spoiled little Maria atrociously. Henry felt shut out by their love for one another. He would have stayed away, but

Tone's mercurial changes of mood fascinated him. He was loving husband, doting father, considerate host; he was lively, audacious, volatile. He aired his dangerous views openly, talking of Ireland's future sometimes with hope, sometimes with despair. An evening spent with him, drinking, arguing, singing, playing the flute, made Henry's mind reel. He felt sapped by Tone's extraordinary nervous energy, while soaking up his philosophy almost without knowing it.

But even as he was captivated by Tone's charm, Henry knew that there was more depth to him than was apparent; that his ultra-radical ideals were far more than bravado. As the clouds gathered in France, culminating with the storming of the Bastille in July, Tone grew feverishly excited. He couldn't sit still, but strode up and down, talking of a new sun rising over Europe, a new dawn for humanity.

Many students at Trinity were wholeheartedly on the side of the Paris insurgents; Henry had reservations. He agreed with the principles of liberty, equality and fraternity, but his mind quailed when he thought of a blood-crazed mob, however just their cause. He hoped that the fall of the Bastille would be the beginning and end of the revolt, and would force the French government to make badly needed reforms. He remembered Boula Rectory – a peasant boy shot, a farm labourer felled by a two-handed blow from a blackthorn stick. He told Wolfe Tone about the incident, explaining how he had tried and failed to help the boy.

'I couldn't have bound up the wound even if I could have caught him,' he said. 'He screamed at me in his native Erse, and I could as easily have bandaged a wild colt on the mountains. Do you intend to enrol lads like him? Surely not.'

'I do. You don't understand the art of leadership. I promise you that an army of such boys would follow me into hell and out again. Of course you couldn't catch him. I daresay he had no wish to be whipped or hanged.'

'Hanged? He was fourteen at most.'

'Henry, my friend, I fear you are naïve. It is easy to tell that you don't attend the public hangings. The best way to help the poor peasant is to show him how he may win freedom. There is no time to bind his wounds.' With a sudden change of mood, Tone began to sing a ditty rhyming 'free' with 'libertee'. 'The Millennium is coming, Henry. The lion will lie down with the lamb and Catholic and Protestant will walk hand in hand. I will be President of Ireland, and you shall be my chaplain.'

Henry laughed. 'A pretty notion, Theo. You almost persuade me to take you seriously.'

'It would be a rare treat to be taken seriously. You think I am a frivolous jackanapes – you are wrong. I am a ruthless revolutionary. Or wait – better still, I am a ruthless jackanapes and a frivolous revolutionary. Oh – to the devil! Whatever I am, I know I am thirsty. Some Burgundy?'

They drank together, and Henry thought that not only barefoot boys would follow Theo 'into hell and out again'.

As the year passed, Henry's fascination with Wolfe Tone's theories grew, and helped to keep him from fretting about Anne. Her mother had sailed to England to visit relatives in Bath. This meant that Anne was in charge of her father's household, and it would have been highly improper for a single man to visit it. Thus, Sarah Walker made certain that Anne was kept away both from Henry and from the more eligible Mr Fetherstonhaugh.

She had made up her mind that her elder daughter must remain single as long as possible.

Storms swept the country that autumn, stripping slates from houses, uprooting trees and wrecking ships at their moorings. Torrents of rain washed the potatoes out of the ground.

Henry attended lectures, balls and meetings. He talked well and argued persuasively in the college debates, attracting the attention of men years senior to him whose opinions resembled his. He became friendly with Sir Lawrence Parsons, a blunt-spoken, coarse-featured man from King's County. Sir Lawrence shared Henry's advanced views and his admiration for Wolfe Tone.

Henry felt he was living in a vacuum. He wondered if he was destined to spend all of his youth waiting. Waiting for Anne; waiting for whatever fate had in store for him.

Chapter Eight

Christmas approached, and Dublin was blanketed with snow. The worst winter for generations, said the old people. At Trinity confinement to the College grounds bred boredom and mischief: a gentleman shot a boy in the library for throwing snowballs at him. One scholar laid a bet that he could walk to Constantinople and back in a year and set off hopefully; another attempted to swim the partly frozen Liffey for a wager and drowned.

News arrived that Henry's father had been taken ill in India, and that his eldest son, James, must go there immediately. The letter took five months to reach Ireland – it was possible that John Fulton was already dead. James embarked for Calcutta, and Henry had to leave Trinity and go home to run the family linen business. His sister, Elizabeth, and his mother welcomed him with relief; the youngest boy, William, had his hands full with the managing of the farms.

Henry detested routine office work, but he tackled it because he had to. Efficient and bored, he remained there all spring. He met his father's friend, Luke Teeling, whose views were much like Wolfe Tone's. Henry remarked on this, and was delighted to hear that Luke's sons were friends of Theo's. He met them soon afterwards. Charles, Matthew and Bartholomew were earnest young men, but lacked Tone's compelling qualities: Henry, while respecting and agreeing with them, didn't feel drawn to them in the same way.

'I am surprised,' he said to Bartholomew, 'that you dare talk so openly to me about your revolutionary ideas. I agree with them, but might they not be called seditious? Even treasonable? Don't you run risks by spreading your views?'

Bartholomew, a thickset young man with a serious manner, replied, 'Just now, our ideas are the last word in modishness. It is our only chance to spread them. Once the flood-gates in France open, we will have to pretend we were only funning, or hang.'

Henry couldn't imagine any of the Teelings 'funning'. They expected Tone to come to Antrim for a meeting, they said, but he did not come. Mr Fulton recovered, James sailed for home, and Henry resumed his interrupted studies.

Anne, confined at home, was bored almost to screaming point. She wrote about her few social outings, about the Hayward girls, hoydens, who danced barefoot at the crossroads although their father was a minister. She wrote about stuffy Miss L'Estrange, haughty Miss Prittie and dashing Lady Cahir, who rode astride and cursed and swore like a man.

Henry's letters darted from one subject to another, random thoughts being squeezed among serious accounts of events – snippets of conversation, jokes, sweet nothings . . . His pen couldn't keep up with his thoughts. Neither mentioned Mr Fetherstonhaugh. Henry lamented that the six-month interruption of his studies would mean waiting an extra year before sitting for his degree. Only his certainty of Anne and his friendship with Wolfe Tone made the prospect endurable.

The Misses Leland welcomed him back enthusiastically. Even Miss Eliza permitted herself a grim smile. Sir Timothy had become a martyr to gout, fussed over by Miss Mary. Old Dan could no longer manage the stairs, so Kate, the maid, ran up and down with messages.

Alexander the Great had been abandoned in favour of a book of Greek odes. Miss Eliza translated, Henry copied in a fair Italianate hand. Miss Mary complained (with truth) that some of the poems were indecent; shrieking and clapping her hands to her ears when her sister read them aloud.

'Nonsense, Mary,' said Miss Eliza. 'The classics cannot be indecent. Your missish vapourings create lewdness where none exists.'

Henry had bought a copy of the *Freeman's Journal*, and when they broke off for claret and biscuits, he read an account of a convict fleet bound for Botany Bay from Britain, which had arrived at the Cape of Good Hope. The convicts were said to be very healthy and orderly, only twenty-one having perished since leaving England. He remarked that, in spite of the horrors of the journey, transportation must be preferable to wholesale hangings and the further crowding of overcrowded prisons. As Miss Eliza's only comment was a snort, he went off into a reverie, imagining a wild but fertile land, waiting to be tamed and cultivated. There, he thought, a criminal might become a new man, being removed from a society where lawlessness was normal. What an opportunity. What a fascinating experiment . . .

Miss Eliza brought him back to earth with a jolt. 'Don't daydream, Henry. You will never preach good sermons if you allow your mind to wander.'

'I don't look forward to preaching,' Henry said. 'I don't feel qualified to tell people how they should go on. And I intend my sermons to be short. Yesterday the Provost made a speech lasting three and a half hours, and lost everybody's attention after one.'

Miss Eliza said, 'You will encourage only unchristian thoughts after half an hour. William Knox is always brief. I have spoken to him about you, by the way.'

'Indeed, ma'am? In what connection?'

'I asked him to mention you to his brother, the Bishop of Limerick. His influence could procure you a living in that area when the time comes.'

Henry's thanks were interrupted by Miss Mary, who exclaimed, 'Only think. Limerick is but a day's ride from Roscrea. Will not that be delightful?' Henry, who was just thinking how delightful it would be, was confused, and knocked over a silver vase. Miss Eliza said that a herd of bullocks would be less clumsy.

'I can see you tumbling down the chancel steps and into open graves,' she said. 'As for baptising infants, no sane woman would give you her child to hold.'

'I beg your pardon most humbly, ma'am,' said Henry, but his eyes were sparkling, and when she rose to her feet he impulsively put his arm round her sharp shoulders and hugged her.

Miss Eliza snapped, 'Impudence,' but her eyes were soft.

Theobald Wolfe Tone was not at his Clarendon Street lodgings. Neither was he at his father-in-law's house in Grafton Street. Here, though, Henry found Matty's sister who told him that little Richard, Matty's second child, had died a fortnight earlier, aged only six months. Theo had taken a cottage by the sea, she said, because Matty was unwell and depressed. It was at Irishtown, north of the city, and the family was going to spend the summer there.

Henry left a message of condolence and turned away disappointed.

As he walked up the street, he heard hurrying feet behind him and a voice cried out, 'Henry, you dog you, where have you been?' It was Tone, paler and shabbier than ever. He grabbed Henry's arm and steered him into the nearest tavern where he shouted for two glasses of cognac.

'I have but now come from Grafton Street,' said Henry. 'Theo, this is a sad business about your little son. I know how proud you both were of him – Sir Jonah told me. Give Matty my condolences, please.' He stretched his hand across the table, and Tone grasped it hard. There was pain in the bright dark eyes. 'He was a pretty babe,' he said, and he seemed to shrink and grow older under Henry's eyes. He swallowed some brandy and spoke again. 'My poor little wife is distracted.'

Henry felt his friend's pain as if it had been his own. 'Is there nothing I can do to help?'

Tone straightened his shoulders and gulped his drink as Henry called for another. 'Yes, Henry, you can come to our cottage and plague us. Are you still set on a career in Mother Church?'

Henry found it hard to keep up with Tone's changes of mood. He was smiling now, that happy smile which, like Henry's own, made others smile back. What an actor he would have made. 'I'd love to visit you if it would not be too much for Matty,' Henry said, 'and yes, I'm for the Church, but God knows when. I may have to go north on business again, or even to India.'

'Go your own way, Henry, or you will waste your life. You were not born to plod in your father's footsteps and you know it.'

'Yes, I know it, and that is the devil of it; but he needs help and I can't do anything for my country as yet, except air my views in debate.'

'At Irishtown,' said Tone, 'you may air any views you please.'

So Henry hired a job-horse one day, and rode north by the river mouth and along the coast road. The thatched cottage stood among gorse bushes, a mere stone's throw from the strand. Here, Henry saw Tone's domestic side rather than his political one, as he helped Matty to prepare the food, played with Maria, and amused them all with his wicked quips and with the nonsense verses he seemed able to invent for any occasion. No wonder children loved him, thought Henry.

They had a picnic lunch on the sand, watched curiously by a

dozen or more ragged toddlers. Maria called them to play with her, but they backed away. Tone won them over with the remains of the meal – chicken legs and apples. They seemed to be free to wander on the shore, gathering driftwood and shells, although the youngest was a tiny girl just able to walk, and the oldest no more than four years old. Henry gave them rides on his horse, and Tone carried them piggy-back in turn, even the filthiest. He raced along the strand, curvetting and whinneying like a horse, then he gave a whoop, set down the child from his back and turned a cartwheel. Small change rained from his pockets and the children fought over it with astonishing ferocity. Tone sat on the ground and laughed at them.

'See the wolf-cubs,' he said to Henry. 'Imagine what the wolves might achieve.'

'Poor babes,' said Henry, laughing.

'No sentiment now, my friend. Do not concern yourself with these brats – at least, not as individuals.'

'How else?' asked Henry. 'They *are* individuals.'

'If you see the future of Ireland as I do, you must widen your views,' said Tone. '"The greater good", is the phrase you will find in the books. When my glass of wine is not to my liking, I open another bottle; I don't analyse the faulty glassful drop by drop – it would take too long.'

Henry watched the children, the coins divided among the strongest, hurrying up the beach towards the village. The smallest toddler toiled along behind, crying, dragged by a slightly older sister. 'You pour away the bad wine,' he said, 'which brings us back to the shedding of blood, and whether or not it can be justified. I want the greater good as much as you, but I fear that too much blood will be poured away.'

'Why, Henry, what a long face. If that should happen, we must change our wine merchant and restock our cellar, perhaps with a different vintage. I thought I had found a man after my own heart and I was wrong. Can you think of one great movement towards freedom which was achieved without bloodshed? Consider America. And I assure you that a vast quantity is likely to be spilled in France shortly. And think of the trail of blood left by the coming of Christianity. Apathy is the great enemy.'

Henry sat back on his heels, feeling the extraordinary pull of

Theo's will; realising how much of his philosophy he had accepted already. Another slight tug and he would tip him into total agreement. The sensation was frightening, the more so because he had experienced some sort of foreknowledge of it. He half wanted to resist but did not. Uncertainty began to give way to conviction.

He jumped to his feet. 'Come, Theo, you are in a fair way to persuade me. There is sound sense in what you say, but I may not stay to discuss it further. I'm supposed to have this old nag back in its stable by seven o'clock.'

'If you must go, I will ride with you, at least as far as the edge of the city.' Tone fetched both horses while Henry said goodbye to Matty, and they set off for Dublin.

Henry allowed his horse to trot on a slack rein. Tone had launched into one of his amusing tales of his time at the Bar, but for once Henry paid little attention – the change was too sudden. He rode silently, with bent head, feeling troubled and shaken. None of the fiery speeches he had listened to had moved him like Tone's earlier remarks, despite their apparent lightness and humorous overtones. He had experienced an urge to throw in his lot with Tone, no matter what he wanted to do. He had wanted to say, 'Tell me what to do and I'll do it – ' and yet . . .

A strange awareness of Anne troubled him. He felt that she was listening and arguing moderation, just as he done himself. By moving to an extreme stance he would distance himself from Anne – perhaps endanger her life when they married. In his mind, he saw her puzzled frown, heard her anxious words . . .

At that point, Henry's horse shied, almost unseating him. By the side of the road, stretched on the muddy verge, lay a sick man covered with an old coat. He was shivering violently with chattering teeth, in spite of the sun. Henry and Tone dismounted, dragged him into a doorway and asked how they could help, but the man shook his head, staring vacantly. Then he turned on his side and retched emptily in the gutter.

Tone rode off to a hostel he knew of while Henry remained. He wiped the man's mouth and supported his head, trying not wince at the stench of him. But a minute later, his head lolled sideways – he was dead.

When Tone returned, having been told that there were no

71

vacancies in the hostel, Henry was standing beside the body. 'He's dead!' he shouted furiously. 'The poor bastard's dead.'

'Calm yourself, Henry' – it might have been Miss Eliza speaking – 'there is still fever in the air. Poor people die every day – every hour.'

'But Theo, he was no older than you or I. Did you see his look of resignation? Of acceptance? Oh, it's infamous! Seeing him, I feel like throwing in my lot with you and fighting for liberty and equality.'

Tone bent, closed the staring eyes and covered the white face in silence; then he turned angrily on Henry. 'You should keep your sense of proportion, my friend. You are not a revolutionary, just a charitable reformer, looking at the result rather than the cause. You should forget the apathy on the dead man's face and attack the apathy in London which is the root of all the ills that befell him and will befall thousands of others. When you can do that, let me know.' He swung himself up on his horse and, as Henry slowly followed suit, Tone's voice changed. 'I'm sorry – I didn't mean to shout at you. Do you understand now why I sometimes turn cartwheels lest I burst into tears?'

'Yes,' Henry said, 'I begin to understand.'

Ned Fitzmaurice had been stationed in Dublin for some time, and he and Henry met occasionally for a drink and a hand of cards. Ned belonged to a hard-drinking set which gambled for high stakes at dice and cards. Henry was of a different age-group and wasn't invited to their sessions – fortunately for his pocket. Sometimes he saw Rachael Fitzmaurice walking in Merrion Square or driving along the North Circular Road, always accompanied by her two plain elder sisters. Once, he called at the house where the couple were living temporarily with Rachael's parents.

When Ned suggested that Henry should join him and Rachael on his week's leave, he jumped at the chance. They were going to the Fitzmaurice mansion near Maryborough, where they would eventually make their home. The vacation would soon be over, and he had no wish to post north again. Most of his friends were, like Tone, out of town.

He called on the Leland sisters in tremendous spirits, taking the stairs three at a time, and found Miss Eliza alone, writing letters, a bottle of claret at her elbow. Her sour expression subdued him instantly; he greeted her soberly.

'You look peaky, Henry,' she said, without bothering to welcome him. 'You should take a mistress.'

Henry was long past being startled by anything she might say. 'My dear ma'am,' he said, 'I am betrothed to your niece. Surely such down-to-earth advice from you is inappropriate.'

'Try to remember that you and Anne are betrothed only in the eyes of one another and, possibly, God.'

Henry smiled. 'I'm afraid I must wait for the news to become more generally known,' he said. 'I could not afford to keep a mistress, even if I wished to do so.'

'Honestly spoken. I cannot understand, though, why, although your father owns a factory and a business abroad, you live on the brink of bankruptcy.'

Henry decided he wasn't going to be asked to sit down, so he sat and crossed one long leg over the other, drawing an outraged glare from his hostess. 'My father's in India, as I think you know,' he said, 'and shortly before he left Ireland he bought a very large house. Business is poor and my brother is finding it hard to make a profit. My sister is to be married soon and must have a dowry; worst of all, a ship in which my father had a share sank with all hands last year.'

Henry was giving only half his attention to what he was saying. Miss Eliza had reminded him of his womanless state, and there was a grain of truth in her diagnosis. Strange how Anne's distant presence supported him, he thought. When he wrote, 'You are always in my thoughts,' the words were literally true. She occupied his mind just as surely as she would one day, he knew, occupy his home and his bed.

Miss Eliza's gaze focused on his swinging foot. He looked and saw that the toe of his shoe was worn almost through. 'I must visit the cobbler,' he said.

'And the tailor. And the hatter,' said Miss Eliza.

'I am going out of town for a sennight,' said Henry hastily. In the past two and a half years, he had received a number of garments which had belonged to the late Doctor Leland. The reversible 'cartouche cape' had been the only wearable item. He now owned a pair of black satin breeches, too wide and too short, and a pair of square-toed boots with heels, too short and too wide. Most useless of all was a great rusty black three-cornered hat. All these gifts had been conferred on him in a way which made it impossible to refuse.

'You would look more mature and distinguished if you wore a wig,' said Miss Eliza, her eyes straying to her brother's portrait. In it, he was wearing a short, fluffy white wig, with side curls and a centre parting.

Henry sprang to his feet. 'I feel sure you are right,' he said, 'but, clumsy as I am, I would probably allow it to fall off when I was making my bow. Thank you ma'am, I won't take wine – I called only to take my leave of you before going out of town.'

Rachael Fitzmaurice, her sisters, her mother, her servants and her baggage had gone ahead to Castlegarry, sixty miles south-west of Dublin. Henry and Ned followed two days later. After riding through the tiny hamlet of Newbridge, they left the high road for a gallop on the Curragh. As Ned was riding a troop-horse and Henry a hireling, the gallop made up in energy what it lacked in speed. They pulled up, breathless.

'I swear I could run faster,' said Henry.

'No doubt,' said Ned. 'Take heart, Harry, my brother has a string of prime hunters. When I tell him what a fine horseman you are, he won't hesitate to lend you one of his best.'

'A fine horseman? I have been thrown as often as the next.'

'I grant you don't look like one,' said Ned, 'but the acid test of a horseman is not remaining clamped on a buckjumper until it is exhausted, but making a heartless beast like that bay of yours appear better than average. Perhaps, on second thoughts, it would be more entertaining to allow brother Gerald to think you are a timid and insecure trider. He is sure to put you up on some tearaway and back it to throw you in three minutes. It would do him good to lose his guineas.'

'He would probably win his bet,' said Henry. 'Do you think so poorly of your brother then?'

'I tolerate him because I see him so seldom.' Ned dismounted in the cobbled square of Kildare town, pulled the reins over his horse's head and let it drink from the stone horse-trough. 'We will put up here for the night. The inn is passable.'

That night, the two men sat late in the tap-room. Ned drank

brandy, which didn't affect him in the least. Henry, whose head was reasonably good, stopped drinking when he felt that, if he continued, he would have to be carried upstairs. He leaned back in his corner seat, twisting the stem of his empty glass, watching Ned swallowing smuggled French brandy like water. The older man's face, always stern, had set in deep lines and creases. His eyes were unknowable.

'When you wed, Harry,' he said suddenly, 'choose an orphaned only child from the foundling hospital. My Rachael has a mother, two sisters, an abigail, an old nurse and a couple of aunts. I appear to have married them all. Oh, don't misunderstand me, Rachael is all that a man could wish, but I would consign the rest to hell with pleasure. And Rachael is twenty years younger than I. Ah well, men are doting fools and always have been. Perhaps you would like to take Clara or Lucy off my hands? I thought not. They have Rachael's faults, I fear, but not her looks.' He drained his brandy. 'I expect to be sent overseas soon. Please God she won't expect to bring the whole menagerie with her.'

Morosely, he refilled his glass.

Chapter Nine

———————◆<·●·>◆———————

Castlegarry House was a vast, square mansion, deathly cold in winter. Even in late August it was dank and draughty; there was no garden, cattle grazed up to the windows, and the drive was a rutted track.

Old General Fitzmaurice, widowed for twenty years, was the nominal master. Deaf and feeble, he snored in his chair, while Ned's brother Gerald frittered away his fortune and his life.

The house looked so forbidding as he approached it that Henry was surprised to find it bursting with guests, mostly uninvited. Colossal meals of a majestic simplicity were served in the dining saloon; whole sheep, quartered and roasted, great slabs of boiled beef, yard-wide pies brought to the table in the pans they'd been baked in. Liquor flowed, and Gerald and his friends swallowed it from any cup, glass or mug that came handy, drinking themselves senseless every night. They rose, yawning and cursing, at noon. Then, if there was no race-meeting or prize-fight to tempt them away, they would ride off to the hills with their dogs, in search of deer.

Henry was sorry for Rachael. Spoiled youngest child of a Dublin banker, she hung about uncertainly with her mother and sisters, saying little and eating hardly anything. Ned treated her with absent-minded affection, Gerald with heavy-handed gallantry. Their father seemed not to know that she was Ned's wife, and often asked her what she was called. Henry couldn't imagine her as mistress of Castlegarry.

'So you're going to be a parson, Fulton,' said Gerald. 'I never thought I'd see Ned in the company of a God-botherer.'

'He acted for me in a duel,' said Henry, not adding that the fight had been forced on him.

'Not such a goody-goody then.' Gerald spoke with more respect. 'Would you fancy a day's hunting after stag?'

'I would indeed. Could you lend me a horse? Mine is but a hack.'

'Something quiet,' put in Ned, with a flicker of a wink at Henry. 'Is old Dapple still alive? Henry is unfamiliar with the sport.'

Gerald's face, made hideous by a duelling scar from eye-corner to jaw, split in a grin. 'I have the very horse for him,' he said.

A groom brought Henry's mount to the door, leading it gingerly: a chestnut stallion with a tiny head and piggy eyes. It pranced about, screaming at the other horses and snatching sideways at the groom's arm. 'A thoroughbred colt?' asked Henry in surprise. 'Will you trust me with him over your rough country?'

'Of course I will,' said Gerald, winking at Ned as they swung themselves up on their weight-carrying geldings. 'You can school him for me. He is a green jumper, having raced on the flat. He is a grandson of Eclipse – Thunder, I call him.'

'He looks as if he could gallop,' said Henry. 'It's good of you to lend him.'

'Gallop as far and as fast as you like,' said Gerald. 'Don't hesitate to give him the spur if he misbehaves. Go on, up with you.'

Henry picked up the reins, asked the groom to stand aside, mounted and trotted away. Gerald's jaw dropped. Ned shouted with laughter. 'Hand over your hundred guineas, brother,' he said.

Thunder's good behaviour came to an abrupt end when Gerald's hounds came yowling out of their kennels. He capered and plunged, gobs of froth from his bit flying back to spatter Henry's coat. A high wind was blowing, enough in itself to make a young horse play up; leaves and twigs whirled about and Henry's coat-tails flapped. He sat firmly, his hands low and very still, speaking quietly to the horse.

Gerald's private pack of hounds resembled his chosen circle of friends – noisy, unruly, greedy and stupid. They roused a buck in the grounds of Castlegarry itself, and chased it through the village of Mountrath. Henry, busy restraining Thunder's wish to bolt, saw out of the corner of his eye a team of coach horses rearing in excitement. The bottle-green coach looked familiar, but no – there were many like it. He shortened his reins and concentrated on keeping Thunder's head straight, while he sent him along so fast that he hadn't time to buck.

The stag headed for the Slieve Bloom mountains, where sheep-tracks led upwards through closely nibbled pastures. There were no hedges, to Henry's relief. He suspected that Thunder had never jumped a fence in his life. Some men cocking late hay – more rushes than grass – stopped working to watch the hunt, while their wives paused in their task of collecting dried cowdung for firing. Barefoot children scuttled out of Thunder's way, shouting what might have been encouragement or abuse in Irish.

Higher up, Henry emerged on to an open plateau, where the full force of the summer gale hit him. Scent failed, and the pack checked, sniffing about aimlessly on the short turf where heather and broom grew. Henry had let Thunder gallop uphill as fast as he liked. If he had to ride him downhill while he was still fresh, he would probably be thrown. Anyway, he doubted if a racehorse could travel down those rocky tracks at speed without a fall. He reined in and gave his mount a breather, patting the sweaty neck, noticing how Thunder bent his head to the rein, the fight gone out of him.

Soon he heard the rest of the party crashing through the under-growth. Gerald, first on the scene, began to shout furiously as soon as he was in earshot. 'How dare you treat my colt like that? Don't you know his value? By God, you'll regret it if he's lamed! Stick to your bible, Fulton, you know nothing about horses.'

Henry choked back an angry retort. Gerald had fought more than a dozen duels, and a fight with his host wouldn't do – especially if the Walkers got to hear of it. Controlling his voice, he said, 'You told me to ride him without mercy, but I have used neither whip nor spur. I told you he was unsuitable for hunting, but you insisted that I should ride him.'

'Do you imagine I meant a fledgling parson to knock him up when I paid three hundred guineas for him at Newmarket? I didn't expect you to stay on his back above a minute.'

'Since you show so little civility to your guests,' said Henry, 'let me tell you that your wonder horse has a one-sided mouth and is touched in the wind. However, if you require him for stud purposes, I will walk him quietly back to his stable.'

There was laughter, and Gerald was told by his friends that he was well served. He was saved further argument when the pack picked up the line and set off in the direction of Kinnitty. Henry turned back, and Ned swung his horse round and joined him.

'You needn't miss your sport on my account,' said Henry. 'I know my way back.'

'You flatter yourself. I think Rachael has been long enough in the company of the young bucks and old goats down at Castlegarry. Pay no heed to Gerald. He is a dissolute wretch, who would gamble on the length of a piece of straw. I warned you.'

'I don't heed him,' said Henry, 'but I am heartily sorry for his tenants.' They were passing the haymakers' dwelling, a cavelike hovel with mud walls, no windows and a hole in the roof to let out the smoke. 'Some of those poor devils could do with the guineas he spent on this horse – and it isn't even a good one.'

Ned glanced vaguely at the peasants. 'They seem well enough,' he said. 'Gerald isn't as bad a landlord as some – in fact he is popular. If you are looking for villains, blame the land agents. Most landlords are a deal too lazy to go chasing rents, so they employ a fat middleman with a foot in each camp, no loyalties and no scruples. Gerald's agent is better than average. Of course he extorts money – how would he get it else? And he isn't too particular about his methods, but without him, Gerald would have been ruined years ago. I think you are criticising what you don't understand.'

'I think I do understand,' Henry said. 'Ned, I'm grateful to you for inviting me here, and I hope you won't think badly of me if I leave tomorrow. I don't care to remain as your brother's guest, even if he wishes it.'

'On the contrary, Harry. I would think less of you if you stayed after his treatment of you.'

Henry left in the morning. When he reached the main road, he saw a milestone: 'DUBLIN 60 MILES: ROSCREA 20 MILES', he read. He turned his horse's head southward.

He reached Roscrea in two and a half hours and rode straight to the Glebe House, trying to devise an excuse. But the blinds were down, the knocker off the door. With a sinking heart, he rode to the stableyard, where a workman was sweeping the cobbles. Henry learned that Mrs Walker, returning from England, had been nine days at sea, the ship being blown offshore by the persistent westerly winds. She had been taken ill at sea and had collapsed after arriving in Dublin where she was now at her sisters' house. Hetty and Thomas were staying with friends; James Walker and Anne had left for Dublin the day before.

★

79

Anne sometimes found it difficult to remember Henry's face. She had made a quick sketch of him explaining something to Hetty as they sat under a tree. It was a good likeness – Henry sitting on the grass, one knee drawn up, the other leg stretched out, giving all his attention to the child at his side. What a good teacher he would make, Anne had thought.

Clearer in her mind was his expression as he had looked down at her, withholding the expected kiss; a stern face with an unfamiliar line between its brows. The memory hurt. Instead, she tried to recall him laughing, teasing her, tickling the back of her neck with a blade of grass as they walked together. Then there was the time when she had seen him at his bedroom window when she was in the garden. Still in his nightshirt, his hair loose, he had noticed her and stepped back. She could hardly believe her eyes when he had appeared at her side, fully dressed, a few minutes later.

Anne knew she shouldn't be thinking about Henry – certainly not about Henry in his night attire. She should save her thoughts for Mama, gravely ill in Dublin. But she had been unable to put him out of her mind since the previous day, when her father's horses had almost been stampeded by a stag hunt as they were being harnessed. There was no reason, she told herself, why Henry should be in Mountrath, and if he were, he would not be riding a wildly bounding stallion. She had been unable to see the horseman's face, but he certainly bore a striking resemblance to Henry. She sat lost in thought, her bones aching from the bumping of the coach.

At last they rattled over the cobblestones of Naas, where they were to spend the night, and the ostler let down the steps. Anne's maid went to see that beds and a meal were prepared, while the two armed outriders accompanied Anne and her father into the saloon. One was her cousin, Ambrose Walker, a lieutenant in the militia, the other was a neighbouring squire, Hilton Fetherstonhaugh.

At the Connolly Arms, they ate cold boiled pork, beetroot and stewed gooseberries, washed down with flat porter. The taproom, adjoining the saloon, was full of soldiers, and Ambrose joined them after the meal. The Reverend James fell asleep. Hilton Fetherstonhaugh, who had a red face and a loud, grating voice, entertained Anne with an account of what he would have done if the coach had been attacked by highwaymen. 'I have long sought an opportunity to prove my worth to you, Miss Anne,' he roared.

'Let us be thankful that no highwayman waylaid us,' said Anne. 'If you will excuse me, sir, I have the headache and will retire early.' She stood up and he accompanied her to the door, caught her hand and kissed it loudly, with an ungraceful bow.

'Dare I hope you will dream of me?' he suggested.

'I wish you will lower your voice. These gallantries are not your style, sir.' Anne snatched her hand away and followed the maid-servant upstairs. Mr Fetherstonhaugh had a thick hide, and was impervious to snubs. She washed the kissed hand which was disgustingly damp, and went to bed. Her dreams were indeed haunted by his coarse features and braying laugh.

In the morning, it was raining hard. The horses were put to, and they set off at nine o'clock on the twenty-mile journey to Dublin. Ambrose Walker rode on ahead to warn the Leland sisters of the party's arrival. The coach rumbled out of Naas on to the churned mud of the dirt road: water filled the potholes, so it was impossible to guess their depth. Some had been filled with loose stones. About a mile outside the town, the back axle broke without warning. The body of the coach was trapped between its in-turned wheels, both doors jammed shut; the pole between the two wheelers jerked roughly up and backward, sitting them almost on their rumps.

Inside the coach, Norah, the maid, was flung violently into James Walker's lap while Anne, who had nobody sitting opposite, hit her head hard on the panels behind the empty seat. Anne heard the horses neighing, and the uneven pounding of their hoofs as they fought their bridles, terrified by the sagging, lurching weight behind. The coachman and postilions cursed and shouted at the tops of their voices as they struggled to hold them; the sound of splintering wood was drowned by their yells. Through the mud-splashed window, Anne saw her trunk fall from the roof and burst open, scattering her clothes in the mire.

She wrenched uselessly at the door, then let down the window, screaming, 'Get us out! Help!' Mr Fetherstonhaugh's damp red face appeared in the opening and he held out his arms to her. Having screamed to be let out, she could hardly choose to remain, so she squeezed her head and shoulders through the window. He pulled her half way through by her arms, and was shifting his grip to her waist when, with a loud crack, the wheel broke and the coach tilted

81

over, held only by its front wheels. Anne found herself hanging with her hands a few inches from the ground, caught fast by the hips, while Hilton Fetherstonhaugh sprang clear of the tottering vehicle. Anne screamed then in earnest, but he stayed out of reach. James and Norah had been thrown on the floor, and one of them was lying heavily on Anne's legs.

'Help us to loose the horses!' shouted someone, the coachman, she supposed. Greatly relieved, Hilton hurried to help. While the team was being cut free, Norah managed to drag Anne back inside the coach. A moment later, it crashed over on its side.

It was a while before the three managed to scramble though the offside door, now above their heads. Hilton was waiting to lift Anne to the ground. 'Thank God you are safe,' he said.

'You are a fine beau, are you not?' said Anne furiously. 'You left me hanging head downwards, stuck in a window frame, when I might have been crushed to death, because you were afraid for your own skin. You who would have overpowered a dozen highwaymen!' She laughed scornfully. 'Well, are you going to assist my father and my maid to alight, or not?'

Sulkily, he did as she asked. Norah, sobbing with fear, held Anne's cloak for her to put on, and she clutched it, shivering. 'How fortunate that the rain has kept the robbers at home,' she said. Her anger was less at Hilton's cowardice than because he had seen her in a ridiculous position and had heard her screams for help. She and Norah crammed her wet clothes back into the trunk . . . Stays, camisoles . . . 'Sir,' Anne said, 'will you kindly take yourself off? You can surely not wish to help me pack my personal belongings.' And, as he still looked on, his horse's reins slung over his arm, his large red hands dangling, 'Oh, for the love of God, go away! Come, Papa, let us walk back to Naas if you are not too shaken.'

They waded through the mud, the Reverend James explaining how and why the accident had occurred. Anne put up her hood, her teeth chattering. Bruised and humiliated, her shoes squelching with water, she was much more shaken than he.

Henry, having left Roscrea, changed his job-horse in Mountrath and reached Maryborough that night. He had no spare money for hired horses or lodgings, so he was delighted when he was offered a lift by a college acquaintance, Peter Holmes from Nenagh. Peter was travelling as far as Naas. They set off early and arrived there in the late afternoon. Peter was not staying in the town, so Henry asked to be set down at the Connolly Arms, where he might obtain another lift to Dublin. Otherwise he would have to finish his journey on foot. The rain was coming down in sheets – he was going to have to stay overnight. Mentally cursing Gerald Fitzmaurice, Henry counted the few coins remaining in his pocket and went into the saloon where a fire was burning.

The saloon was low-ceilinged, dark and smoky. A crowd of men and a few women had come in after the weekly market, and the room echoed with loud voices and all the noises of a busy inn. Henry hadn't the price of a meal left if he meant to stay the night; he ordered coffee and plain bread and elbowed through the crowd to warm his hands at the fire.

An elderly man and a young woman were sitting in the shadows by the hearth, and Henry stopped dead, his heart thumping. It couldn't be. The woman's face was turned to the fire, but he would have known her anywhere. 'Anne?' he said, his voice a croak.

She turned her head, and he saw how white her face was and how her wet hair was pasted to her forehead. He held out his arms and she jumped up and ran into them.

Once before, Anne had thrown her arms around Henry – at Boula Rectory. Then they had been alone. Now she embraced him, crying and laughing and reaching up to kiss him, in a crowded saloon, under her father's outraged gaze.

'Anne!' he gasped, 'what are you thinking of?'

'Henry and I are betrothed,' she said, 'and have been for more than a year. I cannot help it if you disapprove.' Henry led her back to her seat and sat down beside her, his arm round her waist.

James Walker's small store of well-worn phrases was inadequate to express the horror he felt at his daughter's behaviour – in a common inn, too. But his real horror was saved for the day that his wife found out and blamed him. In his heart, he would have liked to say that he didn't care what Anne did, so long as her mother didn't find out. He said nothing.

Anne drew a ring on a hair-ribbon from the neck of her gown with her free hand; the other was holding Henry's. She untied the ribbon and gave the ring to Henry, who put it on her fourth finger

83

and kissed the finger gently. 'Will you give us your blessing, sir?' he asked, looking up.

'Certainly not . . . this is most irregular . . . My wife . . .'

'In that case,' Henry said, 'we must manage without. I trust that you will perform the marriage ceremony. I'm afraid it cannot take place for more than a year.'

'It is most improper to discuss the matter in my daughter's presence,' said Mr Walker, pulling himself together. 'I am prepared to countenance your betrothal on condition that you, Anne, have procured your Mama's approval, and you, Mr Fulton, have graduated. I would of course prefer you to wait until you have been ordained.' His voice trailed off. 'Young people . . . foolish notions . . . should wait a few years . . .'

Anne gave Henry's hand a warning squeeze, as she saw he was about to argue. She agreed meekly to everything her father had to say, and Henry again asked for, and got, his blessing.

They dined together, on tripe and crubeens, and the next day a hired chaise took all three to Dublin.

Norah drove with them in the carriage, and Hilton Fetherston-haugh rode behind in the rain.

James Walker sat silently in the chaise, terrified by the thought of the coming scene with his wife. He couldn't imagine her too ill to revile him for his weakness. Henry was telling Anne about Wolfe Tone at Irishtown – but not how deeply he had been moved – and promised to introduce him to her while they were in Dublin. Anne looked doubtful. 'Isn't he a trifle odd? A grown man turning cartwheels?'

'No odder than I am myself. He worries constantly about the state of the country and England's lack of interest in our problems. He told me he jokes and turns somersaults lest he burst into tears.'

Henry left the coach at the edge of the city, promising to wait on Miss Eliza the following day.

All was confusion at Clare Street. Mrs Walker was being bled by the surgeon, and Sir Timothy had had some kind of fit. His own physician had been fetched and Miss Mary fluttered from one patient to the other, weeping and getting in the way. Sir Timothy's wife, a person whom none of the family had ever met, had arrived but had not been shown upstairs. A tall fat old lady, she was fanning herself in the hall. Miss Eliza had shut herself in her bedroom, leaving instructions that she was not to be disturbed.

James Walker sat down at his wife's side and waited nervously for her to revive. Anne, having kissed her mother and sat with her for a while, disobeyed Miss Eliza's instructions and knocked on her door. Mama was improving, she had been told, and Miss Eliza might be an ally if she proved difficult about Henry. 'Aunt,' she said, 'Henry Fulton and I intend to wed with Papa's full consent.'

'Why, girl, I knew that long since from Henry himself. You are a pair of foolish children. Time enough for marriage.'

'But ma'am, we are twenty-three and twenty-four years old. Why delay? We love each other.' She blushed.

'Love is an illusion,' pronounced Miss Eliza. 'It is a cloak worn by desire to make it respectable. Lust is no excuse for a precipitate marriage – you must needs call it love, then you may be forgiven.'

'You have no right to speak so,' Anne said hotly. 'What about a mother's love for her child, a – '

'Hold your tongue, miss, you forget youself.' Miss Eliza, who was seated at her dressing-table, rose to her feet and looked searchingly into Anne's face. Anne felt that the cold, grey eyes could see into her very soul. 'Perhaps,' said her aunt more kindly, 'you are one of the lucky ones. That old booby Timothy imagined he loved me – aye, and others as well as he. Sentimental moonshine. Well girl, I'll put no rub in your way. Henry has less sense than an unborn babe, but I own that I like him. I will speak to your mother when she is sufficiently recovered.'

Within the hour James Walker went in search of lodgings and Sir Timothy was removed by four servants to the hospital, stretched on a litter. He was followed by his wife in a sedan chair and an interested crowd. Anne sat by her mother's bed until, drugged by laudanum, the patient fell into a deep sleep.

Henry called the next day, and Miss Eliza instantly sent him to the hospital to enquire for Sir Timothy, who was on the mend. When he returned, he met Anne who looked weary and heavy-eyed. To his amazement, Miss Eliza told him that a walk in the fresh air would do them both good. So he and Anne strolled in Merrion Square and made plans for a wedding early in 1792.

Chapter Ten

As soon as Sarah Walker was well enough to travel, she insisted on returning to Roscrea.

Henry, back at Trinity, and in what should have been his final year, was again obliged to go home to Lisburn. Here, he found his family in serious difficulties, his father being still in India, and trade having fallen off. His sister's wedding was a smart one, an effort to keep up appearances, and Henry was angry when he discovered that many prominent citizens had withdrawn their custom and their 'friendship' because of his father's connection with Luke Teeling.

Week by week, the radical broadsheet which was the organ of Wolfe Tone's infant society was delivered after nightfall. As John Fulton wasn't there, only Henry read it. Its smudgy print and inflammatory articles made him dismiss it at first as trash, but soon he began to find his own opinions reflected in it. Usually there were at least two well-reasoned articles written under false names. Henry read them all and wished he could discuss them with Theo.

He got his chance unexpectedly. A large delivery of damask was being made to a Belfast merchant, a staunch Presbyterian called John McGinn. As the consignment was a valuable one, Henry went along too, and saw it safely into the warehouse. Mr McGinn, a friend of his father's, invited him in, and in the parlour sat Tone, talking to a rapt audience of men of all ages, his thin face as eager as boy's.

'Henry!' Tone jumped up and wrung his hand. 'I have often wished you were here. Who told you of our meeting?'

'Nobody. I am here on business – I thought you were in Dublin. It's good to see you, Theo, may I join in?'

'By all means.' Tone plunged back into his rapid, witty talk, which sounded so spontaneous and was really so carefully considered and provocative. Henry again felt the fascination which had half scared him before. But he had matured since the previous summer and was determined not to be wooed into something he didn't approve of. He left when Tone did, and after enquiring for his family, asked him more about his Society of United Irishmen.

'I will put up your name,' said Tone. 'You shall join before I return to Dublin.'

'But Theo, I don't care for your idea of involving the French. Can you be so sure that France and England will fight? It's a fine idea in theory, but all I want is to relieve the terrible suffering of the poor peasants. Surely if we can bring about a new act of Parliament, that will suffice? Your way would plunge the country into war.'

'It would not. I want to frighten Westminster into action, reasoning having failed. Organised charity isn't the answer, we must have a free government, with equal rights for all creeds. If we can't have it without French help, then I shall go to Paris and round up a French army. A pity I can't speak their curst language.' He turned those glowing dark eyes on Henry and said, 'We need men like you, Henry. Men who are young, well-informed and able to work. You could be sworn in at our next meeting – here, take this copy of the oath and read it – I'll swear you will find nothing in it to disagree with.'

Tone was right. There was nothing in the oath except a promise to help to promote justice for all and religious tolerance. Henry was sworn in a week later. The Society was not proscribed, but Trinity students were barred from it, as were the clergy. Henry expected to be ordained within the year, but so optimistic was Theo that he thought it quite probable that the parliamentary reforms would have already come about, making his position legal.

As he held the Bible and repeated the words after Tone, Henry felt a great surge of emotion. This was it. This was the inner meaning and purpose of his dreams. He would be an agent in the movement which would turn Ireland into a democratic country, peaceful, prosperous and happy. Nothing since his first meeting with Tone and his betrothal to Anne had moved him so much, and in some ways his elation now was even greater. Mildly ashamed of this, he postponed telling Anne of his membership. Soon they would be married and he would have no secrets from her.

A year later, Anne wrote to Henry:

My dearest love,
What could exceed the Miseries and Disappointments of the past

87

Eighteen Months? I wish I could be Present to see your Bachelor of
Arts Degree conferred on you – The Excellence of your Results
comes as no Surprise to me – But why have you not told me until
now about Mr Tone's Society? If it as Respectable as you say, why
should I object? Oh, but I don't write to Accuse you when you are to
be Taken from me – Dearest, must you indeed go to India? I do not
think I can Bear it – if only we were already Wed, then I would have
the right to a Second Home with your dear Mama, and the Right to
grieve should Disaster overtake you – Oh, Henry, my Own, only
think of the perils of the Deep, the Pirates, the Ships of War, the
Tempests – and you say you must remain for a Year – perhaps two,
among the Savage Inhabitants of a Distant Land – Your Devotion to
your Papa's Affairs in Admirable, but Consider and Pity your
Deserted and Despairing
    Anne.

This letter, which upset Henry considerably, was followed immediately by another. Henry was waiting, his bags packed, for the wind
to veer to a more favourable quarter; the *Ajax*, fully provisioned,
had been standing off White Head for two days.

Henry, my Dear Life,
I fear my last Letter was such as must Distress you rather than
Console you – I beg you will forgive me – I am now much calmer,
accepting my Sad Lot in Hope of a Long and Happy Life together
when you return – last year was such a dreadful one, it has left its
Mark upon all – Who could fail to be Affected by the Massacres in
France, the Wars raging on Sea and Land – the threats of Revolt here
– I know you Admire Mr Tone, and indeed when I met him in
Dublin, I could understand why – but there is much criticism of his
Society of United Irishmen, and I wish you had not Joined it – As
you say, its Aims are for Common Justice, but Mr Tone would Go
Farther, I am sure – there is a Fire burning in him that will not easily
be Quenched – I beg you to Engage in nothing Lightly – perhaps
when you return you will Reconsider – I had not meant to mention
this again, but I cannot be with you to say Farewell, and will not
Allow you to go from me until I have told you of my Fears – Mama
is in good Health, and is Fretting us to pieces with Fresh Rehearsals
for *The Messiah* – it is to be Performed at Easter – I think the concert
is Fated, and if it ever takes place some Astonishing Thing will
happen, perhaps an Earthquake or a Sign from Heaven – I must not

poke fun at Poor Mama, must I? I fear for you, I Pray for you, I Long for your Return, I Long to be your Wife. . . .

The *Ajax* sailed with the tide, taking Henry away for almost two years.

PART TWO

PART TWO

Chapter Eleven

The autumn of 1796 was cold and wet. Ireland sulked and brooded, on the brink of open rebellion. A thin drizzle was falling, and the trees dropped limp leaves, not yet coloured by the first frost. The pastures beside the road were saturated by weeks of rain; the road itself stretched muddily towards a murky horizon.

The new curate of the Kilmore Union of parishes, with his wife and baby, was travelling in an open carriage, and getting extremely wet.

Henry and Anne Fulton had married in January of the previous year, and the baby, James, was five months old. Anne wrapped her cloak more closely round him as she watched Henry, always an uneasy companion in a carriage, crossing and uncrossing his long legs and looking about him eagerly. As often, she wondered what he was thinking.

Henry was enjoying himself. His life, he felt, was only just beginning; his destiny advancing to meet him. In this mood, he could move mountains, conquer armies, convert nations. Was not Theobald Wolfe Tone raising an army in France. Theo with his frightful French, his persuasive tongue and fifty guineas in his pocket? How much easier to succeed in one's own land.

Henry had marked time politically during his two years in India, and had then been enrolled as a go-between in the United Irish Society. Obliged to renounce his oath when he was ordained, he had ratified it shortly afterwards. By then, he had been appointed to the curacy of Aughrim in East Galway, and was at last about to be married. These years had seen the worst excesses of the French Revolution, and a new regime was emerging. Henry had been sickened by the bloody horrors in France, and was almost as shocked by his own gradual acceptance of terror as something unpalatable but perhaps necessary. He was distressed but no longer outraged – troubled but no longer appalled. Tone's aims and beliefs had taken hold of him, and he looked forward to the founding of a Republic of Ireland.

Henry had kept in touch with William Knox, now bishop of Killaloe, who had consistently used his influence to help him. It was Knox who had helped him to the curacy of Kilmore and the Silvermines, plus the Vicarship of Monsea, near Nenagh in Country Tipperary. His was the glowing testimonial in Henry's pocket, guaranteed to secure him the post of tutor to Francis Prittie whose father owned the living. A tutor's salary would be a welcome addition to his curate's stipend of £30 a year.

In his first parish he and Anne had lived in shabby lodgings, unsupported by either set of parents. Henry had done all the work of the parish for his absentee rector who lived in England, and had learned more about his profession than ten years at Divinity School would have taught him.

He smiled at Anne, wrapped in her blue cloak. She looked little older than when they met eight years before and was both the centre of his life and the source of most of his fears. Alone, he would tread dangerous paths and risk banishment or death without a second thought, but Anne must not be put at risk. She might suspect, but must not know the lengths he was prepared to go to. She shared his concern for the hungry and helpless, but liberty, equality and fraternity were only words to her. He held her hand in his, under the damp rug which covered their knees, and knew that she worried and wondered.

Henry looked older than his twenty-nine years. The Indian sun had darkened his skin and lined it prematurely. He had the keen stare of a hill shepherd, seeming always to be watching something far away. His face would have been stern, but for the humorous twist of his mouth. He scanned the horizon, making a mental picture of the landscape – its silver-bearing hills, its marshes, its empty fields. It was a depressing outlook. The horses' backs and the driver's coat were greyed over by the mist which had settled like hoar-frost.

In the distance, they all heard the muffled sound of a single shot.

Soon, a church tower appeared above scrubby trees, and they turned into a narrow road, bordered by woods. The two outriders unslung their muskets and rode with them resting across their saddles. The sense that someone, probably a number of people, were watching them was acute. Henry felt Anne's fingers tighten in his. For a hundred yards, the trees met overhead, shutting out the daylight, and he put his arm round her, fear for her safety damping his elation. For himself, he felt no more fear than when Joscelyn Darcy had challenged him. He was – he must be – armoured against fate by his purpose.

Dorcas Andrews, her hands on her bony hips, watched her lodger depart from the farmhouse. This lodger, who had been curate of Kilmore and the Silvermines for two years, was a pallid, untidy man with the distressing habit of polishing his boots with his wig.

Dorcas looked on unsmilingly while the curate mounted his horse. Her son, Arthur, who had been holding its head, stood back, and mother and son watched him trot away in silence. Nobody waved or said farewell. Dorcas, who looked as well scrubbed as her step, said, 'Well, that's that. Good riddance.'

She was a sturdy woman, whose broad, weather-beaten face seldom showed any emotion other than displeasure, her sandy hair all hidden by a severe linen cap. A Scotswoman, she disliked Ireland and all things Irish, including, unfortunately, her husband George, agent to Sir Henry Prittie. Arthur was her darling, although she would have rather died than admit it. She wondered how he had escaped the lures of the local girls – perhaps they were afraid because several attempts had been made on his life. She prayed for his safety every time he went out, and gave thanks when he returned safely. Hers was an unforgiving God, sensitive to slights. George, she felt, could fend for himself without intercession.

'Here's the new man now – he's early,' said Arthur indifferently.

Sir Henry Prittie had sent a carriage to fetch the new curate and his wife from the coach. Not the best barouche, naturally, and not the best (or even second best) team. The carriage was drawn by farm horses and driven by a carter. Behind, rode a pair of scarlet-coated yeomen, Ezekiel and Ben Tydd, sons of a tenant farmer.

Dorcas Andrews had lodged half a dozen curates in her time, some married, some single. All had been of the humble and meek variety, destined to be exalted in the next world. Serious, hard-working young men, with wives to match, they had fitted well into the Andrews's solemn, God-fearing household. Now, scrutinising the new couple with cold, grey eyes, Dorcas knew at once that the Reverend Henry Fulton and his wife were not at all the thing.

For a start, the curate was laughing. Worse, he addressed the driver – a common Catholic carter – in a familiar way, and the driver laughed too. Then he jumped down, lifted his wife to the ground and kissed her – actually kissed her! In public, with three grown people watching! A clergyman's wife with a child in her arms. Oh, shameless! She caught some fatuous words about happiness in their new home, followed by murmured words, probably endearments.

Dorcas advanced to greet them, her nostrils pinched with disgust. The woman was far prettier than a parson's wife had any business to be. Arthur was gawping at her, his hat clutched in his hands.

Mr Fulton took off his hat, revealing brown hair cropped short, Frenchie fashion. Dorcas knew that the style was being copied both by men and women in Court circles and by the Irish rebels, who were beginning to be known as 'croppies'. She thought that Sir Henry Prittie would instruct the curate to grow his hair or wear a wig. Mr Fulton clasped Dorcas's unwilling hand firmly and gave her a cheerful greeting. He removed his wife's damp cloak and Arthur sprang forward to take it. Mrs Fulton thanked him smilingly, and he stuttered and blushed.

Dorcas showed the pair into the rooms set aside for them; bedroom and parlour, sparsely furnished, scrupulously clean. Meals were taken in the kitchen with the family. Mr Fulton tried to flatter Dorcas with compliments on her house, but she turned them aside. She was not to be won over.

Kilmore lay on the edge of the Silvermines Mountains, in an area where trouble was known to be brewing. An agent had been shot, and houses burned. The neighbouring landlords, Henry Prittie and Cooke Otway, maintained what amounted to private armies to protect themselves against their own Catholic tenants. Even then they felt insecure, as they couldn't be sure of the yeomen's loyalty.

George Andrews, a typical agent, was descended from one of Cromwell's troopers, Sir Henry Prittie from one of his colonels. Their precedence hadn't changed in a century and a half. George was devoted to the Protestant church and the Prittie family: he risked his life daily for his employer as a matter of course. Third generation Irish, he thought of himself as Scottish and had no particular feelings about King George of England. His world was a tiny one, bounded by the Kilboy estate.

George's arid marriage didn't encourage him to spend his time at home. He didn't drink or play cards, and went to church twice on Sundays. He reserved his affection for his horse, Barney, a thickset roan with a noticeable white blaze. Barney had been a present from Sir Henry Prittie; an ill-chosen gift for a marked man, his white blaze was better known than George's nondescript features. As George jogged home past Bawn and Kilriffith, he talked quietly to the horse — at home he talked hardly at all. He stroked the wiry black mane and the sturdy crest with its wrinkles of fat. He was as happy as it was in his nature to be.

The single shot took George completely by surprise. He couldn't tell where it had come from — it had missed, that was the main thing. Barney leaped forward at a gallop and George urged him on, knowing that he would be well out of range by the time his attacker had reloaded. He was, of course, carrying a pistol, but safety lay in speed, not retaliation. George had been shot at before, more than once. He never asked himself why his neighbours should want to kill him or his son: he dismissed them all as murderous heathens and madmen. He slapped his horse down the flank and hoped the croppies' marksmanship wouldn't improve. Once he reached open ground, he reined in and rode quietly home.

The family had already sat down to dinner. Habitually morose, George didn't feel it necessary to mention that someone had tried to shoot him half an hour earlier. The new curate – great beanpole of a man – rose to shake hands. The wife, thought George, was quite indecently pretty. Arthur was staring at her as if he'd never seen a woman before. George set about his bacon and cabbage with a good appetite.

Henry's high spirits had plummeted. George and Dorcas were cutting up their food and packing it away methodically and in silence. Arthur bolted his bacon, and stared at Anne who was seated opposite to him. He was tall – almost as tall as Henry – handsome in a brutish way. His brown eyes stared from under a low, broad brow. His hair, long, black and greasy, was combed straight back and hung to his shoulder-blades; his teeth were white in a thick-lipped mouth. His linen was spotless – his mother would see to that – but he wore his clothes in a slovenly way and he hadn't shaved.

Henry tried in vain to catch Arthur's eye and stare him down. With increasing anger, he saw Anne involuntarily raise her hand to check that her neckerchief was properly arranged over her bosom. Angry colour rose in her cheeks and Arthur transferred his gaze to his apple pie.

'May we be excused?' Henry asked Dorcas. 'My wife is tired and would like to rest.' He stood up as he spoke, took Anne's arm and led her from the room.

'Thank you, my love,' said Anne, when they were in their parlour, the door closed behind them. 'That puppy was making me feel like a joint of meat in a butcher's shop.' She spoke lightly, but her eyes sparked with anger.

'He had best mend his manners if he wants to keep a whole skin,' Henry said dangerously.

'Pray don't be so hasty, dearest. He's just an ignorant whelp who knows no better. I will contrive not to sit opposite him again – let him stare at you instead.' She pulled him down beside her on the settee.

'Hasty?' exploded Henry. 'What do you expect? I must needs be away for hours at a time, how can I be easy knowing that you are at the mercy of that leering barbarian?'

'Be sensible, Henry. Remember how you left me and disappeared for half a day in Aughrim when the rebels were all about the place? Surely I'll be safer with young Andrews than with the rebels.'

Henry said, 'I think you'd be safer with the rebels, but enough of that. If that young man is a nuisance, we will seek other lodgings.'

'Now you're being unreasonable. When a score of wild United men forced their way into our Galway home there was no talk of seeking other lodgings. And do but remember that fellow with the bloodied cloth around his head who came knocking at dead of night. I was never so frightened. I hope I can put Master Andrews in his place but not, I think at the dinner table.'

Henry stood up and walked about the room, his hands in his breeches pockets. 'I made some good friends in Galway,' he said, 'but as things stand now, it would cause consternation if they visited me here. You know that some of my political beliefs are unorthodox, I would prefer that you didn't discuss them, or not until the threat of rebellion has died down. I could express opinions openly last year which might cost me my living this.'

'Your living?' Anne said, 'I have heard you and your friends say things which would cost you your life! Thank God you have modified your notions. Only think, Theo Tone who used to be your friend is said to be raising an army in France. Imagine if you were still one of his adherents! And I know how much you used to admire him. It must have been hard for you to renounce his Society when it became rebellious.' She leaned back in the corner of the settee, looking up at him with her direct gaze.

'We aren't going to talk politics, you and I,' said Henry, who had gone to the window and was looking out. 'We are going to be happy here, just the three of us, and I hope we will make new friends. I believe Ned Fitzmaurice is stationed in Nenagh, we are bound to meet soon. I own I can do without most of the Barrack gentry though – only remember the Roscommon Militia in Ballinasloe!'

'Horrid, weren't they? When they were stationed at Roscrea, Mama engaged their trumpeters to play in *The Messiah*. They used to come drunk to rehearsals, then they removed to Galway, taking their trumpets with them, and the performance had to be postponed yet again. Henry, are you listening?'

Henry, his back turned, was studying the window which was small, nailed shut and heavily barred. He started guiltily. 'Forgive me, my love, my thoughts were straying. I was thinking that with my parishes so widely separated, I am certain to be given a horse.'

She laughed at him. 'Poor Henry, obliged to ride. You must forsake your notion of walking everywhere so as to be on a level with your fellow men. Will it be hard?'

'No, it will be delightful.' He turned to face her, his face stern. 'Anne,' he said, 'I have heard a rumour that Theo is at sea with a French fleet, about to invade this country.'

'How did you hear it?' She jumped to her feet and looked up into his face, holding his coat lapels. Then, as he didn't answer at once: 'Of course we've all heard rumours that the French might come, but are you saying that an Irish rebel is bringing them here to rid us of the English? Is that what you mean?'

'Exactly that. Never mind how I heard it, and do you keep it to yourself. I couldn't leave you in ignorance. If the French invade, the country will rise to support them.'

'Surely you exaggerate,' said Anne. 'What do Irish peasants know of France? Do the rebel leaders know anything of the peasants? I doubt if they want a French government.'

'They will have an Irish government,' Henry said. 'Justice and equality at last.' Seeing Anne's face he added, 'Naturally, I hope there will be no rebellion.'

'Do you? You sound like Theo himself. Are you sure you don't wish for a rising? I don't want to be ruled by the French, do you?' She looked up searchingly at him, and her eyes were scared. 'Please don't meddle in these things – it's dangerous.'

'I am ruled by none but you, and have I ever complained?' Henry snatched her hands and waltzed her round the room. 'No more politics,' he said. 'We won't speak of it again.'

Matt Gleeson had been drilling pikemen in the hills around Temple-derry for almost two years. His bearing was soldierly, and his great shoulders bulged his tattered frieze coat. He was terrified. Matt had objected to showing his face abroad. There was as yet no price on his head, but one day there would be.

'Go when the men are in the fields,' his captain had said. 'Nobody will see you but the woman of the house, and she won't remark your appearance.'

It hadn't occurred to Matt that he had been chosen for the assignment because his face was unknown in Kilmore parish, or that, once known, he would be considered expendable. The woman of the house. To Matt, orphan and bachelor, the words had a pleasant homely ring.

Dorcas opened the door to his timid knock and flung a monosyl-lable at him. 'Well?' She advanced a step, her chin jutting, her mouth folded so tightly that it was lipless.

Matt opened his mouth and tried to speak. Those cold eyes would never forget him. In his mind, he heard the gates of Nenagh Gaol shutting behind him with a steely thud. 'A message for the new parson,' he managed to say.

'Yes?' Dorcas folded broad freckled forearms on her formidable bosom.

'I have to give a letter to Parson Fulton.'

Dorcas held out her hand. 'Give it to me.'

'I have to give it to his Reverence myself.'

'Who says so?'

'Mr Otway.' On the spur of the moment, Matt chose a name that Dorcas was sure to know and respect. That of his own hated landlord. It worked. The woman went away; Matt fought an urge to run while there was still time, then Parson himself appeared. Matt, with a gesture instilled into him from infancy, removed his hat and held it while they talked. The tall man, to his astonishment, grasped his hand and asked him how he did as if he really wanted to know. Matt looked quickly at the windows. Parsons didn't shake the hands of such as he, and what if that freckle-faced cow was watching?

'Mind out, you'll get us both hung,' said Matt. 'Here's a message for you.' He watched anxiously as Henry studied the letter that Matt couldn't read. Ned Heffernan had given just such another to the Sheriff, not knowing that it contained the message, 'Arrest this man.' He waited for the code. It came.

'Are there good horses for sale in Nenagh?' asked Henry.

Matt sighed with relief and gave the answer. 'Yes, but those in Limerick are better.' He relaxed, wiping sweat from his face with the back of his hand.

'This letter is from a gentleman in Nenagh who wishes to sell me a horse,' said Henry.

'There's another message,' said Matt.

'Not here.' The tall clergyman strolled away from the house, signing to Matt to walk with him. Matt walked a pace behind, conscious of windows and his unprotected back. When they reached open ground, Henry stopped and waited.

'The man with a horse to sell told me that you might see a lot of animals over that way,' said Matt, pointing, 'most evenings around five, near the Church. He might buy a few if he could get near enough. He wants to know how many there are, and if they are trained or not.'

'Does he indeed? I wonder if he realises that I arrived here only yesterday.'

'He does, your Reverence.'

'Don't call me that, or only when my parishioners are there. My code-name is Harry, but I'm sure you won't use it – better not call me anything. And you? What is your name and your position?'

'I lead a troop of the Castle Otway pikemen,' said Matt sullenly. 'My name is Matt. I have no code-name.'

'Are you also a yeoman of Cooke Otway's troop?'

'I am not, then.' Matt thought of his arch-enemy Cooke Otway, stout, elderly and autocratic, combing his desolate estate for croppies at the head of his yeomanry. A noisy bunch – it was easy to avoid them in the silent hills. The pikemen outnumbered the yeomen, since Otway had been obliged to dismiss all his Catholic men, on hearing they had taken the United oath.

Matt recalled himself. The man whom he mustn't call 'your Reverence' and would never call 'Harry,' was asking, 'Are you Mr Otway's tenant?' His confident, friendly manner encouraged a truthful reply.

'I pay rent for rocks and bracken. My house is tumbling about my ears.'

Matt wondered how much it was wise to say. His instinct was to trust Henry, but could you trust a gentleman? The only person he knew who could lay claim to such a title was the detestable Otway himself. Dare he admit to having a hundred pikes stored under his thatch and buried in his potato furrows? He and his brother cut the shafts at night, never cutting two from the same hedgerow, while another brother, Liam, hammered out the wicked three-pronged blades. Liam also forged shoes for the soldiers' horses in his shop in Templederry.

'You don't trust me, do you?' asked Henry.

'Not entirely,' said Matt. 'I'm not used to your kind. I'm not afraid, mind, or not of being killed – I dread prison, that's all. I'd sooner be dead than locked up.'

He shuddered. A mountainy man, doors and windows which could be locked and bolted were unknown to him. His first language was Irish, he knew little of politics. The new dogma, that France was good, England bad, seemed to him of little practical interest. He wanted his landlord dead with an intense, vicious longing. He dug his bare toes into the dirt, ready to run if need be. 'Let me be gone,' he muttered.

'In a moment. Who did you say sent you? Our stories must agree.'

'Mr Otway. I had to tell the old bitch something.'

'Mrs Andrews,' Henry corrected, but his eyes twinkled. 'It was foolish to mention Mr Otway. If it is discovered that he sent no letter, I will have to say that you guessed at the signature or we'll both be in queer street.'

'Somebody's watching,' said Matt. 'Hiding. I know it.'

'Nobody can hear. Let them watch. As far as you are concerned, I am merely someone who needs a horse. Tell your superior that I don't mean to ride far afield at present. I will look at the horses he mentioned, but my knowledge is slight. You understand? I prefer not to write it down. Say that I don't wish to try any more horses until I have made up my mind about the one in Nenagh. Repeat my words, if you please.'

Matt repeated them sulkily. This man's eyes and manner reminded him of others who had given him orders. Others now dead. He supposed this parson was above suspicion. His head would never be displayed over a prison gate – but he was of the same breed as the landlords, or near enough. Could he be trusted with hundreds of lives? Telling him secrets was a crazy thing to do – like putting a knife in the hand of a madman. (Surely he must be mad to take such risks for others.) The madman said goodbye in the same easy way as he had greeted Matt, holding out a large hand with a gold ring on the little finger.

There was a movement in the laurels near the stables. Matt ignored the hand, said 'Good luck', the usual Irish farewell, and almost ran down the drive.

Henry strolled towards the laurels. Sure enough, someone was concealed there. Someone who fled, bent double, round the garden wall. He could have heard nothing. Henry reread the letter, which contained much more than he had told Matt, and later burned it on the parlour fire.

Chapter Twelve

Henry arrived at Kilmore on a Monday, so he had some days there before facing his congregation in church. The day after his meeting with Matt Gleeson, he put on his hat about four in the afternoon and told Anne he was going for a walk. 'Bolt the parlour door,' he said. 'Arthur might fancy some female company. I don't trust him an inch.'

'Ridiculous.' Anne reached up to kiss him. 'I fear Mrs Andrews more than her son. You'll be home before dark, I hope.'

'I can't say. Probably.' Henry picked up Miss Eliza's cape and slung it over his shoulder.

'Dearest, you mustn't be abroad after dark – it's dangerous. Even if you escape hurt, your pistol may be taken and used against some innocent person.' She held him back by the arm.

'I am not armed,' said Henry, gently disengaging her fingers. 'Let me go now if you want me to be home in daylight.'

'Not armed? Henry, you're mad. Everyone carries a pistol – *everyone!*'

He opened the door, laughing back at her. 'Why, my love, there's no pleasing you this afternoon. You insist I carry a pistol, although you are sure I will be relieved of it. You know what a pitiful marksman I am. Farewell – I'll be back as soon as I can.'

George Andrews met him as he went through the gate. 'Don't walk abroad alone,' he said. 'No sensible man does.'

'What about yourself?'

'I ride,' said George tersely. He hesitated, overcoming his natural reserve, then he said, 'Divine protection, eh, Reverend? You have need of it. Please yourself.' He tramped off towards the stables.

Henry paused. He was making mistakes, and over-confidence was one of them. It would arouse suspicion and, as George said, he was in danger from the rebels until he became known – especially when he was lodging with a family so heartily disliked. Another time, he must show some sign of nervousness – too late now. He strode on.

Henry walked fast, hurried by excitement and curiosity. His boots swished through fallen beech-leaves from the trees whose branches met overhead. A squirrel dashed across the path; there was a pungent scent of wet earth. He kept his eyes open for watchers and his ears for unusual sounds, but there were none.

He started violently as a cock pheasant rocketed just ahead of him – first rashness, then timidity, he thought. Locals like Matt must be better agents. Henry hadn't met a revolutionary of Matt's background before, although he had seen them in action. His dealings had been with secret members of the United Irish Society like himself, and, like himself, professional men. Matt was one of the peasantry that the Society was pledged to free, yet to Henry, his would-be liberator, he was as alien as a Chinaman. Altruism, idealism – what did Matt know of these? He was preparing for bloody civil war.

Henry hated the secrecy of his assignment. He would have liked to follow Theo, in person, into battle: failing that, he would have liked to preach his unorthodox gospel in the market place. Either would be a certain road to the gallows; he must content himself with writing reports and swearing in new members. He longed for the day when Tone would land with his fifteen thousand Frenchmen, but with an impractical longing which didn't include such considerations as the feeding of an army, or the three-sided war which was sure to follow when reinforcements arrived from Britain. The year-old war with France would merely shift to Irish soil, and the outcome was anyone's guess.

The trees were thinning out. Henry heard the sound of a number of horsemen on the move, punctuated by ferocious yells. Around a bend in the road, he came on an open space, backed by the church, where a troop of volunteers was drilling. A fat man with white hair and a purple face was bellowing orders: his men, all sizes, shapes and ages, carried them out sloppily, talking among themselves. Their officer, bolt upright on a brown hunter, looked as if he might easily have a fit.

Henry raised his hand in casual greeting as he lounged past, assessing the troop-horses which, like their riders, were a mixed lot. He accurately counted the contingent, and noted how the men were armed. Among them were Ezekiel and Ben Tydd, who had escorted his carriage two days before. An undisciplined crowd of young and not-so-young tenants, Henry thought. They would offer little resistance to regular soldiers. He almost pitied their purple-faced leader. Angry peasants, carrying their unwieldy pikes, would certainly stampede such a troop.

Skirting the parade ground, Henry went into the church.

When Henry had gone, Anne tidied the parlour and drew up a chair to the fire. She opened a box of silks and began to embroider a stole for him. As she worked, she rocked the baby's cradle with her foot. James was sleeping deeply; she could see the curve of his cheek and a dimpled fist. His nightcap and shawl hid all the rest.

The room was silent except for the creak of the rocking crib and the faint mutter of the turf fire. Anne felt a sharp pang of loneliness as well as the worry which never left her. Henry's moods baffled her. Why should a man who had work which suited him and a happy marriage veer between high spirits and silent brooding? Where did he go on his long, solitary walks? He had always been impulsive and outspoken: now, she thought, he was choosing his words. She had feared that some blackguard, knowing of his previous friendship with Wolfe Tone, was trying to blackmail him. But now, it seemed, he was still sympathetic to the revolutionaries.

Gazing into the fire, her hands idle on her lap, her vague suspicions hardened. Henry must be in touch with the rebels. She didn't judge him – she pictured him swinging at the end of a rope or being led out blindfolded to face a firing squad. Cold all over, she wondered what to do. She dared not question him because she feared the answers – or the oathbound silence which would amount to the same thing.

James woke up and whimpered. She lifted him from the cradle and put him to her breast. Looking down at him, she wondered what his future would be. James was a big, sturdy baby who had never been ill in his life. He was wrapped in layers of wool, cotton and linen; shawl, coat, frock, vest and petticoat. She cuddled him tightly to her, feeling insecure and afraid.

The parlour grew gloomy. A sod of turf fell to the hearth in a flurry of sparks. She leaned over the baby who was still sucking intently, mended the fire with the tongs and rang the handbell to summon the maid.

The door opened without a knock, and Arthur Andrews came in. 'You wanted something, ma'am?' he said.

'Please ask the maid to bring me some more turf,' Anne said, hastily detaching James and covering her breast. Arthur favoured her with a devouring stare and left the room. He returned with logs piled on one arm and a creel of turf under the other. He set them down and knelt to make up the fire. Anne stood by the mantel-shelf not speaking, the baby against her shoulder. Arthur again turned his hungry gaze on her, sitting on his heels by the fire.

Furious, Anne opened her mouth to order him out – but suppose he was insolent or refused to go? With an effort, she said lightly, 'You will recognise me when we meet again.'

'Looking is no crime,' muttered Arthur.

'No, but it is remarkably bad manners. Thank you, that will be all.' She waited for him to go.

He got slowly to his feet, his open shirt startlingly white against his black hair and swarthy skin. 'Call me at any time,' he said, 'Ring the bell and I'll be there, ready to do anything you want. You need never lift a finger.'

'Thank you, but it is the maid's duty to wait on us, not yours.'

'The maids are in the dairy,' said Arthur. 'I am here. Let me know how I can help you.' James belched and a milky dribble escaped from the corner of his mouth. As Anne wiped it, Arthur touched the baby's cheek. 'Fine little fellow,' he said, but his eyes were on Anne. Opaque eyes, which showed the white like a nervous horse.

'How dare you touch him! Go away!' She was frightened and angry.

'Go away? I'm not doing any harm. Can we not be friends, then? There's nothing here for me, nothing for anyone young; no singing or dancing or cards, and the women are all Papists – they hate me, and their fathers have threatened to kill me. I have a sad life of it.'

She went to the door and held it open, saying, 'I think you forget who I am. Surely you don't pursue married women with babes in arms? My husband would be angry if he found you here – please go.'

He didn't go. He bent his head, the long, lank hair swinging forward. 'I'm going. Up at Kilboy, they play backgammon for kisses. Can I kiss you? Just one? Please – nobody will ever know. You are so beautiful.' His breath smelled of fried onions. Anne ducked past him and ran into the hall as the front door opened and Henry came in.

Henry stopped short and Anne said, 'Mr Andrews has just mended the fire for me.' Arthur slid past them both with a last smouldering look at Anne. Anne turned her hot face away from Henry as she carried James back into the parlour; she knew his jealous temper where she was concerned.

Henry followed her through the doorway, under the lintel which was little higher than his shoulder. 'What now? What did he want? He's upset you, I can tell. If he vexes you again he shall have a thrashing.'

'Of course he didn't,' Anne said briskly. 'He answered the bell, the maids being elsewhere. Sit down and warm yourself while I attend to the baby.' She took James into the bedroom, hoping that Henry wouldn't follow. She heard the chair creak as he sat down; she heard him breathing. She wondered how she would get through her days knowing that Henry was a target for rebels and loyalists alike, while she herself must bolt her door against the son of the house.

She decided reluctantly to tell Dorcas if she had any more trouble with Arthur. Better by far to antagonise mother and son than to risk adding manslaughter to Henry's possible list of sins.

For some days, Henry and Anne saw little of Arthur, who was busy with the potato harvest. Dorcas left her lodgers strictly alone. A few ladies called on Anne, but having no means of travelling except on foot, she was unable to return their calls. She tried to persuade Henry that Arthur meant no harm, but he wasn't convinced. Perhaps he guessed he hadn't been told the whole truth.

There were three churches in the Union, two within three miles of one another and one nine miles away. This last was Monsea, of which Henry was vicar, and to reach it he had to borrow a horse and ride by way of Nenagh. He didn't act on Matt's message at once, thinking it foolish to associate with suspect people before he knew his way about. He had no idea whether the writer of the letter, one Father O'Meara, was under suspicion or not.

On his first Sunday, Henry had to preach at all three churches, both rectors being absent. The service at Monsea took place in the evening, and he left Anne behind, riding there on one of Sir Henry Prittie's horses. In Nenagh, he passed by the military barracks as an officer in the uniform of the 7th Dragoons was riding away from the building. Henry pulled up, shouting, 'Hey there, Ned!'

'Harry, by my soul. I was going to call on you at the first opportunity. I wouldn't have known you in your shovel hat and gloomy blacks. Where are you off to then?'

They hadn't met since Henry left for India, six years before. They shook hands, Ned's clumsy in gauntlets, while their horses backed and sidled. Henry's trained eye noticed a shabby man, so unremarkable that his ordinariness was noticeable, pausing at the other side of the street to remove a stone from his shoe.

If this was a rebel spy, and Henry thought he was, he would think that Henry was cleverly infiltrating the enemy stronghold. He hoped he would never have to do anything which might endanger Ned, and remembered too late that he should not have shown that he was already friendly with the captain of the garrison. Not only would he be expected to pass on information, he might be used as bait to lure Ned into a trap. As these thoughts chased through his head, Henry answered Ned's questions automatically.

'You are a strange fellow,' said Ned. 'You greet me like a long lost brother, then you have nothing further to say. However, I have finished for the day and I have a mind to ride with you and hear you preach.' He turned his horse, and they rode on together.

Ned chatted easily, telling Henry whom to cultivate, whom to fear. He enquired for Anne and asked about life at Aughrim. Henry answered carefully – it would be easy to slip up – and hoped he could continue to be this man's friend. But he knew that, if he were caught, it would be Ned whose dragoons would arrest him, Ned who would court martial him, Ned who would have him hanged or shot. Henry had no illusions about Ned's opinion of traitors.

By the time they reached Monsea, Henry had forgotten his sermon. Having preached it twice already that day, he hadn't bothered to bring his notes. The church was packed with people who had turned out to hear the new vicar, and Henry felt that he had given his reputation a powerful boost by arriving with Captain Ned Fitzmaurice. Much would be expected of him. With a false air of confidence, he read the prayers and led the singing, then with a sinking heart, he ascended the wooden pulpit and bowed his head.

The church, outwardly plain, with round-arched windows and immensely thick walls, was about to be replaced by a modern building. It had been painted inside by somebody with a fine disregard for beauty. The upper walls were cobalt blue, while the lower three feet or so was painted bright red. Between these colours, a narrow band of black ran right round the building, waist high. Henry looked desperately round for inspiration. It came.

Pointing to the walls, he suggested that the crimson might represent the flames of hell and the blue suggest heaven; the black line between symbolising the hazardous path trodden by sinners. Not bad, thought Henry, as he enlarged on the joys of heaven, the slippery nature of the path, and the danger of sliding down into hell. Once, the scarlet splash of Ned's uniform caught his eye and Henry noticed that he was amused.

'The human soul,' said Henry firmly, 'totters on the brink of damnation. Hellfire – ' he gestured at the wall below him – 'awaits the wretch who – ' Ned gave way to fit of coughing and there were some muffled giggles from children at the back. At last the half hour was over, and Henry brought his argument to a hasty and rather untidy close, gave the blessing and hurried to the door to shake the hands of the departing worshippers. One of these was a heavily whiskered old man of military appearance, who ignored Henry's hand and turned away. 'God is not mocked,' he said, 'And neither am I, young man.'

As Henry and Ned went to the corner of the churchyard where their horses were tethered, Ned said, 'That was Colonel Finch, one of the church's principal benefactors. I told you particularly not to vex him.'

'I didn't. Why did he insult me?'

Ned grinned. 'He had the church painted – at vast expense, I understand – in his racing colours. Crimson, light blue hoops, black cap.' Henry let out a yelp of laughter, but Ned had turned serious. 'You may have made an enemy, Harry,' he said. 'You were never my idea of a cleric and you have some curst unconventional notions. I don't heed gossip, but others might. Have a care.'

'I will do my best to offend nobody,' said Henry, with a carelessness he didn't feel. What has he heard? he thought. How much does he know? When they reached Ned's house on the edge of the town, he almost refused to come in, then decided that to refuse might in itself appear suspicious. He told the groom not to unsaddle his horse as he didn't intend to delay.

Years spent serving abroad had aged Ned. His pock-marked skin was leathery, his eyes screwed up in a nest of wrinkles. His hair was greying, and there were tufts of white in his thick eyebrows. Rachael, however, had hardly changed. The twenty years between them might have been forty. She looked up demurely at Henry with a sidelong sweep of her lashes, tossing back her honey-coloured curls. Henry's devotion to Anne made him almost immune to wiles like these, but he wasn't blind – and Rachael was captivating. She led him to the sofa, chattering artlessly of trivial things. Henry sat down beside her and Ned threw himself into an easy chair and watched them sardonically.

When Rachael made eyes at Henry, peeping up under lowered lids, he smiled at her and pressed the small hand she had impulsively put in his. She was like a little girl playing at flirting – impossible to believe that she was the mother of two children. A ribbon was slipping from her hair, her dress was slipping from her shoulder. He had heard of daring new fashions and supposed (rightly) that he was out of touch. She leaned across him to snuff the candle and, either by accident or design, rather more than half of a neat round breast appeared briefly at the top of her gown. Henry pretended he hadn't noticed, but not very successfully.

Ned drawled, 'Rachael, my sweet life, make sure of your audience, I beg. Harry wasn't watching and you must repeat the performance.'

Thoroughly embarrassed, Henry drank some tea. Rachael flounced pettishly and protested, 'I don't know what you mean.'

'Oh yes you do, my dear,' said Ned. 'You have chosen the wrong man though. Why don't you make your attempt on his virtue when I am out of the room so you may explain the procedure to him?'

'When *I* am out of the room, you may bicker with your wife,' said Henry. Rachael, who had flushed scarlet, jumped to her feet and rushed from the room, slamming the door.

'Spoilt baggage,' said Ned. 'She had been indulged all her life.'

'You were unkind,' Henry protested. 'You humiliated her.'

'I meant to. She is unkinder than I. Too old for her I may be, but

I grow weary of seeing her coquette with every beardless boy who enters the house. I should have stayed single.' He stretched out his legs and yawned. 'At all events, we are now no longer obliged to watch our language and drink tea. I have some capital brandy in the sideboard.'

Several cognacs later, Henry remembered that the groom was still holding his horse. He left hastily, and Ned accompanied him for part of the way, through an area where the dilapidated houses bred dissent, he said, as fast as fleas. 'I must leave you now,' he said at last. 'Go home and don't linger. Keep to the centre of the road. I must be up betimes to attend a hanging. I grow soft with age – it is a spectacle I dislike.'

'I suppose any reasonable man must dislike it,' said Henry, thoughtfully fingering his neck.

'Indeed no. Not if the cheering crowds are anything to go by. Even when some of them doubt the victim's guilt. We grow more inhuman as the years go by.'

'On the contrary,' said Henry, 'I think we are growing more humane.'

'Tell that to the French,' said Ned. 'Bleeding heads piled like so many turnips; women and children slaughtered while other women and children enjoy the spectacle – man has never been so cruel. But I forgot – you used to find excuses for the French murderers when fraternity was fashionable.'

Henry was glad that the darkness hid his face. 'When have I ever condoned murder?' he demanded. 'Anyway, they say the guillotine is more merciful than the rope. Not so long since, a burning at the stake was a family entertainment; now half-hanging and disembowelling are frowned on by reformers. Why, Ned, I believe a day may come when the right to take the life, even of a murderer, may be argued by extremists.'

Ned laughed. 'You are a sad case, Harry.' he said. 'If your fairy-tale comes to pass, I hope I may not live to see it.' He turned his horse and clattered away in the darkness.

Chapter Thirteen

Arthur Andrews did indeed lead a wretched life. His mother hid her fondness for him and his father had none to hide. He worked hard for little money and no praise. He had, as he had told Anne, no fun.

His knowledge of women was almost nil. Belonging to a class thinly represented and unpopular, that of the Protestant agents, bailiffs and proctors, he was despised by the ascendancy and peasantry alike. His sexual exploits had been confined to sweaty fumblings with the gypsy girls who came to glean in the harvest fields. These adventures brought on attacks of guilt as a result of his rigid unbringing. He spent his evenings reading the Old Testament in his room, and praying to a stern God for forgiveness. Thou shalt not covet thy neighbour's wife . . . . How much worse to covet the curate's wife! His passion for Anne was becoming an obsession. Arthur had not been designed by nature for a life of chastity.

Arthur spun fantasies about Anne. He rescued her from burning houses, shipwrecks and wolves. In gratitude, she would look at him as she did at Henry, brokenly murmuring her thanks, and he would carry her away to some imaginary castle where he could make love to her for ever. In his daydreams, sometimes it was the baby that he rescued, snatching it from the jaws of death and earning her undying gratitude. The baby added to her uncanny attraction: he went weak at the knees when he remembered how he had seen her suckling it.

Arthur's most far-fetched and favourite fantasy was one in which Henry went suddenly mad and attacked his wife with an axe. The climax varied – sometimes Arthur killed Henry with the axe, sometimes Henry was carried screaming away to Bedlam. Either way, Anne was his. The knowledge that she wasn't – couldn't be – his, made no difference. He went through his days in a sort of passionate stupor.

Arthur was expected to go to church twice on Sundays, so he had to sit twice through a service conducted by Henry, endure twice the sight of Anne in her blue cloak and velvet bonnet, with its goffered frill of linen framing her face, and its blue ribbons tied under her chin. A beautiful young woman, deeply in love with her husband. Arthur knew it and refused to admit it. His mind and body were in turmoil.

On the Sunday evenings that Henry took service in Monsea, Anne bolted the parlour door, George read improving books aloud and Arthur went to bed at eight o'clock.

One October afternoon, Arthur took a pair of horses to be shod in Silvermines village, and stayed for a sly, forbidden drink at Mrs Ryan's tavern. He had earned a few shillings unknown to his mother, bush-beating and running errands for the Prittie family. He ordered a large pot of porter.

Arthur had grown used to being treated like a leper by his neighbours, and drank alone as often as not. This time, Ezekiel Tydd who was also having a horse shod, joined him. Ezekiel was of the same background as Arthur, with the added slur of being a yeoman. Like Arthur, he was slow-witted: his parents, like Arthur's, imagined he was teetotal. No alcohol was allowed in either household.

'How d'you like the new curate?' asked Ezekiel, and when Arthur grunted 'not much,' he agreed. 'The wife's not my notion of a parson's missus either,' he added.

'Nor mine,' said Arthur, with feeling. 'Parson's a queer fellow too. Away at all hours, walks when he might ride, friendly with Papists – I don't like him.'

Ezekiel held out his mug for more porter. 'Did you hear him gabbing to Ben and me the day he came?' he asked. 'He'll talk to anyone, and joke with them. He doesn't know his place, that's for sure. Then one evening when we were drilling up at Dolla, he comes walking up the road and, only that he seems harmless enough, I'd've sworn he was counting the troops. Then off he goes into church as nice as pie. My Da thinks he's a croppy.'

'Ah, go on,' said Arthur. 'Parson a rebel? Much good he'd be to them.'

'Why? Nobody'd suspect him. Wouldn't it be great sport if the yeos had to hunt him down? Do you watch him close, Arthur, and see if he's up to something. Ten to one he's a United man – see his hair and his Frenchified rig?'

Arthur finished his drink. 'Have sense, Zeke,' he said. 'Can you see him with a pike in his hands? As for the rest, the wife wears Frenchie dress as well.' He felt rather than heard a change in his voice when he mentioned Anne, but couldn't prevent it.

As he rode home, he wondered about Henry Fulton. His powers of concentrated thought were limited, and he relied on emotion and instinct to guide him. Often he was right. Arthur had ridden further afield than his father, following the foxhounds. When he saw Matt Gleeson at the farmhouse, he had recognised him as one of Cooke Otway's men, a part-time helper in the kennels. Arthur had hidden in the laurels out of curiosity. Parson had as near as nothing caught him there, and he hadn't overheard anything, except a mention of a horse for sale in Nenagh.

Arthur's slow mind turned this remark over and considered it. Why send a Templederry man to Kilmore with a message from Nenagh? It was off in the other direction. And Matt had been uneasy. Arthur knew more of feelings than logic – Matt had been afraid. Parson had been calm enough, but he had shaken Matt's hand. Aye, and would have repeated the eccentric gesture if Matt hadn't taken himself off in a hurry.

As Arthur rode into his own yard, his thoughts rushed back to Anne. Anne who had no intention of allowing him near her, who had changed her seat at table so that he couldn't watch her. Anne whose kind eyes and smiling mouth seemed to make promises; whose cold words unmade them. What would she say if she heard that her husband was a traitor? That would wipe the adoring look off her face . . . . Arthur slowly worked out the implications. If Zeke was right, the family was in Arthur's power. Anne might be prepared to trade his silence for kisses, if nothing more.

Autumn turned to winter, and Arthur, his obsession sharpening his faculties, watched and waited. He also listened behind doors, but heard nothing except some home truths about himself.

Henry had been to Nenagh, supposedly to try a horse, but had returned as he went, on Sir Henry Prittie's borrowed nag. Young Francis Prittie was thought to be too delicate to attend university, and Henry taught him Latin, Greek and mathematics every morning except Saturday. Anne never walked abroad alone. She would stroll about the garden with James in her arms, provided Dorcas was about, otherwise she sat in the parlour with the door bolted. The Fultons were looking for different lodgings, Henry's excuse being that Anne would prefer to be near the village. Nobody was deceived by this.

December gales blew away the leaves, and made the old house creak and rattle at night. It was a squally day with a threat of snow when Arthur set off for Nenagh on his father's business. His jealous hatred of Henry was now almost as strong as his passion for Anne, and he trotted along on his father's roan horse, absorbed in his thoughts.

Arthur was in a pitiable state of misery and frustration. His fantasies had taken a new turn. Now, the renegade parson was arrested and hanged, while Arthur was at hand to comfort his sorrowing widow. Naturally, her disgust at her late husband's behaviour would prevent her from sorrowing for long.

Lost in his daydream, Arthur barely noticed the band of youths who ran behind him as he approached the town, booing and jeering. They insulted him in Irish, a language no Andrews would dream of learning, but their meaning was clear enough. When they began to pelt him with dung, he spurred his horse and left them behind, but he was so accustomed to this sort of reception that he felt no more than irritation.

Entering the town by Thomond Gate, he rode to the Market Cross, passing a dozen people he knew by sight. None greeted him except the butcher and the constable, with whom he had dealings. There had been rioting at the week-end, and the wine merchant and the apothecary had barred their shops, although it was market day. The main street was busy, and so was the tap-room of the Star and Garter Inn. There, Arthur greeted the landlord, Jack Cantrell, and got a surly nod in return. He listened, only half understanding, to a couple of travellers discussing the war with France, downed two swift pints and left.

Arthur was in town to collect money for barley from the maltster. Although George considered alcohol to be cursed, he had no objection to earning money from the making of it. The malthouse was a few doors away, with a hop garden at the back; Arthur left his horse and walked there.

As he crossed Chapel Lane, he noted with disapproval that the priest's new house was finished – a neat, slated building with green railings in front. A wicked waste of money, thought Arthur. Ten to one, they'd be raising money to repair the Catholic church next – its thatched roof was said to be leaking. Money was scarce among Father O'Meara's congregation and his new house was a measure of his popularity.

The maltster was busy, and sent Arthur to wait in an upstairs room at the back of the building. Bored, he stood at the window, his hands in his pockets, idly surveying Father O'Meara's house. Then he hastily stepped back out of sight; he had seen Henry Fulton in the yard, talking to the priest.

Arthur's boredom vanished. True, there was no law which said that the two might not speak – no law was normally necessary. The Protestant bishop of Killaloe, Dr Knox, was notoriously lax in such matters, so Arthur had heard, but even he would have taken a grave view of one of his curates talking to a priest who was strongly suspected of subversion. Proof of Zeke's suspicions was tantalisingly close: Arthur watched eagerly, keeping out of sight.

There was nothing suspect in the men's behaviour, it was broad daylight, anyone could have seen them. No papers changed hands, there were no signals, no covert glances or attempts at concealment. They chose to talk in the middle of a yard where they couldn't be overheard, but that might have been chance. Arthur would have believed anything of Henry – all he needed was proof. When Joe, the maltster, entered the room quietly behind him and spoke, he almost jumped out of his skin.

His business completed, Arthur set off for home as snow began to fall, blown horizontally by icy gusts from the north east. Crouching low in his saddle, his hat pulled down, his collar up, he overtook Henry a couple of miles outside the town.

Henry had been successfully limiting his encounters with Arthur to the dinner table and the Communion rails. He feared his own quick temper, and Arthur was impervious to the chill in his manner and kept trying to ingratiate himself. Having looked back and seen the roan's white-blazed face behind, Henry had spurred his herring-gutted bay, but it was a wretched animal, and Arthur continued to gain on him. Henry knew that his face was alight with excitement

117

and his eyes shining. He suddenly realised when he saw Arthur's muffled face and his mount's laid-back ears that he himself hadn't even buttoned up his coat. He tried to assume a polite mask as Arthur overtook him and reined in his horse.

The two rode on together, and Henry, having greeted him, waited for Arthur to speak first, wondering at the change in his usual sullen looks. Arthur seemed to be, like Henry, excited about something.

'I heard at the Star and Garter that the French are beat,' said Arthur at last. 'Two ships sunk, maybe more. I had the story from a traveller. He said the traitor Wolfe Tone was on one of the ships and drowned with the rest. Good enough for him, say I.'

'You were misinformed,' said Henry flatly. 'The French fleet is in Bantry Bay – if it hasn't been blown out again. By now, the French may have already landed. Cork may be in a siege. I suppose we will know tomorrow.' He had the utmost difficulty in keeping his voice low and controlled.

'Priest tell you that?' asked Arthur nastily.

Henry gave him a quick look. 'Yes,' he said. 'Father O'Meara had it from a friend who arrived from Mallow this morning.'

'It'll be lies,' said Arthur. 'Sure to be.'

Henry bit his lip. 'We shall see,' he said.

The news of the attempted French landing at Bantry Bay took two days to penetrate to remote areas and longer than that to be accepted. As Christmas approached, and the gales and blizzards continued, the country was alive with rumours. Some said the British guns at the Cove of Cork had annihilated the French ships, others that a French army was advancing unhindered on Fermoy. All agreed that Theobald Wolfe Tone was with the invaders.

Henry was kept informed as far as possible by other agents. He found it hard to remember how much he might legitimately be expected to know and how much he must conceal. He discovered from Francis Prittie that the Kilboy butler knew as much as he did, and wondered if the man was an agent for another cell or if his information was now common knowledge. He rode home on Christmas Eve, his mind entirely taken up with the reports he had heard and the instructions he had to pass on to Matt Gleeson. He had almost forgotten to buy Anne a present.

What a wretched Christmas she would have, he thought. He

would be taking two services and assisting at two more, while Christmas dinner with the Andrews family wasn't an event to look forward to. Oh, but she deserved better! He would make it up to her when they had a home of their own. He thought of the lace shawl he had bought, and wished he had the means to give her jewellery and keep a carriage for her. Their only Christmas call together had been to widower Benjamin Tydd, a man whose friendliness seemed overdone. 'Your good self', 'your lady wife'. The well-worn phrases were spoken with an oily deference which he disliked.

Henry overtook George and Dorcas, returning from a visit on foot. Probably they too had been to see Mr Tydd who was their nearest neighbour. Arthur wasn't in the yard, so Henry stabled his horse and walked into the house, pulling off his gloves, his riding whip under his arm. He had an odd, detached feeling which reminded him of a frosty morning in Phoenix Park. A feeling of foreboding mixed with powerlessness to avert whatever was going to happen. He let himself into the house, his thoughts elsewhere.

James was screaming. Not the normal cries of a teething baby but screams of fear. Henry tried the parlour door and found it unbolted.

Arthur hadn't heard him. One arm was tight around Anne, while with the other hand he forced her to turn her face to his. Her back was to the sofa and, as Henry opened the door, she fell, half on the sofa, half on the floor, Arthur crashing down with her.

Henry sprang forward, grabbed Arthur by the collar, dragged him to his feet and flung him violently into a corner. Arthur came out with his fists up, shouting incoherently, but he was no match for Henry's fury as his knuckles split flesh and snapped teeth. Anne caught at his arm, crying, 'Let him go!' when she saw blood streaming down Arthur's chin, but Henry took no notice.

They fought all over the room, Arthur protesting in spluttering half-finished sentences, Henry in vengeful silence. Henry got a painful blow on the nose, another in the eye and a third which split his lip, but Arthur hadn't either the skill or the power to follow them up. He took a crashing blow to his jaw and another which floored him. He got up shouting, 'Enough!' turned and ran to the door, but Henry hadn't finished with him. He picked up the riding whip he'd dropped and pursued Arthur out of the room, landing several painful cuts on the seat of his breeches and finally breaking the whip in two. He threw it away as Arthur made off towards the stable yard.

Henry ran back to the parlour, his nose pouring blood, his lip swelling and his right eye closing fast. He caught Anne in his arms, panting and speechless. As she was weeping hysterically and James was still howling, words would have been wasted anyway.

They clung together until Anne got her tears under control and pulled away from him to comfort James. Henry wiped his mouth, mumbling, 'Lecherous pig. How dare he? Leave the baby be, sweetheart – he'll soon quieten. Why, your face is all bruised.'

'It doesn't signify, the fright was much worse.' She flopped on the sofa, mopping away tears.

'When I saw him throw you down – '

'He didn't, I fell. But he handled me roughly. . . .And talked all the time of love, which made it somehow worse.'

Henry strode up and down. 'If I lay my hands on him again, I'll break his neck. Why, in God's name, did you let him in?'

'He knocked and knocked. Then he called through the door that if I didn't open, he was going to the magistrate to – to inform on you. Oh, Henry, what have you done? Please – you *must* tell me, I have been so worried since we came here – ' She began to cry again.

He sat beside her, took her kerchief from her and wiped her eyes with it. 'Hush. Dry your eyes while I go to the kitchen for warm water. We look a fine pair, all bloodied.'

'What have you done, Henry?'

'Nothing. Nothing that creature could harm me with. Don't fret, lovey, who would listen to him? We'll pack our bags as soon as we can and go to Kilboy. That should reassure you. Sir Henry is a magistrate, and I won't stay here another night.'

'We can't go there. It's Christmas Eve and you told me yourself they have a dinner party. Fine figures we would cut.'

Just then, they heard Arthur's voice in the hall. 'I won't go! Why should I be turned out for a canting parson? He attacked me first . . . .' The words were shouted loudly but indistinctly. Henry charged through the door, but stopped when he saw Dorcas. George was there too and shouldered his way between the two men, looking from one battered face to the other. Arthur dived into the kitchen and Dorcas followed with a measured tread, closing the door behind them.

George's usually passive face was brick red. 'I beg your pardon, Reverend,' he said, getting the words out with difficulty. 'Arthur told us what happened. He will never set foot in this house again.'

'It is we who must go,' Henry said. 'I must admit I would cheerfully have killed him in the heat of the moment, but I don't expect you to turn your son out of doors, especially tonight, on our account. We will see if Mr Tydd has a room for us.'

George almost smiled. 'Not Ben Tydd,' he said. 'That's where Arthur's going for now. He isn't our son – he'd be different if he was. No, he was a merry-begotten brat the wife took pity on, seeing we have none of our own. Some Papist's by-blow. I told her how it would be. Go back to your room, Reverend – there's naught else to do tonight.'

Chapter Fourteen

The Protestants of Kilmore had a rare treat on Christmas Day. Parson Fulton appeared with a black eye, and lisped the service through split and swollen lips. The sermon – not his own, but the work of a long dead bishop – concerned peace and goodwill. It failed to convince. Mrs Fulton, heavily cloaked and hooded, was trying to conceal a bruised face, and Arthur was not in his usual place. Outside, stories circulated, none of them true, as Henry's parishioners waited to get a closer look. They were disappointed. The curate and his wife left hurriedly after the service.

The Fultons had moved to a disused gate-lodge at Kilboy, home of Sir Henry Prittie. Built like a miniature fortress, it was dark, cold, and infested with cockroaches. Anne, practical in most ways, had a horror of these creatures which swarmed over the kitchen floor at night and were hard to see by candlelight. The roof leaked, the fire smoked, the walls ran with damp and there was hardly any furniture. They had been promised the services of a maidservant from Kilboy, but a week later she hadn't arrived.

On New Year's Eve, the Fultons, Henry carrying James who was growing big and heavy, walked up the drive of Kilboy House to have three o'clock dinner with their benefactors.

The house was huge, about twenty-five years old. Some day, trees would soften those gaunt walls and shelter the mansion from wind. At present, the neo-classical portico and shining rows of windows – four rows of five on each side – looked staring and ostentatious.

'It seems excessively large for four people,' Anne remarked. 'I think they might have found room for us here.'

'I dislike the house. I'm glad we don't live here,' said Henry. He looked up at the long rows of windows, counting them to take his mind off the uneasy feeling that there was something wrong somewhere. That something unpleasant was about to happen.

Suddenly, he saw the house ablaze – one of those strange visions which had plagued him in the past, now almost forgotten. Flame, a solid sheet of it, behind the blank faces of the windows: black, oily smoke hiding the sky. He thought he could hear the glass shattering, the pistol-shot cracks of the slates.

'Henry. What are you looking at?' Anne took the baby from him and followed his gaze.

'I thought for a moment the house was afire. A trick of the light, I suppose. Hurry – we're going to be late.'

In the great hall, the butler took Henry's coat and hat, while the housekeeper carried James away through the baize door to the servants' quarters in the basement. The meal was an uneasy one, as Sir Henry Prittie and his sons were silent, while Lady Prittie chattered feverishly about nothing in particular. Afterwards, Henry joined his host, a magistrate, in the library, where he had to give a more detailed account of Arthur's attack on Anne and the fight which followed. His temper had gone off the boil; he blamed himself for not taking better care of Anne. 'I don't believe Andrews is normal,' he said.

'A common plea of rogues,' said Sir Henry Prittie, a lean, hawk-nosed man with a habitual sniff.

'My wife is a charitable woman,' Henry said. 'In spite of all, she insists that Andrews is a poor wretch deprived of affection all his life, whose wits were temporarily deranged. I was misled myself at the time. I thought he had thrown himself upon her, but it appears that my wife stumbled, bringing both of them down. She says Andrews had demanded no more than kisses.' He bit his scabbed lip, making it start bleeding again. 'Crazy or not, I thank God that I returned when I did,' he said.

'The law is not concerned with emotions,' said the stern man in the wing chair. 'Chained in a Bedlam or chained in a cell, where's the difference? I can have the man arrested and tried, but I presume you do not want that, or you would have suggested it yourself. It would, of course, draw much attention, and cause vulgar speculation which would be undesirable in your position. I can, if you wish, see that the affair is hushed up and that Andrews leaves the district.'

'Thank you, sir, I think that would be best. I hoped you would suggest something of the kind.' Henry rose to his feet. 'I won't take up any more of your time – '

123

'Wait. There is something else. I must request that you confine your tutoring of my son to the subjects we agreed. These do not include the scriptures. It may appear in Holy Writ that Our Lord sought out the company of the lower orders, but it is not a point on which one cares to dwell.'

'Does one not? I find that aspect of the gospels fascinating.'

'Understand that others do not share your somewhat eccentric notions. And I want no sermon about fishermen, shepherds and the like. Kindly confine your religious instruction to a recital of the Lord's Prayer and a reading of the collect for the day. That is all. You may go.'

Henry remained where he was. He dabbed angrily at his bleeding lip, saying, 'I am grateful for your hospitality and your understanding in the matter of Arthur Andrews, but I don't care to be dismissed like a naughty child.'

'Don't you Fulton? Where is your Christian humility? Now, if you will allow me – ' He rang the bell which summoned a footman. 'Take Mr Fulton to the drawing-room,' he said, and nodded a curt goodbye.

There was no arrest and no trial, but vulgar speculation was rampant.

Arthur disappeared abruptly, and his foster parents offered no explanation. However, their groom spread a highly coloured account of the affair, and the story created more interest locally than the fate of the French fleet, which had been blown out of Bantry Bay by the worst gales for a decade.

Henry expected criticism for his rough justice, but none came. Instead, he found he was more popular than before with the capricious young bucks of the neighbourhood. They urged him to attend prize-fights and to train with them, and offered to lend him valuable horses. Henry declined regretfully. He rode his borrowed nag, wore sober clothes and tried to merge into the background as a model curate should.

As she cooked and cleaned and sewed, Anne was glad of her practical upbringing. Many of her social equals, deprived of their servants, would have been at a loss, unable even to mind their own children.

Sir Henry Prittie was having a larger house decorated for the

Fultons, and it was to be ready by summer. Anne was almost sorry. In the cut stone lodge with its thick walls and tiny windows, she felt safe; she could see carts and carriages going up and down the road a few yards from the door. The new parsonage was up a laneway, nearer to the Silvermines. There they would be isolated, far from the road and served by people who might be planning to murder them. She thought of the grisly deaths of the tithe proctor of Knockgrafton and his wife, and shuddered. Henry swept her doubts aside. 'I promise you we will be safe,' he said.

She remembered his confident words as she knelt outside in the pale January sunshine, weeding dead grass from a clump of snow-drops. Where had he got to this time, she wondered – he should have been back from tutoring Francis Prittie two hours since. Henry liked the slight, fair-haired boy with his round shoulders and sweet smile. Perhaps he was giving him extra tuition. . . .

At that moment, Henry was quite close – in a roofless cabin not two hundred yards away. He was talking to Father O'Meara, who had walked from Nenagh to meet him – or rather, Father O'Meara was talking.

'What, in the name of all that's holy are you trying to do?' he demanded. 'I hear a tale that you gave one of your own parishioners a thrashing. And they say you insulted Colonel Finch from the pulpit about the way the church was painted. Are you mad? Are you *trying* to be noticed? The balladeers have the story of yourself and young Andrews on a penny broadsheet. Oh, and a fine likeness of yourself with a whip in one hand and a bible in the other. The ballad's sung at every wedding and wake in North Tipperary. Make no mistake, you're watched wherever you go.'

'I was obliged to act as I did,' said Henry. 'The man attacked my wife. It will soon be forgotten if I lie low for a while.' He smiled down at the priest, an elderly man whose eyebrows had stayed dark while his hair whitened. Beneath them, his eyes were deep-set, clever and dark.

'You didn't hear the last of Andrews,' he said. 'He's working in the Latteragh woods with Otway's gang. He was seen in Nenagh yesterday, and he waylaid Captain Fitzmaurice in the street. My informant didn't hear your name mentioned, but you may be sure it was. Fitzmaurice sent Andrews about his business all right – cursed him up, down and across. Half the town heard him.'

'I can imagine.' Henry smiled reflectively. 'I don't believe Arthur will be heeded by anyone in authority, and his understanding isn't strong. He suspects, I daresay, but he knows nothing. I'd hoped he'd be sent further than Latteragh, though. I don't want him to see Matt heading this way.'

Father O'Meara glanced quickly up and down the road. 'I've a job for you,' he said. 'When it's done, you would be advised to keep quiet and confine your activities to teaching heresies to young Prittie. Oh, and tell him to keep them to himself if you don't want to be hanged by your own friends. Jesus Christ a rebel against society, indeed!'

'I begin to wonder who my friends are,' said Henry quietly. 'Francis, perhaps, but I am obliged to use him. He is in love – or thinks he is – with Otway's daughter, Selina. They exchange letters clandestinely, and who better to carry them than Matt Gleeson?'

'Convenient. I hope the affair prospers.'

'I dislike my position in all this,' Henry said. 'I am not supposed to know about these letters. Francis trusts me.'

'The old predicament of the gentleman spy,' said Father O'Meara. 'And you are not cut out for the work. Why did you take it on?'

'For an ideal. And I never intended to spy on my friends. Now I am in a position when I don't know if I will be shot by the dragoons or piked by the rebels – either seems likely. What was the work you said you had for me?'

'Do you know Hervey Morres of Knockalton House?'

'I think I met him once. A magistrate? About my own age?'

'That's the man. He fought in the Austrian army and married an Austrian baroness. He's a Catholic – I baptised him myself – but he has the entry into all the big Protestant houses. He quarrelled with Cooke Otway – '

'Who has not?'

'Indeed. Morres complained to Otway about the trouble the Orangemen were giving and got no satisfaction. Now he wants to join the United Men.' The priest paused, listening, as a horseman passed their hiding place, then he went on, 'I'll need your assistance in swearing him in and will let you know the place and time. After that, no more assignments for a while.'

'Surely you aren't suggesting that I should stop swearing in new members?' said Henry. 'That's honourable work. It's spying and lying that I object to.'

The priest sighed. 'I am acting in your own interests. I know you are brave, but surely you must think about the consequences if you are caught. You speak about being shot or piked, but not as if you believed it might happen.'

'I believe it – and I have a wife and child to consider. I don't intend to be caught.'

'Consider yourself first. Listen, this rebellion which is coming may go either way. We believe it will succeed. But even if it does, every revolution has its aftermath, when rebels turn respectable. How can you do that if you are respectable already? Be warned. People like you make handy scapegoats.' He peered through the glassless window. 'I must away. Is the coast clear?'

They went their separate ways, walking. Henry, whose feet were blistered, often had to remind himself that Rousseau wouldn't place himself above his fellow men by riding. A coach and six overtook him, travelling full pelt through the mire. Henry limped home, keeping his thoughts on Rousseau with difficulty. It was better than dwelling on Father O'Meara's warnings.

Henry ate his supper, read the *Limerick Chronicle* by the light of a candle, then threw the paper aside. He folded his arms and leaned back in his chair, gazing at the ceiling. Anne, sitting in the firelight, idle for once, asked him if he was weary. Henry answered vaguely that he supposed he was.

'Oh, you are impossible!' Anne jumped to her feet and stood in front of him, obliging him to look at her. 'What is wrong with you? You hardly speak, sometimes you forget that I'm here. There are times when I feel that I could go away and you wouldn't notice until the next mealtime.'

She was between anger and tears. She had never raised her voice to Henry before, and he was startled. Guiltily, he pulled her down on his knee and kissed her, reassuring her, saying that he had been neglectful and selfish. 'I have much on my mind. Forgive me, my dear love – it won't happen again.'

She snuggled against him, mollified but not altogether convinced. She felt that she hadn't his whole attention, even now. He said, 'You know how much I love you. You know I am all yours.'

'No I don't,' Anne replied with spirit. 'I own about two-thirds of you, your heart and your body. Your mind is your own – I don't know what goes on in your head. When you came home this evening, hours late, you almost bumped into me before you saw me, and your manner was so strange I felt half afraid of you. You aren't still brooding about Arthur Andrews?'

'I am not. That dog? Do you think I give him a thought now that he has gone?'

'What then? He threatened me, and when I asked you what hold he could have on you, you turned the question aside. Yet he implied that he knew something disgraceful about you, and he thought I knew it too. Don't be angry but – are you working for the United Irish Society? Don't lie to me, I have a right to know.'

Henry didn't answer at once. The desire to tell Anne everything was strong and he knew he had already told her too much. 'Anne, my darling,' he said at last, 'There are things I cannot tell you, and which you must not know. This is because I have information which could be dangerous. The fewer people who share it the better. If you knew as much as I, you would have no protection against blackmailers. Please believe that there are things that I can't tell you, and trust me. If you do, I promise we will all be safe.'

There was a note in Henry's voice which told Anne that he would tell her no more. Frightened and bewildered, she said, 'Of course I trust you.'

'I know you do. One day, I'll explain everything. Come, my dear, let us go early to bed.'

Chapter Fifteen

The spring and summer passed in tense waiting. The country seemed to hold its breath.

Arthur Andrews was happy when he was cutting wood. He was strong and had a good eye: each time the axe struck exactly where he intended with a satisfying smack and a sharp wedge of wood sprang from the trunk. He bent and straightened and swung his axe and sweated. Sometimes he thought that if he had been as fit on Christmas Eve as he was now, he would have settled Parson's business. Mostly, he pushed Henry Fulton and his wife to the back of his mind.

Arthur no longer found himself a loathed member of an alien class. His workmates were all Protestant labourers recruited by his employer, Cooke Otway – one couldn't turn local men loose with axes. They had their camp, and a store where they spent their wages. Otway's money never left his estate. The other foresters, nourished on rumours, thought of Arthur as a man moved by mighty passions. They admired his silent strength, thinking him something of a hero. Arthur let them think what they liked.

He hadn't meant to hurt Anne – not even to touch her. Neither had he been able to keep his hands off her. He had lived on dreams until they fused with reality. Then his dreams had failed him – he had woken up.

Arthur stood back watching, as the wood cracked and snapped. The great beech fell with a swish and rattle of breaking twigs and he at once attacked its branches. His muscles ached but he ignored the pain. When the foreman blew his whistle, there would be plenty of porter to drink. Life wasn't so bad now – or wouldn't be if he could get even with Parson. He had forgiven Henry for breaking his teeth but not for beating him with a whip.

His thoughts had been murderous when he had waylaid Captain Fitzmaurice in the street. He knew now that he should have waited for more evidence and that he shouldn't have stated his price to the redcoat officer. He swung his axe with all his strength as he remembered the roared oaths and the insults spoken in a voice of bitter scorn. Arthur remembered every biting word: he was slowly hatching a different plan.

The camp had moved to a wood on the border of the Castle Otway estate, about a mile from Kilboy. Sir Henry Prittie's land lay all about them; a farm tenanted by Jona Tydd, brother of Benjamin and uncle of Ezekiel. Jona had got work for Zeke helping in the store, when he wasn't with the yeomanry. Arthur clung to his slight friendship with Zeke, seeing him as his only link with Henry Fulton, the man he would ruin, or even kill.

'Does Reverend Fulton still visit your Da?' he asked Ezekiel over a pint of porter.

'Oh, he does, and so does his good lady. My Da don't like him because he seems to think well of the United Men, but he lets him keep coming. Says he'd like to trip him up. Says he has a feeling about him.'

'I rode home with him once,' said Arthur, 'and he was saying how the French would come and kill all the English and we'd have a French king.'

'G'way! He never said that, did he? Sure, the French cut off one another's heads for fun!'

'It was something like that. He got it from that Nenagh priest they said was a croppy last year. You know – Father William, they call him. He was taken in and let go again.'

Zeke digested this. 'I'll tell my Da that,' he said. 'There's good money for information.'

'I'll want half,' said Arthur. He drank in silence for a while, then said, 'I don't think she's mixed up with the rebels.'

'You wouldn't,' said Ezekiel Tydd.

While the woodcutters were working away from the Castle, Matt Gleeson took out his employer's foxhounds for exercise. As he walked them, he thought over the message he had been given, memorising it. The words made no sense to him because he wouldn't allow them to. His mind received words as wax received the impression of a seal, to be passed on and then erased. Once discarded, they were gone from his mind for ever. Neither threats nor torture would bring them back.

The hounds back in their kennels, Matt set off loping through the woods as silently as a fox. He carried a package containing an emotional note from Miss Selina Otway to Francis Prittie, and a lock of her straight mouse-brown hair. It was the perfect cover if he was caught. The message in his brain was to be delivered to Parson Fulton, then swiftly forgotten.

Matt always delivered Selina's letters to Francis in a little gothic summerhouse – a suitably romantic spot, and the place where the two young people had twice managed to meet. Today, Matt wondered if he should perhaps leave the letter in a crack in the wall and go. There seemed to be some sort of military exercise going on at the back of the mansion. He hid among the trees, listening. He heard carriages on the front drive. A party no doubt. It was going to be tricky. And if he was delayed, he would keep Mr Fulton waiting.

He began to work his way closer to the outbuildings, wishing there were trees to hide him.

Meanwhile, Henry and Anne had been invited at short notice to luncheon at Kilboy. Bishop Knox was to attend, as well as a number of proud ladies who had not so far felt that they need take any notice of the curate. Anne had accepted the invitation, and Henry had somehow to intercept Matt and meet him first.

Striding along on the edge of a wood, hoping he hadn't missed the other man, Henry knew he would be late, that he would have to dream up some tale of visiting the sick. . . . The sort of needless lie he tried to avoid.

He had learned a little about self-preservation, although not nearly enough, and thought there was someone following him. Pausing, he cut a switch from the hedge with his pocket knife and glanced idly back. The man was too far away to recognise, but he was running, and the morning sun gleamed on the blade of an axe.

Henry sidestepped, dropped neatly into the ditch and waited. He heard the thump of heavy feet and the sound of somebody panting. Holding his breath and willing the twigs he stood on not to snap, he craned his neck. Arthur Andrews had run past, his head low, his axe held short, near its head. Henry climbed out on the other side of the ditch, made his way quietly through a belt of young trees, then took to his heels and ran in the other direction. The country was open all the way to Kilboy – he *must* be seen. He slowed to a walk and when his breath was coming more normally, he knocked at the door of the nearest house – that of Benjamin Tydd, mentally cursing all luncheon parties.

Mrs Otway, Mrs Holmes and Mrs Waller had nothing in common except rich, land-owning husbands. They sat in a row on Lady Prittie's gold brocade sofa and looked stonily at their hostess.

Stout Mrs Otway spoke for all of them. 'My dear ma'am,' she said, 'do you mean to say you have invited us and our husbands here, and the Bishop too, to lunch with the curate and his wife? We have called on Mrs Fulton – that should suffice.'

Lady Prittie's faded face wore its usual anxious smile. 'You don't understand, Augusta. Like you, I thought the curate, son of a linen merchant, had married a woman of his own standing, but I was mistaken. Her father's family is a titled one, and her mother is a sister of Doctor Thomas Leland.'

'The historian? I met him once at the viceregal ball, oh, it must be twenty years since. He was expecting to be made Provost of Trinity. He and Lord Claremont were for ever visiting.' Mrs Otway paused. 'As a matter of fact,' she said, 'I always thought that Mrs Fulton was of a different class to her husband. She has great address.'

'Yes she has, has she not? And sweetly pretty too. Fulton is well enough in his way, but I sometimes wonder if he is a trifle crazed. He would have us live in the fashion laid down in the gospels – as if one could. People in our position . . . .' Lady Prittie glanced side-ways to make sure that Bishop Knox couldn't hear. 'Mr Fulton has many of the dear bishop's liberal notions, but Dr Knox knows they are not intended for practical living. One has one's standards.'

The other ladies nodded their agreement. If they remembered the parable of the needle's eye, they dismissed it as a mistranslation or a joke.

Lady Prittie, a great chatterer, chattered on. 'Imagine,' she said, 'poor Anne has not seen her mama and papa since the birth of her child. Her mama is about to present a performance of Handel's *Messiah* in Roscrea. She is a sister, you know, of the celebrated writer, Miss Eliza Leland.'

132

'I've heard of her,' said Mrs Holmes. 'Is she not the bluestocking who recently published a life of Alexander the Great?'

'Yes indeed. Brilliant, I'm sure. I must endeavour to read it, I suppose. What can be keeping the Fultons? The barouche was sent for them more than an hour ago. No trouble, I hope, though one can never be sure. Thank God for our yeomen.'

As she turned away to speak to another guest, Mrs Otway murmured to Mrs Holmes, 'We should have had entertainment if Eliza Leland had graced the dining table – all Dublin is talking about her and her ninety-year-old paramour, Sir Timothy Boyle. She has decided to live a virtuous life and has returned him to his wife. I cannot imagine how she gets away with such behaviour – she has the entrée everywhere.'

'Hush, Augusta, here's Mrs Fulton.'

Anne Fulton was late and alone. This extraordinary circumstance, a lady arriving unattended, made her hope fervently that the party was a small one. Where, oh where was Henry?

Lady Prittie greeted her kindly, agreeing that Henry must have been detained by a parishioner with a pressing problem. 'He is so good, my dear, so charitable. I'm sure he would put his Christian duty before any social obligation.'

Anne made her excuses automatically, hardly knowing what she said, for all the county was there, and apparently delighted to see her. Bishop Knox was always friendly, but she fancied that he watched her closely when she said that Henry had been unexpectedly detained. He looked sympathetic, agreeing almost too readily that Henry must have been called to somebody's bedside when out on his morning stroll.

Anne, who was well aware why she was suddenly in favour with the Pritties' friends, answered their eager questions about her health with an inward smile. Augusta Otway, almost as forthright and rude as Miss Eliza, asked her if she was increasing and, when she admitted that she expected a second child in February, said sharply, 'In that case, you should wear stays or you will lose your figure.'

Anne blushed. Her loose high-waisted gown might have been cut from the same pattern as that worn by Mrs Waller. The French empire style was sweeping the country.

A servant opened the door, and Henry came in without waiting to be announced. Anne, so relieved that she forgot to be vexed, noticed how Lady Prittie's chilly greeting melted into warm smiles and kind words. The various men present took longer to thaw out, but soon all had forgotten their annoyance. How did Henry manage it? Anne asked herself. He had almost ruined a party and, within minutes, he was the centre of it. He had called at Ben Tydd's house, he said, and what a to-do! Ben had tumbled off a ladder and was in a fair way to have cracked his skull. 'I offered to gallop post-haste for the surgeon, but he wouldn't hear of it. So I remained at his bedside until he felt able to sit up and drink some terrible tisane which he concocts himself. He has now recovered, except for a bump on his crown big enough to set his wig askew. I thought I'd never get here.'

'So did your hosts and your poor wife,' said Bishop Knox, giving him an interested glance. He offered his arm to Anne, and they went in to luncheon.

As Anne went across the hall on the bishop's arm, she noticed that the butler was watching her. A fat man with cunning eyes and an ill-tempered twist to his mouth, Grogan was married to the cook. Meeting his eye, Anne smiled, and saw his face relax and break into an open friendly grin. A strange expression for an upper servant, she thought – as if they were equals, or shared a secret.

During the meal, a scared footman came into the dining room and whispered to Sir Henry Prittie who gave him a curt order and helped himself to more beef. 'Some tale of croppies hiding in the summer-house,' he said when the man had gone. 'In broad daylight. I don't believe a word of it,' he glared round, inviting dissent.

Nobody argued with him, but young Francis asked, 'Should we not go and look?' half rising from his chair.

'Certainly not. I maintain the yeomanry in order that I may dine in peace.'

Francis was silenced. Anne risked a glance at Henry, sitting across the table from her, but his expression was bland as he turned to speak to Mrs Holmes, who had dropped her fork with a nervous gasp. 'This house is in no danger from the rebels,' he said. 'Neither is mine, so I have been told.'

A noise of clattering hoofs, shouts and a couple of shots made everyone start, but Lady Prittie, taking her line from her husband, rang the handbell for the footman to remove the covers.

This time, the man entered at a run. 'The croppy's been shot, your honour!' he cried. 'Matt Gleeson from Castle Otway. He's killed!'

Everyone rose at this, but Henry and Francis made for the door so fast that they collided, Francis bursting through and tearing down just ahead of Henry. Matt was lying in the yard with blood streaming from his shoulder. A trail of it showed where he had been carried in. Henry ran to kneel beside him, with a snapped, 'How did this come about?' to Ezekiel Tydd and two other yeomen who were looking on.

'We didn't see who he was,' said Zeke. 'He didn't answer our challenge and he was running through the bushes like a rabbit.'

'Get on that horse and ride to Nenagh for a surgeon.' Henry took command without noticing that he was doing so. 'As fast as you can now.' His expression made Zeke step back involuntarily. Henry spread his coat over Matt's body against the October chill, and tried to plug the bullet hole with his handkerchief.

Francis, looking on helplessly, mouthed at Henry, 'Has he a message for me?' and Henry said quietly, 'Later,' By now, the whole party was in the yard, all asking if the man was dead.

'Not even dying,' said Henry. 'But his shoulder seems to be broken and he is faint from loss of blood.' He had extracted Francis's letter from Matt's shirt and transferred it quietly to his black, clerical breeches. Eight years, he thought. Eight years since the Whiteboys' raid on Boula Rectory, and nothing has changed. A man wounded. A group of people trying to pretend for as long as possible that nothing is amiss. He saw his rosy dreams fading, but he was committed to his ideals. Would any good come of them? he wondered. There was no turning back now, even had he wished to do so.

Matt was whispering something, and Henry bent his head to hear. 'I lost it. I lost it when they shot me.' Matt never lost anything. It was some moments before Henry understood that the message for him was blanked out in Matt's mind. The surgeon would attend to him in the military barracks, but nobody there would learn anything from Matt, even in delirium. There was nothing there to learn.

Later, Henry gave the letter to Francis, and told him to show it to his father. It was a scented note from 'Your own sorrowing Selina'.

'I can't.' Francis protested.

'You must. Matt was badly hurt delivering your letter, and until you explain what he was doing, he is at the risk of being thought a croppy. You heard the footman at lunch? The soldiers would think nothing of torturing him if they couldn't get information any other way. They might even hang him. Without the letter, how is he to explain himself? Take it to your father at once.'

Francis obeyed, trembling, and his father lectured him at great length. However, he startled his son by saying that he had already planned an alliance with the Otway family. Francis, his grand passion reduced to a breeding programme, slunk away to his room.

Henry now had to find a replacement for Matt, if possible without attracting attention. Between him and his superior in Thurles lay the forest where Cooke Otway's men were now helping the yeomanry as the situation worsened. Armed with axes and slashhooks, they guarded their area and watched the road. Even when Matt recovered, he would be no more use. Neither could Henry risk being seen by Arthur Andrews anywhere that he had no business to be. He had to make a detour over the hills towards Cureeney, a desolate place inhabited mainly by grouse. Often he arrived home after dark.

The little parsonage was undefended. Anne had two maidservants, but no man to scare away raiders when Henry was absent. The maids, Johanna and Mary, had both worked at Kilboy and were supposedly loyal. They had been trained by the Kilboy housekeeper to try to please their employers with flattery. Feeling at ease with Anne, they behaved more naturally, but they talked to one another in Irish. Once, Anne would have told them that this was impolite in her presence; now she listened to every word, hoping and fearing to learn what they thought of Henry.

She was amazed at how well informed the girls were as she heard them discussing the purge of United Irishmen in Belfast the year before. Seventy from Monaghan alone had been shot, standing beside their coffins. It was this act which had spread dissidence to the midlands. It was from the girls that she heard that King's County had been proclaimed 'free'. It was in the papers a week later. 'How did they know?' she asked Henry.

'Travelling labourers on piecework carry news from town to town. Tipperary will be next. Why, the rebels are training in the hills when they are supposed to be picking potatoes.'

'Picking potatoes in January?'

'Certainly. The Militia know the truth, but don't fancy riding into an ambush. The rebels will still be picking potatoes in April, I don't doubt.' He put on his low-crowned black hat and looked out at the cold, swirling mist outside. 'I must be going. I have business to see to off Killoscully way.' He fetched the 'cartouche cape' given him by the Leland sisters and slung it round his shoulders.

Anne straightened the black cloth so that none of the bright blue lining showed. 'Dearest, please don't go running into danger. If you can't tell me why you do it, I'll try to understand, but think of James and the baby I'm carrying now. Someone is going to mistake you for a rebel and shoot you.'

'I'll take care. Both sides think I am touched in the head. Who would shoot a poor crazy parson?' He kissed her and was gone.

In mid-February of that year, 1798, Mrs Walker travelled to Kilmore from Roscrea to be with her daughter at the birth of her baby.

Sir Henry Prittie provided armed outriders for her carriage, who occasionally fired warning shots in the air as they approached the wooded drive of the parsonage. Mrs Walker travelled with her maid, Higgins who, too well trained to speak without being spoken to, sat clutching her valise in terror whilst tears poured down her cheeks. Her mistress was totally absorbed in her thoughts; the shots were no more than a mild irritant. She wasn't thinking of her daughter, but of *The Messiah*, now planned for the middle of May. At last, a regiment with an outstanding band was stationed at Roscrea. She had started drilling the trumpeters and all had promised to practise daily in her absence. 'Oh, for heavens' sake, Higgins, blow your nose,' she said.

She had come at Henry's insistence. Anne had doubted whether she would be of much use and she had been right. The baby, a girl, was born a few days early, after a brief labour, during the afternoon. Mrs Walker might as well have remained in Roscrea, as the child was washed and dressed by the time she saw her. No midwife was sent for; Henry was away. As Johanna and Mary bent over Anne, she could tell by their faces that they were longing to chat to one another. At last, Mary murmured in Irish, 'Parson ought to be ashamed – away at a time like this. Suppose Missis needs a physician?'

'How can he stay?' asked Johanna, who supported Henry right or wrong. 'He has to obey orders like you and me. He's wasting his time trying to recruit anyway. My father says nobody'll believe he isn't a spy or crazy or both.'

Anne kept her eyes closed, hoping the girls wouldn't notice that she'd understood. Here was the news she had dreaded, at a time when she felt unable to stand it. Her muscles tensed as Johanna added, 'I think he's gone to Killoscully again. He'd better watch out – Waller's yeomen are looking all over for Liam Flaherty.'

'Everyone knows that,' said Mary scornfully, and Anne opened her eyes as Higgins bustled in importantly with a glass of cordial.

Henry arrived home as night was falling, tore upstairs and fell on his knees by the low feather-bed. The baby was a little angel, Anne the best wife in the world. He made no excuse and gave no reason for being late. With his arms round both Anne and her infant, he bent his head to kiss the baby. His hair smelled of damp earth and there was a fragment of moss in it; there was drying mud on his sleeve. Anne reflected that most wives would have suspected an assignation with another woman, despite the chilly weather. Henry had a look about him which she had learned to dread – tense, alert, his eyes brilliant with excitement. She said, 'Henry, listen. The maids know – they were talking Irish. So you may as well tell me.'

'The maids have been listening to gossip.' He looked shaken but recovered himself. 'Remember, *you* know nothing.'

She held the bit of moss under his nose. 'I know nothing, you say. Are you trying to make me guess? For God's sake let it rest – and change your coat.' Her voice dropped to a whisper as Mrs Walker opened the door, humming a too familiar air. Henry winked at his wife and went downstairs to wash.

They decided to call the baby Jane. Henry baptised her at home, with Mrs Walker standing godmother. Bishop Knox, passing through Silvermines on Church business, made a detour in order to call on the Fultons. Handsome and energetic, he was conscious of his effect on the peasantry as he rode by on his black horse, but he was no longer the ambitious socialite Henry had known at Trinity. Few churchmen of his rank would have dared to ride unattended just then, but Bishop Knox's popularity protected him. He had helped to finance a Catholic school and was an ardent social reformer.

After admiring little Jane and taking tea with Anne and her mother, he went for a stroll in the garden with Henry. 'There are times,' he said, 'when I wish I had not obtained this living for you. First, I hear you are a bad influence on young Prittie, now there is a rumour that you are secretly helping the disaffected. Try to remember that what was once fashionable at Trinity is now a matter for the hangman.'

'I do remember it,' said Henry. 'I also remember your own enthusiasm for the French Revolution. Did you not say that you recognised no king but the Almighty?'

'I did. I backed the French even when they were killing priests and desecrating churches because I thought it was a temporary madness. Then ideals and visions turned to blood and death, Christianity was officially abolished, the "Supreme Being" replaced God, and Temples of Reason replaced churches. How can you associate yourself with that kind of thing?'

Henry considered before replying, head bowed, hands behind his back. 'I believe,' he said at last,' that others will learn from France's mistakes. Nothing has changed for the oppressed peasants of Ireland because nobody has thought them worth bothering about. The so-called reforms of the last few years are scribblings in the statute book, not real improvements – just as I call you "My Lord" instead of Willie, but you are not a new person.'

'Am I not? Henry, I fear you are making a mistake and are likely to make others. Calamitous mistakes.' He hesitated, then said, 'I know you will tell me nothing, but that wild, visionary gaze of your frightens me. Events will run away with you. You will be like Mazeppa, lashed to the back of a wild horse.'

Henry, seeing the other man's concern, swallowed the laughter that this picture conjured up. 'I have read the legend,' he said, 'and if I remember it correctly, the horse dropped dead and Mazeppa lived on.'

Henry rode with the bishop for a short distance, then left him in order to call on Benjamin Tydd, whose health had never been good since his fall from the ladder some months earlier. A tall, colourless man, Henry found it hard to understand why he had become so friendly.

While Benjamin bolted the door, Henry glanced through a copy of the *Limerick Chronicle*. It was folded open at an article about the activities of the United Irishmen. He looked at it absently, his mind still on the bishop's words. He had so nearly been caught by the Castle Waller cavalry on the day of Jane's birth that he felt cold when he thought of it. Well, the message had been delivered, but he doubted if there would be another. He was too conspicuous a messenger. His mind straying back to the mossy ditch where he'd hidden for three hours, he only half heard Benjamin say, 'The United oath is written down in there. It isn't as dreadful as I had thought.'

'No,' said Henry vaguely. 'It was a fine oath when I heard it at College. A promise to make the country a better place for everyone. Nowadays, they have added the words, "Union, Truth, Liberty or Death".'

'Where does it say that?'

'It's hearsay,' said Henry, noisily turning a page.

'I have a notion to join the United Men,' said Benjamin. 'I thought you might help me. Can you tell me who to talk to? I'd be prepared to take an oath.'

Henry lowered the paper and stared at the older man. True, it was his duty to recruit new members and he had sworn in over twenty, including the new leader, Hervey Morres. None had been of Tydd's sort – a bigoted Protestant with Calvinistic views. But Benjamin had been unfailingly friendly and supportive for the best part of a year.

'Membership is a capital offence,' Henry said.

'I was told you'd get me in, Reverend. I was told you were one of them yourself. For friendship's sake, help me.'

'I can't believe you're serious,' said Henry. 'If I told Sir Henry Prittie of this, you would lose your good name and your farm – you realise that?'

'I do.'

Henry went to the door. 'I must go home,' he said. 'I think you should forget this conversation, and so should I.'

Benjamin made no move to stop him. When the clatter of Henry's horse had died away, he scrawled on the margin of the newspaper, 'Union, Truth, Liberty or Death'. Then he folded it small and hid it in the chimney.

Chapter Sixteen

Ned Fitzmaurice was disgusted with life. When he had joined the 7th Dragoons, he had had visions of an exciting life in exotic places. Cool and courageous, he would have made an excellent commander, for he was also a good organiser and had natural authority. Commanding the Nenagh garrison wasn't Ned's idea of soldiering. He found himself the leader of a sort of armed police force, feared and disliked by the vast majority of the townspeople.

Ned's duties included quelling riots started either by rebels or Orangemen, sending out armed escorts for the Mail and for anyone who could afford them, listening to the stories of informers for both sides and (hateful duty) seeing that they were paid. He also meted out punishment by flogging for drunkenness and petty crime, and by firing squad for desertion. His favourite recreation was foxhunting, a sport which continued regardless of the political situation, and which was getting to be far more dangerous for any follower in a red coat than for the fox. By tacit consent, the huntsmen avoided places where the rebels were known to be well-armed and spoiling for a fight.

In the evening, Ned visited the houses of gentry, and watched his wife flirting with a succession of men half his age. He suspected that she was carrying on an intrigue with Lancelot Finch, one of his own junior officers, but couldn't prove anything. No wonder that his temper was shocking. He felt old, and couldn't decide if the deference shown towards him by his men was caused by respect or dislike.

As the country advanced steadily towards the open rebellion which Ned knew to be inevitable, he saw his chance of being posted overseas disappear. He was sitting at his desk, crossly writing a report, when his adjutant, young Richard Falkiner, son of the regiment's chaplain, knocked and entered.

'Another informer, sir,' he said. 'He looks respectable enough, but he wants to endorse information laid against a public figure last year. Do you remember that Andrews fellow that you sent packing?'

Ned jumped up, rocking the rickety desk and upsetting the ink. 'Do I not! The scoundrel who attacked a clergyman's wife with a child at her breast, then, when he had got the thrashing he deserved, tried to lay information against the man he had wronged. Hanging is too good for such swine.' He was shouting as he made for the door, and Falkiner stopped him with difficulty.

'With respect, sir, it isn't Andrews who is here, but a well thought of tenant from the Kilboy estate. I believe that he learned enough from Andrews to put him on his guard, and he now has real evidence.'

'Against Harry Fulton? I don't believe it. Tell him to go to hell.'

As Falkiner opened the door so as to deliver this message, Benjamin Tydd slid round and through it. Seeing his frail appearance, Ned said shortly, 'Very well, Richard, let him stay. Now, sir, what have you to say for yourself?' He remained standing, glaring at Tydd. Ink dripped unheeded on to the floor.

Benjamin Tydd was fifty-eight years old and would have passed for seventy-five. His pale, leathery skin seemed glued to his bones, showing every corded sinew. His lips and nails were purplish and he wore a threadbare grey wig. His small eyes were an unexpected bright blue, without depth. 'I'm a poor man. . . . ' he began.

'Very likely,' said Ned. 'To the point, if you please.'

'My boy Zeke works at Castle Otway, or he did before the yeomanry was put on permanent duty.'

Ned drummed his fingers. 'My time is limited, Mr Tydd, and so is my patience.'

'Your pardon, Captain.' Tydd was offensively humble. 'Zeke knew of parson's sympathies from a fellow-worker.'

'Andrews? Forget him. I want to hear none of his evidence.'

'And so,' Tydd might not have heard, 'Zeke warned me to have nothing to do with Mr Fulton, but I, being His Majesty's loyal subject, thought it advisable to find out what I could. I encouraged Mr Fulton to visit my house, which he did regularly.' Tydd delved into his pocket, and produced a filthy newspaper which he held under Ned's nose. 'The amendment to the United oath. The Reverend told me of it on the date of that paper. It wasn't made public for another two months. I made so bold as to write out a formal confession of the Reverend's knowledge of rebel activities. When your soldiers have caught him, he can be forced to sign it.'

He held out a sheet torn from a rent-book, and Ned snatched it and glanced at the ill-written lines. 'What's this nonsense? "Sayeth – That in Mr Ben Tydd's parlour, in a Conversation about United Irishmen, that the said Informant took a Limerick newspaper up . . ." Ned's eyes skimmed down the page – ". . . . that the Person to whom said Tydd applyed to, said he would not tell him any more unless he took an Oath . . . Said informant further sayeth that he has a Knowledge that there were frequent Meetings at Ballyard of Croppies assembled to exercise with Farm men at the McCarthy's. . . ." Do you seriously call this farrago a confession? Do you imagine that it proves anything? We all know that the croppies drill in the mountains – it would take any army to surround the area, and the rebels would be long gone and laughing at us.' He took a menacing step towards Tydd, who stood his ground. 'You scum. You expect payment for attempting to ruin an honest man. You make me want to puke. Get out of my sight, God damn your soul!' His voice rose to a bellow, and Leutenant Falkiner came to drag Tydd from the room by force.

Tydd held on to the door jamb. 'You want proof?' he asked. 'I have it.'

Ned snapped his hunter watch open. 'You have one minute,' he said.

'At this very moment, Fulton and the parish priest, Father O'Meara, are engaged in swearing in new members. They are at the priest's house in Chapel Lane – the house which is openly called the Rebel's Den. Papist and Protestant in hellish and unnatural alliance.'

Ned put his watch away. 'Out,' he said.

Father O'Meara's house was a sound modern structure, unlike his church, which had unplastered walls and a thatched roof. The parlour faced the narrow laneway, and the kitchen the vegetable plot at the back. Beyond that was a hop-garden where the plants twined round cords stretched between stout posts. It was early May, and the rows formed walls of greenery. Between them, two saddled horses

143

were tethered. One belonged to Henry Fulton, the other to Cornelius Murphy, a cordwainer from the neighbouring town of Borrisokane.

Cornelius was to be sworn in before a dozen members of the United Irish Society, all solid citizens considered above suspicion.

'I don't like it,' Father O'Meara was saying. 'Cooke Otway has Father Kennedy, and God only knows how much information he may have screwed out of him. We know his methods. I should have insisted on a remote meeting place when I swore him in.'

'Templederry is remote enough,' remarked Henry. 'Safer than Nenagh for a swearing, I would have thought. Don't fret – I doubt Father Kennedy knows about the arms dump.'

'No? Why then is the blacksmith hanged, and the joiner? To me it suggests the two ends of a pike. Come, we'll get on with our business without waiting any longer. We have more than enough witnesses.'

They formed a circle in the darkened kitchen, and started going through the form which both clerics knew by heart. Presently, Cornelius, a fat man, sweating heavily from nervousness, took the bible in his hand and began to repeat the oath, phrase by phrase, after Henry.

'Hush. Listen.' It was a young man standing by the window who spoke. Clearly, they all heard the sound of bugles. 'Evening stables,' said someone. 'Think nothing of it.'

'Fool,' cried Henry, 'it's the call to arms.' They all went into the parlour and listened at the outer door. Soon they heard the sound of troops on the move, accompanied by the usual jeers and insults from the streets. Henry recognised Ned's voice raised as he led his men at a slow – a very slow – trot down the main street. The United men had ample time to leave the house by the front door, and disperse. Some coolly waited to see what would happen. Cornelius Murphy dived into the tavern at the other side of the street. The two priests were left alone.

'Run for it,' said Father O'Meara.

'Not without you. Father Kennedy must have had your name tortured out of him. Murphy's horse is out there with mine. You can lose yourself in the hills. Come – don't waste any more time.'

Nearer now, Ned's voice roared, 'Turn right, men, and surround the priest's house. Take prisoners – I want no bloodshed.' By the time he had finished shouting, Henry was untying his horse. Moments later, both men were crashing through a small stand of poplar trees, planted to protect the hops from the wind. They galloped their horses across an open common, grazed by tethered cows and goats; in a few minutes they reached the Lisboney river and forced their mounts into the water, bearing righthanded towards the line of hills between them and Templederry. There were no sounds of pursuit – they pulled up at last on a wooded hillside overlooking the tiny village of Killeen.

There was no one to be seen, and no sound except the rustlings and twitterings of birds and small animals. It was about seven o'clock in the evening, and growing chilly after a warm sunny day. White mist swirled in the valleys.

'Great weather for losing ourselves,' remarked Father O'Meara, 'whether we want to or not. Where are you heading for, anyway?'

'Home. Then Wexford. I am committed to the rebellion now.'

'On that spavined crock? How far have we come? Six miles? Six more will founder him, and Wexford must be nearer a hundred. As for home, you'll find your friend Captain Fitzmaurice waiting for you there.'

'The horse must do as well as he can. He was the best I could afford.'

'Take one of Prittie's. You're well in with his grooms.'

'Steal my employer's horse?' Henry was horrified. 'I'm not a common criminal.' Then he and Father O'Meara looked at each other and both began to laugh. 'I'd prefer to steal from a man who hadn't befriended me,' amended Henry.

They had to wait two hours or more for darkness, then Henry went on foot down to the village. Two mounted patrols had passed, and the road, leading as it did from Limerick to Dublin, was normally fairly busy. This mountainous stretch, from Newport to Toomevara, had latterly become too dangerous for any vehicle to travel without armed escort. The priest expertly picketed the horses as Henry's black-clad figure disappeared in the cold, white mist.

Henry knew of two 'safe' houses in Killeen, and he called at both, being greeted by the small tenant farmers who owned them with surprised promises of help. He realised sadly that, even now, they didn't take him altogether seriously and, while they knew he was risking his life for them, they felt obscurely that he should have known better. They looked upon him as a gentleman bent, for some reason, on disgracing himself and his family.

He found his way back to the wood with a bag of cold boiled potatoes, a large, lidded crock of milk and a chunk of fat, boiled bacon. He hadn't however been able to find any disguises.

'I'll get something at home,' he said, as Father O'Meara opened a large, sharp knife and attacked the bacon.

'Want to kiss the wife goodbye? You can go alone. I'll wait near the old mine workings and I'll give you an hour. If you aren't back, I'll go on alone.'

'As you wish. Here, have my bacon – I'm not hungry.' Henry stood up, unrolled the cartouche cape which he had been carrying on the back of his saddle, turned it inside out and put it on. He mounted, and his horse, just as inferior as Father O'Meara had said, sighed and moved stiffly away.

Henry rode parallel to the road and about fifty yards above it. The going would have been bad, even in daylight: in the misty darkness, his horse lurched in and out of holes, crashed through briars and constantly stumbled. Pausing to get his bearings, Henry recognised the squat shape of the Andrews's farmhouse. A moment later, he was joined by George Andrews's brown-spotted spaniel. Whining with delight, it ran about, almost under the horse's feet, feverishly wagging its tail.

'Go home, damn you,' hissed Henry. The dog panted, wriggling its fat body; thrilled to meet its old friend. Henry gave it a fairly gentle tap with his whip and it backed off with a shrill yelp. There was an answering yelp from another dog, somewhere in the farmyard. Henry knew that the spaniel was the sort of dog which would respond to a kick with the most piercing howls. He dismounted, looped his reins over a gatepost, and furtively made his way towards the stableyard, eagerly followed by the dog. All was in silence and darkness. He pushed open the first door he saw, and stepped back startled. A glimmering white shape – what in heaven? He smiled as his eyes got used to the gloom and he saw that it was the white-blazed face of George Andrews's horse, Barney. Henry hesitated, then made up his mind. He fetched his own tired nag, and, as quickly as he could, transferred its saddle and bridle to the other. He found a piece of rope and tied the spaniel to the manger. Then he set off again in the direction of his home, on the back of George Andrews's sturdy roan.

Well mounted now, Henry made good time. Once he stopped

and bound his handkerchief round the horse's bit to prevent it from jingling, then he decided to risk riding on the grassy verge of the road. He would hear approaching hoofs as soon as his pursuers, and firearms would be useless in the mist.

In order to reach the parsonage by road, he had to pass Benjamin Tydd's neat farmstead. As he quietly walked his horse towards the tall pine trees which flanked the white-painted gate, it occurred to him that Ben would very probably give him shelter and a disguise. He had not wanted his friend to risk joining the United men – not with two sons in the yeomanry – but plainly he was sympathetic. Would his sympathy stretch to helping Father O'Meara? Henry wondered. Only the tops of the pines were visible in the mist, faintly illuminated by a rising half moon. In the inky darkness behind the nearest tree, the silence was broken by a tremendous sneeze.

Henry, his heart thudding, shortened his reins as his horse, sensing the presence of others, whickered gently and a startled voice cried 'Halt'. There were more than a dozen uniformed and mounted men backed into the gateway: among them, Henry could see Ben Tydd's lean figure. Two of the men would be his sons – the voice had been Zeke's.

At the sound of the sneeze, Henry had pulled off his well-known black hat and hidden it under his reversed cloak. Quickening to a trot, drawing up his long legs and riding crouched down, he rode past with a surly, 'Night', in a good imitation of George Andrews's voice.

'Good night, George,' came the answer from three or four, while Tydd called after him, 'Keep your eyes peeled for the Parson.'

Henry forced himself to call a gruff 'Aye', thankful that George's horse was so familiar and his voice so husky.

He had ridden a bare twenty yards when someone called, 'Here, George, wait a minute,' then more loudly, 'Hey, come back here.' One or two began to follow, riding cautiously. No doubt they were wondering why George was riding out at one in the morning.

Thankful that he had encountered some fairly slow-witted yeomen rather than a detachment of cavalry, Henry abandoned any idea of going home and set off to rejoin Father O'Meara at the old mine workings.

147

Chapter Seventeen

Anne had been uneasy all day. The news was all of killings and burnings, of pitch-capping and half-hanging to extort confessions, of rebels massing in the south-east and the French fleet approaching the north-west. Strangers were presumed to be rebels or French spies until proved otherwise.

The great houses were barricaded and their gates guarded. Soldiers fearful of being posted overseas were selling their commissions so as to be free to protect their homes and families.

The parsonage garden was really only an acre of land divided from the surrounding field by a low stone wall. A man could have stepped over it. There was a newly built stable block at the side, which housed Henry's horse and the family's cow and her calf. In front, Anne had started a flower garden. A short drive led to the roadway, and the gate stood open all day. Henry had been gone – to Nenagh on business, he said – since noon.

Johanna and Mary were beating the parlour carpet which they had draped over a bush. Spring-cleaning was in full swing. Anne, who normally joined in with a will, sat on the short grass rocking three-months-old Jane in her arms, while James charged up and down the path pretending to be a horse. Anne's head ached. She no longer wondered if Henry was a rebel, or even if he would be caught. She listened unashamedly to the maid's chatter and asked herself whom she could turn to if her husband was captured, whether his profession would save his neck, how she would fend for her children. She no longer questioned Henry, knowing that he was under oath to keep silence. The strain of keeping silence herself was affecting her health.

She had learned from Johanna and Mary that by virtue of his superior education and his social position, Henry had become a local leader, in charge of the insurgents of Kilboy estate, and acting as go-between with the estates on either side – Castle Otway and Castle

Waller. She knew too that Henry was not cut out for leadership. He wanted to avoid bloodshed, and he hadn't any hatred in him – except for the oppression of the helpless. He needed a vital, compelling adventurer like Wolfe Tone to follow. Idealism was not going to be enough to save his skin – the time for honour and integrity was disappearing.

During the afternoon, a party of men with turf-spades came to the door and offered to dig the back garden for her.

'I cannot pay you,' Anne said. 'And it is too late in the year and too dry to plant vegetables.'

'We want no money,' said the spokesman, a thin redhaired lad. 'Won't we be turning the weeds under the sod? Preparing a fine seed-bed for next year.'

'Oh, very well,' said Anne wearily, 'thank you.' The men went away with their spades and for a short time she could hear them working, out of sight behind the stables. Johanna ran giggling to see and the men cursed her roundly for her pains.

At six o'clock, Anne put the children to bed. She noticed that the diggers had left unheard. Mary, the elder of the maids, came up to ask if Henry was to be home for supper. Anne said she wouldn't wait for him, and presently sat down alone to a light meal. She was interrupted by the arrival of a dozen yeomen who collected in front of the house, demanding to see Henry. The spokesman was unknown to her, but she saw Zeke Tydd, son of Henry's friend Benjamin, hanging about at the back. When he caught Anne's eye, he edged his horse behind another rider.

Anne said coldly that Henry was not at home, and before she could say more, the whole party rode past her, over the flower-bed and round to the back. Thinking they meant to question the maids, or even force their way into the house, she ran through to the back door, but the yeomen had disappeared behind the stables. There was silence for a moment, then a furious voice yelled, 'Gone, by God, but the earth is fresh turned!' With that, the leader jumped his horse over the wall at the end of the garden and galloped off towards the hills, followed by all but two of the others. These took up positions on either side of the front gate.

Turning to Mary, who had run to the window, Anne asked, 'Do you know what that was about?'

Twisting her apron in her hands, the girl replied, 'They were after the pikes, ma'am. The lads just got them in time.' She began to sob. 'They'll be caught for sure. Oh ma'am – '

It was only then that Anne realised that not only did the girls know all about Henry's activities, and approve of them, but they supposed that she did as well. And *did* Henry know there were pikes buried in his garden? She suspected that he didn't. But . . . the world was turned upside down. It appeared that the pleasant young clergyman she had married was a calamity-prone revolutionary. 'Mary,' she said firmly, 'Mr Fulton would never allow weapons to be concealed here. Now dry your eyes and eat your supper.'

When the girl had gone, Anne went to Henry's desk and found it unlocked. She rapidly sorted through notes for sermons, letters and bills. A few scraps of paper had scrawled notes on them. There were no names or dates, and they were almost illegible. They might be harmless – probably were – but she daren't risk keeping them. She burned them in the kitchen fire, then went to their bedroom and systematically went through Henry's pockets. Their very emptiness was suspicious. She went into the little room where the children were sleeping and sat down with her head in her hands.

It was about nine o'clock and still light when Captain Ned Fitzmaurice trotted up to the parsonage with a detachment of the 7th Dragoons. Anne had last seen him at a party where she had tried to chat normally to him while a few feet away his wife Rachael was playing backgammon for kisses with Lt Lancelot Finch. Even now, her face burned with embarrassment at the memory, and she was glad to see that Finch was not there.

Ned dismounted, throwing his reins to his groom. He greeted her formally, although they had been on easy terms. He came in without waiting for an invitation, and turned to face her in the narrow hall.

'Mrs Fulton, where is your husband?'

'In Nenagh, I believe. Ned, I beg you – '

'I regret to have to inform you that Mr Fulton escaped arrest this afternoon. He, in company with the parish priest, was engaged in seditious activities in Nenagh. When he returns here, it will be my duty to arrest him, and I and my men will remain here until he does return.' Relaxing his grim tone slightly, he added, 'It's a devilish business, ma'am, I wish myself a thousand miles away, but I am obliged to search the house.'

Anne's thoughts raced as she wondered how she could warn Henry to stay away. The maids? 'You make a mistake, sir,' she said stiffly. 'However, if you wait for my husband's return, I feel sure he will be able to explain. Excuse me if you please.' Then, as he moved to prevent her from going, her composure deserted her. 'I must go to the children . . . . Ned, for God's sake – ' she tried to dodge past him, but he placed a firm, not unkind hand on her arm.

'Don't oblige me to restrain you by force,' he said. 'Stay where you are.' As he spoke, she heard Johanna scream, and a crash from the direction of the kitchen. Tears of fear and anger filled her eyes, blurring the scarlet of the dragoons' jackets as they crowded into the hall: cavalrymen looking clumsy and topheavy without their horses, with their high boots and plumes and trailing sabres.

A lieutenant sketched a salute. 'Nothing so far, sir, and the servants don't know anything.'

'Carry on, Mr Falkiner,' said Ned.

With that, two soldiers raced up the stairs: Anne heard the opening and shutting of doors, the banging of drawers. In the kitchen, the maids' screams grew hysterical and James woke and joined in. Anne wrenched her arm free and sprinted upstairs. James was sitting up in his crib, bawling, and she lifted him out and cuddled him, standing by Jane's cradle while the soldiers thrust daggers into the curtains and the clothes hanging in the cupboard.

Ned had stayed in the hall and, almost before she knew it, the men were gone again, making as much noise as a herd of cattle. Outside, Ned spoke curtly to the two yeomen who were still guarding the gate, and replaced them with two of his soldiers. Three more took up positions at the back of the house with much clanking of equipment, creaking of saddles and shouted orders. It occurred to Anne that Henry would be able to hear them half a mile away, and she wondered if it had also occurred to Ned. If it had, he gave no sign.

James had stopped crying – he struggled to be put down saying, 'Ned, Ned.' It was an easy name to say. He repeated it a dozen times before Anne's patience ran out, and she silenced him with a hard shake.

Anne spent the remainder of the night sitting by the bedroom window, straining her eyes as she stared out into the thickening mist. Ned sat in the parlour alone. Neither slept.

★

151

As Henry rode towards the disused mine workings, he met Father O'Meara coming to meet him. They turned their horses lefthanded up a muddy laneway, intending to cross the lonely Slieve Felim Mountains. They would head for Cashel, Clonmel and Carrick-on-Suir, thence to Wexford, where the country was on the edge of open revolt. Neither man was certain of the way, and there were no stars to guide them. A pale sickle moon had risen, and they steered towards the mountains by its fuzzy light. Up in those wild heights plenty of men with prices on their heads were hiding. They were less to be feared than the yeomen, who fired first and asked questions afterwards, but only because the outlaws lacked efficient firearms.

Behind the first line of hills lay a marshy plain dotted with gorse bushes, and beyond that was a lonely road where small villages such as Cureeney, Kilcommon and Milestone were almost completely given over to the rebels and their families. A military barracks stood deserted, where the besieged soldiers had fought their way out and afterwards burned every cottage in the area. As the two men started to ride across the flat land, Henry's horse suddenly planted its feet and stopped, while Father O'Meara's took another step and plunged up to its shoulders in a boghole, hurling the priest over its head and squealing with fear.

Henry jumped down and, stepping cautiously on clumps of rushes managed to reach the priest, but he had to lie down at full length in order to drag him to dry – or drier – land without sinking himself. Then both men hauled the struggling horse free of the clinging mud. 'I'm too old for this sort of thing,' grumbled Father O'Meara. 'We'll drown or catch our deaths if we continue. It'll be dawn in a few hours' time.' So they tethered the horses, rolled their wet bodies in their wet cloaks and lay down in the shelter of the gorse. The priest fell asleep at once and began to snore.

Henry lay awake shivering. Father O'Meara's body was a dark hump silvered over with damp. The eerie cry of curlews, a sign of coming rain, accompanied the priest's snores. Henry had a profound respect for the older man, although he had no love for the Catholic faith, believing in religious tolerance while adhering to the teaching of the Protestant church. He had been taught the doctrine of free will, which seemed to him at odds with his occasional flashes of almost prophetic vision. Often – usually between sleeping and waking – he imagined something which turned out afterwards to have happened.

He knew that by now his house would have been searched and his wife questioned, but not who would have been responsible. 'God send it was the army, not the yeos,' he muttered to himself. Distressed at his betrayal by Tydd, he blamed himself for being so naïve as to think that anyone so bigoted would want to join a proscribed society. Henry had always found it hard to believe ill of those who were friendly with him. He turned over, his eyes hot and gritty with fatigue.

As soon as he settled down to try to sleep, a picture presented itself to Henry. Himself in cassock and bands, standing at a graveside in blinding sunshine. His eyes flew open again, and he saw a number of bright lights approaching across the bog. They came from the direction of their line of escape, bobbing and flaring. The horses stopped grazing and threw up their heads and Henry forgot his dream, although the feeling of tears on his cheeks persisted. He scrambled stiffly to his feet and roused Father O'Meara with difficulty. The priest watched the advancing lights for a moment, then shouted a greeting in Irish. It was faintly returned, and Henry thought he really should have tried to learn the principal language of his allies: allies whom he had never so far met except singly, although he had acted as go-between for two and a half years. 'Croppies?' he asked.

'Aye. A meeting, I daresay. They'll shelter me, but I'd be on that horse ready to run if I were you. They mightn't know about you, and you haven't the right looks for a rebel.'

Henry however thought that a readiness to run might give the wrong idea, so he stood his ground. The lights were sods of turf soaked in oil, set alight and carried on pointed stakes. The men who carried them were typical of that part of the country – tall and lanky like Henry himself. Their leader was white-haired, and surprisingly few of them were young. There were about a dozen of them, running on the bog as if it it had been a paved street; mountainy men owning practically nothing, but calling themselves farmers and despising paid work. Henry was relieved to find that they could speak English if they had to. They gathered round the two men excitedly, all asking questions of Father O'Meara. Henry got only suspicious looks.

153

'I am Harry Fulton,' he said, when at last someone asked him who he was, thinking that it was ironic that nobody outside the Society called him Harry except Ned. 'I have been responsible for communications between the United men of Kilboy and Castle Otway. Father William, as he is known, and I are on the run, making for Wexford.' There was something about these wild men that appealed to Henry – they were lacking in the ingrained servility of the labourers, and even the small tenant farmers. They looked straight at him, sizing him up.

'You may come with us if you fancy some action,' said Father O'Meara.

'I wouldn't if I were you,' said Henry. 'We haven't a weapon between us and we don't know the way.'

That raised a laugh. The croppies threw their torches into a pile, where they burned fiercely, giving out both light and a scorching, oily heat. All crowded, steaming, around the fire, and Henry saw the light flicker over thin dirty faces, ragged shirts and breeches, bare legs and feet. 'I like you,' said the grey-haired man. 'You tell the truth. You have no guns and you're lost. The last outlaw we saw gave us a great yarn about freedom and glory and victory. The yeomen caught him and hanged him over Doon way.'

'Ah, and we caught a couple of yeos after,' said another. There was a reflective silence.

'What arms have you?' asked Henry. 'We don't want followers without guns – you'd be butchered by the first soldiers we met.'

'We have twenty muskets and some ball,' said the spokesman, 'but our powder is all wet. We'll use our guns as clubs if we use them at all. We have pikes enough for all, slashhooks, sickles and knives.' His hand strayed to the waistband of his breeches.

'I still think we should save the hay first,' said a discontented voice at the back, but a dozen angry voices were raised at once.

'Ah, you can talk, Timothy, your house isn't burned. Stay and save hay and be damned.' To Henry's secret relief, they decided to wait until there was definite news of a major rising. Then they shared out their rations of baked potatoes, and Henry washed his down with brackish water, lying on his face, sucking it up from the swampy ground.

'Keep the rising sun on your left,' the leader advised. 'The country's heaving with redcoats over Thurles way. You'd be safer to try and join Liam Flaherty's lads near Newport.'

Henry wanted to ignore this advice and press on over the hills towards the Suir, but Father O'Meara disagreed. 'The two of us haven't a chance of escape,' he said. 'We might lie up in the hills until Christmas, but as soon as we take to the roads, someone will betray us to the redcoats. Either of us could be worth a hundred guineas to an informer. No, my friend, we must join a fighting unit or be captured. Flaherty has a hundred deserters from the militia with their muskets. We should aim to meet them and hope they haven't already marched for Limerick. I thought from the first that we should join them.'

'Why didn't you say so?' Henry asked irritably. 'Very well, we'll do as you suggest.' He mounted George Andrews's horse, which still made him feel guilty every time he looked at it, and both men set off slowly riding across the bog, with a sure-footed lad to guide them to sounder going.

That day, May 10th, 1798, they rode from grey dawn for two hours across the hills without meeting a living soul. There was silence except for the twittering of birds and buzzing of bees. The mist had gone, and the sun drew a heavy, pungent scent from the acres of gorse coming into bloom. In a fold of the hills, they took off their coats and stretched out on the springy grass to rest and to finish their food. Henry was thoughtful; his meeting with some of the men who might be opposing the 7th Dragoons or the Ormond Union Cavalry or – God forbid – both, hadn't been encouraging. He was ashamed that he still knew so little about the forces he helped to control. 'Do you think those men would really benefit if we had a Republic of Ireland?' he asked. 'I begin to wonder if they even know what they fight for.'

'Don't fret about them.' The priest's voice came hollowly from under his hat which he had laid over his face. 'They fight for no republic. They fight because the soldiers burned their houses – who wouldn't? Don't talk politics to a mountainy man with a grievance and a pike in his hand, not if you want to stay alive. Now keep watch, will you, while I sleep.'

The familiar snore started almost at once. Henry wondered how Father William managed it. At best, they were going to join a rabble of insurgents and army deserters and fight their way to Wexford. At worst, they were heading for the firing squad or the hangman's rope, with a strong likelihood of being tortured for information thrown in. And Anne had no idea where he was. The knowledge that he had dragged her into all this and had now abandoned her to fend for herself filled him with a shame so excruciating that he could face it only in flashes which he instantly blacked out.

Never did a day pass so slowly. Henry sat with his arms round his knees, listening to the gentle sounds of the countryside, watching the horses grazing and restively stamping as the flies bothered them. He had been so sure of the rightness of what he was doing. He still believed totally in the cause of freedom from English dominance and of religious tolerance, but now realised as never before how one-sided any military struggle was likely to be. Barefoot peasants might overcome seasoned veterans by mere force of numbers – but at what a cost!

Hungry, thirsty, hiding, outlawed – what had happened to his ideals? And Anne . . . Wolfe Tone had never lied to his Mattie, and had seen to it that the children were now safe in America. That was how a rebel should deal with his divided loyalties, but he, Henry had . . . And again he veered away from the shame and pain of it.

It began to drizzle. Henry woke Father O'Meara with some difficulty. 'It's raining and I'm starving. All this time the army is looking for us. Don't you think we might risk moving in daylight? How are we to find Flaherty's men in the dark?'

'Have it your own way.' The priest scrambled yawning to his feet. 'What time is it?'

'Six o'clock, and another three hours of daylight at least.' Henry vaulted into the saddle. Still without a disguise, he had brushed his hair straight back from his forehead. It had grown since he first affected the Napoleonic cut, and he was able to tie an end of tape round it. The bright blue cape was far too warm, but concealed his black coat and breeches. 'I believe I look different,' he said hopefully.

'Devil a bit,' said Father O'Meara, adjusting a stirrup leather. 'You can't change that long thin nose of yours nor yet your long black legs. Come on, so; we'll see what lies at the far side of the ridge.' He turned his horse and set off towards the edge of the basin-shaped dell where they had spent the day.

Henry set his horse at the steepest but shortest climb, while his companion trotted away up a gentler slope, fifty yards to the right. Henry's roan, fresh and full of itself, bounded up the hill and breasted the summit in minutes. At the far side lay another small glen, where about fifty yeomen were sprawled on the grass eating chicken legs and drinking porter from stone jugs.

There was a second when they all stared up at Henry, their food in their hands, then with a yell they flung themselves on to their horses. Henry, regardless of direction, turned away from the line taken by Father O'Meara. He raced right across the clearing and in among a stand of pine trees, the only cover in sight. As he guarded his knees from the tree-trunks and kept an eye out for low branches, he urged the roan forward. The yeomen, he knew, unlike the regular army on their questionable remounts, were foxhunting men riding good hunters. Behind him there were a few wild shots; he found them less alarming than the whoops of his pursuers. Useless to expect a stout cob to distance blood horses, however willing it might be: his only hope of escape was to take the roughest line of country he could find. He raised his head to see if he was nearly through the wood and almost ran it into a thick branch. Just in time, he dropped flat in the saddle and felt its bark graze his shoulders.

He felt rather than saw the trees thin out. Emerging on to a sandy lane, he glimpsed Father O'Meara disappearing far to his right. He wrenched the roan lefthanded and galloped uphill, a sitting target, he thought, between lines of trees. Over the hill, and he was in the open again facing bogland. He remembered how his horse had jibbed the night before rather than step on quaking bog. He set off straight across the plain with its outcrops of rock and heather and its sinister patches of bright green. The roan pricked its short ears and galloped hard with lowered head; once it swerved abruptly without slowing down, another time it jumped in its stride across an unexpected ditch with crumbling banks of black earth.

Henry risked a backward glance and saw that no more than ten yeomen were in sight, well-mounted tenant farmers. They hallooed as they rode, and one blew a hunting horn. A large village lay ahead, and Henry recognised Newport, said to be Liam Flaherty's head-quarters. The rebels, he knew, met in Clare Glens, and there, if he could get round or through the town, the yeomen would probably hesitate to go. Too late, he realised that he was too far west. Had he continued up the lane, he might have reached the head of the glen and avoided the town.

It was teatime in Newport, the single street was deserted. People ran to doors and windows at the sound of the galloping horse, and out into the street to look when it had gone. When a dozen yelling yeomen arrived a minute later, they had to check rather than knock down parties of women and children who had instinctively barred their way.

The roads around Newport were hardly worthy of the name, except for the coach road which led to Limerick, nine miles away. Henry reached the bridge outside the town, and discovered that it had been blown up. He spurred his horse towards the river bank, but it had had enough. Its dislike of bogs extended to water, and the river ran deep and fast between steep banks. A view halloo behind him decided Henry. He doubted if there was a horse which would willingly attempt the river, and on the other side were Flaherty and his men. He jumped to the ground, discarded his cape and dived in.

Chapter Eighteen

Major Digby Smyth of the South Cork Militia felt he had reason to be pleased with his men. They had relieved the Devon and Cornwall Fencibles in Limerick Barracks less than a month earlier, and he had a high percentage of pressed men, often reluctant fighters, and raw boys from the slums of Cork City.

Major Smyth had been alarmed when he got the order to clear the rebels out of the Limerick/Tipperary border area. They were a strong force and had been holed up in a narrow glen for months. But he could honestly report that the rebels were gone and his force still intact. He smiled to himself, a stout red-faced man sitting at a folding table eating a dish of gruel. Captain Elton Reeves at the other side of the table noted the smile, a rarity on the major's heavy face.

'A good day's work,' said Captain Reeves, who generally waited for his superior to speak first.

"H'm. Up to a point.' Major Smyth's remarks were a series of short sharp barks. 'Didn't lose a man. Valuable experience. Better than a battle. Flaherty'd have crucified us.'

'We have three of his.' Reeves jerked a thumb in the direction of the gibbet where three bodies swung gently to and fro in the evening breeze.

'Pah! A groom and two shopkeepers. Couldn't run fast enough.' Smyth gave a sudden shout for wine which made Reeves jump.

There were about a hundred men bivouacked in a large field near Newport. They had been on the move all day, and were not going to ride the twelve miles back to Limerick that evening. Liam Flaherty had given them the slip with his pikemen – all but the three laggards on the gallows – but who knew how many more croppies might be hiding in the glens? Major Smyth was as cautious as he was short-tempered. Earlier in the day, a messenger had brought news of two priests on the run – one Catholic, one Protestant – but Smyth had paid him little attention. The tale sounded unlikely, and unless the two crossed the river and entered County Limerick, he would not be expected to give chase. They were Ned Fitzmaurice's concern, and his men were welcome to any prize money that might be going.

It was an unusual meal to say the least. The drivers of two baggage waggons had deserted, taking most of the rations with them. There was plenty of excellent Burgundy and plenty of oatmeal. Captain Reeves dared to joke about their dinner of porridge washed down with wine, but the major merely glared at him. 'Good for you,' he snapped. 'Can't beat porridge. Opens the bowels.' They drank another bottle of wine in silence.

Reeves raised his head, listening. 'What was that, sir?' Far away but unmistakable, they both heard the sound of a hunting horn and a faint cheer.

'What? Can't say. No hunting in May. Close season.' Major Smyth drank deeply and glared at Reeves.

All over the field, soldiers jumped to their feet, pointing in the direction of the sounds. A lieutenant approached, and saluted. 'Permission to join the hunt sir?'

'No, by God! See what's afoot. Report back to me.'

Crestfallen, the young man, Martin White, mounted his horse and trotted away, accompanied by another subaltern and half a dozen troopers.

Martin White was, he felt, only marking time in the militia. One day, he would inherit his father's seat in Parliament and then there would be an end to rebellion and civic strife. He believed that there was nothing better than a regiment of horse for dealing with a discontented peasantry. If they remained discontented, two regiments would certainly teach them to keep quiet, if nothing else. Although of Cromwellian descent, White had a face which might have modelled for a cartoon Irishman of the day – low-browed, long-chinned and with an upper lip like a spoon. He was aware of this, and it had the effect of making him even more aggressive than he would otherwise have been. He was a good horseman, a champion amateur boxer and a useful athlete. He led the way at a canter across the crowded field, letting the soldiers, now busy erecting tents, get out of his way as best they might.

The tally-hos had come from the direction of the Mulcair Bridge, but that had been blown up a week earlier in an effort to contain Flaherty's rebels before attacking them. White led his party left-handed to the nearest ford, half a mile downstream.

When he reached the river bank, he saw a dozen yeomen trying to ford it from the other side. The water was about four feet deep, and they were having trouble persuading their horses to go in. They shouted and swore, while some still whooped as if they had viewed a hunted fox. White urged his horse forward, and yelled at the yeomen, but his voice was drowned by their own noise and the rushing of water. Then he saw that everyone was gazing into the river. He looked too – under the near bank – and saw a body caught up in a submerged tree.

White shouted an order to his soldiers, and two of them slid down the bank and caught the body by an arm and a leg. They dragged it free of the branch that held it, and bundled it up the bank to their comrades. As they turned it over, White saw blood streaming from a cut on the forehead. 'He's alive!' he cried.

The yeomen, who were being joined all the time by more men, had started to cross the river in ones and twos. 'He's ours!' shouted the leader, as his horse scrambled up the bank and emerged dripping. 'It's Parson Fulton, the man the croppies call Harry. There's a price on him and we claim it for the Ormond Union Cavalry.'

'Go to the devil,' said White. 'He's mine – I caught him.'

'Caught him! You fished him out of the river when we had hunted him down for you.'

White didn't answer. He instructed the two soldiers to lift Parson Fulton on to a horse, hanging him head downwards over its back. After a few moments, the sodden body heaved convulsively, and vomited quantities of water. 'He'll do,' said White. 'Hold his legs, you, and lead the horse.'

Lieutenant de Courcy, a very young, very new officer, said, 'He has a nasty head wound. Should we not bind it up before jolting him half a mile in that position?'

'Later,' said White. 'I have every intention of dressing it with hot pitch. How fortunate that we brought some with us.'

'But Mr White, you cannot! He's a clergyman after all. My sister lives in his parish, he baptised her child. She knows Mrs Fulton well – their infants are of the same age.'

'Indeed. Young children, I daresay.'

De Courcy was pleased by White's show of interest. Perhaps he had a spark of humanity after all. 'Yes, very young,' he said eagerly. 'A boy not above two years old and a baby girl. I do not know Mrs Fulton, but my sister says she is quite ravishing – all the young men are in love with her – but she and her husband are the most devoted couple imaginable.' He added awkwardly, 'I know it isn't my place to speak, but I feel sure you cannot mean to punish such a worthy man.'

White turned his long, sour face and surveyed the young man up and down. 'He's a renegade,' he said. 'A disgrace to his nation and his calling, and a traitor to his rightful king. I am obliged to you for your information about his family. It should prove useful. As for this "worthy man",' and his voice went thin with scorn, 'when I have discovered what I can from him, I shall have pleasure in hanging him.'

Henry's first sensation when he regained consciousness was that of nausea. Nausea made worse by his unfed stomach which was knotted with cramp. He was draped over a horse's back, so the blood had rushed to his head. The gash on his forehead, although it was throbbing sharply, was the least of his problems. He hung limply on the slowly walking animal, pretending to be still unconscious, while he tried to think of a means of escape. Two men seemed to be discussing him, but he found it hard to concentrate on what they were saying. He wondered if Father O'Meara had been caught too. Even stronger than fear and pain was his anger at himself. He was much younger and fitter than the priest, and had a better horse. Yet, far from helping his companion to escape, he had been captured himself – mainly because he had been thoughtless enough to dive into a river without knowing how deep it was. Most of the masonry of a triple-arched bridge was now in the river bed. No wonder he had knocked himself out.

His hands weren't tied and nobody seemed to be attending to him. Somebody was steadying him with a hand on one of his ankles, but it was a careless hand. Certainly its owner was expecting nothing. Cautiously he opened his eyes. The upside-down view was not helpful, consisting of a sweaty bay flank and a saddle girth. Squinting sideways, he saw another horse's hind-quarters, and, on the other side a powerful thigh, clad in white breeches, very much muddied, and a beefy fist holding a gun with fixed bayonet. They were moving slowly through woodland.

It wouldn't be too difficult, Henry thought, to get a leg across his horse and trust to surprise to get him clear, but he sensed that he was surrounded by more than the dozen yeomen he had evaded. The reins lay on his horse's neck, tied in a knot. He flexed a knee slightly, and dug an elbow into its shoulder. Then he suddenly twisted himself round so he was face down, brought his leg over the horse's croup and, lying flat along its neck, dragged it around and urged it forward with his heels.

Henry succeeded in surprising everyone, including the quiet old troop horse. It yanked its headrope free of the man who was leading it and swung round. Henry forced it into a clumsy gallop and rode straight through the party of yeomen who were riding behind, still arguing about their share of the blood-money.

This time, exhausted and half drowned as he was, Henry had little chance. He had neither whip nor spurs, and his long legs dangled a foot below the stirrups. A musket ball knocked a chip out of a tree as he passed it, and another zipped unpleasantly close to his ear. The shooting had the effect of making his mount find an extra turn of speed, but just as Henry was wondering how and where he could recross the river, it caught its hoof in a root and turned head over heels.

Back at the camp, Major Smyth poured the last drops from a third bottle of burgundy into his glass. 'Damned young hothead, White,' he grunted. 'Probably chasing croppies still. Should have sent you, Reeves.'

'Perhaps he's caught the renegade priests,' suggested Reeves, picking up the bottle, up-ending it to no avail and setting it down with emphasis

'No. He'd have brought 'em in.'

'From what I know of White,' said Reeves, 'he'd have strung both of them up by now . . . or shot them,' he added, as two musket shots echoed from the direction of the river.

Smyth jumped to his feet, steadying his considerable bulk by holding the edge of the folding table, which rocked and finally collapsed. 'Not his job to execute prisoners. Bloody upstart. Go and stop him.'

Reeves shouted for his horse to be brought to him, but before he could mount it, a soldier came cantering across the field towards them. He pulled up and saluted. 'We have the rebel parson, sir,' he said breathlessly. 'The Ormond Union say he's theirs. Mr White's on his way now with the prisoner.'

Before he had finished speaking, the rest of the party appeared: White and de Courcy leading the way, while behind two soldiers walked, one leading a horse, the other holding the ankles of a man who was securely tied to it, face down across the saddle. For good measure, the man's wrists and ankles were also tied. Behind came a shouting, cursing rabble of yeomanry, all dripping wet. Major Smyth, less steady on his feet than he had thought, gave a furious roar from where he stood. The procession finished crossing the field in silence.

The rebel parson was dragged off his horse and dumped unceremoniously at Smyth's feet. He lay there, unable to move, his face covered with blood which poured from his nose as well as from a wound on his head. His coat and boots were gone and he wore a white shirt and black breeches. His face was twisted with pain and, when White stepped forward and tried to heave him into a sitting position, he fainted.

White saluted, and launched into an account of his own daring and resource in making the arrest. He emphasised that Parson Fulton was a dangerous man, glossed over his almost successful attempt to escape and finished with a request to be allowed to hang the prisoner 'as soon as he had come to his senses'.

Smyth was beginning to wonder if porridge and Burgundy were as beneficial to health as he had thought. He felt queasy. White was clothing his report in flowery language, at odds with his wolf-like face. Smyth loathed all rebels without exception, and was prepared to hang this one when it suited him, parson or no parson, but cruelty for its own sake revolted him. 'Call the surgeon,' was all he said, and when he had been fetched, 'Clean the prisoner's face. Dress that wound. Find out if aught else ails him.' Then, turning in fury on the yeomen, 'Go home to your kennels!'

These men, well used to being detested by civilians and the army alike, retreated sulkily, muttering threats. They conferred among themselves for a few minutes, then trotted away towards the nearest road. There were no senior officers with them and they knew they had no chance of a hearing without.

'Broken collar-bone, sir,' said the surgeon, looking up from his task. 'With his arm in a sling, he should do – or shall I bleed him?'

'Bleed him? Of course not. Make him as comfortable as you can.'

'I'd make him comfortable at the end of a rope,' murmured White. Smyth had to feign deafness, rather than reprove an officer in front of his men. Another fit of nausea assailed him, and when White asked permission to interrogate the prisoner when he should have come round, it was grudgingly given.

Smyth made his way to his tent, a handkerchief to his mouth, and lay down on his straw mattress without removing his boots.

It was almost dark in the tent. Henry lay on the ground, his back propped against a truss of hay, his arm strapped across his chest. The surgeon had accompanied the soldiers who had brought him to the tent, and had seen to his comfort, as far as was possible. A groom had brought him a dish of cold gruel to eat and, unexpectedly, a mug of wine to drink.

He ached all over, but the excruciating pain of being roughly handled with a broken collar bone was gone. When the clumsy troop horse fell, it had pinned his leg and bruised it badly. The man who tied him up had pulled off his boots, and he would never forget the agony of having a close fitting riding boot dragged off a rapidly swelling and strained ankle.

He wondered what time it was, but his watch had gone along with his coat. Anyway, the water would have stopped it. He judged that it might be nine o'clock at night. The tent was just high enough for one man to stand upright in the centre. Outside the flap, a sentry stood on guard. Henry cursed himself for his impulsive actions – especially his final attempt to escape – but his natural optimism surfaced and refused to let him despair. The South Cork Militia were quite unlike Ned Fitzmaurice's dragoons; he recognised the weakness of their commander, who overlooked impudence in a subordinate and then took himself off to bed. But still . . . these were officers and, he supposed, gentlemen. Even if discipline were a trifle slack, he could expect to be treated with the respect due to his calling. He had felt the soldiers' reluctance to treat him roughly, but he had lost that advantage by trying to escape.

He saw the light of a lantern glimmer through the canvas, and three men came stooping in. The light jumped and flickered; they stood all together under the peak of the tent, the tallest, White, in the middle. He was flanked by a sergeant who looked like a fist-fighter and the young lieutenant who had been with him at the river. This young man, who looked extremely unhappy, carried a note-book and pencil. The sergeant held the lantern so that it shone in Henry's eyes, and White did the talking.

'We've got your fine Papist priest,' he said. 'He told us all we wanted to know – yes, about you too, you traitor – so questioning you will be no more than a formality. First – '

'What priest are you talking about?' Henry interrupted. And when White hesitated for a second before saying, 'Your associate in your treasonable activities,' he knew he was lying.

When formally asked his name, Henry replied, equally formally, 'The Reverend Henry Fulton, B.A., curate of the union of Kilmore and Silvermines; vicar of Monsea.'

'Write merely, "Henry Fulton",' White said aside to de Courcy, who was miserably licking his pencil.

'Who, apart from the priest, are your associates?' White demanded, as de Courcy scribbled on his pad.

'This is not a court of law,' said Henry. 'I have the right to keep silent until my attorney can be fetched.' He was pleased to note that his voice, though weak, was steady.

'Attorney! You are living in fairyland, man. You'll be hanged long before your man of law knows you have need of him.'

Henry said, 'If you are going to hang me, what point is there in answering your questions? I doubt if a confession of guilt would save me.'

White snatched the lantern away from the sergeant and advanced, holding it close to Henry's face. 'Reverend sir,' he said, 'I think you will confess. Have you heard of half-hanging? Of being slowly raised from the ground by a rope thrown over a branch? Of feeling the noose bite tighter and tighter, throttling you bit by bit? Of being lowered to the ground, allowed to recover then hoisted up again? I can assure you, the confessions come thick and fast after an hour or so. Well, we shall see.'

Henry, cold sweat breaking out all over him, did his best to sound nonchalant. 'Certainly I have heard of half-hanging, who has not? It

166

is done by drunken mercenaries, taking the law into their own hands. Even in these troubled times, I'm sure the army will not countenance torture.'

'Perhaps it will not be necessary,' said White. 'I might obtain equally good results in the privacy of this tent. I might ask you to consider the safety of your lovely wife and those two sweet infants of yours. I might try the effect of a well-aimed kick on that left elbow.' De Courcy looked as though he might be going to be sick, and the sergeant folded his thick arms across his barrel chest.

Henry's stomach lurched, but he said, with all the bravado he could muster, 'I don't imagine you are serious when you threaten innocent women and children. As for kicking my injured arm, why, then you would have an insensible body on your hands. I'm sure you can do better than that.'

'Who gives you your instructions?' White shouted suddenly, bending over Henry, menace in his eyes.

'The Reverend Woods, rector of my parish, and Sir Henry Prittie, whose son I tutor in mathematics, Latin and Greek. Incidentally, Sir Henry is a man of influence and would certainly see that anyone harming my wife and children was punished.'

White's fragile temper snapped. He began to curse Henry with a torrent of barrack-room abuse. Hoping he would work off his temper harmlessly, Henry listened, his fear of White lessening as his contempt grew. Sensing this, White's control left him and he lashed out, aiming a kick at Henry's elbow, immobilised in its sling. De Courcy grabbed White's arm, making him miss his target and fall backwards. The lamp sailed through the air and landed on the straw mattress beside Henry, pouring oil. Within a minute, the light from the burning tent was illuminating the camp, and Reeves was turning out the guard.

Major Smyth, roused from boozy dreams by Reeves, emerged from his tent, buttoning the tunic he had been sleeping in. The fire had been put out and no one hurt except the sergeant, the only able-bodied person present who had kept his head. He had carried out the prisoner, scorching his hands severely. Smyth wished himself back in the barracks in King John's Castle with all his heart. He also wished that the prisoner had been shot at the outset, saving everyone trouble. He felt his head tenderly and flinched. 'Carry on, Mr Reeves,' he said, and went back to bed.

When he rose in the morning, as his men prepared to strike camp, he was annoyed to see that there was a deputation to see him. Mr Tydd, a grey-haired man mounted on a mule, was accompanied by a couple of yeomen. Tydd wished to lay information against the prisoner, and repeatedly waved a piece of paper in the major's face, saying it was full confession which Fulton must sign. Fulton, who was feverish, was fetched, and refused to sign. One of the yeomen threatened reprisals against his family, and Fulton asked to read the confession. Having done so, he said, 'This is mainly true, but it is not a confession and proves nothing except that I should be more careful in my choice of friends. If it will keep my wife and children safe, I'll sign.'

When the prisoner had signed, the informer asked for money, and was told to apply to the commander of the Nenagh garrison. This he seemed reluctant to do, but at last the three rode away grumbling.

By then, the company was ready to set off for Limerick, and Smyth hoisted himself on to his horse and moved off in front. On reaching the main road, however, there was another delay. Captain Fitzmaurice, who had ridden the twenty-four miles from Nenagh that morning, came trotting up and accosted him. Bloody regulars, thought Smyth, think they're little gods. Fitzmaurice wanted to know Smyth's plans for the rebel parson, and, on hearing that a court martial was planned as soon as possible, objected.

'Mr Fulton carries no arms,' he said, 'and has harmed no one. He comes from my area, not yours, and is entitled to be tried in a civil court and to be legally represented.'

Smyth argued, but Fitzmaurice was adamant. A diversion was caused by a civilian who claimed that Fulton had stolen a horse – a matter for hanging or transportation. 'The same punishment as for treason,' said Captain Fitzmaurice scornfully. 'The statute book should be rewritten.' Then he asked to see the prisoner, and Smyth, scenting collusion, watched them closely, but neither gave anything away.

'Did you steal a horse, Mr Fulton? Surely not.'

Fulton, swaying with weakness on the back of a pack mule, was trussed up like a parcel. He said, 'No Captain. I loaned one from George Andrews, and I trust by now it has been restored to him.'

168

Fitzmaurice made an explosive sound which might, in other circumstances have been mistaken for a laugh. He turned to Smyth and said, 'No court martial, or you will find that a number of influential people are out for your blood. You had better take him to Limerick gaol. Good day to you.' He turned his horse and clattered away.

Chapter Nineteen

Henry's treatment at Limerick gaol was better than he expected. His head wound was dressed, not gently, or with much regard for hygiene, but effectively; while lack of exercise helped to set his collar bone and mend his strained leg.

He would have tried to escape, given the smallest opportunity, but common sense told him that prison was the safest place for him. News of drumhead courts martial and summary hangings filtered in from outside every day, the militia being far harsher than the regular army. Lieutenant White, foiled in his designs on Henry's life, was leading a platoon on a round of reprisals. Every village had its gibbet and its 'triangle' for floggings: the air was bitter with acrid smoke from burned cottages and ricks.

Recurring fever kept Henry awake and restless on his lumpy mattress. At night he would first shiver under his dirty grey blanket, then throw it off as his skin grew burning hot. He had not been chained at any time, and discovered from a warder that this was because Sir Henry Prittie had written to the governor on his behalf. He was kept in solitary confinement, with poor food, little light, nothing to do and no letters or visitors, but he was far better off than the poor wretches crowded in the common cells. Every so often, a batch was taken away to be tried, and public executions were commonplace.

For the first time in his life, Henry was deprived of clean linen, still wearing the filthy, bloodstained shirt and black cloth breeches in which he had been taken. Bugs, fleas and lice attacked him, waking him from his fevered dreams. At times he was delirious, his mind seething with emotions so violent and so muddled that he couldn't sort them out, but fears for Anne and the babies tormented him night and day.

Henry had been in gaol for a week before he heard anything of Father O'Meara. He had hesitated to ask for news of his friend, for fear of implicating him further. The priest had run straight into a patrol on the road, an hour after he and Henry had separated, and he was in the same prison, suffering from a putrid sore throat. That much Henry overheard, and afterwards he presumed that the priest must have died, as he heard no more of him.

On May 18th, as soon as he had finished his breakfast of weak gruel, Henry was brought out of his cell by two warders. News of his escape had preceded him, and they propelled him along between them while a guard with a horse pistol brought up the rear. Henry blinked, blinded by his first sight of daylight for eight days. So alarming were the prison rumours that he quite expected to be taken out and shot without more ado. He wondered whether, in that case, he would be allowed to talk to a chaplain or not. The immediate fear of death had left him along with the fever. His left arm was still in a sling, but the collar bone had set and his other injuries were healing fast.

As his sight returned, Henry saw that he and another dozen or so prisoners were being hustled into a group in front of the main building. A double cordon of foot soldiers, bayonets fixed, surrounded them, and beyond these the whole population of Limerick seemed to be collected, jeering or cheering, according to their sympathies.

Henry had thought that being unwashed, unshaven and lousy was the ultimate in degradation, but he was wrong. Now he was to endure the humiliation of being chained to a fellow prisoner. Two men in leather aprons strode across the yard, carrying fetters, hammers, and rivets. As Henry stood there with feet bare since his boots had been pulled off him, one of the men clapped an open iron ring around his ankle, closed it, and held it while the other man hammered a rivet into it. Henry tried to joke with the smith, saying, 'I thought you were going to nail a set of shoes on to me.' The man grinned up at him but didn't reply. A warder led another prisoner across, and he was shackled to Henry, ankle to ankle. Henry greeted him, but the warder told him to shut his gob.

Next both men were prodded into line with a dozen others, all leg-shackled, and marched, if that was the right word for their hopping, stumbling progress, to a large waggon, drawn by a pair of horses. Henry asked where they were going, and the man who had told him to shut his gob hit him across the mouth. As an afterthought, he hit Henry's new companion, just as hard. This was sound psychology. Henry kept quiet and behaved himself after that. His companion looked no more than sixteen.

Half an hour later, the waggon deposited them at the magistrate's court where they were formally charged. Henry was surprised to hear that he was accused, not of treason, but of the lesser crime of sedition. As he stood in the dock, he could feel the violent trembling of the tall boy beside him; a lad who had never needed to shave. He was charged with possession of a pike and with attending an illegal meeting. Both men were remanded in custody to the Sessions in August.

As they were being loaded into their cart afterwards, the magistrate, William Osborne, came out of the courthouse and surveyed Henry up and down for a minute before speaking. 'You are a fine ornament to your profession,' he said.

Henry looked straight into close-set grey eyes under an over-sized wig and said expressionlessly, 'Thank you, sir.'

Osborne seemed uncertain how to treat this meek reply. His frown deepened. 'You are fortunate not to have horse-stealing added to your record,' he said grimly. 'It was lucky for you that Andrews chose to come forward and say that you had his permission to borrow the animal.'

'Very lucky,' said Henry, hoping that his astonishment didn't show.

Osborne said, 'I cannot mete out heavy sentences in this court, as you know, but I hope to try you in due course. Men like you are a danger to all decent people.' His voice rose. 'Viper! Judas! Traitor!' He swung round on his heel and strode away.

Mrs Fulton and her children were a cause of embarrassment, both to the soldiers keeping them under house arrest and to those whom Anne had thought of as Henry's friends. It was the last straw, said these worthy souls. Rebellion was spreading through the midlands, the insurgents growing bolder every day, and now came this dreadful loss of face. The curate they had chosen had bitten the hands that fed him, they said.

Anne had seen Ned Fitzmaurice riding away from the parsonage the morning after he had questioned her. She had gone to rouse Johanna and Mary, only to find that both girls had escaped from the house in the night, given the guard the slip, and presumably returned to their homes in the hills.

Anne fed little Jane and prepared a bowl of bread and milk for James. Then she opened the door and said 'Good morning', to the soldier standing outside. 'May I go out? she asked. 'I must milk the cow.'

'You must not leave the house,' said the man, as if repeating a lesson. 'You must wait until the Captain returns.'

'Will you milk the cow for me then? And see if there are any eggs? I have very little food in the house. Oh, and bring in some cabbage too, will you? Thank you.' Anne went into the kitchen and laid the fire, then she began to tidy the room which had been ransacked the night before. James pattered after her, banging his spoon on his wooden platter and asking for an egg. He looked like a little girl, with his long brown curls and his white frock. She hugged him absently.

Anne was making a great effort to behave as if everything was normal. As if it were an everyday matter to be alone save for the children and half a dozen dragoons. She knew she was being kept at home as bait to lure Henry back, and that if she were let go free it would probably mean he had been captured. She got on with the job of putting the house to rights and tried to keep her mind on what she was doing.

Outside, she could hear the soldiers arguing, and presently one of them came in and told her that she was free to milk the cow and go to the garden. Anne smiled. The cow was not fond of strangers.

All day, she busied herself, trying not to think. One of the soldiers rode off and returned an hour later with a laden mule. He gave Anne a large joint of beef and asked if she would mind cooking it for them. Anne's resolve to be polite and reasonable deserted her and she snapped, 'I'd mind very much. Cook it yourselves.' The man went away in a hurry, and presently a column of smoke rose from a camp fire in the front garden.

It was midday the following day when Ned Fitzmaurice came back. His face told her all she needed to know. She said simply, 'Where is he?'

'He's in Limerick gaol, ma'am.'

Anne stared at the rock-like face, guessing that her questions wouldn't be answered. The loss of Ned's friendship hurt more than she had thought possible. 'Will they . . . will they hang him?'

'He won't be charged until the magistrate comes on his rounds.' Ned's voice was expressionless, but she fancied that there was a slight softening – she tried again.

'How can I help him?'

'I wish I knew,' Ned burst out, then, with a return to his earlier stern tones, 'I have asked Sir Henry Prittie to send a carriage for you. A new curate has been engaged already and you will have to leave the house.'

'But where can I go? Not to Kilboy. Where can I turn with a two-year-old child and a baby?'

'I wish I could advise you, ma'am.' Ned stared bleakly over her head. She thought he was struggling not to express the sympathy he felt, and wondered whether the sentry, watching with unconcealed interest, had noticed as well.

Anne said briskly, 'I suppose I had better pack our things. If the carriage arrives soon, I might be in time to catch the Dublin stage and then I would be in Roscrea before night. I can leave James with my mother while I find out how best I can help my husband.'

She stepped back alarmed as Ned suddenly roared, 'Look to your front, damn your idle carcase!'

The soldier jumped to attention with a snort like a startled horse. 'I beg your pardon, ma'am, I was never at home in a drawing-room.' muttered Ned. 'Set those two maids to pack for you.'

'I cannot. They both ran away last night. Perhaps it's as well – I couldn't take them with me, and would have hated to leave them here alone.' She detached James who was clinging unheeded to Ned's boot. 'Excuse me, if you please, I have no time to lose.'

When Anne had gone into the house, Ned, in the fond belief that she was out of earshot, told the soldiers just what he thought of them. The maids gone, nobody lifting a finger to help a lady, a fire lit in front of her windows with greasy bones strewed about. Then he followed Anne indoors.

Ned could never speak to Anne without realising once more what a fool he had been to marry Rachael – who had recently transferred her attentions from Lieutenant Finch to the even younger Second Lieutenant Head. Unfaithfulness he could understand, as he blamed it on his own age and lack of charm; disloyalty and mockery hurt him much more. He found Anne on her knees in the parlour, packing china into a hamper. Lovely woman, he thought, looking at her and envying Henry with all his heart. Anne would always be beautiful . . . provided she didn't allow herself to grow fat, thought Ned with his usual honesty. Those dark blue eyes; that enchanting mouth – was Harry blind? And what character! How could he let his ideals put such a marriage at risk? Ned knew the answer. Knew that, had he been in Harry's shoes, his wife would have had to take second place to his convictions.

He said sharply, 'You can take with you only what you can carry in a one-horse carriage. Your clothes and valuables. Harry's are forfeit. I will lend you some money if you need it.'

She sat back on her heels, saying, 'Don't speak so roughly, Ned, I can't bear it. Thank you for the offer, but I have enough money to see me home.' Turning her face away, she left the room, the hamper half packed. There was a teacup lying on the carpet, Ned picked it up and flung it at the wall. Then he went out and was much relieved to see a horse and carriage turning into the drive.

Sir Henry Prittie's driver had been pelted with stones and handfuls of horse dung on his way from Kilboy. These had been thrown from behind trees and walls, so he didn't know if his assailants were children or dangerous outlaws.

Anne recognised the carter who had brought them to the Andrews's farm eighteen months earlier, and remembered how Henry had scandalised Dorcas Andrews by chatting to him. Ned was complaining because no escort of armed men had been provided, and detailed two of his own men to ride alongside as far as the coach stop at Dolla.

'And don't leave, either of you, until Mrs Fulton is safely on the stage,' he said.

There was room for only one modest trunk and a couple of bundles in the carriage. 'I'll see that your household goods are safely stored,' Ned assured Anne. He picked up James, who was again clinging to his leg and passed him to his mother, banged the door and stood back as the carter cracked his whip. Anne thought she had never seen anyone look quite so angry.

The Dublin stage was late, or they would have missed it. It had been held up by a band of croppies, but the outriders had shot two and the others had run away. There were no other women or children travelling, and there were several empty seats. Anne secured a corner seat inside, and they set off on the ten dangerous miles to Toomevara. Six yeomen rode with the coach on this stage, while a trained marksman sat on the box with the coachman. 'Spring the horses!' shouted a nervous passenger, but there wasn't much spring in the four elderly draught horses. Anything with a turn of speed had been commandeered by the army. The coachman beat them along, and everyone was glad when the road widened and they reached Jim O'Meara's inn at Toomevara.

It was another twelve miles to Roscrea and, even with fresh horses, Anne thought they would never get there. Nothing travelled at night except the mail, and the stage stayed overnight at Roscrea. It arrived about half past eight and drew up at the Castle Inn near the Church. She remembered how often she had run down to collect the mail there, hoping for a letter from Henry. She hadn't been home since her marriage.

As Anne got down and reached up to help James, she wondered how much, if anything, her parents knew. If nothing, how could she tell them? Hetty would understand and Thomas would very likely get into trouble for siding with Henry. But Mama?

'Do you stay at the inn?' asked the guard, as she stood on the cobbles, the trunk and bundles beside her.

'No, but I would be grateful if I might leave my trunk there until it can be collected.' Anne had decided that she needed more time to think. Jane was asleep in her arms, James leaning heavily against her. She thought she would go into the church to pray and to prepare herself to meet her parents.

She was surprised to see the flickering of candles through the windows – all the candles, not the few used at evening prayer. Then she saw carriages – dozens of them, and servants standing in groups, talking. A wedding? At this hour? Well, she could slip in quietly. She pushed open the massive oak door which made the building virtually soundproof, and was almost deafened by a flourish of trumpets, followed by fifty voices raised fortissimo.

HALLELUJAH! HALLELUJAH! HALLELUJAH HALLELU-JAH HALLE-E-LU–UJAH!

Mrs Walker had achieved her ambition at last.

Chapter Twenty

Anne Fulton knelt unnoticed at the back of the church. She still held Jane in the crook of her arm, fearful of waking her; James sat dozing on a footstool. She put her right hand over her eyes, and felt the tears hot on her fingers.

She wept for Henry, the children, and the family life which she was sure had gone for ever. She wept at the needlessness of it all. Then the soaring crystal notes of a pure soprano voice silenced the more restive members of the congregation. 'I know that my redeemer liveth . . . .' Anne wiped her eyes, angry with her mother who had turned her against the music and words she had once loved.

Next, the trumpeters of the Prince of Wales's Fencibles accompanying a fine bass, launched into 'The Trumpet shall sound, and the dead shall be raised incorruptible . . . .' Brave words from a man of rock-like faith. She believed them literally, as she had been taught, and believed that she and Henry would meet in an after-life. But what if he were hanged as a traitor? Must she spend all eternity as well as the rest of her life without him? She managed to control her tears before the end of the performance, and walked out with the rest of the congregation, glad of the failing light.

She stood in the doorway, waiting for her mother, but Sarah Walker was surrounded by her friends, all congratulating her on her fine contralto solos. She sailed past Anne and the children without seeing them. Plainly, news of Henry's capture hadn't reached Roscrea. Anne waited. Her mother had gone to her carriage. She must tell her father herself. She waited for him to come out with the visiting clergy, and followed him down the shadowed footpath, not speaking until he was alone.

James Walker greeted his daughter in astonishment, and when she had told him her story was all sympathy at first, but soon began to say that he had known how it would be from the start. Anne interrupted hastily to ask where Hetty and Thomas were.

177

'Why, we have sent Thomas to college in England. He left at Easter. Henrietta has gone to Dublin, and is staying with your aunt Eliza who is unwell. Did she not write?'

'Probably,' said Anne. 'I'm sure she did. But the mail is intercepted as often as not. I have had no word from Mama this past month.'

'Your mother has been much occupied with musical endeavour.' The Reverend Walker's colourless voice gave no clue to his views, if any. He patted James's head dutifully and inspected his baby granddaughter with no sign of interest.

'Papa, will you please tell Mama about Henry? I would rather not.'

'Poor girl, poor girl . . . . Such a disgrace, such a scandal – I feel it would come better from you, my dear.'

So Anne had to face the person who should have been first to console her, knowing that she would have to listen to a scolding. Her father went to fetch her, while Anne sat drooping on a gravestone, too tired to hold up her head.

It was worse than she expected. Mrs Walker was still elated after her success, but news of her son-in-law's arrest easily killed any maternal instincts she might have had. 'What are you doing here? What do you want?' she demanded.

'I don't want anything for myself, Mama. May I leave James with you so that I can visit some people who might help us? Jane is the quietest baby imaginable, but I cannot manage to take a lively toddler with me too. I'm sure I can find someone who will help Henry.'

'Help?' Mrs Walker was so outraged that she could hardly speak. 'Henry is beyond help. As for you, I have no idea what can be done for you. Your children would prevent you from getting a situation as a companion or governess, even if your circumstances could be concealed. As for James, I shall never forget that he is a Fulton, although I imagine you intend to change your names.'

Mr Walker gave a nervous cough and protested feebly. Anne, furious, bit her lip until she tasted blood. A quarrel with Mama would make matters worse. She turned away and walked down the footpath, leaving the carriages and the lights behind. Her mother made no move to follow, but her father plucked at Anne's arm and, when she half turned, offered her five sovereigns. Instinct told her to reject them and run, but common sense prevailed and she accepted the money.

'Husband!' cried Sarah, 'What are you about?'

'Nothing, dearest, I shall be with you directly.'

With little James, a dead weight hanging from her arm, Anne hurried back to the Castle Inn and engaged a bed for the night and a seat on the Limerick coach the following morning. She meant to go to Nenagh and plead with the colonel of Ned's regiment. They had got on well at their only meeting.

Anne was breakfasting early when a chaise arrived from Dublin, attended by cavalry in the familiar scarlet and gold of the 7th Dragoons. They changed horses without entering the inn, and she saw Colonel Longfield himself in the carriage. She ran into the street as the coachman picked up his reins. As the horses began to move off, a young mounted officer almost knocked her over, and stopped to apologise.

'It wasn't your fault – I ran in front of your horse,' Anne said. 'Does the colonel stay in Nenagh or travel further?'

'We all travel further, ma'am. The regiment is transferred to Tullamore, forty miles to the north.' He saluted, and trotted after the others. Anne returned to the inn, and changed her booking to the Dublin coach which left half an hour later.

The rebellion had been planned for the summer, to coincide with another landing by the French. But Lord Edward Fitzgerald's formation of a Directory of United Irishmen, and his alliance with the militant Catholic 'Defenders', was far more worrying to the government than any peasant uprising. Reprisals grew more severe every day, and there were public floggings in the Co Kildare market town of Athy. News of fresh atrocities on both sides spread rapidly, and more people feared a general massacre of civilians. The worst affected area was the midlands, and events there thoroughly disorganised the preparations for an open revolt. The rebel army would wait no longer, and went into action on May 24th.

News of the rebellion reached Limerick gaol the next day, by way of ballad singers. One in particular, a large-breasted young woman with dirty yellow hair down to her waist, who was usually to be found near the prison, sang the news of the day in clumsy rhymes.

Her voice was loud and piercing, and Henry, whose tiny barred window was at the front of the building, was better supplied with news than many a subscriber to the *Freeman's Journal*.

One day, Henry's door was unlocked, and a warder slung a fat man into the cell. The door clanged shut, with a grinding of rusty bolts, and they were left alone. The man, who might have been forty years old, had been flogged almost unconscious. He lay on his face on the filthy floor, groaning; wearing nothing but a pair of stuff breeches, tied with string below the knees.

Henry knew that flogging was the standard form of punishment in the army and the navy. Nobody had protested about it except the sufferers, who were not heeded. He was prepared for angry weals, for cuts even, but not to see a man's back reduced to torn, bleeding raw meat. He had no water or rags to clean the wounds; sick with rage, he shook the bars in the top of his door violently, kicked it and shouted furiously. At last a warder came. They treated Henry well, compared to the other prisoners, but he had been amenable and they had orders from the governor not to strike or even swear at him. Instead, they joked at his expense, disconcerted when he laughed at their jokes.

He wasn't joking now. 'Send a surgeon at once,' he shouted. 'This man needs attention or he will die.' He added more quietly, 'How could anyone use a living human being so?'

'Ask him,' suggested the warder. 'And why don't you pray he may recover? I'm sure we don't want to bury him – the fat pig.'

Henry choked down his temper with an effort which made him feel ill. He was slowly learning diplomacy. 'Have you heard of Sir Henry Prittie or Colonel Waller?' he asked. 'Both are magistrates, and I know them well. It will go hard with you when I am acquitted.'

'Acquitted!' The warder laughed, and spat on the floor, but he looked thoughtful as he went away. Henry, who knew he hadn't the slightest chance of being acquitted, was surprised at the success of his tactics when the man returned with warm water and a damp and greasy towel. 'We've no surgeon here,' he said. 'Attend to him yourself – although you'll wish you'd let him die.'

There was little Henry could do, and in the days that followed, the wounds putrefied and stank so that neither man could eat. However, the fat man had a sound constitution and began to recover. His name, he said, was Anthony Ross, and he had been flogged for information about the seizing and burning of the Cork Mail. But he knew no names, so they might have flogged him to death in vain, and nearly had.

'What, the coach from Dublin? I think I heard a woman singing about that,' Henry said.

'That's the one. It was captured, plundered and burned by pikemen as it left Dublin last week, and that was the signal for the uprising. But I was a poor passenger and knew nothing, except that a young officer was shot and fell dead at my feet. I kept a hedge-school in Kilmainham and tried to teach children to be fair-minded. That was enough to damn me. And maybe I did know more than I should. No matter; when the Irish militia regiments join the rebels, Ireland will be ours.'

Henry laughed shortly. 'When pigs fly,' he said. 'I was captured by the South Cork Militia, and I never saw a bunch of men less likely to join. I fear we took too big a risk in mobilising the poor country people in a struggle for an ideal. It will end in butchery.'

The cell, ten feet by six, had been cruelly cramped for one. For two, it was a squalid cage, and there they remained for two months. Ross was a tall man, whose belly hung over the top of his breeches, but suffering and hunger soon thinned him. Together, they listened to the ballad singer, trying to catch her words. She started in traditional style, 'Come all ye lords and ladies gay – ' (A cruel jest, said Henry), or 'Come all you young lads and listen to me

> My brave croppy boy is lying in a ditch.
> With iron rings for jewels and a crown of burning pitch.'

'I know of pitch-capping,' said Henry to Ross. 'I was threatened with it. Is it true that a cap covered with hot pitch is put on the victims' heads?'

'Worse,' Ross said. 'They add gunpowder and set fire to the mixture. It is the most abominable torture. I have seen it done, and think myself lucky to have got the lash instead.'

As June succeeded May, the yellow-haired tinker sang of towns overrun and freed, of garrisons put to flight.

'All lies,' said Ross. 'What could that trollop know?'

'I wonder,' said Henry. 'The towns she mentions are all in Kildare, where I doubt if she has ever been. Kilcullen, Athy, Clane, Prosperous, Naas – why choose those names? Someone is passing news to us.'

'I grant you the rebels may hold some of those towns,' Ross admitted, 'but Naas? No, they couldn't subdue Naas until the French come.' But even Henry wondered as the list of towns progressed steadily southwards, through Carlow and Wicklow. Then they heard the girl sing a rousing song, in which she was joined by a dozen fresh prisoners. If the words were true, half of Wexford was taken, and the whole eastern half of the country with the exception of Dublin was in the hands of the rebels. At this, two soldiers grabbed the girl roughly, clipped her arms to her sides, and dragged her away, screaming and cursing. They never saw her again.

Another ballad singer, an old man, took her place soon afterwards, singing about masses of United men swarming out of the Antrim glens, a few miles from where Henry had been born. His song was cut short in minutes, leaving the prisoners to guess the rest. Whatever the truth of actual defeats and victories, it was plain that Ulster and Leinster were deep in civil war. Henry could hardly bear it. Where was the expected rush to join the rebels from army and yeomen? Where were the French? Where was Wolfe Tone? The sudden coup they had hoped for had not materialised. Instead there was a bloody sectarian dogfight with no rules. He knew that much from what he could overhear.

They lived through June and July, and it seemed the time would never pass. Anthony Ross was taken away one day and did not return. Henry asked the warder if he had been freed.

'Aye. He's as free as air this minute.' The warder chuckled at his own joke. 'He's dancing on air outside – croppy bastard.' He slammed the door and was gone.

Henry came closer to despair that night than ever before. Ross wasn't a man he would have been likely to strike up friendship with if he had been free, they had little in common. Yet misfortune had united them and made their captivity bearable. Henry mourned the fat man sincerely.

Alone once more, Henry existed through the first half of August. The rebellion had been extinguished except in parts of Wicklow, and nobody felt like singing. The prison was crammed to the doors, in spite of daily deaths from typhus. A company of cavalry delivered more than fifty rebels together, most of them wearing tattered green jackets over naked chests. Herded into a shed, they sang defiantly.

> 'The French are on the sea
> And tomorrow we'll be free . . . .'

They were quickly silenced by the soldiers who beat them with the flat of their swords, but when the cavalry had gone, they began again – 'The French are on the sea . . .' and the tune was taken up by voices outside in the street. Warders yelled for silence as they waded in with whips, but they were outnumbered and backed off. 'The French have gone home – remember Bantry Bay!' shouted the warders, dealing out blows. 'The French are on the sea – remember America!' screamed the prisoners.

Henry, who could just see through his window if he pulled himself up by the bars, believed they knew the truth. He imagined the French warships sailing up the Shannon estuary and landing at Limerick with Wolfe Tone at their head. Surely the yeomen would desert, join them and free the prisoners. Then together they would march on Dublin.

No French fleet arrived, and the prison subsided into gloom. Henry's warder, in a better mood than usual, told him. 'You'll be tried tomorrow, and we'll be rid of you at last. Say your prayers now.'

He supposed that he would have to face the magistrates unwashed. He knew that, under martial law, they had power to hang him without a jury. However, he was hosed down through the bars of his door – there was no soap. His beard had grown and he hated the feel of it, loathed it, longed to get rid of it. His hair grew below his shoulder blades and he was allowed no tape to tie it lest he try to choke himself. He reflected how dirt and unkempt hair made most men look like villains.

As he waited for the cart, again in irons, he tried to combat his misery with an effort to detach his mind from it – to watch from the outside – and was partly successful. But the wrenching effort of doing this reminded him of his dreams when he had watched himself from some sort of disembodied state. He had an obscure feeling that, if he persisted, he might be unable to return to himself and madness would be the result.

He had any normal person's fear of death, but stronger was his fear of being chained in a Bedlam.

The trial was not at Nenagh, greatly to Henry's relief, but at Tipperary. He was one of a dozen chained together and loaded into a cart. Leaving Limerick, they were surrounded by crowds; some pelting them, some shouting, 'Liberty or death!' Their escort of Longford militiamen closed round the carts uneasily. They were outnumbered by fifty to one.

Out on the road, the crowds fell back and Henry blessed the sweet air and clean August sky. Wild thoughts of escape chased through his mind. Somehow, he expected things to have changed – that he would emerge into a different world like Rip Van Winkle – but everything was the same except the season. He slumped on the straw, defeated for the moment.

There was a long procession of carts – Mr Osborne was eager to proceed. The prisoners had no legal representatives, but a seedy little man was said to be pleading for leniency for all. The trial was completed within the hour, and Henry listened with numb disbelief as the charges against him were read out. Seditious practices – yes, he had expected it – and administering the United oath, but what was this about fifty pikes, buried in the parsonage garden? He pleaded ignorance and his plea was swept aside. He listened – he had no choice – to a summing-up which placed him among the vilest traitors in history.

He was sentenced to be transported for life.

Chapter Twenty-One

Henry had been certain he would be hanged. He had been trying to resign himself to it, and to persuade himself that Anne and the children would be cared for by her parents. Transportation opened up new vistas. Not many criminals had been sent from Ireland to New Holland – that vast naval base in the middle of nothingness which was said to have an unexplored hinterland full of strange beasts and black savages. England was now using this new land as a prison overflow in place of the lost colony of America. Henry wished he knew more about it.

Those of his fellows who had received the same sentence looked stunned. All had expected to hang, and some seemed almost disappointed – they had grown used to the idea and feared more of the misery they had been suffering. They were herded into a yard at the back of the courthouse. There, unfit elderly men and wild mountain boys milled together like cattle at a fair and, like cattle, jostled aimlessly with no understanding in their eyes. Many carried the marks of floggings. Henry felt obscurely ashamed because he himself bore no scars.

He was shackled to a surly, low-browed man, a labourer, who had been found guilty of owning a pike. 'We'll be worked to death in chain gangs,' he said. 'I'd sooner swing. They might let you off, I suppose, being what you are.'

'We've been treated alike until now,' Henry said. He wondered if he would in fact be expected to haul a timber carriage or break stones to make roads. He would certainly not be allowed to practise his calling. Although he had entered the ministry as a matter of convenience rather than conviction, preferring mathematics to dogma, he had become a conscientious minister with a deep interest in his chosen vocation. He hadn't realised how much it meant to him until he was deprived of it. He wondered too if he would be allowed to say goodbye to Anne and the children before he sailed, never to see them again.

Henry was jolted out of these gloomy thoughts by the arrival of a mounted escort: not the Longford militia, but a jingling, stamping squadron of the Iverk Cavalry. He expected that this Waterford-based regiment would take them straight to a transport vessel and begged for writing materials.

'Going to write a sermon?' sneered the driver from Limerick. 'Save it for the niggers who walk on their heads. Into the carts now.'

As they jolted south-east, the sun beat down on backs, shoulders and faces which hadn't known fresh air for months. By sunset Henry's fair skin had reddened, blistered and peeled. It was dark when they reached the town of Cahir, with its towering Norman castle, and there they were given bread and water and left all night in the castle courtyard.

The next day, the procession travelled to the garrison town of Carrick-on-Suir, by way of Clonmel. The road was appalling, and it took all day to complete nineteen miles.

Carrick bore more of the marks of rebellion than Limerick. Bodies dangled in chains from the gallows, and soldiers were everywhere. The townspeople had an apathetic look about them, and the prisoners were neither cheered nor jeered. This put some of them in a mood to risk fresh punishment. 'The French are on their way, they'll be here without delay,' they sang, and the words were echoed from the alleys and by-ways of the town.

Towards morning, when Henry had given up trying to sleep, he heard the sound of a horse galloping on the cobbled street and the sentry's challenge. The rider, out of sight behind the wall yelled, 'The French have landed!' and galloped on. There was a confusion of shouts and trampling feet and someone fired one shot, then silence.

All around Henry, men raised themselves on their elbows rubbing their eyes and asking, 'Is it true?' Even in this crowded yard where everyone was chained and on his way to banishment, excitement and tension filled the air. Henry's ragged shirt stuck agonisingly to his burned shoulders, every bone ached from the bumping cart and from lying on paving stones, but the atmosphere of unreasoning hope made him almost happy. As he climbed back into the cart two hours later, he half expected to see an approaching army.

'It *must* be true,' he said to his companion.

The man shrugged. 'Let's hope we sail before the war starts,' he said. 'I've seen enough fighting.'

As they set off along the riverside, great crowds of country people were thronging into the town. 'The French have landed!' The word passed from mouth to mouth. 'Where?' 'Dublin!' 'No, Cork . . .' 'Waterford . . .' 'Kinsale . . .' A woman threw an apple and Henry caught it neatly. The feeling of the people was changing – yesterday it could have been a rotten egg.

The crowds fell behind, and the broad, trampled road narrowed. The carts creaked along twisting lanes between wooded hills and a winding river. The soldiers' stirrups knocked against the shafts as they pressed close to protect the convicts from a rescue attempt from the hills, which could have concealed an army. But the slopes were silent and deserted.

As they jolted through a village where the houses jutted out across the street, an upper casement was thrown open and a man leaned out shouting, 'Liberty or death! The French have landed in Mayo! Wolfe Tone is there with fifty thousand Frenchmen at his back!'

An officer drew his pistol, but the man vanished and the window slammed.

Mayo? Henry was certain that this man knew the truth. If he'd been guessing, he'd have chosen a likelier place. 'Where are we going?' he shouted to the nearest soldier.

'Shut your bonebox,' was the reply. 'You'll know when we get there.'

The slow day wore on and the fierce heat went out of the sun. The countryside was beautiful, if anyone had been in a mood to appreciate it, with gently undulating meadows and the tumbling river beside them. The road wound downwards, following ancient tracks made by animals seeking water. It was amazingly rough. Henry's cart lurched sideways, throwing its twelve occupants into a heap. The wheel was smashed and the cart had to be abandoned. The driver rode the horse, while the convicts struggled along as best they could in their leg-irons. This whole area might have been designed for the concealment of outlaws; the soldiers' nervousness showed as they cursed their horses, the prisoners and each other.

Another cart collapsed, this one with a broken axle, before they

187

reached the outskirts of Waterford City, where two fresh carts were commandeered. Henry, seeing the estuary and harbour ahead, and beyond that the sea, scanned the various ships in the distance. They swung at anchor, and there was no sign of panic; no sign of the French. 'Is this the Cove of Cork?' he wondered.

'No,' said his companion, Tom Meagher, who had scarcely spoken in two days, 'It's Duncannon, outside Waterford. That's Duncannon Fort up there on the cliff. I worked here for a while.'

At the harbour side, the prisoners were lined up and counted. There were a number of small sailing vessels on the river, and Henry wondered in which one they would travel to their convict transport. Most were river craft and barges, but a few larger vessels were manned. If only their fetters were removed. He was a strong swimmer . . .

His thoughts were interrupted as his name was called, and heads turned with interest. There were many Catholic priests involved in the rebellion, but a Church of Ireland clergyman was a rarity.

Some of the prisoners, when their names were called, protested that they hadn't been tried, but the guards ignored them. Many wept, asking to see their wives and families. Henry kept quiet. If Anne had wanted to see him, he thought, she could have done so. He wasn't sure that he wanted her to see him in irons anyway.

They were taken off the jetty, a dozen at a time, in fishing boats, and rowed to a dismasted sloop which lay, a sodden hulk, in mid-river. The stench from the ship was almost visible, and flies swarmed around her in clouds. Her planks were yellow green with weed and slime, her deck tilted at a slight angle and strewn with rubbish and filth. They were exchanging a prison on dry land for one which was floating – just.

Anne had arrived at Miss Eliza's house in Clare Street two days after Henry's capture, hoping the old lady would use her undoubted influence in high places. Hetty, who had heard nothing about her brother-in-law's pursuit and arrest, started back in amazement when she opened the door to Anne and her family. Hetty at twenty-one was a slightly-built girl with a timid manner which had developed as a result of her mother's bullying. (She found Miss Eliza's bullying easier to deal with.) She was as sweet-natured as her sister, though not as practical, and Anne found enormous relief in telling her everything. It was an almost inconceivable comfort, not having to choose her words or consider the impression she was making. Hetty's hugs and kisses made her cry again and it was some time before she asked, 'Where is Aunt Eliza? I thought our noise would have brought her downstairs to scold us. Is she still unwell? And where are the servants?'

'Did you not hear? Aunt had an apoplexy after a quarrel with old Lady Boyle – Sir Timothy died, you know, and she is his widow. Aunt Eliza is not expected to recover. As it happens, we deal very well, and she won't have anyone else near her. I don't mind, I had rather look after her than live at home with Mama and Handel. As for the servants, there's just one poor old thing, scarce able to look after herself.'

Both children had fallen asleep. Anne left them on the parlour settee, and went to see Miss Eliza. 'Aunt Eliza, it's Anne. I hope you feel a little better?'

Red dye was fading from the old woman's hair in patches. Anne hadn't seen her without powder and rouge before. Her face was colourless, with sunken cheeks and clouded eyes. She rolled her head sideways. 'Timothy?' she said.

'Sir Timothy died, ma'am. Do you not remember? He was carried off at Christmas by a seizure,' Hetty said from the other side of the great four-poster. 'This is my sister Anne, who is in terrible trouble.'

'Stuff and nonsense. She's married to Henry Fulton and lives in Tipperary.' Miss Eliza roused a little, then slipped back down her pillows. Her tiny, skeletal body was kept alive by willpower. 'Mary', she whispered, holding out a withered hand, her eyes closed.

Hetty took the wrinkled little claw in silence and held it tight. Miss Mary had died two years earlier.

There was a faint cry from downstairs. Miss Eliza's eyes flew open at once. 'I dislike children,' she said clearly. Anne slipped away and removed herself and them to the housekeeper's room and the bedroom next to it, both being unoccupied.

Incredibly, in the weeks that followed, Miss Eliza began to mend. Anne sat with her when the children were asleep, glad to be able to help Hetty. The only servant who had stayed with the tyrannical old woman was Kate, who had worked in Clare Street for seventy of her eighty-two years. Anne cooked and cleaned, cared for James and Jane and wrote letters. She wrote to Bishop Knox and Sir Henry Prittie, to Canon L'Estrange in Roscrea and Canon Bayly in Nenagh, and to any member of parliament who was known to have liberal views, but the mails were in chaos, many letters being lost. Her only reply was from Sir Henry Prittie.

> . . . Your husband is to be tried in Tipperary town rather than Nenagh because he has been on friendly terms with all the local magistrates, including myself. It would be painful to be obliged to condemn a man whose intentions, I believe, were good, and who has sunk into crime through mistaken ideals rather than real wickedness. The trial will be in August, and the magistrate Sir William Osborne. Meantime, Mr Fulton is confined in Limerick, and I have asked the governor to see that he is made as comfortable as possible. He has a room to himself, and the gaolers have instructions to treat him with the respect due to his profession. He has been charged with the swearing of seditious oaths, for which I myself would recommend banishment for seven years.
>
> Osborne is a harsh man, as we all know, but he is just, according to his lights. It is unfortunate that the political situation is deteriorating just now. If the rebels persist in their present activities, it is bound to influence the course of justice. I regret extremely that Mr Fulton is not allowed visitors, but you will understand that, in the present disturbed state of the country, this rule must be adhered to . . .

Anne thought the last paragraph cancelled out the rest. She wrote again, thanking Sir Henry Prittie for his intervention. She finished:

> . . . If, as you suggest, my Husband is banished – I suppose to some Distant Land – I would Hope to Accompany him. I know the importance of Family Life in the Colonies – James is a fine, sturdy Boy, over two years old. I cannot Bear to Think of my Husband alone in a Strange Land – with his Wife and Children, his Fate might be Tolerable. Together we could build a New Life – perhaps more Easily than if he had been imprisoned here for a Number of Years . . .

As she sanded the letter, there was a knock on the basement door. She opened it to a beggar woman with an infant and a babe in arms. She went to fetch them some bread and milk, noticing that the woman had two babies like herself, yet her hands were free while she carried both. She saw how the new baby lay in a fold of its mother's shawl, swinging in a sort of hammock, while the year-old boy straddled her hip.

When the beggar had gone, Anne fetched an evening shawl and settled Jane in its folds – why hadn't she thought of it before? All country women carried their babies so. James, quick to understand, scrambled on to her hip, but he was too heavy to carry. It didn't matter, he had been walking since he was a year old. Hetty was dubious. 'You can't go about Dublin like that – you will be mistaken for a gypsy.'

'I don't care,' Anne said. With Jane wrapped in her shawl, she called on all the influential men she could get introductions to. Each day, she was disappointed. She was never flatly refused, but got a variety of excuses for non-interference in the course of justice. She didn't give up, even when the rebellion had broken out, and few women were seen in the streets.

Miss Eliza continued to make progress, and finally one day in August got up for an hour. She had taken a fancy to James which she was at pains to conceal, calling him 'that brat', but James wasn't deceived. With her, he was as good as gold; with Hetty he was always into mischief.

That day, Anne came home limping – her shoes needed mending. 'It's useless,' she said. 'I can't go on.' She dropped into a chair and buried her face in her hands.

'Fiddlesticks,' said Miss Eliza. 'You don't aim high enough. Go to the Viceroy. Better still, I will go with you. Stuff! Of course I am well enough. We will leave for the Castle early tomorrow.'

The rising had never affected Dublin in the same way as the rest of the country; it was still possible to go about freely, although the Naas and Bray roads were choked with families of the country gentry, fleeing their estates in Kildare and Wicklow. The next morning, Anne ordered a chaise, and told the driver to go to the viceregal Lodge at Phoenix Park, as Lord Cornwallis was said to be in residence.

'Phoenix Park? Lord Cornwallis? Camden is Viceroy, and never shows his nose outside the Castle.' Miss Eliza scowled at Anne, tapping her cane.

'No, Aunt, Camden is recalled, and Lord Cornwallis has been Viceroy for some weeks now.' Anne looked worriedly at her aunt. They had talked about the new appointment many times.

They had reached Sarah Bridge when their driver hurriedly pulled into the side of the road. A moment later, a brigade of cavalry swept by at the gallop, followed by the viceregal coach-and-six. Several smaller carriages and about fifty more soldiers brought up the rear.

Miss Eliza let the window down and stuck her head through.

'What's afoot?' she screamed at one of the riders.

'The French have landed!' he shouted back.

There was no point in continuing. Both had seen Lord Cornwallis in the coach. Anne ordered their driver to return. By the time the chaise had reached Clare Street, the whole city had the story. 'The French have landed in Mayo!'

A packet had arrived while they were out; a short note for Anne. It was from Ned Fitzmaurice and told her of Henry's trial and sentence. She read it in silence and handed it to Miss Eliza who was sitting down, looking as if the drive had been too much for her. She glanced down the single sheet, and gave it back to Anne. When she spoke, her voice showed no surprise or emotion of any sort.

'Well, niece, are you going to accompany that hare-brained boy to the Antipodes with your brood?'

Anne put the letter in her pocket. 'I haven't the means to do so, but oh, I would give anything – '

'Stop vapouring, girl. I will pay your fare if it will make you happy, and I will put my fortune in trust for that brat of yours. For heavens' sake, no thanks – you won't thank me later on. Now take me up to bed and fetch me a hot posset.'

Miss Eliza didn't visit her bank – she sent for her banker. He arrived the next day, along with her attorney. She chased Anne and Hetty out of the room, and they waited downstairs until the two gentlemen left, looking shaken. 'A most remarkable woman, your aunt,' remarked Mr La Touche, wiping his brow.

'*Most* remarkable,' echoed Mr Bagshaw. Together, they hurried to the nearest tavern to recover.

Chapter Twenty-Two

There were changes at number 18 Clare Street. Miss Eliza grew stronger every day, her mind cleared and she went about the house finding fault with everyone. James trotted at her heels like a little dog. When he tried to creep on to her lap, Miss Eliza went rigid and said, 'There are plenty of chairs in the room, I believe.' James philosophically climbed down and found another seat. But she gave Anne her purse and told her to go to Dawson Street and buy him new frocks and shoes. She took no notice of Jane, who could now sit up in her cradle and coo. Even at six months old, Jane sensed that cooing at Miss Eliza was a waste of time.

Anne, able at last to leave both children with Hetty while she went out, had run out of liberal men with influence. The French had routed the army at Castlebar, and were now marching towards Longford, so nobody was much interested in the fate of a single rebel prisoner, however deserving.

'Your approach was incorrect,' said Miss Eliza. 'You played the part of a sorrowing wife with two helpless babes.'

'I *am* a sorrowing wife with two helpless babes,' Anne protested.

'Possibly, but the worthy men you approached are sated with tales of hardship and pathos. How old are you?'

'Thirty-two,' said Anne, surprised. 'Why do you ask?'

'You would pass for twenty-two when you leave that shawl at home and when you aren't hung about with babies. You should go to a good *friseur* (I'm sure I see a grey hair), and find out what violet eyes, raven locks and a heart-shaped mouth can do – not to mention a pretty bosom. You should call on Charles Tighe – he's as old as I but a fool where women are concerned. Use the weapons God gave you – surely that is Christian behaviour.'

'Oh, sister, do try,' said Hetty. 'Let me do your hair in the Grecian style – I know it would suit you.'

Two days later, Anne walked up the road to Nassau Street,

accompanied by a Mr and Mrs Blake – an impoverished couple roped in by Miss Eliza to give her countenance. It would have been unthinkable for her to visit Mr Tighe alone in his rooms, he being a bachelor.

Charles Tighe, a rich man who had spent an idle life dabbling in the arts and writing *belles-lettres*, had at one time supported the United Irish Society. He had been quick to drop it when it ceased to be fashionable, and he didn't want to be reminded about it. But his foolish heart melted when he saw Anne. Her beauty and her gentle manner were enough to win him over, which was as well. She would have found it hard to practise those god-given wiles on him. He promised to see what could be done and to write to Lord Castlereagh, the Lord Lieutenant, a personal friend.

Mr Tighe was a tall, fat old man in an unfashionable velvet coat. He bowed over Anne's hand and kissed her fingers, vowing that she was 'beauty's self'. He presented her with a volume of his essays, bound in limp leather, entitled, *Leaves From the Tree of Life*, and almost forgot to say goodbye to the Blakes.

He was as good as his word, and Anne received letters from two members of parliament who were sympathetic but helpless, and one from Bishop Knox.

The bishop had not received Anne's letter, written when Henry was still in Limerick gaol, but he had kept in touch with the magistrates and knew that he was now 'awaiting removal to Cork in a prison ship'. A petition was being drawn up and signed by three hundred parishioners on his behalf, and the bishop thought there was a sporting chance that his sentence might be reduced 'as he had confessed under threat of torture and of reprisals to his family'.

The letter ended, 'I know you are in a wretched position, but there is no point in your following Henry to Cork when he is removed, as visiting is stopped while fighting continues. I think you should stay where you are, and join your husband if and when he is taken on board the transport. I personally will try to see that he is well treated in Cork gaol.'

Henry spent almost two months on the prison hulk. Conditions were unspeakable, even by prevailing standards. He was still chained to the taciturn Tom Meagher, ankle to ankle. They stood and sat and lay down together like unwilling Siamese twins. The miasma under the decks was such that it was impossible to see more than a few yards; the food was scanty and bad, the water warm and tainted.

On the third day, Meagher said he felt ill; on the fifth day, he died, not having had any medical attention. Henry had done his best to attract help, but being shackled to a man who was unable to stand and who was both tall and heavy, he could only shout for aid. He shouted in vain.

He had heard of a prisoner on a convict ship who remained fettered to a corpse for a week. Henry's skin crawled at the thought, and he fairly bawled for help. At last, after several hours, a smith and a striker were brought on board, and Meagher's irons were struck off. Henry said a hasty prayer over the body, the guards weighted it with lead and slung it over the side into the river. Henry still wore a leg-iron, or he would have been over the side too and swimming. He leaned against the bulkhead, wondering who his new companion in irons would be.

They were an odd number after Meagher's death, so Henry was chained up like a dog, on his own. Then another man died, and his comrade was dragged over to have his irons riveted to Henry's. He was a pale, elderly man in tattered black, and looked as if it would soon be his turn to be thrown over the side. Incredulously, Henry recognised Father O'Meara.

'Father William! What a wonderful surprise! I thought you had died in Limerick.'

'I would have been better off. Purgatory could be no worse. I am to be imprisoned for life. And you?'

'Botany Bay for me. If only my wife and children could be with me, I would count myself fortunate.'

Father O'Meara turned his gaunt face and studied Henry. 'I think I have never known anyone quite so resilient,' he said. 'Well, there are no first- and second-class prisoners here as there were in Limerick. There you were favoured – here we run in double harness.' He yawned widely. 'I am tired – let us sit. Careful . . . together now . . . that's it.' He thumped down, knees raised, on the deck. 'Is it true that you could buy special food in Limerick?'

'I might have done, and drink too,' said Henry, 'if I'd had any money when I was arrested. All my gold is at the bottom of the Mulcair river. Have you been in Limerick all this time?'

'Yes. Too ill to stand trial. When the rebellion was in full swing,

195

the cells overflowed, and there were men chained to the walls all around the yard. Their friends used to bribe the beadle to let them go. He would take their money and leave the prisoners where they were.'

Early in September, the weather broke. It had been hot and humid, which made conditions on the hulk almost unbearable. The warped timbers leaked steadily, and the pumps were manned night and day; the food was sour within hours of being brought on board, and the ship was overrun with rats. One day, it grew suddenly colder and huge, heavy drops of rain began to fall, dimpling the scummy surface of the river. The prisoners welcomed the coolness, but as the hatches had to be kept partly open to keep them from suffocating, the boat was soon awash with filthy water. The bedding was of straw, thrown down on the planks, and it was sodden in moments. Not surprisingly, there were several more deaths in the weeks that followed.

One advantage of being on the hulk rather than in a prison was that the convicts heard news of the rebellion. This was shouted from the river banks by their supporters, whenever the guards were absent. Henry knew that the French and the rebels had been defeated at Ballinamuck, and he knew that this was the end. But nobody seemed to know what had happened to Wolfe Tone. Plainly, the rumour that he had landed with General Humbert was untrue. Henry felt that, as long as his friend Theo was at large, there was hope, however slight.

As the weather got chillier, Father O'Meara began to suffer badly from both asthma and rheumatism. Henry, fit and active, had to spend his time sitting still, as the other man was unable to walk more than a few steps. It was an appalling existence, made bearable for each by the presence of the other. 'Whether we like it or not, we are United Irishmen,' said Henry, rattling his fetters.

It was a frosty October morning when the prisoners were lined up on deck and counted off into boats like so many sheep going to market. Like sheep, they were lifted and dragged and cursed by their gaolers. They were transferred down river into a dingy vessel named the *Princess*. Henry and Father O'Meara were in the last load, and the guard who had helped to push and pull them from one boat to another, handed a scrawled paper to the master of the *Princess*.

'Two hundred and eighty-two,' he said, 'but fifty are diers, I'd say. They need no irons to keep them from running away.' He laughed heartily.

'They won't be ironed aboard my ship,' said the master. 'I have a prison below, as safe as Kilmainham. But I want no deaths. If the winds are unfavourable, it could take a while to bring the ship round to Cork. Two hundred and eighty-two is more than I bargained for.'

About forty soldiers gathered round the prisoners while their irons were removed, then they were taken below, to a prison which was thirty yards long but only fifteen wide and seven feet high. There were a few hammocks stowed there, but no room to hang more than half what were needed. There was a scattering of straw on the floor, and the usual communal privy tub. They waited seven hours for the tide, then the wind changed and they tacked about the harbour all night.

On the hulk, Henry had stayed in one corner almost all of the time. Here, he was free of fetters and moved about to stretch his legs. He asked another prisoner to help him to rig a hammock for Father O'Meara, and they lifted the priest into it.

The footsteps of the guard sounded loud and close above their heads; the hatches were down and bolted from above. There was no physician on board to help a boy who screamed hysterically on the edge of madness until someone knocked him out with a heavy fist.

As the night crept on, Henry sat awake on the floor beside the hammock, listening to the noises of the ship (the hulk had hardly counted as a ship, her only sounds had been the slop of bilges and the scurrying of rats). About fifty fairly able men were talking in a close group nearby. One boasted that he had murdered half a dozen without being caught, and was charged with the theft of a goat. This man was telling the others to pull up the planks for weapons, club the guards when they brought food and seize the ship.

'What chance have forty recruits against three hundred desperate men?' he asked. 'We must be careful to make sure they are all dead though – we are too near the shore to take chances.'

Henry listened, and was frightened at his own reactions. He had always advocated peaceful reforms, but when he heard a gang of convicts, some of whom had already murdered, planning to club forty men to death, as well, presumably, as the crew, his first thought was of escape. He saw Father O'Meara's eyes, bright in the gloom – he had heard too.

The agitators moved towards the far end of the prison, and Henry said quietly, 'We must stop them, and we can only do it by telling the guard. I never thought to turn informer.'

The priest grunted. 'No victim of an informer likes it. But your problem isn't a moral one, it is that when you inform, they will probably manage to kill you. If not now, then whenever you meet again. Ah well, I suppose there's nothing for it. I will support you.'

Henry tried speaking to some other prisoners who had kept clear of the plot, but they edged away nervously. Henry stationed himself close to the hatch used by the guards, and waited for morning.

There was no light in the hold, except the glimmer that seeped through the chinks in the boards – just enough to tell when it was day. When morning came, and there were busy footsteps around the hatch overhead, Father O'Meara began to groan and retch realistically, and to throw himself about, shouting, 'Give me air! Give me air!' Henry first raised the priest's head, almost convinced himself, but reassured by a wink, then hammered hard on the underside of the hatch, shouting, 'Help! Help for the priest!'

After a time, the bolts were grudgingly drawn. Henry was ready, and, catching the sides of the opening, pulled himself up until his head was through the aperture. The guard who had opened the hatch stamped hard on one of Henry's hands, but he didn't let go and had time to say, 'The prisoners are plotting to kill you all and seize the ship!' Then he cried out and dropped back, shaking his bruised hand. Father O'Meara, who had forgotten to groan while this was going on, flung himself about so violently that he fell out of the hammock on to the straw as he had intended. Henry helped him up, and both men backed into a corner. 'I believe help is at hand,' Henry said.

Some of the plotters had succeeded in prising boards loose during the night, but they were by no means prepared for a fight. They muttered together, wondering if they could catch the surgeon and his guard and hold them to ransom. 'Too close to shore,' said the leader. 'No, let them bring us our rations while we cache more weapons and bide our time. You,' he added to Henry, 'where are we? You had your head out.'

'I couldn't see much,' said Henry truthfully, 'but there were treetops on our left.'

'As I thought. We must wait for night.'

His words were drowned by a tremendous noise of running feet overhead. Orders were shouted, a bugle blown. Then both hatches were lifted at the same time, and every available armed man dropped down into the prison. The ringleader of the gang gave himself away by shouting, 'That bastard has betrayed us!' He was overpowered and put in irons.

For the remainder of the journey, rather more than twenty-four hours, the prisoners were closely guarded, all the able-bodied men being ironed except Henry.

When they reached Cove, Henry and Father O'Meara were thanked and congratulated by the commander, a man too good for his job. In time of peace, he carried grain to the city of Cork from Wexford.

'I am more than obliged to you two gentlemen,' he said. 'If the plot had come off, I'd not be standing here. I will recommend that you are treated as well as possible in gaol, and I will try to see that you, Father, get medical attention as soon as possible.'

This wasn't very soon, as they were all counted again, and a dying man taken away. Then, as they stood under guard on the quay, all their so-called bedding was brought up and burned. Henry, watching the crackling blaze, didn't feel particularly proud of himself, although he knew he'd been right. His own experiences had left him with a dislike of informers which he would never overcome.

Later, they were marched – except for Father O'Meara who was carried – to the new gaol, which was still being built. As each block was completed, it was filled, and, as almost all the convicts had life sentences, only transportation or death could relieve the congestion.

Chapter Twenty-Three

Sir William Osborne had sentenced hundreds of men during the years he had been a senior magistrate. In his eyes, a defendant was almost certain to be guilty and, as such, not entitled to any pity or consideration. His judgments were harsh and his sentences heavy, but no more so than those of many others like him. As he convicted one man after another, they made little impression on him. One criminal was much like another.

One prisoner that Sir William would never forget was the renegade parson, Henry Fulton. He had conceived a violent dislike of him when their paths first crossed. This young man, captured red-handed, disgraced, a traitor, had stood in court as if he were visiting friends. He was a filthy object, with his torn, bloodstained clothes, but he had worn them with an air, and had behaved as if he thought he had a chance of acquittal. This had so infuriated Sir William that he had not been able to resist seeking the wretch out afterwards to tell him what he thought of him. He had been received with something suspiciously like a joke. He had looked forward to having the man hanged.

But first a petition had arrived from some of Henry's friends, then a recommendation to leniency from his employer, then another from his rector. What was the matter with them? thought Sir William. Didn't the fools know that Fulton would think nothing of murdering them in their beds? Such a man was capable of any crime, no matter how foul.

When Fulton came to trial, Osborne had just received another letter actually praising the prisoner, this time from no less a man than the Bishop of Killaloe. Reluctantly, he had sentenced Fulton to transportation for life, feeling that he had let him off more lightly than he deserved. Hanging, however, would have made him into a martyr – that didn't bear thinking of.

Ever since the trial, he had been bombarded with letters. One from the wife – you'd expect that, they all wrote, those that could write. One was from the officer who had committed him to gaol. Well, Captain Fitzmaurice should be cashiered for expressing such unbecoming sympathy, no doubt about that. There were no letters from either set of parents; doubtless they were too ashamed to write, but there was one from Mrs Fulton's aunt, which reviled him with a variety of biting phrases and ordered him to release Fulton at once. Naturally, he didn't reply.

Even more puzzling, he was visited by a deputation from Fulton's parish, all pleading for clemency. He dismissed them, and put the matter out of his mind until he received a long letter from old Lord Claremont, still a prominent figure in politics and a man of great influence. He had, he wrote, received a petition signed by three hundred people, both Catholic and Protestant, on Fulton's behalf. Immediately afterwards, he had been visited by an old friend, Charles Tighe, who had pleaded most eloquently for the prisoner. He would be grateful if Sir William would write and say whether, in his opinion, the sentence of transportation for life might be shortened to seven years.

Sir William assembled his writing materials with hands which shook with rage. How dared all these people doubt the wisdom of his judgment? He wanted to write a blistering rebuke, but he also wanted to keep his job and, with luck, to be promoted. How to damn Fulton while assuring Lord Claremont of his unfailing co-operation? He sharpened his quill, a scowl on his narrow face.

> . . . if I am to give my unprejudiced Opinion as to the Guilt of Mr Fulton, I cannot hesitate in pronouncing him *Guilty* in a most heinous Degree – inasmuch as, disregarding the Sacred Duties of his Function, he turned that Influence he had gained from an apparent Shyness of Demeanour bordering on Methodism – in the Destruction of those committed to his charge. I cannot conceive a more Compleat Wolf in Sheep's Clothing.
>
> He wormed himself into the Confidence of a Gentleman of the most respected in the County by the apparent Sanctity of his Manners, undertook the tuition of his Son and the defence of his House at the time that he had seduced a Principle Dependant. . . . I mean a Mr Tydd – whose name your Lordship will see on the enclosed hasty scrap of paper, taken at the moment of Apprehension, which is a very incompleat Confession indeed . . .

He used to go on Foot, with the Affectation of Humility, to visit the Parishioners; but in reality to Seduce them from their Allegiance. He deceived in a very high degree, his Patron, the Bishop of Killaloe, and disregarding the Noble and highly Meritorious Example set by his Bishop, forgetting all Obligation and Gratitude, endeavoured to destroy that very man who had taken him up, activated only by a Wish to do good and reward the deserving. . . .

I will pronounce Mr Fulton to be one of the last Men I would turn loose among the People . . . He will be guilty of a gross Libel on the Magistrates if he perseveres in saying that he confessed himself guilty under threat. No threats were held out, on the Contrary, he was treated with mildness he has ill requited . . .

I have thought it my Duty to state my Opinion, I have no Resentment to gratify, no Feelings to Combat . . . I cannot see the Justice or Prudence of turning him loose on society, degraded as he is. From the very nature of his Office, he should endeavour to hide. He is unfit to return to it, and should rather wish for Banishment . . .

I beg pardon, My Lord, for detaining you so long, and shall conclude by enforcing my Protest against Mr Fulton's Memorial. Tis untrue in all its parts, except when he seems to allow some small Guilt. It seems to me there has been some good-natured Interference for him. I do not wish to step between him and Mercy. . . .

Sir William leaned back in his chair, pleased with his efforts. Deference and decisiveness, neatly balanced, he thought. He considered adding a postscript, drawing attention to his own hopes and ambitions, but decided against it. His Lordship must be in his dotage if he really thought that renegades like Fulton should be spared. He hoped there were no busybodies in Cork, trying to ease the prisoner's lot.

The prisoner, meanwhile, was better lodged than at any time since his arrest. The new prison was well supplied with small cells for 'first-class' prisoners, and the six- by ten-foot space was even provided with an iron bench and a thin mattress. Washing materials were not considered necessary, and Henry had to save a little of his daily pint of drinking water in order to make a pathetic attempt to wash himself.

There was no window, the grille opening on to the corridor, so he knew nothing of the outside world. He thought his family and friends had abandoned him, and told himself sternly that they were right. He didn't know that money, clothes and food, sent by Anne, by Sir Henry Prittie and by Bishop Knox, had been quietly hived off by the governor. He was in the same case as in Limerick – alone, without occupation or exercise and apparently forgotten. As winter approached, he was also very cold. He thought about Father O'Meara with his asthma and his rheumatism, and asked the warders for news of him. One of them said that a priest had died a while back. 'Could've been him,' he said, without interest. Henry had no cash for bribes, so he was of no interest to anyone.

As he sat on the bench, walked three steps this way – two steps that – or did exercises, he wondered why he was bothering to keep fit. Escape was pointless; he would find himself without shelter or allies. Now that the rebellion had become a sectarian feud, there was no longer any place among the rebels for a Protestant clergyman, however revolutionary his ideas. Neither had he a place among the people he had deceived in the cause of freedom and democracy. He wondered how Wolfe Tone would deal with the situation – a Protestant like himself and with the same aims. He decided that Tone would be obliged to return to France or America, and to make his home there, and thought wryly that he too would be settling abroad.

In November, Henry had a visitor.

The Reverend Tobias Bell was an earnest young man with a social conscience. When a member of his flock in the village of Carrigaline was imprisoned for forgery, he went to the prison with a Bible, a blanket and a bottle of wine. To his disgust, he had to give the wine to the warder before he could persuade him to lead the way to the cell. When he was leaving, in a glow induced by virtue, the warder, who was also glowing, but with Burgundy, offered to take him to see 'another Protestant villain', the traitor Parson Fulton.

Mr Bell felt nervous as he waited for the key to be turned and the bolts drawn. He hadn't intended to visit a traitor, wasn't sure what to say to a fellow cleric so disgraced. The forger, while accepting the blanket, had refused the Bible with some emphasis. Could he offer it to a hardened criminal, a man guilty of far worse than embezzlement? Feeling positively saintly (but very uneasy), he entered the cell and heard the door clang behind him.

The man sitting on the low bench stood up and came forward,

holding out his hand. He was a head taller than Mr Bell and three or four years older – about thirty-three. His long brown hair was greasy, and had obviously been combed with his fingers, he had an untrimmed beard and moustache. There was little left of his shirt which hung in tatters at his waist, and he wore a pair of the cheapest frieze breeches. His legs were bare, and he had wrapped his feet in rags. His face was emaciated, but his eyes were bright and intelligent. His smile was so infectious that Mr Bell, who had schooled his unremarkable features into an expression of pious sorrow, found himself smiling back.

They said their 'how d'you dos' as if they had been at a vicarage tea-party, then Mr Bell said diffidently, 'Shall we pray?'

Mr Fulton shocked him by exclaiming, 'Good God, no,' but he recollected himself and explained, 'Forgive me, but for months I have had no confidante but the Almighty, who must be heartily sick of my pleas. I want so much to talk to a man from the outside world, neither a convict nor a gaoler: I have been caged now for six months or more without visits or letters.'

Tobias Bell began to tell him about the parish of Carrigaline and his ministry there, but Fulton could scarcely conceal his impatience. Clearly, he wanted an account of the rebellion, and Bell began to outline the story of the fighting in Wexford, the rebels' defeat there and the French invasion. He felt deeply embarrassed at discussing such matters with a self-confessed insurgent, and made his account brief. 'After their defeat, the French officers were entertained in Dublin at the best hostelries,' he said. 'I believe they have been allowed to go home. It is all very strange.'

They were sitting on the narrow bench, and Bell, although far from perceptive, felt the tension in the other man: a fiercely controlled emotion which showed only in his white knuckles, and a pulse which beat visibly in his temple. 'What of Wolfe Tone?' he asked. 'I suppose he was captured. The warders have told me so often that he was taken or dead that I don't know what to believe. Is he a prisoner of war?' His low-pitched voice shook slightly.

Bell said uneasily, 'I am afraid you will find the story sad, but he had only himself to blame.'

Fulton jumped to his feet. 'What story? Out with it.' He was shaking from head to foot, and, for the first time, Bell could see that this was a man with ideals which were more than skin deep. He edged away to the end of the bench, alarmed.

'I beg you will calm yourself, Mr Fulton,' he said. 'Wolfe Tone was arrested while fighting on board a French man-of-war. He was brought to Dublin in irons a fortnight ago – early in November. He was wearing the blue and gold uniform of a French colonel – and fetters. Even so, the audacious fellow waved to a lady of his acquaintance. I believe he petitioned for a soldier's death, by firing squad.'

Henry Fulton folded his arms, gripping his forearms hard. 'Go on,' he said quietly.

Tobias Bell was thoroughly frightened now. Fulton was between him and the door, and his wild stare was at odds with his level voice. Breathing hard, the prisoner closed white teeth on his lower lip and waited.

Bell continued, speaking very fast, 'Tone impressed many in the dock, I believe. He said he had sacrificed all for Irish independence, and he sincerely lamented the atrocities committed in the name of freedom in his absence. He was sentenced to . . . I'm sorry, I know this is painful for you . . .'

'Continue.'

'. . . to hang, but he cut his own throat. He died a week later, just three days ago.'

There was silence except for the breathing of the two men. At last Henry Fulton said, 'I am grateful to you for telling me this.' His voice was devoid of expression.

Bell's racing heart returned to normal, and he pulled the Bible out of his pocket and held it out to Mr Fulton with all the caution of someone offering an angry tiger a meat pie. 'A gift,' he muttered. 'Please don't take it amiss.'

'Amiss? Mr Bell, this is water in the desert. I haven't read a word of print for months, and boredom has almost killed me. Many, many thanks. I suppose it is too much to expect that you might have writing materials about you? A pencil? Capital.'

'I fear I have no paper,' Bell said, but Fulton wasn't listening. He was scribbling as fast as he could on the flyleaf of the Bible. When it was covered, he turned to the endpapers and wrote on those. He tore out the flimsy pages carefully and gave them to Bell, who was almost physically hurt by this misuse of the gospels.

'I would be grateful if you would send this note to my wife,' said Mr Fulton. 'I'm not sure where she is, so will give you her parents' address.' Mr Bell memorised it and was emboldened to suggest again that they should pray. This time the prisoner agreed, and Bell took his leave in a rosy glow of virtue.

Henry wasn't allowed a candle, and the times when there was enough light in his cell to read the Bible were limited. He read it as if for a bet, from beginning to end, and with much more concentration than when he had been obliged to read it and to learn whole chapters by heart. By these means, he tried to put Wolfe Tone's death out of his mind. When it was too dark to read, he tried to fix his mind on what he had read last, and to remember passages he had learned. But when the small print gave him eyestrain and he had to put it away, his thoughts raced back to Theo with his throat cut, dying in a prison cell, probably much like his own.

Sadness and anger on Tone's account almost made him forget that Bell was going to pass on his note to Anne, and indeed the days and weeks passed without a word. His visitor had impressed the warder – or perhaps he hoped for another bottle of wine. Whatever the cause, he brought Henry a piece of gritty soap and a tin pan half full of cold water. Henry, scrubbing away, reflected that he had been more grateful for these things than for anything he had ever been given. He asked for scissors, but was refused.

At Christmas, Tobias Bell came to see him again. Henry asked him to sit down, and chatted easily, trying to entertain this plump, unhappy young clergyman. They had nothing in common except their profession, and he suspected that Bell was rather afraid of him. 'I wrote to your wife,' Bell said, 'enclosing your note, and received a reply from her mother. Mrs Fulton has been staying in Dublin with relatives, but has left.'

'Where is she now?' Henry's heart sank like lead.

'Mrs Walker did not say. Her letter was very brief – here it is.'

Henry read the single sheet, and wrote another note, this time on a pad which Bell had brought him. 'Would you be so good as to send this to Miss Eliza Leland at 18 Clare Street? I am sure you will get a reply. My wife can't have gone far, she has two young children with her – unless perhaps she is on her way to visit me – I can't believe she would let me go without a chance to see my family again and to say farewell.'

Mr Bell had a habitual nervous laugh which Henry found irritating. He wanted to say, 'Calm yourself – I don't mean to attack you,' but thought he had better not.

'How old are the children?' asked Mr Bell, laughing nervously.

'James was two last April, and Jane will be a year old in February. I won't recognise Jane when – if I see her. I don't know how Anne will manage; her parents don't seem to want her, and her aunt is an old lady and not over-fond of children.' Henry slumped in his seat. He wished Bell would go.

The warder came to show Bell out, and he said nothing about another visit.

A month passed. Henry divided his time between reading Mr Bell's Bible, huddled in his blanket, and trying to keep warm and stave off infirmity by stamping, swinging his arms and even dancing. Of these activities, the Bible reading was by far the more valuable.

To begin with, he had fallen on Mr Bell's gift chiefly as an antidote to boredom – he would have read almost anything with the same avidity, so starved was his mind of occupation. But solitude and loneliness had sharpened his sensibilities, and the familiar words began to sound in his mind with an astonishing freshness. There were times when something would strike him so forcibly that it almost knocked the breath out of him. 'These things I have spoken unto you that in me ye might have peace. In the world ye might have tribulation: *but be of good cheer; I have overcome the world.*' One afternoon, on reading these words, he found himself on his knees, so full of gratitude for the sense of God's presence they gave him that his prayer could not express itself in words. Henry was always to feel that if he became a minister worthy of the name, it was because of Mr Bell's Bible.

Then one day, there was a great commotion and he heard doors opening and shutting all along the passage. When it was his turn, his door was opened by several men, including a smith. He was put in irons again, but not shackled to another prisoner. Rings were riveted on to both ankles, with nine heavy links between: enough to allow him to walk with short, jerky steps. About fifty prisoners were assembled in the quadrangle and, in spite of the cold, ordered to strip. Then they were hosed down with icy water and roughly scrubbed by warders. Henry shut his eyes, wondering if it was possible to humiliate human beings any further. They scrambled into their filthy rags, still wet, and set off in a long line for the harbour at Cove.

Walking was difficult, and it was a considerable distance. Henry was glad he had kept as fit as possible in his cell. All around him, men were stumbling and falling. Those who could walk were prodded along, and not allowed to help the others.

Henry's feet were soft from inactivity. He set his teeth and went on, head down. The smell of salt made him look up at last and there, ahead, was the harbour. He saw the *Polyphemus*, a man-of-war, and lying close to her, an East Indiaman, a tea clipper, like the one he had sailed in to India. He saw the name on her side, *Minerva*, and wondered what a ship like that was doing there. To her right lay a tubby-looking merchant ship, the *Friendship*. Henry supposed they would sail in her. His unquenchable spirits rose. Anything, *anything* would be better than his solitary cell.

On the quay, they were halted, and told they were getting their issue of clothes. While they waited, prison barbers went up and down the rows, shaving each man's hair, beard and moustache. Many protested loudly, but Henry thought it the least unpleasant thing he'd had to suffer. His head felt cold without its matted mane of hair and the razor was blunt, but what of that? The hated beard was gone and he felt cleaner than he had for months.

The prisoners' clothing was brought to them in packs – quite large packs, Henry was pleased to see. Later, he discovered that he had received two jackets (too short in the arms), two pairs of trousers (too short in the legs), two pairs each of stockings and shoes, a narrow mattress, a blanket and a rug.

A lighter came to the quayside to take the prisoners to the ship. They slipped and tripped with their fettered feet as they tried to walk down the gangway which was wet and slimy. Their hands stuck to the icy rail as they pulled themselves up. At last the boat pulled away, and Henry saw to his joy that they were going aboard the *Minerva*.

The *Minerva* had been built for speed rather than comfort. Her purpose was to bring cargoes of tea from India to Tilbury in the least possible time. She was capable of twelve knots, and was the pride of her master, Captain Salkeld.

Captain Salkeld was in the worst of humours. He and his ship had been detained in the Thames for six months while a legal wrangle was sorted out, then he was told by the owners to sail to the Cove of Cork, collect a cargo of Irish convicts and transport them to Botany Bay. He stood on the bridge in a towering rage, watching the shaven-headed wretches in their chains come aboard.

Henry came up the gangplank, forgetting his cold and discomfort. He remembered how he had wanted to be a sailor as a boy, and had read everything he could about ships. Barefooted sailors, with straw hats and pigtails, were coiling down ropes on deck. Henry was one of the very few passengers who knew the purpose of each rope.

A scowling man in a greasy peajacket appeared with a list in his hand. 'Fulton, Henry,' he bawled.

'Here,' Henry said. The man gestured to two sailors who grabbed him by both arms and hustled him below. He saw the accommodation for the prisoners in the hold and remembered the hulk with a shudder, but the *Minerva* was clean – as yet. The sailors propelled him into a cabin, slammed and locked the door. The cabin was eight feet by six, even smaller than the cell he had left. There were three narrow berths and a hammock neatly stowed. Nothing else.

The cabin was above the water line, and had a small window, whose sloping curve followed the side of the ship. Kneeling on one of the cots, Henry could see the next load of convicts being brought out on the lighter. He watched for some time. Some of the prisoners were women, and many clung to weeping children and spouses on the quayside. The loading was businesslike and methodical; farewells were cut short, but no one was beaten or kicked. He lay down on the cot and fell asleep.

The ship didn't sail that day or the next. A fortnight later, more prisoners were embarked, that was all. Henry had been obliged to leave his Bible behind, and although far better off than in Cork gaol, he was wretchedly bored. The arrival of his meals was an event. No more watery gruel or mouldy bread. He ate hardboiled eggs and jellied beef, and food had never tasted so good.

February was almost over when he heard more passengers coming on board. He was tired and depressed and didn't bother to go to the window. After some time, his door was unlocked, and he looked up, expecting food. A woman wrapped in a shawl had looked round the door. She began to make an apology and go away, then their eyes met. It was Anne.

PART THREE

Chapter Twenty-Four

————◆<·●·>◆————

'I beg your pardon – 'Anne was about to tell the guard that he had unlocked the wrong door. There was a tall, thin, completely bald man in the cabin, dressed in a canvas jacket and trousers designed for somebody shorter and fatter. Then their eyes met – his full of incredulity, as though he were seeing a vision, and she realised the truth. She could feel the blood draining from her face at the shock of it, and feared that she might faint. Setting Jane down on one of the cots, she slowly took the three steps which separated them. He reached out and took her by the shoulders, hardly daring to do so in case she should prove to be an illusion, and she put her arms round him and pressed her face against his jacket, less for the embrace than to hide the turmoil of conflicting emotions which was shaking her.

Everyone had assured her that Henry was being well treated, with his own room, good food and wine, and the clothes and books she and Bishop Knox had sent. She had expected him to be thin and shabby, not a shaven scarecrow with irons on his legs. She clung to him, sobbing. As he took a step, the iron links clanked on the floor. She couldn't bear the sight of his fettered ankles or his shaven crown; she kissed him with closed eyes.

Henry held her close, overcome by joy; but joy was clouded by fear that they would soon be parted for good. 'Don't cry, sweetheart; you make it harder for both of us,' he said. 'Tell me how long you can stay – ' His voice broke as he saw Jane watching, big-eyed, from the cot.

'Didn't you get my letters?'

'What letters? I have heard not one word of you since I was taken. I thought you had washed your hands of me.'

'How could you? Oh my dear, how could you? I am coming with you. Aunt Eliza has paid for the children and myself, a hundred and twenty guineas, and has willed money to James. We will all four travel in this little cabin to start our new life together.' She reached up to kiss him again, forcing herself to look, wondering if she would ever get used to his appearance.

Jane sat watching, her fat little legs dangling, her face thoughtful beyond her years. She could stand and walk if she had something to hold, but was making no attempt to talk yet. Her dark hair still had the downy sheen of babyhood, but there was nothing babyish about her expression. She was watching her father attentively now, although she had given a startled cry when her mother had embraced the ragged stranger.

Henry, who was asking questions much faster than Anne could answer them, turned to Jane and dropped on his knees beside her. 'Are you afraid of me?' he said gently. 'I wouldn't blame you if you screamed.'

For a second Jane shrank back, her lower lip trembling. She turned her face away, then peeped back at him, curiosity overcoming fear. Henry held his breath – and when his child smiled at him, shyly at first, and then with a glow of trust, Anne had to thrust into his hand the kerchief with which she had dried her own eyes.

'It's her birthday,' she said. 'She's a year old today.'

'Bless her heart, I had forgotten. Where's James?'

'I left him with one of the ship's officers. He's a mischievous child – not a bit like Jane. They are letting him play to his heart's content. I thought I would bring them to you one at a time.' As she spoke, a key turned in the lock, and a guard shoved James through the door and relocked it, shouting, 'That's the last time I play nursemaid to you, you limb of Satan.'

James stopped just inside the door and studied Henry. 'Croppy,' he said, backing up against the wall, his mouth trembling.

'It's Papa, Jamie love,' said Anne. 'He's not a croppy – he had to have his hair cut off, that's all.'

James pointed to Henry's legs, and his face began to turn red. 'No, no, he's a croppy! Look at his irons! He'll kill us!' he cried, and began to scream, battering the locked door.

Anne caught hold of him and turned him round gently, and he burrowed his head against her skirts, while his screams turned to whimpers; but as soon as he looked up and saw Henry again, he renewed his shrieks. Henry half moved to pacify his son, but the inevitable clank provoked fresh yells. Only time would accustom him to a croppy father. Henry understood and left him to Anne.

214

'What have you got in that basket, love?' he asked her. 'You mustn't blame the boy – nine months is an eternity at his age. Perhaps some goodies will help.'

Anne removed the napkin which was spread over the hamper she had brought with her, and when James saw his parents and sister eating a delicious picnic, he accepted a chicken leg which kept him quiet. He hid behind Anne, gnawing it, a boy outgrowing his clothes, tall for his age, with brown hair in a fringe to his eyebrows.

'The cabin will be cramped for four,' Henry said, 'But my fetters may be removed when we sail, and you will be free to go on deck when the other prisoners are below.'

They were finishing their meal when the door was unlocked again to admit a strongly built man of about forty, who filled the remaining floor space with untidy parcels of clothes, and a torn military greatcoat which he dropped at his feet. He at once turned to bang on the door, shouting, 'Open up! No one turns a key on General Joseph Holt – I travel free.'

'Not in a convict's cabin you don't – or not until we sail,' came a faint reply.

'And when will that be?'

'God knows – we don't.' The voice receded with the slap of bare soles on deckboards.

Holt turned to his fellow travellers, not particularly put out, and Henry introduced himself and his family. Anne was looking stunned. Must she share a cabin with a large, noisy strange man for several months? There was little enough space for themselves. Practical and unfussy as she was, her upbringing hadn't prepared her for anything like this. She shook his offered hand murmuring that she was delighted to make his acquaintance.

''Servant ma'am. I am General Holt, he who led a thousand rebels in Wicklow. I have consented to join this ship as a matter of expediency. No doubt you have heard of me.' Holt wore a thread-bare scarlet jacket faced with blue, much the worse for wear. When he bowed over her hand, she noticed that he had powdered the curls which clustered round a hairless pate. He ruffled James's hair and wrung Henry's hand. 'When my wife arrives, we shall be a snug little party, shall we not? She brings my son Joshua – a fine lad of twelve summers, and she expects another child in July. It will be delightful for her to have such a charming lady for company.

Imagine if there is a storm when her time comes – she will be glad of your support. Well, never mind, my Hester is as stouthearted as I am myself.'

'I am delighted to hear it,' Anne said faintly, throwing a desperate glance at Henry, but reading only amusement in his face. He hasn't changed after all, she thought.

It was a further two months before Holt's wife and son joined the ship. He was a strange mixture, this rebel general, having a respect for all things military combined with a vitriolic hatred for the British army. He boasted constantly about his campaign in Co Wicklow, battles won, prisoners taken, justice done. It seemed unlikely that everything he said was true, but there was something endearing about his innocent bravado.

He and Henry had many discussions in the cabin which Henry wasn't allowed to leave. Henry had hoped for first-hand news of the state of the country, but was disappointed. Holt's view of the rebellion was entirely personal, and he seemed to hate both sides equally.

Anne, glad that Henry had someone to talk to, went about the ship, trying to find a bribable official who would remove Henry's irons. She met with sympathetic refusal. The cook, however, gave her a basin of goose-grease to salve the sores. The smell of this was strong enough to make her eyes water, but Henry's gratitude was worth it. Afterwards, she passed on what was left to the other prisoners, and was severely rebuked by the officer of the watch.

Meanwhile, Holt tried to find out why Henry had become a rebel. He himself, he said, had been a thief-catcher and tax-collector as well as being in charge of the mending of roads. The first two occupations had given him a thorough knowledge of the Wicklow hills, while making him intensely unpopular locally. A Protestant 'strong farmer', of similar background to George Andrews, Holt made up in imagination what he lacked in education. Henry soon tired of the loud, boasting voice which only softened when he talked about his wife and family.

'Damn my soul if I see why you turned on your own kind,' Holt said.

'I have tried to bring what you call "my own kind" to a different way of thinking,' said Henry. He was sitting on one of the cots, trying to tuck a handkerchief between leg-iron and blister. 'I failed, like better men than I, and found myself caught up in a struggle unlike anything I had been prepared for.'

'But why? Why worry about the thoughts of others? You had your living, a position in society, a house – was your house burned, perhaps?'

'No. Who should want to burn my house?'

'Mine was. By a bastard called Hugo who had a grudge against me, and some scum of militia from Monaghan. Oh, we dealt with Hugo, me and the boys, he'll burn no more. But you – I am at a loss – were you robbed? Or taken in battle, maybe?'

'I was taken out of a river,' Henry said, 'that was my first brush with the army. It was my own fault however; I fear I lost my head. You, Holt, rebelled on account of a personal grudge, I worked for a free parliament, religious tolerance and equal rights for everyone. Surely you can understand. My ideals were no different from Wolfe Tone's, leader of us all.'

'Faith, I can't. Your work was light and your wife and family had need of you, yet you turned on the powers that kept you. You are a man in rebellion against yourself.'

'Have it your own way,' said Henry. 'I will never be able to explain it to you.'

Hester Holt was a quiet woman in her mid-thirties. She seldom spoke, as her husband spoke for her. When she and young Joshua arrived, Anne began to wish she had waited to come aboard until the ship sailed.

They slept an adult and a child to a bed. She shared hers with James, and Henry his with Jane. Holt slept in the hammock and his wife and son squeezed into the third bunk. The first night, young Joshua fell out on the floor twice, the second he slept on the floor. Then Captain Salkeld suggested that he join the bo'sun's mess and get some schooling. He would take his turn at the watch, and relieve the crowding in the cabin. Henry had tried to make friends with James in every way he could think of, but with no success. The child no longer cried out at the sight of him, but his fear of the chains remained. He watched Henry like a wild animal, always ready to run to Anne.

Shortly after Mrs Holt's arrival, James fell into the harbour. Anne,

217

who had her hands occupied pegging out their washing on deck, had taken her eye off him for a second. She screamed, and a sailor fished him out with a boathook. He had bobbed to the surface and was dog-paddling in the flotsam of rubbish surrounding the ship.

She took him down to the cabin, which was now sometimes left unlocked, Henry having promised not to try to escape. 'You will start your new life with but one pair of trousers, my dear,' she said to Henry. 'I am going to make some pantaloons for this rascal out of the other pair. He is young to be breeched, but the weight of his petticoats could have drowned him.'

James's pantaloons seemed to boost his confidence, and he began gradually to accept Henry, whose skull was now covered with inch long hair. He caught cold, though, after his ducking, and soon all six were coughing and sniffing. This especially annoyed Holt, who declared between shattering sneezes that he never caught cold. One by one, they recovered, but James developed a dry cough which worried his parents.

Then an epidemic of fever swept the ship, and six of the prisoners died. Mrs Holt became very nervous, as her baby was due in less than a fortnight, while Anne worried about James and Jane. Jane escaped the infection, but James was seriously ill, and Surgeon Price had to be called in. The crisis came, and all one night he lay on a cot, while Henry and Anne took turns to bathe his burning skin with cool water. In the morning the fever had gone, leaving him weak and white. Anne lay down to sleep, while Henry watched over the child. James opened his eyes, and Henry whispered, 'Don't wake your mama,' expecting tears, but James managed a mischievous smile. 'Croppy,' he said.

Mrs Holt had been obliged to leave her seven-year-old daughter, Marianne, behind with a Mrs La Touche. She was depressed, and her husband's cheerful assurance that she would probably have another girl – perhaps two – didn't console her. As she never took any exercise, she grew enormous, and she spent her days silently sitting on her bunk, occasionally wiping her eyes.

One day, Captain Salkeld came below to talk to Holt about his son's progress, and was amazed when he saw his wife's girth. Taking him aside, he said, 'Mr Holt, you never told me your wife was going to have a child. You must get a room in Cove for her.'

'Not I,' said Holt. 'What more natural than that she should have a child? If this old tub doesn't soon put to sea, she may well have another. Mrs Hobbs will see to her – she has attended six convict women already.'

The captain said, 'Take care how you call my ship an old tub. You aren't sailing in *Friendship* remember.' But he made some of his free passengers move temporarily into another cabin, leaving one vacant for Mrs Holt. It wasn't a moment too soon, as she produced a son the following morning at six o'clock.

This was July 17th, and Henry had been on board for five and a half months, Anne and the children for more than four. Henry, never a patient man, had reached a state of nervous agitation which he found hard to control. Two days after the birth, Holt asked him to baptise the child, but he snapped, 'I refuse to do anything of the kind while I am chained like an animal. It's not fitting. Get the captain to do it.'

Captain Salkeld's temper had improved radically during the months spent in Cork, as he had been courting a Miss Graham, and had married her shortly before. He came down to the cabin wearing a pair of white gloves and with his best cocked hat under his arm, and said to Henry, 'You have promised to stay on board; your door isn't locked. I will have your irons removed immediately, so that you may baptise Holt's boy.'

'And replaced afterwards?' Henry realised with annoyance that his voice wasn't quite steady.

'I think we can contrive to forget to replace them. We should sail within the month.'

'Another month,' groaned Henry.

The chief mate, a Mr Harrison, had become friendly with Holt, and the baby was named Joseph Harrison. When Henry took the baby in his arms, he could hardly say the prayers. He was free, free of fetters, and being treated like a responsible man who could be trusted to keep his word. He found his voice, and never was the christening service delivered with more passionate fervour.

While chained, Henry had refused to wear any but his convicts' issue of clothes, but now he wore the dark coat, breeches and stockings Anne had brought him, and clean linen bands at his throat. Harrison offered him a wig, but he declined it. He found that his feet had swelled so that he couldn't wear his black shoes with cut steel buckles, so his black silk stockings descended into his prison

219

issue of loose rawhide shoes which came in three sizes, large, larger and enormous.

Holt clapped him on the back with a heavy hand. 'Why, you are a well-favoured fellow when you are decently rigged out,' he said. 'I declare until now I couldn't see what your lady wife saw in you.'

A few more prisoners joined the ship on August 19th, and on the 24th, she sailed with the tide. Henry wasn't allowed to go on deck until she was some miles out to sea, he stayed below with Mrs Holt and the children. When he opened the door, he saw a marine outside, his hat jammed well down on his head above his pigtail, his scarlet jacket and white flannel waist-coat immaculate. He stood there woodenly, taking no notice of Henry, but there was no need to ask him why he was there.

Henry went back and pressed his face to the window, watching the low wooded hills recede.

For the first part of the journey, the convoy stuck together, the *Minerva* having to wait for the *Friendship*. Captain Salkeld was right to be proud of his ship, which could have sailed rings round the others. After three weeks, he signalled that he could not keep her back to the speed of the *Friendship* and that he was proceeding alone.

The nights were terrible for the Fultons and the Holts, who were as tightly packed as the convicts in their tiny cabin. Fortunately, the weather was good and no one was sick. Joseph Harrison Holt seemed likely to take after his father, having a loud voice and a hearty appetite; James still had his dry cough. The cabin door was opposite the place where the female prisoners were confined, and very noisy they were. Tears, songs, shrieks and laughter enlivened the nights.

In fact, the Fultons' cabin was part of the steerage, where the convicts lay, partitioned off by moveable bulkheads which would be discarded at the end of the voyage. As she went up on deck, Anne could see them through their iron bars, lying four to a bed; a 'bed' being a seven feet square platform made of planks. They were built in two tiers, with a walkway between.

'I cannot sleep for thinking of those poor wretches,' Anne said to Henry, as they stood at the rail. (Now that they were out of sight of land, Henry was allowed up on deck at stated hours, in daylight.)

Henry said, 'Listen, they're singing again. They didn't sing in Cork, or on that accursed hulk.'

'I don't know what they have to sing about here.'

'I do. I could sing with them.' Henry stared at the horizon and she watched the breeze whipping the growing hair about his face. 'They have something to look forward to at last,' he went on. 'This ship is a palace compared to the gaols I've been in. The convicts are allowed on deck without irons every day, and they have something in view other than a living death in the cells. You can't populate a country with criminals – there are free settlers there who will employ them. If these men and women behave, they may be pardoned and allowed to work for wages, or even granted land.'

Anne said, 'You speak as if we were free settlers ourselves. You almost persuade me that you expect a better life than in Ireland. Surely you will be pardoned in New Holland – even if only because of a shortage of priests.'

Henry didn't answer. He was afraid that his convictions would prevent him from ever following his profession again.

On the first of October under a blue sky, far out on the Atlantic, Henry and Anne watched the women washing the prisoners' clothes. Great tubs stood on deck, full of sea water, and the women scrubbed and laughed and splashed one another with water. The soap wouldn't lather, and the clothes, which were pegged on lines along the length of the ship, dried rough and salty. There was a light breeze from astern and the great sails creaked overhead. They were sailing easily to allow the other ships to catch up.

The look-out yelled from the cross-trees, and in seconds everything had changed. A Portuguese ship was overtaking them fast. Minutes later, the tubs were stowed, the women sent below and extra sails were going up as the washing came down. Henry kept out of the way and watched, fascinated. He saw the light guns run out by the marines, but they wouldn't be needed. *Minerva* was a flyer, as her captain had said. Henry was reminded of a good horse taking hold of his bit and settling into a gallop. The bubbling of water under the bows grew louder as the ship accelerated.

Twice, Henry saw a puff of smoke at the other ship's side, followed by the dull bang of a cannon, but the shot fell far short. Within half an hour, the Portuguese ship was out of sight. He wished that Anne shared his love of the sea, and went below for his dinner in a buoyant frame of mind.

There was plenty of salt pork and beef to eat, and often fresh fish, but little drinking water. They drank wine and porter instead. They settled into a routine, broken by the death of a prisoner, an innkeeper from Limerick who had been jailed at the same time as Henry. Henry took the burial service, and watched the body, properly sewn up in sailcloth, slide under the oily green swell. Captain Salkeld was particular about the treatment of prisoners, even dead ones. Other masters were less fussy, Henry had heard.

Later that month, Rio de Janeiro came into view. Henry strained his eyes, trying to see what the country was like. There were hills clothed with forests to the right and sandy beaches to the left, while a conical mountain guarded the bay.

Holt had been saying for some time how he meant to spend his time in Rio, so he was very cast down when he wasn't allowed ashore. The ship remained in the bay for more than a fornight, taking on fruit and perishable food. Henry and Holt found themselves in agreement for once as they leant on the rail, watching the sailors bartering the passengers' salt pork and flour for tobacco and rum. These could be sold in Sydney for an enormous profit.

'We sail at noon,' cried Henry, catching Anne round the waist as she arranged food on the table which led down from the wall and doubled as Henry's bed.

She turned a laughing face – 'Be careful. How many plates have you smashed since we left Cork?'

'I lost count long ago. Just think – we must beat back across the ocean to Africa, then we enter the Indian Ocean where we will see flying fish and it will be summer at Christmas.'

'Oh, dearest Henry, what an optimist you are. After all you have suffered, your mind is all on happy days ahead.'

'Why dwell on wretched days gone by? I achieved nothing that I intended in Ireland, perhaps I am destined to do better in the Antipodes. By all accounts there is much to be done. Justice, they say, is as wanting as ever it was at home. If only I am allowed a living . . . Listen! They are weighing anchor.' He dived through the door and was gone.

Back they sailed, across the South Atlantic, heading for the Cape

222

of Good Hope, the other transport and the convoy left far behind, the wind astern.

They were chased for five days by a Spanish frigate, but distanced her. Then two more Spanish ships began to close on the ship, and the decks were cleared for action. One of the ships fired a broadside, but missed, and the *Minerva* took to her heels again. Henry was most relieved, as Holt, who had been put in charge of a gun, had said he intended to surrender to the Spaniard because she was England's foe.

On Christmas Eve, the fresh breeze suddenly increased and veered, as the Fultons and Mrs Holt were at breakfast. Everything slid on to the floor, including poor Jane. It was impossible to clear up the mess, as the wind seemed to be coming from every quarter at once; hail rattled on the window and the wind screamed through the rigging.

Holt had gone to get the prisoners up on deck for exercise, but they were quickly hustled below again, and the hatches battened down on them. 'We're shipping water fast,' said Holt, coming in wearing a sacking cape. Water washed into the cabin after him. 'Say your prayers, Parson.'

'All in good time. I might be of some assistance on deck.' Henry went out, and was nearly washed overboard. The gallery at that point had been swept away. The jolly boat lay broken in two and each roll put the rail under water. Above the shouts of the sailors and the uproar of the sails and the protesting timbers, Henry could hear the screams of the prisoners under the hatches, where the water deepened every second. All were in irons except six women who had young babies, born since they embarked. Henry saw that there was nothing he could do, so he took Holt's advice and prayed.

Amazingly, the only casualty was a sailor with a broken leg. The wind steadied into a full gale dead astern and the ship tore along through squalls of hail and sleet. Christmas day was spent repairing the canvas, pumping and tidying up. The prisoners had to spend it below, but the hatches were propped open a few inches. Father Harold, a priest who had been arrested in Kildare, recovered from a bad bout of seasickness in time to say Mass, while Henry held a brief service for such of his flock as felt able to attend.

Day after day, the *Minerva* tore eastward, sailing sixteen hundred miles in a week, as the weather changed from winter to spring to tropical summer. Then the wind dropped as suddenly as it had risen, and Captain Salkeld fumed at the delay. His run had looked like breaking records.

Henry was impatient too – he was growing tired of sailing. The ship lay becalmed on translucent green water, and anyone who could swim did so. The children begged to swim too, so a sail was lowered over the side and allowed to fill with water for the children and non-swimmers to splash about in. Later, those prisoners who had given least trouble were allowed a dip. The next day they sighted land.

All convicts, including Henry, were kept below for that last lap, but they could smell vegetation and hear the cries of unfamiliar sea-birds. They changed direction, sailing along the coast of Australia, mile after featureless mile. Henry had no glass, so could see only a blur of shoreline from his window.

At last, the ship turned in towards the land, passing a small island which was the first part of the continent he saw close. Its main feature was a gibbet, on which hung the body of a man in chains.

Chapter Twenty-Five

Anne was on deck when the *Minerva* anchored in Sydney Cove, having found a place in the shade from which to watch. There was little in the scene to give any strong impression of her new homeland. White sand and ridges of rock, trembling in the heat . . . small boats crammed with people swarming round the ship . . . some cheering, and shouts for 'Letters!' . . . soldiers on the beach – a rough and ready lot by the look of them . . . No women among the few civilians coming and going around the landing place. She had expected something more dramatic.

Only the captain and an officer of marines left the ship that day. Next morning, when their door was unlocked, Henry was first at the head of the ladder, but was sharply prevented from leaving the ship – he had forgotten he was still a prisoner. Holt was having a noisy argument with a boatload of fishermen. Anne gathered that the convicts were about to be brought up, and the soldiers were afraid that they might commandeer some of the little boats and escape. They shouted at the rowers to keep back, but were ignored. At this, a soldier levelled his musket at a young man in the nearest boat and shot him dead.

Anne backed away from the rail, horrified at the murder, but nobody else seemed particularly concerned. The soldier was pinioned by two others and taken below, protesting, 'I did but do my duty.'

Some Australian soldiers were coming on board, hardly sparing a glance for the young man's corpse. Captain Johnston, commanding the New South Wales Corps, or the Botany Bay Rangers, to give them their more usual name, ordered the prisoners to be assembled in rows and their irons removed. Henry was stationed at the end of a row, a little apart. Captain Johnston checked names and occupations, and went ashore.

As soon as he had gone, a dozen soldiers and a crowd of men burned dark brown and wearing only trousers and leather hats, swarmed over the side, shouting and arguing. They barged past Anne who shrank into a corner, pushing Jane behind her. She would have gone below, but the hatches were down.

The heat was extraordinary. The sun was a brighter spot in a bright, white sky. The few marines who had travelled with them looked ready to swoon in their thick scarlet jackets and high collars. The Australian soldiers, whose uniform was shabby and haphazard, wore their jackets open.

Mr Harrison, chief mate, said to her, 'If you want a maidservant, you had better choose quickly, before all the strong ones are spoken for.'

Anne saw that the soldiers and other men were choosing from among the twenty-six female convicts as if they were at a cattle market. 'That one – no, not her, the one with red hair – I'll take her.' The man was shouting at the top of his voice. 'You, girl, speak English? Bloody Irish whores, why can't they talk a Christian language? Who talks English? You with the shaven head? You'll do.' The speaker was a bull-headed man with thick arms and three fingers of his right hand missing. He reeked of rum, but so did almost everyone.

Finding her voice, Anne said, 'I need a servant. I will take the red-haired girl.' The girl seemed to know more English than she pretended – she turned towards Anne who smiled, expecting some sign of relief or gratitude. She got a suspicious scowl. The girl remarked to her neighbour, in Irish, 'I'm going to be a parlourmaid, Hannah. Jesus, what'll I do at all?'

'Same as always, I daresay,' said the other, bored.

Henry was allowed to land with his family after the emigrants but before the other convicts. They were taken in a small boat some little way from the anchorage. On dry ground at last, ground which seemed to heave under her feet, Anne saw, not the expected town, but a scatter of buildings, only one of two stories, and beaten earth for streets. Here the whole population seemed to have gathered. An old man in naval dress uniform, plumed hat under his arm, hand on the pommel of his sword, was talking to the captain. His eye wandered over the convicts with a mixture of boredom and disgust, before he turned and went into the large house. Anne guessed he must be the governor, Captain Hunter.

James and Jane wilted in the January heat. They held hands in

226

silence until James spotted some thin black figures hovering on the edge of the crowd and eagerly pointed them out to Jane. 'Look, Janie – cannibals.' She looked, not understanding the word. All were naked and carried long spears.

When Henry joined them, his eyes bright with elation at having arrived safely, Anne told him about the girl, Caitlin. He surprised her by saying, 'She's a hardy one that – Croppy Cait they call her. She could have fended for herself, so young and handsome as she is. I would have chosen some poor creature no man wanted, to get her away from the work gangs.'

'A pity you did not tell me,' Anne snapped. 'If it turns out that we are entitled to a manservant to chop wood and draw water, I will leave it to you to choose some decrepit wreck for me.'

Then they realised they were arguing before they had well landed and begged one another's pardon. Henry took Anne's arm and led her towards the settlement, dominated by its stockaded prison. Nobody seemed to be taking any notice of them, so they put down their bundles in the scanty shade of a grey-green tree with ragged bark, sat on them and waited.

For the rest of that day of confusion and heat, they hung about, hoping to be told what to do. The girl Cait, shuffling sulkily in light shackles, was brought to them by a guard.

'Set her free,' Henry said sharply to the guard.

'She'll run away.'

The girl said something to the guard which made Anne blush, but Henry, who of course hadn't understood, said, 'I'll risk that. You won't run away, Cait, will you?'

'I will if you beat me.' Cait's English was slow and uncertain. The guard laughed, but he called a smith to strike out the rivets.

While they waited, he stared at Henry rudely, chewing a plug of tobacco. 'The governor doesn't know what to do with you,' he said. 'He's not over fond of Specials. You can't be put on the chain gangs and you can't be let free, so you'll be no use to anybody, just another mouth to feed.' He turned aside and spat.

Anne had never heard anyone speak disrespectfully to Henry, even on the ship. She longed to speak up for him, but really there was nothing she could say. Henry put a hand on her arm. 'Don't ruffle up, my dear,' he said. 'The governor is right. Think about it.'

★

Their first home in Australia hardly merited the title of 'house'. It was a shack, or hut, built of great baulks of wood with clay bricks between. It was thatched with reeds, and raised above ground level on blocks of timber, against snakes.

At first sight Anne didn't share Henry's delight in this dwelling. It was ideal for the sweltering heat of that day, but looked inadequate to protect from heavy rain or cold. It was partitioned in two with a wall which appeared to be made of bark.

The children, once they had overcome their shyness, took to Cait. She set about gathering firing, while they skirmished round collecting twigs and bits of bark. In the evening it became cooler; the sky was an amazing shade of violet and the setting sun shone on unfamiliar slender trees with silver bark. Animals and birds barked, chuckled or whooped. To Anne's eyes, everything in nature was almost as it should be but not quite. She leaned against a tree, watching Cait as she slouched about, her red hair swinging in a long rope, her apron full of kindling. There were angry red marks on her bare ankles and she had a black eye. Henry had gone in search of food.

Anne sat down and wrote to her mother. '. . . we have a charming Cottage here – close to the Sea – and I have been Fortunate in Managing to Engage a Maidservant – ' Not for anything would she have admitted that the cottage was a shanty and the maidservant a rebel prisoner. She found it hard to understand Henry's satisfaction with his situation.

'Eighteen months' imprisonment has taught me to count my blessings,' said Henry, 'and at last we have some privacy, and enough room to turn round.'

He had come up from the harbour with fish, fresh from the sea. They toasted them at a wood fire for their first meal ashore, and washed them down with milk. They were all ravenously hungry and very tired.

By the time they went to bed on straw mattresses laid on the floor, Anne was beginning to understand Henry's keen appreciation of small mercies. This hut smelt of woodsmoke and thatch, not of sweat and urine as their cabin had done, however hard she worked to keep it clean. The plank floor didn't heave; beyond the walls there was space and silence into which they could move at will; and above all they were alone. No boisterous smelly Mr Holt, belching and snoring within arms' length of them; no gloomy Mrs Holt, wincing whenever one of the children brushed against her skirts. During the voyage Anne had sometimes felt that if she let herself dwell on her loathing of life in that cabin she would rush up on deck and jump overboard, so she had gritted her teeth and shut her eyes to it. Now, cautiously letting herself believe that it was over, she felt a blissful relief. She put the children to sleep with Cait, and she and Henry made love for the first time in eighteen months – shyly at first, but Henry's hunger for her soon carried her away. She, who had always loved him a little less than he loved her, and who was nervous of conceiving in this inhospitable place and with her husband still a convict, found herself responding to him more eagerly than ever before. When she woke up next morning she felt at least a small share of his optimism.

She was going to need it all.

While Anne tried to make the hut into a home, and Cait did as little as possible and took orders from nobody, Henry looked about for work. He called on the Reverend Johnson, who had come out with the first fleet, and found him to be a stooped elderly man with fair hair streaked with white, ruled by his wife. Outside his house grew a row of orange trees, raised from pips he had collected in Rio on the way out. They were still the only ones in the colony.

Johnson pointed out that there was nothing to stop Henry holding services in private houses – if he could get anyone to go to them – as he had not been unfrocked. He was prevented only from taking services in church and from receiving payment.

'But you have no church yourself,' Henry said.

'I had one, but it was burned down. A new one will be built shortly.' Johnson had been in Sydney long enough to be quite touchy if he thought it was being criticised.

Henry exclaimed to Johnson when he saw prisoners setting off to work in heavy irons, and when he heard the distant but unmistakable sound of a man being flogged. 'Haven't they suffered enough? Isn't banishment for life sufficient punishment? I had heard that this country would reform criminals by giving them an incentive to improve their lot. As far as I can see, the poor wretches are still ruled by the lash.'

'They are, they are; it is indeed unfortunate. We must pray for them, and hope that true repentance will bring their misery to an end.' Johnson shook his head sadly.

'I should think,' retorted Henry, 'that bad food, overwork and beatings are like to end their misery, repentant or not.'

He returned angrily to the hut which two men were re-roofing, this time with wooden shingles. They were Englishmen, skilled workers, transported for theft many years before. They had served their time twice over, but had neither the means nor the inclination to go home. Their Cockney twang was infectious – Henry had to scold James for mimicking it.

June and July came, and with them winter. Anne was pregnant and for the first time was suffering from nausea and heartburn. Their diet of salt pork, charred fish and hard greyish bread upset her stomach; she was depressed and out of sorts.

One day, she declared that the hut was too stuffy to bear, and she and Henry went walking down to the cove. It was a silent, heavy day, and white mist hung over the sea. Henry sat on a rock, his mind going back to his flight from Nenagh, and the white mist which had helped him to escape. He wondered what was happening in Ireland now.

The fog crept in off the sea with an air of silent purpose which was uncanny. Anne felt it too and shivered although it was quite warm. Then the sky darkened, and sluggish drops of rain began to fall. 'We had better go home,' Henry said.

'It won't be much – it never seems to rain in this country,' said Anne. As she spoke, the clouds opened and rain sluiced straight down in a cataract, drenching them in a few seconds. They turned to run, but Anne's sodden skirts hampered her, and anyway it was impossible to be any wetter. Near the house, they saw Cait and the two children plunging through the wall of water which almost hid them, and soon they were all indoors and pleased to see that the new roof hardly leaked at all.

Anne dried James and changed his clothes before her own, as he hadn't lost his cough. He submitted with a fairly good grace but, when both his parents were getting out of their soaked garments and Cait was busy with Jane, he ran outside again. There were no more dry things, so Anne put him to bed with a scolding. As she tucked him in, mud began to dribble down the wall in half a dozen places. The bricks were made of common clay, and disintegrated fast. In a few hours, their neat house was no more than a shingled roof supported on wooden posts. The wind rose and it grew cold, and Henry insisted that Anne take James and ask the Johnsons for shelter for the night.

As a result, they were assigned a house built of real brick, but they had to live in their shed for several days. James's cough was worse, and Anne was bent double with backache.

They made no friends. The free settlers were kind to Anne in a patronising way but didn't want to know Henry; the prisoners were jealous of his partial freedom. The New South Wales Corps kept to themselves. Anyway, they had the habit, distressing to a minister, of using rum as currency to buy everything from groceries to women. The Reverend Johnson asked Henry to dine, but nobody followed his example.

Cait had become fond of Anne, never having been treated kindly in all her nineteen years. Guiltily, Anne talked Irish to her, learning all manner of things which startled, shocked or amused her. Both women doted on Jane, who was growing into a lovely child, almost unnaturally good.

The arrival of a ship was the most exciting event in the new colony. One sailed in from Ireland, and Anne got a letter from Hetty. Miss Eliza had died suddenly, in the middle of giving Lord Cornwallis a piece of her mind. Enclosed was a copy of the *Tipperary Vindicator*, which mentioned the death of Benjamin Tydd at sixty years old, also that of Father O'Meara's crony, Father White, a rebel priest from Cloughjordan.

In September, there were rumours of a fresh insurrection among the Irish convicts. About twenty men were suspected, on the information of another prisoner, anxious for government favours. Captain King was recalled from Norfolk Island, and made governor in place of old Captain Hunter, who made plans to go to England as soon as possible. He had seen more than enough of Australia.

Henry, drinking rum with Mr Johnson, found him as excited as a child. 'I go to England with the governor,' he said. 'I hope I can contrive to stay there. I will take all my possessions so that I may be independent.'

'Will Parson Marsden take your ministry? He will need a fast horse and will be for ever travelling.'

'No, no – impossible. I have suggested that you might take over the Hawkesbury district in my absence. Don't mention it anywhere – I ought not to discuss it with you – in fact I have been censured for inviting you to dine. But I think there are a lot of great rogues wearing the cloth, and see no reason why you should not preach.' Tactfully put, thought Henry, but he went home walking on air. Perhaps this was the start of his new life.

At this time, when one governor had left and another had just arrived, Parson Marsden as senior magistrate took it upon himself to crush the rebels.

His dubious informant said they had pikes, but nobody knew where. Marsden set about flogging information out of the suspects. As there were no pikes, his floggers laboured in vain, laying on as many as a thousand lashes in some cases. The surgeon, who had power to limit beatings, allowed some to be flogged to death. Suspicion fell on Henry, as a United man, and he was harshly questioned by Marsden. Henry, who had taken an instant dislike to the pudgy-faced tyrant, didn't trouble to try to ingratiate himself. Instead, he protested against the punishments being meted out, calling the parson an inhuman wretch. As Marsden dared not have him flogged without concrete evidence, he was obliged to let him go with a warning. Henry knew he had made a dangerous enemy and achieved nothing. Although no pikes were found, the floggings continued with as much ferocity as ever.

The Reverend Richard Johnson had gradually accepted a way of life which had been utterly repugnant to him when he came to the colony. A humane man, he had tried in vain to get the governor to forbid the shipping of old, infirm felons. The practice had been stopped, but only because it was uneconomic. Johnson had gone down among the sick, verminous prisoners, lying in irons between the decks of the infamous *Neptune*, where there was so little oxygen that a candle wouldn't burn. He had almost fainted, and had vomited when he reached the deck.

Twelve years later, he had given up trying to influence those in authority.

Johnson had not known what to make of Henry Fulton. The Reverend Marsden, known with good reason as the flogging parson, had warned Johnson not to be taken in by Fulton's obvious education, good manners and apparent rectitude. 'Shun him,' he had said. 'Firstly, he is from Ireland, home of Popery and all sorts of villainy, secondly, he has been found guilty of plotting to overthrow his most sovereign majesty King George, and thirdly, he has no respect for his betters and is without shame or penitence.' He glowered at Johnson, daring him to contradict.

Johnson, who liked Henry, had found himself in a tricky situation. He feared Marsden and his own wife about equally, and she too had warned him, so he approached the rebel parson's home with a feeling of guilty defiance. It was November 8th 1800 and he had gained permission from Governor King for Fulton to hold Divine Service at the Hawkesbury river as soon as he, Johnson, had gone to England. He had also got a half promise that Fulton, whose behaviour had so far been exemplary, would be granted a conditional emancipation. How delighted he would be – what a Christmas present! And he had been looking worried lately, his wife was soon to be confined and his son was unwell. Johnson knocked on the door, looking forward to seeing Fulton's face when he heard.

The door opened slowly. Henry Fulton stood there, his face white and drawn. His wife sat by the table in tears, while in the other room the convict servant howled like a dog. Johnson stepped back. 'I have come at a bad time – ' he said.

'Yes. Our son James died a few minutes ago. Convulsions. We had no time to call a physician. You had better come in.'

Johnson prayed briefly over the small body, made a few consoling remarks to Mrs Fulton and suggested that the burial should be as soon as possible. 'In this climate, it is inadvisable to wait.' He could, of course, understand the mother's grief, and those Irish girls were always wailing about something, but he found Fulton's evident despair hard to fathom. 'You are still young, and your wife is again with child,' he said bracingly. 'A great many infants die out here – they always have. I came today to tell you something which will cheer you – '

'It would be hard to cheer me today.' Fulton had gone to his wife who was holding their little girl in her arms. 'But for my blundering stupidity we would be in Ireland and James alive.'

'I'm sure you must regret your previous career. . . .' Johnson began awkwardly.

Fulton cut him short. 'I regret having been caught,' he said.

★

233

Anne walked with Henry to the graveyard in George Street. He had urged her to stay at home, but she angrily refused, so he had accepted Johnson's offer to read the prayers, leaving him free to accompany Anne. Her new baby was expected within a week. One of the Irish prisoners, John Flahavan, a Waterford carpenter, made a wooden box for a coffin, and he and Henry carried it, while Anne followed with Johnson. Cait stayed behind with Jane, who didn't seem to understand what had happened.

After the burial, Anne delayed at the graveside, while Henry erected a rough cross, made of two pieces of board. On it he had written, 'James Walker Fulton. Died 8/11/1800 a. 4yrs 7mths.' She watched him dry-eyed and he went to her and put his arm round her shoulders saying, 'Come home, my love. We will put up a proper headstone when we can.'

She looked up at him dully. 'Babies die. They always have and they always will.'

'What kind of talk is that? Come, it's time you were away from here.'

'That's what my mama said to me. She lost five of us. Parson Johnson said much the same.'

'We'll prove them wrong. Jane's as healthy as could be, and now that we are settled here, things will be easier.' He led her firmly back, noticing worriedly that her face was streaming with sweat. No tears. When they reached the house, she went in and lay down on their mattress.

'See if you can get some help. My labour is beginning.'

Cait sat with Anne while Henry went in search of a midwife. There were two in the colony and both were hopelessly drunk. He returned home with a Mrs Jones, a pickpocket, mother of twelve children. Cait had helped to deliver a convict girl's baby on board ship and was capable if rather rough. Neither woman was over fussy about hygiene.

At dawn Henry, who hadn't slept, left Jane in her cradle and went in search of a doctor. He had to wait until the hospital surgeon felt like getting up, and then he wished he had let him lie. This, he realised too late, was the man who was obliged to attend the floggings. The man who would feel the victim's pulse and say how many more blows he could stand.

He gave it as his opinion that the labour might continue for another day, but that a strong woman should be able to stand it. He asked for rum, accepted currency instead and left.

Twenty dreadful hours later, Anne had her second daughter, a big baby who showed signs of dying at once. Mrs Jones turned her upside down, slapped her and cursed her, while Cait called on the saints to preserve her. When they told Anne that the child was alive and put it to her breast, she was past caring.

Henry knelt beside her, whispering endearments under Mrs Jones's cold eye, trying to get her to take a little broth, but she turned her head away muttering, 'Babies die . . .'

The baby didn't die. Henry baptised her with water in a sugar bowl, Sarah Leland Fulton. Anne recovered slowly, and was still very weak ten days later when Henry burst open the door and rushed into the room, tripping over the mat.

'Great news! The best yet! I am conditionally pardoned!'

Anne couldn't share his excitement, try as she might. Too many disappointments had come her way. 'Why, so you should be,' she said. 'And what are the conditions?'

'I may not leave the colony. A conditional emancipation – think of it! and I am to preach at the Hawkesbury next month. I was never more delighted.'

Richard Johnson had left for England, so Samuel Marsden was the only free clergyman in the area. Henry disliked being answerable to the man who was known as the Christian Mahomet of Botany Bay. He disliked excessively having to ask him for the loan of a horse. But when he was in the large hall which served as a church, he felt so happy that he preached better than ever before to his sullen and unappreciative congregation.

'Never thought I'd see a convict in the cackle tub,' muttered one of them as Henry entered the pulpit.

After that, he took the service at one parish or another each Sunday.

Anne came to hear him on Christmas Day, pale, but much stronger. Parson Marsden preached while Henry read the service. Jane had started to talk at last, and when Marsden began to intone in his loud booming voice, she cried, 'Look, Mama, is that God?'

Muffled guffaws greeted this question, and Henry, caught unawares, gave a slight hiccup. Marsden glared balefully at him and, the following Sunday, sent him to a distant village and had no horse available to lend him.

On January 11th, just a year after Henry had landed, the governor set for him. 'Mr Fulton,' he said, 'I am sure you would like to be assigned to a parish where you would be in sole charge.'

Henry, who had not been asked to sit, replied, 'Indeed I would. Mr Marsden and I do not always agree, and I believe we would both prefer to be separated. I have heard I might be assigned to the Hawkesbury, but hardly dared hope the rumour was correct.'

'The Hawkesbury? No Mr Fulton, you go too fast. I am sending you to Norfolk Island, where you will be the first Anglican minister. A Mr Haddock was to come from England to take over, but he has not arrived.'

'Norfolk Island? The place where you yourself were governor? It has since gained a sorry reputation. For myself, I wouldn't mind, but I doubt if it's a suitable place to take my wife and little girls.'

The governor laughed shortly. 'I doubt if it is. Leave them behind.'

'Sir, I cannot. The baby is but two months old, and my wife has been unwell since the birth, which occurred only three days after the death of our son.'

Governor King rose to his feet. 'For a man only recently granted a conditional pardon, you are very particular. First your wife cannot go to Norfolk Island, then you cannot leave her behind. With her or without her, I order you to go.'

There was no more to be said. Henry went home and told Anne, hardly knowing whether he wanted her to say yes or no. A thousand- mile voyage to a place called a living hell – could she survive it? Would she survive in Sydney without friends? Supposing she were ill?

Anne said, 'Where you go, I go. We have been separated long enough.'

A month later, they embarked on HMS *Porpoise*.

Chapter Twenty-Six

The *Porpoise* was no flying East Indiaman, just a stoutly built vessel designed to stand rough weather and to carry heavy cargoes. No ship was especially designed to carry convicts – *Minerva* had been fitted with moveable bulkheads and special hatches. The *Porpoise* had a partitioned iron cage amidships, below her heaving decks.

Here, the hard cases which didn't quite merit hanging were chained up on their thousand-mile voyage to Norfolk Island.

The ship was so heavily loaded with supplies of flour, tea and sugar that she wallowed low in the water. Not many vessels went to 'Norfolk'. Goats, pigs, calves and sheep were penned on deck, leaving only enough room for the mariners to work the ropes. The prisoners were never freed from their double irons and manacles, far less allowed out of their enclosure. The hatches were propped open a couple of inches, and secured with chains, admitting little light and less air.

Henry and Anne shared a stateroom far larger than the cabin which had housed four adults and four children on the *Minerva*. There was a berth big enough for two, a cradle for baby Sarah and a small bunk for Jane. She, however, wanted a hammock, so Henry slung one for her. In this, the sea rocked her to sleep, and it pleased her more than any toy.

Henry was in a sombre mood. He had been finding it hard to forgive himself for landing his wife and children in Botany Bay – doubly so after James died. Ever since he had been ordered to Norfolk Island, he had been hearing horror stories about the conditions there, and the new governor, Major Fouveaux.

'There must be *something* there besides dangerous criminals,' Anne said. 'Mrs Cox told me that the scenery is considered very fine.'

Henry leaned on the rail, watching the fishing lines trailing from the stern. 'The island has giant pines and fields of flax, so they tell me,' he said. 'It was to have been a haven for boat building; the pines to make the masts, the flax to provide canvas for the sails. But I believe that neither firs nor flax proved suitable. Look' – he held out his hand – 'I have brought pips from Richard Johnson's orangery. Remember how he told us that he gathered them in Rio? We will grow oranges.'

'I intend to keep chickens,' said Anne, 'and perhaps a goat. I believe tainted meat had much to do with James's illness.' She paused, and continued more cheerfully, 'If we eat fresh eggs and drink milk, Jane will surely grow up healthy. I wish we had been allowed to bring Cait with us.'

On Sunday, Henry held a short service for the crew and passengers, and suggested to the captain that he should visit the convicts. The captain laughed until he had to mop away tears. 'What do you intend to say to them?' he asked. 'Don't you know that Norfolk is a dumping ground for the irredeemable?'

'Nobody is irredeemable,' said Henry mildly.

'No? You'll find different. Norfolk is hell on earth, and there's no redemption from hell.' He laughed again, a huge, ugly man, with a mouth so full of teeth that he couldn't shut it. 'I'll take you below if you like,' he said, 'but I'll warrant you won't ask me again.'

When Henry's eyes had become accustomed to the half light and his nostrils to the stench, he asked the captain to leave him. The bars reached to the ceiling, about seven feet, and men and a few women, chained hand and foot, crowded up to them to see him. He had to admit they looked a villainous lot until he remembered how he himself had looked after a long spell in prison.

Nobody spoke. He had to make the first move. 'Good day,' he began, and, thinking the day was the reverse of good for his audience, he hurried on. 'You will be glad to hear,' he said, 'that a Catholic priest has already gone to Norfolk Island – Father Harold, whom you probably know. . . .'

No response. He battled on. 'Before reading some prayers for our safe arrival, I would like to say. . .'

'Ah, go to hell,' said a loud, somehow familiar voice. 'I'll get you on Norfolk, I will, even if I swing for it, you rat.'

'You'll get the cat if you talk like that,' said another voice nervously. 'He don't mean it, sir.'

Henry peered in, trying to see the first man's face. He had no doubt that he did mean it. And if the man was loosed when he

238

reached land, it would be easy for him to carry out his threat. A face came thrusting through the others, one that he recognised. It was Jim Bohan, the man who had been planning to capture the *Princess* between Waterford and Cork. The man he and Father O'Meara had handed over to the authorities.

Fourteen days out, they anchored at a small island to take on fresh water. Then the ship resumed her lurching, rolling progress over the enormous swell. She was much smaller than *Minerva*, and the waves towered above her as if carved from green glass. Henry, who had never been seasick in his life, would have enjoyed the voyage if his thoughts hadn't been on the half-suffocated convicts below and on Anne and Jane. Dragged right round the world in his wake.

Then the wind dropped, and they were becalmed for three weeks, rocking gently on the everlasting swell, bored and hot and cross. Easter came, and he held services on deck and – against the captain's advice – below. The prisoners' resentment was less apparent now. Some were too ill to care, others grumbled apathetically. Afterwards, Henry tried hard to have the sick men freed from their fetters and brought up on deck, but he got the same reply as before. With so much livestock penned there, room could not be found for the sick.

Anne's depression had returned, and she spent hours lying in their cabin, while Jane followed Henry everywhere. She was a timid child, holding his hand as he walked about, and climbing on his knee when he sat down. Fond as he had been of naughty James, he doted on Jane, whose face was her mother's in miniature.

Six weeks after leaving Sydney, the look-out sighted land. It was an hour before it was visible from the deck – a startlingly beautiful mountain, rising from the frothing surf, its black and basalt cliffs crowned with tall pines and surrounded by coral reefs. There was no harbour, merely a passage through the rocks to a small beach. The sound of the thundering surf brought Anne up to look and exclaim at the craggy grandeur of the scenery. 'It is like one of the places in those novels Mama reads,' she said. 'And, see, those stone houses look better than ours in Sydney. I'm sure we will be happy here.'

'I'm sure we will,' Henry agreed, but his whole being was filled with foreboding. Although they were too far away to get more than a general impression, he felt cold and weak with dread and with the certainty that the worst was yet to come.

The ship anchored, and they waited for the tide to cover the sharpest of the rocks. Then a whaler, an ocean-going row-boat with a shallow draught and a broad beam, appeared heading for the reef. Pitching violently, she shot through the gap: at one moment, she was a yard clear of the sea, all her oars pointing upwards, then she crashed down and was through, toiling through the surf towards them.

Sailors brought her up beside the *Porpoise*, and called for the women and children to be handed down to the bosun, followed by their men. The only free woman on board was Anne, and hers were the only children. Her courage failed – not for herself but for them, and she screamed as she was put over the side. She tried to keep her balance in the whaler as Henry handed Sarah down, but he couldn't prise Jane's hands loose, and jumped with her, having had the forethought to take off his shoes.

The boat grounded in about two feet of tepid water, and Henry waded ashore with Anne in his arms and Jane astride his shoulders, while a sailor carried the baby.

Henry had expected a large island with a landscape similar to the mainland, and perhaps a small town set among pinewoods. He found a towering rock crowned with pines, no more than seven miles long by four miles wide. The band of marines who were assembled to take the convicts inland were brutalised types, men with a criminal record on the mainland. They were redcoats only in name, as most were stripped to the waist and looked like well-fed convicts. Major Fouveaux smiled broadly as he welcomed Henry and Anne, but it was a wolfish smile. Henry thought of some of the tales he had heard of this son of a French cook, and shuddered.

Anne had asked whether there would be children there, or any women other than the most hardened criminals. It seemed unlikely. But as soon as they landed, they saw scores of barefoot boys and girls, from about twelve years old down to crawling infants.

The sailors threw them pieces of sugar-cane, and they fought for it, screaming, kicking and biting: a memory stirred. A pack of small children fighting for the small change that fell out of Wolfe Tone's pockets as he turned cartwheels on the beach. Henry watched the children of Norfolk Island morosely. He tried not to think about Theo.

There was a missionary on the island who was presented to the Fultons, but he was almost too drunk to stand. He had come to see the rum landed – great casks of it which were taken away with an armed guard.

A tidily dressed young woman who looked sadly out of place introduced herself to Anne as Mrs Sherwin, wife of one of the soldiers. She took Anne by the arm and led her away from the beach to a place which had been cleared, and a stone house built on it. It was small but solid, with three rooms in a row, in the style of the cottages in Ireland. Like them, its roof was thatched, but with flax, not straw. 'The Vicarage,' she said, smiling. 'You are but a stone's throw from Government House and well removed from the prison.'

'Come in. My husband will be with us in a few minutes, I daresay.' Anne sat down, settling Sarah on her lap, looking forward to talking to another woman, even one who seemed to be extremely nervous about something. 'Perhaps you can tell me how to obtain a milking goat and a few hens – I have a little money. Won't you sit down?' she added.

Mrs Sherwin didn't seem to hear. She said hastily, glancing over her shoulder, 'Listen to me. Whatever you do, never vex Joseph Fouveaux. You are a thousand miles from the mainland and he holds you in the hollow of his hand. He censors every letter that leaves here, and he punishes people as he thinks fit – he hanged two Irishmen without trial a short time ago, and he thinks nothing of flogging prisoners to death. You will be outraged, and determined to stop him, but I warn you he is unstoppable. Warn your husband – watch your tongue!'

She had gone. Anne, who had tried to interrupt her more than once, saw her disappear among the stone huts.

The *Porpoise* took on no cargo, so she returned to Sydney two days later. She carried three men, all ironed together and scarred from repeated floggings. They had deliberately committed crimes so as to be sent to Sydney for trial, even at the risk of being hanged there. Fouveaux had experienced some mild criticism from Governor King after his summary execution of two Irishmen, and was afraid to repeat it.

The ship also carried mail to Sydney – after Major Fouveaux had read every letter. This time there were three written by the new ex-convict minister, one addressed to King, one to the clergyman who had taken his place and one to Bishop Knox in Ireland. Fouveaux read them through.

'. . . sickening cruelty to helpless prisoners . . . at least two hundred bastard children, running wild, without care or education . . . worse than a brothel, unfit for decent women . . . no draught animals, so men do the work of oxen until they drop . . . stone buildings erected by exhausted – ' Fouveaux swore. He would have to coach this new broom in the art of letter writing. He crumpled the sheets and threw them away.

Henry's congregation consisted of a few soldiers and their wives or mistresses. Convicts had given the last ounce of their strength to build the stone barn which served as a church when it rained. He read prayers and preached sermons and gave Communion to perhaps thirty. Fouveaux attended, as a matter of form, and grinned his toothy grin and enjoyed knowing he was hated. He sat where he could conveniently watch Mrs Sherwin's pretty face.

Outside, Father Harold said Mass to the convicts. It was said that only the intervention of a woman that Fouveaux fancied had saved the priest from being flogged.

Almost all the men and most of the women on the island drank steadily. Rum was their only solace, deadening their despair. The missionary, who drank more than most, advised Henry not to concern himself with the running of the island. 'You'll go crazy if you do,' he said, 'or turn into a sot like me.'

Stories of orgies at the governor's house reached Henry, so startling that he thought they must be exaggerated. A boat called with some women on board, and he discovered on his return from a sick man's house that they had been auctioned off at from £8 to £10 each to the soldiers. He went and hammered on Fouveaux's door and was turned away by the guards, both very drunk and waving guns. He went home: there was nothing else to do.

That day, he wrote a fresh batch of letters to the mainland. Major Fouveaux, who had told Henry how he liked letters to be phrased, sighed as he put them on the fire.

Henry had no outlet for his anger. Fouveaux laughed at him when he managed to bluff his way past the guards, and advised him not to meddle if he valued his freedom and his family's protection. Fuming, he walked among the pines on the cliff top, where a breeze from the sea relieved the scorching heat, and brilliantly coloured parrots flew shrieking through the wild jasmine which clothed the tree trunks. He thought how the island must have been when Captain Cook discovered its deserted shores, many years before. Now, men who called themselves civilised had turned it into a hell on earth; a graveyard of hope.

He returned to the cliffs often, but feared to leave Anne alone for long. One evening, as he returned home, she ran out to meet him, and her expression made him say, 'Is Jane all right?'

'Yes. She's making a garden of shells, and Sarah's asleep. Henry, a dreadful thing has happened, only you can help. Major Fouveaux has taken Nan Sherwin for himself.'

'The sergeant's wife? What do you mean? Has he abducted her? Impossible.'

'It isn't. A party of soldiers have taken her to Fouveaux's house. She was here with me. She had come to tell me that John – her husband, Sergeant Sherwin – had been gaoled for being drunk. We couldn't believe it, he drinks, of course, they all do, but no more than the next man. She had just said to me that it was a trumped-up charge, when somebody called her outside. I went to the door a minute later and saw the soldiers taking her away.'

Anne hid her face against Henry's chest as he put his arms round her. 'Take me away from this horrible, horrible place.'

'My darling, I can't. I'm a prisoner in everything but name, and I haven't been given my pay. Bribery is the only way to get favours, and I haven't enough to feed my family. Come indoors and tell me about Mrs Sherwin. How do you know where they were taking her? Did she resist?' He led her into the house and made her sit down.

'I ran after them. Oh, Henry, they said Major Fouveaux wanted her for his mistress and when I said you would prevent it, the man said – oh no, I can't repeat it. . . .'

'Don't. I don't want to hear their filthy talk from you.'

Anne said in a rush, 'He said, "Parson can't have her until the Major's done with her." And Mrs Sherwin told me to go home and forget about her. What are we going to do?'

Henry said slowly. 'I don't believe we can do anything, if Mrs

Sherwin put up no struggle. I will try to see her husband and find out whether or not his wife was already carrying on an intrigue with that insufferable man. If not, and if he wants her back, I will do what I can, but I have written to Governor King by both ships which touched here since we came and had no acknowledgment.'

He called to Jane, who was playing outside the open door, and she ran in laughing, carefully carrying an exquisite pink shell to show him. Obediently, he let her hold it to his ear and listened to the sea, although he could hear the real thing from where he sat, booming endlessly on the reefs. 'I dread the day when she is too old to stay with us all the time,' he said.

'That will be soon – she's three and a half after all. I am teaching her her letters already.' Anne stroked Jane's dark ringlets.

'A is for Australia, B is for boat, C is for convict,' said Jane proudly.

'And C is for cruelty and chains and corpse and curses – by heaven, Anne, she will learn a strange alphabet here.'

'Don't confuse the child.'

'Do you suppose she isn't confused already, poor infant? I wish I could start a school here – I might be a poor teacher, but I could fill the gap until they let Mr Hart out of gaol.' He gave the shell back to Jane. 'Off you go to the garden, Miss. I must go at once and try to see Sergeant Sherwin.'

The sergeant was in the guardroom, locked up but not ironed. He was an Englishman who had joined the New South Wales Corps, now popularly known as the 'Rum Corps', at the same time as Major Fouveaux himself. A corporal, who seemed to be much amused, let Henry in, and left them.

Henry handed over a small bottle of rum to Sherwin, who seemed startled to see him, although he was aware that Fouveaux had made off with his wife. He didn't sound too surprised. 'He's had his eye on her for weeks,' he said. 'Offered me money for her, then promotion. Now he has her and I have nothing. Was she taken against her will? Did she scream – struggle – call for me?'

'I believe she made no protest, except at the soldiers' rough treatment.' Henry looked in amazement at this man who discussed his wife's abduction so calmly. 'I have since spoken to one of the soldiers, and he said she had been told you would be flogged if she

244

objected. This is the most abominable thing I have encountered since I came here. I don't know how I may help you, but I will try. You want your wife back, I take it?'

There was a long pause. Sherwin, a stocky man in his thirties with a thatch of ginger hair, stood thinking and Henry didn't interrupt. Most of the soldiers were out, guarding the chain gangs, and the building was silent.

Sherwin spoke at last. 'She shouldn't 'a gone so quiet,' he said. 'I want her back, of course I do, but he'll keep her if he wants. No, I'd sooner lose my wife than my life, thank you, Parson. If I lose that, I lose her too. He'd have me killed for spite and who'd stop him?' He turned away, and Henry saw that he was crying.

Henry stayed with Sherwin until the corporal came back and asked him to go before the gangs returned from work. He was obliged to accept that there was no stopping Fouveaux. This very ordinary man, a year younger than Henry, invested with absolute power, had turned into a sadistic monster. If he chose to break every law of civilisation, he could, because officially the convicts had no legal rights. Rape was not rape if the victim was a convict; murder was not murder if it was a prisoner who was beaten to death.

Sherwin had had rights until he was charged. Now, if Fouveaux could find an informer, he must forfeit his possessions, which included his wife. And the island was full of informers – men who would send their comrades to the gallows for a twist of tobacco or a pint of rum.

Henry walked away from the military barracks and past the prison so deep in thought he didn't notice the chain gang until the leading men were beside him. It had rained heavily that day, as it often did, and they looked even more abjectly miserable than usual. Their harsh grey and yellow clothing with the broad arrows was sodden. The chains on their bare ankles chafed festering sores. Thousands of flies buzzed round their heads. Guards walked beside, behind and ahead of the column, carrying muskets, while the overseers carried whips.

He stood back as they shuffled by, their eyes on the ground. All but one. The sallow face was unmistakable – it didn't burn like the others – and so were the broken nose and long, cleft chin. Jim Bohan turned his head and looked at Henry with a face made wooden by implacable hatred.

★

245

As that wretched year dragged on, Henry worried that he was growing callous. He was deeply sympathetic to the sufferings of the convicts, but the frustrating knowledge that he could not help them made him shut his mind to their plight. He knew that Anne was terrified that, by angering Fouveaux, he might have his conditional emancipation revoked and become a prisoner himself. Although their house was a quarter of a mile from the prison, the whistle and thud of the lash was a background noise like the roar of the surf.

As for his ministry, he felt like a missionary among hostile barbarians. The mainly Catholic Irish prisoners wanted only their own priest. Deeply religious, they dreaded dying without a priest. They rated murder less serious than suicide, because murder could be confessed, suicide could not. The Protestants of the island had mostly become indifferent to the Church, tolerating Henry as a mere symbol of lost respectability.

Henry found a small white goat, little more than a kid, wandering on the cliffs, and took it home for Anne. She tethered it near the hutch where she kept her chickens. He engaged an old man, so old that he claimed to have forgotten what his crime was, to look after the garden in return for a few eggs. Anne's talent for home-making hadn't left her, but it was impossible to be happy. Henry's promised salary hadn't been paid, and he wrote again to Governor King.

Fouveaux removed those pages which might have spelled trouble for himself, and allowed the rest to go.

Late in November, when the baking heat was affecting everybody, Fouveaux sent for Henry. He sat smiling in his armchair – the same happy smile that he wore as he urged the floggers to strike harder. 'Mr Fulton, I wonder if you know that information has been laid against you.'

'Against me? By whom? And what am I supposed to have done?' Henry, sweating in his coat and neckcloth, sounded as indignant as he felt. In a corner, Nan Sherwin sat sewing, and had not been asked to leave.

'An Irish convict, name of Bohan, claims that you stole a goat, the property of an old woman, and gave it to your wife. I had him flogged for his impudence – a hundred lashes, but he persisted with his story. He said further that you had bribed an old man, name of McLean, to leave his employer and work for your wife. Also that you tried to bribe another convict to have him – Bohan – murdered.

Naturally, I had him flogged again, but to no avail. He says he has witnesses to all these charges.'

'I need hardly tell you they are untrue – ' Henry began, hotly.

'No, indeed. Although I can see a pretty white goat from my window, and an old man feeding chickens.' Fouveaux's smile widened. 'I wouldn't listen to a convict's information against a free settler or one of my soldiers, of course, but your position here is rather – delicate, shall I say? Your record will have to be blameless indeed if you are to receive your free pardon within the next ten years.' He leaned back, crossing his legs and beamed at Henry.

'What do you want?' Henry asked bluntly.

'That's more like it. A little consideration, a little discretion. I don't need informers to tell me that you tried to take Nancy here away from me – ' (Nan Sherwin blushed darkly), 'and you talk too much. Surely we understand each other.'

All thought of discretion gone, Henry shook his fist in Fouveaux's face. 'How dare you threaten me, sir! I will not be bribed or coerced by any man. You waste your time flogging Bohan, he is consumed with hatred for me and wishes me dead. Your morals are not, I am glad to say, my concern. Good day.' He turned on his heels and stormed out.

Nan Sherwin was the only person on earth who had the slightest control over Joseph Fouveaux. Henry never knew it, but he owed his continued freedom to her, and probably his life. Many a time, she came to the flogging triangles to plead for some poor victim, and Fouveaux often heeded her. He loved her, as much as he was capable of loving anyone, and also he was afraid that she might complain of his treatment of her husband to Governor King.

Henry went home, his temper cooling, wondering if he and Anne would have to spend the rest of their days on Norfolk Island.

Chapter Twenty-Seven

———◆—⟨·●·⟩—◆———

The children who formed such a high percentage of the population had a better life than the adults – all, that is, except the older girls who often had babies while they were still children themselves. The younger ones spent all their time at play, as did the boys.

They sunned themselves naked on the rocks, swam like ducklings, fished for red snapper and mullet, and collected huge, delicious crabs. They were as wild as hares, and when Henry found a party of them playing they made off as fast as they could.

Henry didn't follow. He baited some hooks and settled down to wait for his dinner. The small payment he had been given soon after he arrived hadn't been repeated, and he was determined not to ask Fouveaux for it. In the meantime, he eked out the produce of Anne's garden and chicken-house with fish.

His first missionary zeal, when he had wanted to educate every child on the island, had abated. They wouldn't keep still long enough to be educated. But he watched their games and saw with horror that they played at flogging and hanging one another. He couldn't accept the governor's view that little bastards, sired by soldiers on convict women, were born evil and certain to remain so. He tried to tame them, like wild animals, and so far had failed.

It was a hot day and the fish weren't biting. Henry stripped to his drawers and dived into the deep inlet where the water was cool and translucent. There were a few advantages in being sent to such a place – a British or Irish clergyman couldn't possibly risk the scandal of being seen by a parishioner without all his clothes on. He swam about idly, thinking of a cruelly cold day long ago in Co Galway, when he had been a newly ordained curate, and the parish clerk had called at the lodgings where he and Anne were living to ask if he would mind baptising four foundlings, all a month old or less. It had been left to Henry to choose both Christian and surnames for them. He had discussed it with Anne – who begged to keep one of the babies herself – and decided on Mary Snow, John Frost, Sarah Gale and Charles Winter. They would be about six years old now. . . .

His thoughts were interrupted by a pebble which splashed into the water a few inches from his nose. Looking up, he saw a fringe of brown faces round the place he had dived from. A boy stood there, wearing Henry's black clothes and hat, and pretending to pray, with downcast eyes and folded hands. He had no idea how fast Henry could run.

Henry walked quietly out of the ripples at the sand's edge, and limped up the slope as if he had trodden on a stone. Then, with a sudden bound, he was among the children and running after the boy who was hampered by his overlarge suit. Henry caught him, saying, 'You should be beaten for that,' but he was amused rather than angry. The boy's mimicry was good, and Henry had no illusions about himself.

'Tie him up and flog him.' 'Take him to the gaol and give him to the skinner.' The other children weren't quite joking. They waited out of reach to see what Henry would do.

Henry trapped the boy's head under his arm, and peeled his clothes off, then held him at arm's length. 'What is your name?' he asked.

'Jack,' muttered the child.

'Jack, I think you will make an actor. Do you know what a play is?'

'Yes.' Jack hung his head, still expecting a blow.

'I know some good stories,' Henry said, and as he spoke the children moved closer. 'I could tell them to you and you could act them when you were tired of fishing. Stories about pirates and battles – all sorts of things.' He pretended not to hear the comments of the older children, whose vocabulary was gleaned from the Rum Corps and the convicts. One thing at a time. He let the boy Jack go, and pulled on his trousers. The children backed away but didn't run. When his head emerged from his shirt, they had moved a little closer. He sat down on a rock, and started to tell them the most exciting story he could think of. The story of a young clergyman trying to escape from a company of cavalry on a dark night.

★

249

Most of the children were too wild to sit still and listen to stories, but about a dozen of the younger ones took to hanging about near Henry's house, and following him when he came out. Within a few weeks, he was alternating fairy-tales with bible stories; stirring tales like David and Goliath. They listened fascinated: the first and probably the last Sunday School on Norfolk Island.

Henry worried less about leaving Anne alone now that she had the old man, Charlie, working for her. He was tough and sinewy for all his years, and said he would split the skull of any intruder with his hoe. Perhaps he had split other skulls. Both Henry and Anne found that they didn't care if he had. 'Even if Charlie is a murderer, he is not half as wicked as Major Fouveaux,' said Anne. She had no maidservant, and was glad to be able to leave Jane in his care while she washed their clothes and cooked their meals of fish – always fish. Henry would pick fruit and berries in the woods, and the little savages, now known as 'Parson's Chickens', would tell him which were safe to eat.

The most amenable of them were starting to learn their catechism, and all could do simple sums.

Convicts were felling pines up on the cliffs. For this work, the guards were trebled, as the prisoners had their hands and feet free, being chained round the waist. By blowing themselves out, breath held, when they were being chained, some men had managed to keep the chains loose enough to wriggle out of. As they were using axes, all were kept within range of the soldiers' muskets. Their axes were taken from them whenever they weren't actually swinging them.

Henry, picking wild plums, had passed close to them. The guards laughed and argued and cursed the convicts, who worked, on pain of flogging, in total silence.

He sat down at the foot of a palm tree. Its top had been blown off, but it offered the shade of a thick trunk with a few fronds at the top. He was dozing when one of the large, noisy birds which abounded there flew up, clapping its wings and squawking. Henry woke startled, and in that second knew that he was in danger. He didn't see anyone – didn't need to – he could smell him. His reflexes had been permanently sharpened by his time on the run. He rolled over and sideways, throwing up an arm to protect his head.

Something grazed his ear, and a length of hoop-iron with an edge bright from polishing hissed past his shoulder and embedded itself in the root of the tree. By then he was on his feet, ready to defend himself, but his attacker had plunged into the undergrowth. Henry pulled the piece of iron out of the root and waited, listening. He heard a sudden uproar from the direction of the workers' camp, and a moment later a soldier appeared, running down the path. A gaggle of children were following, copying his bow-legged progress and shouting unheeded insults. The soldier paused when he saw Henry. 'If you see a convict loose, kill the bugger,' he said and ran on.

Henry looked at the makeshift knife in his hand and shuddered. He was beginning to accept some things which would have appalled him once, like leaving his beloved Jane in the care of a man who was probably a murderer, but he knew that he could not use this piece of hoop-iron on a prisoner, whatever the provocation. He turned and threw it, and watched the sun catch its edge as it arched through the air and fell into the sea, far out.

The cliff top curved just there, overhanging the black rock, veined in places with red. He saw a figure creeping, bent double, along a crevice, just below the edge. Someone else had seen him too; there were yells from the children who had been following the soldier. They began rolling large stones over the edge, but they bounced harmlessly. Henry ran, shouting, 'Stop. Leave him be.' The memory of being hunted was strong.

He was too late. As he rounded the bluff, he heard the bang of a musket. Two soldiers had gone to the lip of the cliff and were looking down. Henry looked too, and saw Jim Bohan's body, bright with blood, rising and falling on the tide. The children saw Henry's face and melted into the pines.

Henry walked home, feeling sick.

The anniversary of James's death passed, and three days later, Sarah's first birthday. She was a fractious child, whose system seemed not to have recovered from her difficult entry into the world. She was thin too, and Anne worried often about her health. Jane joined Henry's bible class, where the children were acting out simple stories with great verve; the more violent the better. They didn't fully accept Jane, although many of them were no older. Her long muslin skirts and her shoes set her apart. (There were no cobblers on the island. Charlie had made Jane's slippers from the skin of a young goat.)

At that time, there were about a thousand people on the island: two hundred children or more, about a hundred soldiers and government employees and the rest prisoners. Skilled labour was non-existent, and the convict's work, which had to punish as well as to achieve, was arduous, done badly and at a snail's pace. The digging of drains progressed slowly, and in hot weather the built-on area stank and was alive with rats.

No wonder that diseases like typhus, dysentery and diphtheria were common. There was no cure; the patient was given rest and rum if an adult, rest and lime-juice if a child. The children, 'Parson's Chickens', seemed to be proof against most maladies. Probably the weaker had died as infants.

It was a boiling day early in December when Jane complained of a sore throat and asked if she might stay in bed.

Henry didn't wait to see if she felt better later on. He took one look at her flushed face, and set off for the hospital, his long, loping stride eating up the ground.

William Redfern, assistant surgeon at the hospital, was a convict. An Ulsterman in his mid-twenties, he had had a hanging sentence transmuted to transportation. His crime was encouraging – some said leading – the mutineers at the British naval base at the Nore a few years earlier. He had come to Australia in chains, and had deep sympathy for the men and women in his care, but, of course, he had to do as he was told. Henry had met him twice since his arrival, and liked and admired him. At the hospital, he asked if he might take Redfern to his home.

'No,' said the overseer flatly. 'Take Hobson – he's a free man. Unless,' he added, 'you have a little something to spare.'

'I have no rum. When Dr Redfern has attended my child, I will send you milk and vegetables and a few eggs. I have nothing else.'

The overseer asked, 'Will you add a couple of fowl?'

'Yes, laying hens – anything, only let Redfern come at once.'

William Redfern looked red-eyed and haggard after a sleepless night. There was an outbreak of disease in the gaol. The prisoners had the 'yellows'. A helpful medicine existed, but there was none of it to hand. In fact, there was almost no medicine of any kind. Rum was used to revive the weak, to deaden the pain of the injured and to cheer the dying.

Henry hurried the doctor back to his house as fast as he could. 'We lost our son in a convulsion a year since,' he said. 'My poor wife is near demented with worry. I am myself.'

Doctor Redfern greeted Anne with a warm smile, and bent to lay his square, freckled hand on Jane's forehead. 'Open your mouth, my dear – that's right. She has fever and a putrid throat, ma'am. I cannot say how serious it may be. Some types are more dangerous than others. Keep her cool and give her as much clean water as she will drink. I'm sorry – I wish I had the means to do more for her.' He turned back the sheet and examined the child for a rash, but there was none. Her breathing was quick and light. Her eyes followed his hands anxiously. He replaced the sheet gently, and Henry saw the look in his eyes and put his arm round Anne, holding her tightly.

'What are you called, pet?' Redfern asked, propping Jane's head up while Anne held a mug of water for her.

'Jane Fulton.' The voice was clear but faint.

'Jane. Fancy – that's my favourite name. Well, Jane, you must lie still and try to drink two full beakers of water every day. You need not eat unless you want to.'

Jane's irresistible smile made him bite his lip. He doubted whether she had a chance. He bent down and lightly kissed her. Then he shook Anne's hand and left, carrying a sack of food for the overseer. Henry offered him one of his last coins for himself, but he refused it. 'I could do nothing,' he said, and spread his hands helplessly when Henry and Anne begged him for an opinion on Jane's chances.

Redfern was kept under lock and key at night, so Henry's frantic battering at the hospital doors was fruitless. It was past midnight, and he went to Doctor Hobson's house knowing what he would find. The door was open, and the doctor was snoring, face down on a dirty mattress. A woman snored beside him, and there was an empty gallon jug on the floor. Henry failed to rouse the doctor and ran home.

Jane died at four in the morning on the twelfth of December.

There was no shortage of convict labour for the digging of graves. A small party toiled sullenly in the sweltering heat. They felt that

Bohan would have been better left for the sharks. He had been a trouble-maker, and had repeatedly informed on his mates.

Not far away, Henry punished himself with the only means to hand, by digging Jane's grave himself. He broke the handle of his shoddy spade and went to find another. Convicts got twenty-five lashes for breaking a tool – sometimes more. He dug deep into the crumbly soil of the cemetery, high up on the island. A hibiscus grew beside the spot, and it was well away from the exposed side, where erosion sometimes uncovered bones.

Later, as he stood by the graveside, sweating in cassock and bands under the cruel sun, he could hardly speak for tears. He knew he had foreseen the moment long before, and the knowledge scared him.

Anne had nobody to support her but old Charlie, who took her home down the hill, Sarah wailing in her arms. When they were out of sight, Henry tore off his surplice, rolled up his sleeves and filled in the grave at furious speed. Father Harold, who had said a few prayers over Bohan, came over to speak to him, but, seeing his face, he murmured a platitude or two and went away.

As Henry straightened his back, and hurled away a second broken spade, he saw Nan Sherwin watching him, but, like the priest, she hurried away.

Henry put up a cross made of planks from a packing case with the words: Jane Fulton. d. 12/12/1801 a. 3 yrs 10 mths.

Chapter Twenty-Eight

———◆<•●•>◆———

'Have you caught some mullet? How lovely – my favourite.' Anne looked up from her task of making a shift for Sarah as Henry came stooping through the low door. When the last ship had left, in February 1804, she had exchanged two baskets of fresh vegetables from her garden for a length of white Indian cotton.

'We eat mullet five days a week and red snapper the other two.' Henry threw down the basket of fish he had caught and kissed the top of her head. 'You are a jewel,' he said. 'What other woman would have put up with as much? Do you know, I have never once heard you complain, except for others, in the whole three years we have been on this accursed island.'

'What good would complaining do?' Anne nipped off the thread and laid her sewing aside. 'If the governor had kept his word about a free pardon for you, and if you received the wage due to you, we wouldn't live badly.'

'If I hadn't angered that brute Marsden, we wouldn't be here at all, but you have never blamed me.' He drew a wickedly sharp cutlass from his belt and began to gut the fish, sitting cross-legged on the earth floor. 'Even in an outlying parish on the mainland, you would have a maid to help you and woman friends. And I could go to the governor and demand money. Shall I shell these peas for you when I've cleaned the fish?'

Anne pushed the basin of peas towards him. 'Yes please. Why should I need a maidservant? You leave little for me to do, bless you. We could be happy but for the sufferings of the prisoners under that – that Nero.' She lifted baby John out of his cradle and cuddled him to her. 'We have become used to the sights and sounds which used to shock us so. That frightens me. I don't want our children to grow up indifferent.'

Anne had been horrified when she discovered that she was pregnant again, but the birth of her fourth child had been an easy one. Dr Redfern, who had become friendly with Henry, had attended her, and shortly afterwards had received his free pardon. Since then, eight months ago, he had often spent the evening with them. He had a new house, but it was close to the hospital, and he was glad to get away from his assistant, ex-highwayman D'Arcy Wentworth, a womanising adventurer who was to become a pillar of Australian society.

Sarah was past four years old, and had outgrown her childish illnesses. Anne's fruit and vegetables, goat's milk, fresh chicken and eggs were keeping the family in good health. Even Henry had put on a little weight. Anne had grown plump, but it suited her. They lived in a contained world, insulated from the wars being waged in Europe. Napoleon Bonaparte – Nelson – Sir Arthur Wellesley – these were names of commanders on another planet fighting battles heard of six months after they had been won and lost. They heard nothing of Ireland except that it was being ruled from London – news which had made Henry groan.

Charlie still gardened, and sometimes minded the baby. There was no woman on the island that Anne would have cared to engage. The soldiers' wives did no work, and the convict women had all been sentenced a second time after reaching Sydney. Parson Marsden had dismissed them collectively as harlots, but prostitution was never punished by transportation and most of them had been convicted for thieving. They drank almost as heavily as their men. A small percentage were Irish rebels, but these were kept in the prison or at work. Major Fouveaux enjoyed having them punished. Occasionally they were stripped naked and flogged, more often their heads were shaved and they were put in irons for a while, day and night, in solitary confinement.

Both Henry and William Redfern had risked their chances of freedom and wasted their breath by complaining bitterly to Fouveaux about it. He was always present when a woman was beaten, deriving enormous pleasure from the sight.

Anne had asked Mrs Sherwin to find a woman to help her, but the other woman had laughed. 'Bless you, ma'am, I could send you a dozen, but you wouldn't thank me. As you treat a woman, so she becomes, and these have been treated like wild beasts.' (Mrs Sherwin's luckless husband had taken the first opportunity to leave the 'Rum Corps', and had gone to the mainland.)

Anne did nod really need a maid – she liked to keep busy – but life was monotonous and she remembered Cait with her long red hair and her proud, sulky manner, and wished she could have her back. She had grown fond of the girl, whatever her deficiencies as a maidservant, and would have liked the company of another woman.

The number of children on the island who knew their tables and their catechism was now substantial. 'Parson's Chickens' usually flew the nest at ten or so, but there was an endless supply of toddlers growing up to join them. Anne was uneasy when she saw Sarah with them – in fact she was afraid whenever the child was out of her sight, but she couldn't be kept in the small enclosure round their house indefinitely.

Around April of that year, the ship *Betsy* arrived at Norfolk, and anchored, not outside the reef near the settlement but at the other side of the island. From there she sent signals that there had been a rebellion on the mainland and that she carried dangerous criminals. The soldiers quickly put on their uniforms, armed themselves to the teeth and went down to the beach. Here, the prisoners were driven ashore through the surf, carrying the cargo of tea, sugar, wool and other necessities on their backs. As each man stepped on to dry land, workmen took his load from him and he was manacled and ironed before being taken to the prison.

Henry, who had been baiting eel-traps, watched from a rocky bluff a quarter of a mile away. He saw a man with a crate on his back lose his footing in the surf and fall. His head disappeared under the water, but nobody moved to take his load. Henry left his traps and dashed down the hill, as the man crept out of the sea on all fours. He spat out sea water and began to curse, loudly and fluently. A guard hit him in the mouth and dragged him away, but not before Henry had recognised Joseph Holt who had been their shipmate for so long. Holt had claimed that he was not a prisoner previously, but had been treated as a 'Special' rather than a free man.

Although he had never liked Holt, who had informed to save his skin and was arrogant and boastful, Henry was pleased to see any familiar face. He shouted to the soldiers who were hauling him up the beach and Holt turned his head and saw him, but his guards took no notice.

Henry followed them half way across the island to the gaol,

furious at being ignored. At the gaol gates, the master, Robert Jones, another highwayman whom the convicts called Bobby Buckey, told Henry to come back when the new prisoners were in and counted.

Henry turned away and went home. There was nothing else to do.

He had missed seeing the last prisoners landed. Some of them had to be carried, weak with dysentery, their backs a tangle of scars, their legs covered with ulcers. One of the last men to wade ashore unaided carried a woman on his back. She was young and strong, and even a shaven head didn't disguise her looks. When the man set her down, a soldier went to the guard in charge, and bought her for a gallon of rum.

The 'Castle Hill Rebellion' had been ill-managed and brief. Its outcome was what might have been expected – bodies hanging, rotting in chains; mass floggings and a boatload of Irish rebels for Norfolk Island. This boatload included some only suspected, like Joseph Holt, and many who had already been subjected to brutal punishments by the magistrates, led by Parson Marsden.

'Croppy Cait' had not been allowed to go to Norfolk with the Fultons, allegedly because there was no room on the boat for domestic servants, actually because a sergeant major in the Rum Corps had been waiting his chance to get her away from the parson's wife. He still had a problem when the ship had sailed. He was English, and had to abduct the Irish girl by force. Holt had seen him pursuing Cait with a gun, swearing that he would shoot her if she did not go with him.

He had kept the girl locked in his house for weeks, and had beaten her black and blue, but she had managed to escape and had been hiding out in the bush. There she met a man called Bourke who was a freed convict working for a settler. She had moved into his shack and had been more than eager to help when he told her of the plans for an uprising. Her only contribution had been to light a small fire to draw the attention of the guards, but she had been seen and was hunted down relentlessly. Even then, she might have escaped with a spell of hard labour, but she was unfortunate enough to be found by the sergeant major who was still suffering from the blow to his pride. Cait was sent to Norfolk Island on the good ship *Betsy*.

Bourke had been hanged, and Cait rode ashore on the shoulders of a blacksmith called Mick Fry who had promised to keep her safe. He got no chance to do so. Cait's feet had hardly touched the ground when she was seized by a soldier who might have doubled for the sergeant major. She screamed and fought all the way to his house, using all the English she had learned elsewhere.

She knew Parson Fulton had gone to Norfolk, and had noticed a long-legged man in ragged trousers who reminded her of him running up the path after a party of prisoners. Could that wild figure be Parson? As the soldier pulled her along, they were joined by a dozen wild, brown children who kept their distance, watching them.

On impulse, she yelled, 'Find Parson Fulton! Go on, you little bastards – get him! Tell him it's Croppy Cait.'

The children stopped, looked amazed and fled. The soldier, even more amazed, said 'Were you Parson's woman?' slightly loosening his hold on her. She spat full in his face, kicked him in the crotch and ran. She was too weary and footsore to run fast, but the soldier was in no state to follow. Half a mile down the track, she collided with Henry, overtaken near the gaol by the children, dashing back up the path to find her.

Later, when Anne was treating Cait's bruises with a brew made from herbs, the soldier arrived at the house, demanding a gallon of rum in exchange for the woman he had legally bought. Henry turned on him furiously. 'What kind of man are you? Are you not ashamed to come to your pastor's home with such a request? No, I can see you are not. Clear out before I throw you out, and never come back.'

Three years had hardened and coarsened Cait, but she did her best to behave and would have stolen and possibly killed in order to please Henry. She tried to moderate her barrack-room English for him, while Sarah learned Irish with the speed of a small child. Cait also taught Sarah rebel songs, and verses which they sang to the tunes of popular hymns. Anne reluctantly put a stop to this – she hated scolding Cait.

'You are still a convict, Cait. If you don't conform, you could be taken away to prison, where people are flogged for singing rebel songs.'

'Not women,' said Cait defiantly. 'They shave your hair, if you've any left, and give you a few weeks on the treadmill, that's all.'

'Major Fouveaux flogs women and humiliates them in horrible ways. If you must sing, learn some new songs.'

Soon Cait, not having enough work to keep her busy, began to help Charlie in the garden. Charlie resented this, and complained to Henry, who told him it was time he took life easier. Charlie muttered and bided his time. When handsome Mick Fry's good behaviour got him released from his irons and a job mending a gate in the governor's orchard, Cait was over the wall like a shot and Charlie went straight to Anne.

He waited for Cait to be dismissed, but she wasn't. Anne had been very much annoyed and had told Cait so in plain language, but she knew what dismissal would mean. She didn't mention the incident to Henry, but Charlie assumed that she had. Cait's manner towards Charlie, which had been scornful of his age and uselessness, now became truculent. 'Too old to do anything but inform – you're jealous of Mick,' she said.

There was a grain of truth in it. Charlie turned his back, and attacked the weeds viciously with his hoe. When one of the governor's guard went up the road, he left his work and hobbled over to talk to him. That night, Henry found Charlie lying uncon-scious on the doorstep. 'Cait,' he shouted. 'Here's Charlie dead drunk. Help me get him indoors. How on earth did he manage to pay for rum, I wonder.'

The next day was Sunday, and Henry preached as usual. There was a swampy area between the group of houses where both he and the Governor lived, and the other group which housed the soldiers and the convicts. He held his services in fine weather on the flat land between the swamp and sea.

The attention had grown, especially of children, and his sermons, which he kept short and simple, were popular. Anne had Sarah beside her and little John in her arms. This left Cait and Charlie free to attend Father Harold's Mass if they wished.

When they got home, there was no sign of Cait. Charlie was in bed, recovering from a hangover. They waited, then Anne prepared their Sunday dinner herself. Afterwards, Henry walked over to the barrack side of the swamp to see William Redfern, and noticed Joseph Holt shaking out his mattress in the prison compound. Holt, a strict Protestant, had not been at service, and he called out, 'Come and give me your blessing, Fulton.'

Mildly surprised – this was not Holt's form – Henry did as he was asked. Holt bent his head in acknowledgment, and said quietly, 'That rebel wench of yours is taken. Somebody saw her lying with a convict right under Fouveaux's windows. She's to be punished tomorrow – stupid bitch. Thought you'd like to know.'

Not waiting for an answer, he winked, picked up his mattress and went indoors.

Even Major Fouveaux usually hesitated before accepting information from criminals in their eighties unless there was a witness, so he felt obliged to try to flog a confession out of Mick Fry. But Mick was a blacksmith by trade, and skilled labour was at a premium – it wouldn't do to kill him. Mick escaped with fifty lashes, a mild punishment by the Major's standard, and confessed nothing, but Fouveaux didn't want to miss the opportunity of having a woman flogged.

As was his practice, he told Cait that her sentence of fifty lashes would be reduced to ten if she would strip naked. Cait, who had seen Mick's bloody back as he was taken back into the cells, was very glad to oblige, but screamed and swore when she found she was to be marched naked past all the male convicts. Her screams reached Henry who was trying to argue his way past the prison guards. Hearing them, he rushed forward, shouting 'Let her go!'

Cait was being tied to the triangle, while Fouveaux, a pistol in his hand, grinned in anticipation of his treat. When Henry appeared, he hesitated, but said, 'Mr Fulton, I beg you will confine yourself to your duties. I have had to mention it before. Will you go, or must I have you taken away?'

Henry, with a line of convicts between him and the triangle, knew he meant it, and that if he had to be forcibly removed by the soldiers, he would never get his pardon. He changed his tactics, saying, 'Major Fouveaux, that girl is my wife's servant. Any punishment she may merit is my wife's affair. Wait until she is dismissed from service before you touch her.'

Fouveaux turned purple with rage, but he knew he had gone too far. Anne Fulton was a free woman, and he was not entitled to punish her servant on the information of another of her servants.

261

Not, that is, unless she herself complained. 'I never intended to flog her,' he said, 'merely to frighten her a little. But I cannot have my convict labourers seduced from their work by any doxy. Take her down, men. And you, Parson, kindly go home unless you want Governor King to hear of your extraordinary interest in this woman.'

Henry knew this was bluster. He now had the whip hand of Fouveaux – or would have when he, Henry, was returned to the mainland. He walked away as he was told, but slowly, and Cait, in cloak and petticoat, frightened and furious, overtook him before he reached his house.

Major Fouveaux flogged no more women. He had already had trouble when one of his floggers refused this duty, and a soldier asked to take his place had barely flicked the prisoner's back with the cat. There were too many government officials about, and Redfern's pardon had made the Major nervous. Who knew what he might tell Governor King if he were returned to Sydney? He wondered if his floggers were getting soft. 'Pack of old mollies,' he muttered to himself.

About the month of August, a rumour reached Norfolk Island which spread excitement and happiness like the promise of a pardon. Major Fouveaux was recalled to Sydney, and would be departing on the next ship. Some said he was going to have to answer to Governor King for his methods, others that he was afraid of being murdered. William Redfern told Henry that neither was the case. Fouveaux suffered from asthma and was being allowed to go to London to set his affairs in order and receive treatment.

Henry knew that one of Anne's herbal remedies was a sovereign cure for asthma, but did not mention it.

September came, and with it a ship bound for England. Fouveaux was going on extended leave, so no new governor was appointed. Captain John Piper, a cheerful, inefficient man, saintly compared with Fouveaux, took over the running of the island.

The night Fouveaux left, every man, woman and child celebrated. Even his bullies of the Rum Corps were getting sated with cruelty. Soldiers and convicts alike sang, danced and drank themselves senseless. The next day, Piper freed a number of well-behaved prisoners who he felt could be trusted to work without the handicap of irons. These included Joseph Holt.

Henry hoped for a complete reform in the running of the settlement, but Piper hadn't the strength of character to achieve it. The Rum Corps were the true masters now, and they knew it. The French had scored a number of sea victories, and Piper allowed himself to be persuaded that, if the French fleet came to Norfolk – an unlikely event – all the Irish rebels would somehow kill their guards, rise and join them.

One hot November day, as Piper and D'Arcy Wentworth were talking together, they saw Holt running down the hill towards them, waving and shouting, 'Ships in sight! A dozen sail at least!'

Piper and Wentworth climbed Mount George as fast as they could, and sure enough fourteen ships were approaching. Piper looked to his junior officers and his Chief Constable for advice – service with Fouveaux had undermined his confidence.

Henry was showing Sarah how to plait rushes to make baskets when they heard a tremendous commotion in the direction of the gaol. At the same time, a sergeant came running to the barracks and breathlessly turned out the guard. Henry told Sarah to stay with her mother and went to investigate.

He found a scene of the utmost confusion. Soldiers were helping the prison guards to round up all the convicts and lock them up in gaol. 'What's afoot?' asked Henry. 'Has there been a break-out?'

A chorus of voices answered. 'The French! The French fleet is standing to off Cascade beach. We'll be attacked at first light.' The soldiers rushed here and there, demoralised without the brutal dictator they had obeyed for so long. It was getting dark, and Henry went home. He feared the drunken rampaging soldiers far more than any Frenchman, and knew that no boat would face the treacherous landing in the dark.

In the morning, all able-bodied men on the island, whether soldiers, emancipists or government employees, were at the shore. The island's two ancient and rusty guns were dragged out, and old men and children were told to gather rum bottles and smash them, so that the guns could be loaded with broken glass. Henry, refusing a suggestion that he might like to help, squinted at the group of ships. Certainly one was a French warship – a ship unlikely to be discouraged by a volley of rum bottles. The others appeared to be traders.

About ten in the morning, one of the ships lowered a boat which was rowed to land. The garrison shamefacedly greeted a dozen Chinese seamen, landing in search of fresh water for their convoy of trading ships, accompanied by the French frigate.

Some miles away, the prisoners trembled in the darkness, for all their windows were blocked up. All night, the soldiers had been piling brushwood against the walls. Some of the older convicts knew why. Major Fouveaux had left orders with his civilian staff that, if the French landed, the Irish rebels were to be burned alive in their prison and any who escaped were to be shot. The ships sailed away, the brushwood was removed and Holt told Henry about it. They went together to see Captain Piper, but he seemed genuinely to know nothing of Fouveaux's plan.

The next ship that arrived at the island carried the first mail from Ireland the Fultons had seen in three and a half years. Henry had heard nothing from his own family since his arrest – plainly they were at pains to forget he had ever been born. Anne's letter from Hetty contained a cutting:

> Died at sea: John Henry Fulton, passenger from Calcutta in the ship *Minerva*.

The notice was followed by a date in April and a short obituary. Henry read it in silence. He had admired his father for his advanced ideas, and had expected his support after his arrest. He felt they had never really known one another, but couldn't mourn his death. It was ironic that he had died on board the same East Indiaman which had carried his son to Botany Bay in chains.

Chapter Twenty-Nine

Christmas that year was Henry's happiest since leaving Ireland. His large congregation was made up of convicts and soldiers as well as a swarm of moderately clean children, dressed in light cotton garments mostly made by Anne or by Cait, who had shown unexpected talent with a needle.

The white heat of the sun, so fierce that it took the colour out of the scarlet blossoms on the trees and the gaudy parrots that perched in them, was tempered by a little breeze off the sea. Anne and Cait had made a tremendous dinner of roast fowl, potatoes and green vegetables, followed by a suet pudding stuffed full of dried fruit and drenched with rum. There was a syllabub for the children, who included such of 'Parson's Chickens' as had no homes to go to. Henry had tried and failed to get a dispensation for Joseph Holt, and had sent him a pair of fowl. The only adult guest was William Redfern, who arrived with a quart of rum as his contribution.

After the meal, Henry and Redfern sat in the shade under the trees, recovering. Redfern wasn't yet thirty years old, but he treated Henry, a parson and eight years older, as a contemporary. He tipped his straw hat over his eyes, and watched Henry from under the brim. Nobody was more cheerful than Mr Fulton, he thought, or better able to make the best of his circumstances. But about the clear hazel eyes and the sensitive mouth was an expression of great sadness.

Redfern said. 'Forgive me if I am inquisitive, but I often wonder how a man like you came to join the insurgent peasants in Ireland.'

Henry's quick temper flared. 'It occurs to me,' he said, 'that a man like you should not have joined the mutinous jack tars at the Nore.'

Redfern sat up. 'Mutinous jack tars? You must have no knowledge of the circumstances –'

'Exactly so,' said Henry. 'And neither have you. You come from

Ireland, but I suppose you left it too young to know of all the misrule and oppression of its unlucky people. I was at University, and had only a hazy notion myself until Wolfe Tone opened my eyes.'

'An audacious rascal, so I have heard, but perhaps I am wrong about him also. Tell me about him.' Redfern clasped his arms round his knees and listened as Henry described his meetings with Tone, his admiration for the principles of democracy and republicanism and his joining the Society of United Irishmen.

'Oddly enough,' he said, 'nobody since my arrest has asked me anything about my views, or why I followed the path I did.'

'I doubt if I would dare if I hadn't drunk so much rum at dinner,' said Redfern. 'Tell me then, you must have forsworn the Society when you were ordained, how did you become involved a second time?'

Henry stared out to sea for a minute before he answered. 'I was ordained into a remote parish – Aughrim, scene of a famous siege –'

'I have heard of it. In County Galway, is it not?'

'Yes, between Loughrea and Ballinasloe. Just a fortnight after my ordination, a friend of mine, Walter Burke, suggested we ride to the great fair of Ballinasloe, and offered to lend me a horse for, poor hungry curate that I was, I had none. Herds of cattle had passed bellowing along the road all night, horses tied head and tail and vast flocks of sheep. It would make a welcome change for me. We set off early in the morning, and dined at a truly terrible inn.

'I was choking down the last of my tough beef, fried with quantities of onions, when I heard a voice I knew, and who should it be but Theo – Wolfe Tone, that is. Burke had gone to buy cattle and I saw no more of him, so I spent the rest of the day with Theo, who was on his way to see the United men of Mayo. You call him an audacious rascal, and perhaps he was. So was Sir Francis Drake, so is Bonaparte. Tone was a visionary who never faltered and had the courage of his convictions. His bravery was extraordinary and so was his resource. He was convinced that he could persuade the French to invade Ireland, and he did. Backed by the Irish, they could have deposed the British. It might have been done. Nobody knows how nearly it was done.'

'Surely not. I thought the rising was a brief, bloody affair between Catholic and Protestant.'

'So it became. The French invaded the wrong corner of Ireland, too late to be of use. We who supported Tone were flung into an insurrection which couldn't succeed. I was fortunate to be arrested before the real butchery started, otherwise I would certainly have been hanged.

'That day in Ballinasloe, I agreed to keep a safe house for the passing of messages, and later I carried many myself, as well as recruiting for the Society and swearing in new members. But for my wife and family, I would have played an even more active part, but I was not designed by nature to lead men. I missed Tone's friendship and leadership equally when he took his own life – I still do. And nobody has taken his place in my life. I feel I have a vocation other than teaching the catechism in this spoiled Eden, but I need another Theo to lead me.'

Redfern said, 'Perhaps you should be converting the heathen.'

'I doubt it. One thing incarceration has taught me is to respect the privacy of others. If the heathen want conversion, I am here to baptise and instruct. If not, perhaps they are as good as I. Oh, William, I have eaten far too much. Have you a cure for the bloat?'

Redfern explained the properties of bicarbonate of soda at some length. When he had finished, he saw that Henry was sound asleep.

During the year that followed, Redfern had many a Sunday dinner at the Fultons' house. Following his pardon, Henry had been advised that his full pay of £96 a year would be sent to him, retrospective from the beginning of 1801. When no money arrived, he repeatedly wrote to Governor King and, when Fouveaux departed, his letters were no longer destroyed or censored.

King having received only one letter, but that a desperate plea, replied in surprise that the Colonial Agent had sent the money. Henry was fairly sure that Parson Marsden had intercepted it, but thought he'd better keep his suspicions to himself. He told Redfern, always a sympathetic listener. The surgeon was developing a brusque, rather didactic manner, probably because he worked with convicts who couldn't answer back. But he was clever and popular, seeming far older than he was.

As they walked up from the beach one day, he said abruptly, 'I notice that both your wife and your maidservant are with child.'

Henry laughed. 'You are observant. Yes, Anne expects our fifth some time in September, but Cait – are you sure?'

'Naturally I'm sure. And if I'm not mistaken, the two will be confined about the same time. Inconvenient.'

'I can see that my sermons and Anne's lectures have been wasted. However, the girl isn't a wanton, or if she is one could hardly judge her. Dear me. I suppose even on Norfolk Island a pregnant maid is out of place in a parson's household. I must talk to her.'

Cait had for some weeks been expecting a harangue, followed by instant dismissal. She trembled before her idol.

'Don't you think you ought to be married?' Henry asked her. 'Mick Fry is more than willing – I've been speaking to him. You would not be able to live together at present, but a wedding ring would be no harm, would it?' He watched Cait's face pass through fear and disbelief to joy.

'No harm? I have his mother's ring around my neck. What I'd give to wear it on my finger! You're a dote, Parson, that's what you are!' She sprang away to boast to Charlie.

'Anne,' said Henry later, 'while the two of you are fashioning tiny garments, do you think you could persuade Cait to behave a little more conventionally? As a married woman, we should promote her to housekeeper.'

'As a housekeeper, we should contrive to give her a wage. As long as she works for her keep, there isn't much I can say.'

Cait and Mick were married in August, and a month later, as William Redfern had predicted, the women gave birth within a week of each other. Redfern attended both births. Anne named her daughter Lydia Margaret, and Cait called her son William. Anne dissuaded her from choosing 'Henry' as a second name, so she chose Henry's other name, which was James.

Within two months, Mick Fry, to his great surprise, was given a conditional pardon. This was not for good behaviour, but because blacksmiths were so scarce on the mainland. A great number of Irish blacksmiths had been hanged for making pikeheads, and even in Ireland smiths were hard to find. Mick had made Henry a sort of miniature pike for spearing eels, which might have cost him his life if Fouveaux had seen it. Captain Piper admired its workmanship and agreed to send Mick back to Sydney on the next boat. Cait and the baby would go with him.

Another passenger for the boat was Joseph Holt, who was like a boy let out of school. He had long been free of his chains, and spent his time fishing or lazing in the sun. He would be going to an overseer's job, and was overjoyed to be returning to his wife.

'Hester was in great flesh when I left,' he said. 'I daresay she is worn to a thread by now.' He and Henry were sipping rum in the little porch newly built on to Henry's house.

'I'm delighted for you,' said Henry sincerely. 'And also for Mick Fry, although we will miss Cait sadly. I wonder if any other women travel.'

'I can tell you of one, if you can keep a secret.'

'Lower your voice if you have a secret,' said Henry laughing. 'It can be heard all over the house.'

'Is that so?' Holt continued in a hoarse whisper, 'you know Mary Ginders?'

'Yes,' said Henry grimly. 'A popular young lady in Fouveaux's day. She broke another woman's arm out of jealousy. Redfern, who set it, told me.'

'Ah, don't be hard on poor Mary. As you may know, she is a convict married to a freed man, William Ginders, and as you very likely don't know, the Chief Constable took her by force to be his woman and she must make the best of it. Well, Kimberley means to keep Mary, and so he's sending poor Ginders back to Sydney. Anyway, Mary is at this moment hiding near the anchorage and she is to be stowed away in a sack of cabbages. Not a word now.'

Holt's vice had risen steadily as he talked, but Henry judged that none of his household would be likely to tell the hated Chief Constable, Ted Kimberley.

When the ship was ready to sail, Henry and Anne went down to the beach to wave Cait goodbye, and saw soldiers swarming on to the decks armed with bayonets. 'They're looking for Mary Ginders,' said an old woman, doubled up with mirth. 'I'll lay they don't find her.'

The soldiers searched in vain, and finally the ship sailed, carrying William Ginders, Joseph Holt, Mick Fry, Cait with her baby and Mary Ginders, sewn up in a sack of cabbages.

Ships had been calling at Norfolk Island rather oftener of late, and it was no more than two months before another one arrived.

She carried a few prisoners, but was mainly loaded with supplies for the twelve hundred people on the island. They could grow almost anything there, but there were no factories – not even a mill or a plough. Everything was still done as inefficiently and slowly as possible, and there was no way of processing the raw materials. Sugar, flour and tea had often run low when the boats arrived, while the rum made on the island was a beverage which would strip paint.

Mrs Sherwin, who had not gone to London with Fouveaux, came up from the beach with a packet of letters, one of which was for Henry. He took it from her curiously. It was a large rectangular package, wrapped in oiled silk. Inside the wrapping was a parchment envelope, and inside that a sheet of vellum inscribed in copperplate and heavy with seals. His heart missed a beat or two as he read it. Then he gave a whoop which brought Anne and Sarah running, with John toddling behind. He threw his arms round Anne and whirled her round and round the room. 'I'm pardoned! I have a free pardon from the governor! My darling, I'm free!'

Sarah, like any Island child, knew the meaning of the words, and the three of them clung together, then collapsed on to the rickety couch which immediately fell over. They hugged and kissed and repeated the wonderful words over and over. Sarah spotted a sheet of writing paper which had fallen from the packet and tried to read it. 'King,' she said, picking out a word she recognised.

Henry read it through, and looked thoughtful. 'See,' he said to Anne. 'This letter is from that pharisee, Marsden. According to this, my pardon must be ratified by the Prince Regent in England before it becomes law. It is signed by Governor King, who in any case may not have complete power, as Captain Bligh was appointed in his place last May.'

'But Bligh is still in England, is he not? Anyway, you are free – it says so. You can go where you like.'

'Yes, and what is as good, we will be returned to the mainland and I will get a parish. The snag is that my commission won't be legal by English law until the Prince acts, so I could be superseded by a free settler. We will cross that bridge when we get to it. I may be worrying unnecessarily. . . . Put on your best dress, love, we'll have a party tonight'.

Henry free was much the same as Henry conditionally emancipated in their closed society. The main difference was that, in theory, he was free to leave Norfolk Island. Lacking transport, money and anywhere to go, he stayed where he was and awaited the next ship impatiently. He waited for four months.

The brig *Nancy* arrived in mid-April, with instructions for Reverend Henry Fulton and family to proceed to the mainland immediately. Parson Marsden was going to England to recruit missionaries to convert cannibals in New Zealand, and required Mr Fulton to take his place as acting chaplain in Sydney in his absence.

They had two days in which to get ready with the children, now aged five, two and five months. Old Charlie had died a few weeks earlier aged ninety. This was as well for him, as no passage would have been available and he would have had a miserable death alone.

Anne gave her goats (four of them) and her hens to Nan Sherwin, and asked William Redfern to distribute their vegetables to the convicts in the hospital. She had made a happy, comfortable home against all the odds, and wept when they left it.

They had a worse trip going out to the ship than they had had coming in, five years before. The whaler, leaping against the incoming waves, stood on her tail as she crossed the reef, deluging them with water. But Anne didn't scream or hesitate this time. Henry swarmed up the side of the ship and a sailor handed the children up in turn, then Anne stepped across, clutching the ropes, not daring to look down at the boiling surf.

The sea was rough all the way back to Sydney, but the wind was astern and the ship tore along, completing the thousand miles in thirteen days. She sailed up past Pinchgut Island, where a corpse had hung in chains on their first arrival, up the channel where small boats swarmed, and anchored at Sydney Cove. The passengers came ashore in a flotilla of little boats, and the Fultons saw that Sydney appeared to have more than doubled in size – had changed completely – they wouldn't have recognised it. But they had no trouble in recognising the two elaborately dressed figures approaching to welcome them. They were the governor, Lieutenant Philip Gidley King RN, and the Reverend Samuel Marsden.

When the Fultons had arrived at Sydney Cove in 1800, there had been few buildings, and those little more than huts. Instead of roads, there had been stretches of cleared land, fringed with tree stumps.

All was now levelled and built on, and long streets had appeared with large stone houses on either side. There were shops, offices and private houses. Fashionably dressed ladies strolled down to see the ship, accompanied by little girls in long dimity dresses and hats with ribbons, and little boys in nankeen trousers braced up to the armpits, and ruffled shirts. A few aborigines hung about, both sexes wearing cotton aprons. They carried containers of every shape and size. When they found that the ship had brought no rum, they slipped quietly away, discarding their aprons as they went.

Henry wore his black suit, now discoloured by weather, and neatly mended where it had been chewed by rats. He had long since lost his black hat, and found it again with a hen laying in it, so he had left it behind. His shirt was snowy; brand new, made from the same length of cotton as every garment the children wore. Anne's faded green dress had started life in Dublin ten years before.

Governor King, having greeted them in a kind if patronising manner, walked off to his residence. Relieved of his office but not yet replaced, he was marking time. When Captain Bligh took over, he would be leaving for England. Marsden went with Henry and Anne to show them their new home, or barrack, as it was called. It was a stone house with a wooden verandah and green shutters, facing the harbour. There was no garden.

Henry called on Marsden the next morning. He had to wait his turn for two hours, in a queue of wool-graders, dealers and graziers. When at last he faced Marsden across his cluttered desk, he felt the other man's enmity like something visible.

'I suppose you are looking for money,' said Marsden, without preamble. 'You had better make an appointment with my agent.'

Henry had almost forgotten the impotent rage which Marsden could arouse in him. He swallowed. 'My money can wait. It has waited for five years. No, I came to see you about another matter. When the *Nancy* brig arrived at Norfolk Island, there was no clergyman aboard to take my place. I am worried about the islanders – the children especially.'

'As far as the records go,' said Marsden, 'you were merely *in locum tenens*. The parson appointed by London was the Reverend Charles Haddock.'

'But that was years ago.'

'Precisely. There is a missionary on Norfolk – he must suffice.'

'Mr Marsden, the missionary abandoned his vocation long before I arrived. He keeps a small store and a convict mistress.'

'What a pity. Well, Mr Fulton, I mustn't detain you – '

Henry stood his ground. 'If a parson on Norfolk Island is not necessary, why did you send me there? When I went, you were the only clergyman in this whole colony. You yourself complained of overwork.'

Marsden's large, round face assumed an unpleasant smile. 'Why, Mr Fulton, you were but conditionally pardoned. I knew how uncomfortable you must feel here, in a position of authority, but unable to command respect or to be accepted in polite society.'

Henry turned white, and his whole body trembled. He controlled an urge to jump over the desk and strangle his superior. 'I think I should have been the judge of that,' he said, when he could speak. 'Do you mean to tell me that you sent me and my family to that hell, a hell where our little girl died, to save me from some imaginary social embarrassment? I don't believe you, sir. It must have been personal spite.'

'That is your opinion. Do not goad me, Mr Fulton. I have not your violent temper, but I have power. Restrain yourself.' Marsden surveyed Henry up and down offensively, taking in every detail of his threadbare dress, then he opened a ledger and began to write. 'My servant will show you out,' he said, without looking up.

Gripping the edge of the desk, Henry said, 'Before I go, you must listen to me.'

Marsden sighed and laid down his quill. 'Be brief, I beg.'

'I will. I am concerned for the children of Norfolk Island. They were learning to trust me and much besides – the younger ones, that is. The older children are beyond help. Girls of twelve and thirteen give birth in the bush. They have nobody to care for them. Dr Redfern is most sympathetic, but he has his hospital. . . .'

'What children? Not those of freed men, surely? Ah, I thought not. If you are talking about the bastards of felons and whores, what can you expect? Irish too, most of them.' Marsden picked up his quill again.

'I insist that you hear me out.' Henry had control of his voice now, and Marsden looked up impatiently. 'You, Mr Marsden, are a good farmer, I believe.' This was acknowledged with a slight nod.

273

'You wouldn't allow your lambs to interbreed and reproduce in their first year, and I am talking about human beings.'

'Your business is with their souls. Baptise, bury – marry, if they are co-habiting.'

'As to their souls,' said Henry, 'All the younger ones know the Lord's Prayer and the Creed, some have learned their catechism, all enjoy singing hymns. Are they to revert to the state I found them in?'

'Probably.' Samuel Marsden suddenly shouted, 'Robinson! Greene! Here!' And when two hefty labourers appeared, he said, 'Show this gentleman out. Goodbye, Mr Fulton.'

Chapter Thirty

Anne now found herself in a society unlike any she had known. New South Wales was still a young colony, thought of as a naval base rather than part of a continent, and accordingly governed by a naval commander. Shiploads of convicts still arrived from England and the old system of brutal punishments persisted.

A closely-knit female community had developed, determined to ignore everything that was not quite pleasant. Anne was introduced to women who were all trying to be as much like English middle-class ladies as possible. The emancipists' wives had little in common other than a mutual desire to forget any shady incidents in their husbands' pasts. They hungered for social equality with the wives of the free settlers, who looked down their noses at them.

Anne, although an ex-convict's wife, found herself accepted by some of the free settlers on account of Henry's profession. After five years on Norfolk Island, she was impatient of these niceties. She drank tea with ladies who were trying as hard as they could to be like Lady Prittie, Mrs Holmes and Mrs Otway back in Ireland. Anne found the talk of servants, the price of flour and the latest flirtations boring.

Mrs Marsden, next after the governor's wife in order of precedence, made a fuss of Anne. It was hard to say if she was genuine – Anne thought she was. A solidly built matron, she reminded Anne of her mother, and, like Mrs Walker, she had a strong contralto voice.

Over a cup of tea on Anne's verandah, she said, 'I am thinking of getting a choir together, my dear. I don't intend to go to London with my husband, and will need something to do. If I can find enough voices and a competent player on the forte piano, we might put on Handel's *Messiah* at Christmas.'

Memories of her mother's obsession rushed back to Anne. She set down her cup. Then, as if a stranger had taken over her voice, she cried, 'No, ma'am, not *The Messiah*! Not that – anything you like – anything but *The Messiah*! I cannot, cannot bear it!' She was shaking, and there were tears in her eyes. Making a tremendous effort, she apologised. 'I beg you pardon, I don't know what came over me.' Too late. Mrs Marsden, having no cold water handy, flung a glass of lemonade in her face.

'Sunstroke often brings on hysteria,' she said. 'You had better lie down.'

The choir, never popular, performed some choruses from Haydn's *Creation* instead.

Henry's chief worries were trying not to fall out with Mr Marsden, and to live on less than three pounds ten shillings a week. The two were directly connected, as he was certain that Marsden had appropriated his money. On Norfolk Island, the Fultons had lived on very little, because they were almost self-supporting; in Sydney, everything had to be bought at inflated prices. The assistant chaplain must not be seen going off with spear or fishing rod to catch his dinner, and in any case fish was called 'convict food', and heartily despised. The family might eat it, provided nobody was sharing the meal. A grim housekeeper had been provided for them – a pious elderly woman who lost no opportunity of mentioning that she had come to the colony free. Soon, she would have to be paid. The whole family urgently needed new clothes, and they had hardly any furniture.

Henry took Sunday services at Port Jackson and Parramatta, and at Sydney turn and turn about with Marsden. To get to Parramatta, sixteen miles away, he had to borrow a horse. Sometimes he went off to the Hawkesbury district, returning the following day. His boots wore out, and he couldn't buy more. He went to see Marsden again.

Henry was determined to be polite, quiet and restrained, but as usual, he failed, and presently demanded, 'Where is the £140 due to me since my arrival? You say the balance was sent to Norfolk Island, I never saw it. I am asking for what is due to me since my return. Do you want to see your assistant and his family hungry and in rags? Why must I beg for my rightful wage?'

'Surely you exaggerate.' Marsden's voice was as smooth as soap. 'I have nothing that is yours, but, out of good nature, I will pay in

276

kind. You shall have a horse worth £70 to ride to Parramatta each Sunday, and the balance in sheep, let me see . . . about ten wethers. These I will keep for you and give you what they fetch when they are fat. You might even find you had gained on the deal.'

'I am entitled to the use of a horse free when I have to ride to distant parishes. I am in no case to buy one. As for the sheep, I am obliged to you, but they won't feed my family.'

'Please don't raise your voice to me, Mr Fulton.' Marsden stared straight at Henry with small, red-rimmed eyes. 'I am told that you fed your family wonderfully well on Norfolk Island. Even when the maize failed, your children never wanted for anything. Perhaps you would like to return there, especially as you are so worried about the souls of the islanders. I'm sure I could arrange it.'

'I'll take the horse,' said Henry, violently.

'Somehow I thought you would. Good day, Mr Fulton.'

The horse was an ancient white mare, which took almost as long to reach Parramatta as Henry would have done on foot. Having been brought up to good horses, he detested riding an animal which was worn out. The price of £70 was ten times its value. If he had been single he would have considered returning to Norfolk, but he was determined not to take Anne back there. Neither would he leave her behind. He jolted about on his antique mount, his brains poached by the heat, wondering what to do next.

By August, he was borrowing money at a high rate of interest. His family was clothed and fed, the housekeeper paid, and Henry was able to appear in a new suit of clothes when the *Porpoise* arrived, carrying Captain Bligh.

Ex-Governor King, whose departure had been postponed because he was in poor health, was there to greet Bligh, along with some civic officials. Marsden, bland as ever, his hands folded on his stomach, said, 'I trust, Fulton, that you will not start begging favours from our new governor before he is well off the boat. I felt it my duty to warn him of what he might expect.'

'Samuel dear,' said his wife at his elbow. With these two words, she silenced him.

The ship's boat was rowed ashore to the sound of fife and drum. This regimental band of the New South Wales Corps was popularly known as the 'fife and rum band', as most of its members were likely to be drunk. The music was played with more regard for

277

volume than correctness, the banging of the drums echoing in uneven rhythm across the harbour.

The man in the stern wasn't wearing nearly as much gold lace and braid as King, although he had put on a powdered wig for the occasion. His shoulders were broad in his dark blue uniform. The first words Henry heard him say were addressed to a lieutenant who was probably trying to help him off the boat. 'Damn your blood, Mr Floyd sir! Out of my way!'

'Just what this colony needs,' murmured Marsden with satisfaction.

Bligh's reputation as a stormy petrel had preceded him. First there had been the mutiny at the Nore, where William Redfern had been involved. True, when the rebels were told that the officers to whom they objected would be removed from their ships, nobody demanded the removal of Bligh – this when more than a hundred officers were taken off. In fact, Bligh himself had been chosen to act as intermediary by the Admiralty. Still, a small doubt hung over all the commanders at the Nore. Later, Bligh had done well at the battle of Camperdown, helping to defeat the Dutch flagship, and being decorated. Lord Nelson thought highly of him and praised his resource and courage at another famous battle, Copenhagen.

Next, he was sent on HMS *Bounty* to carry breadfruit plants from Tahiti to the West Indies, where a British colony was being established, and was catapulted into the headlines. Some said he was a brutal captain, others that the crew didn't want to leave their lovely Tahiti girls. They had spent six idyllic months on the beautiful island, and many considered themselves married. Whatever the reason, most of the men mutinied and Bligh and eighteen loyal members of his crew were turned adrift in an open boat. In this, they sailed 3,618 miles to Timor, in the Dutch East Indies – an unparalleled feat of seamanship.

Afterwards, some of the *Bounty* mutineers were court-martialled in London. Unfortunately for Bligh, he was at sea when the trial came up, so was unable to defend himself against the accusations of their supporters. He returned to find that his name had been blackened, and there was nothing he could then do about it.

He must have been unique among sea captains in having been called to order by the Admiralty for bad language. 'Calling a ship's officer "rascal" and "scoundrel" and shaking his fist in his face'. The cloud over Bligh's name deepened when the court decided that Bligh be 'reprimanded, and admonished in future to be more correct in his language'.

Bligh seemed the ideal man to sort out the problems of an infant colony; to deal with the drunkenness and corruption of the Australian soldiers. He would punish the convicts harshly but fairly, and he would obey orders from London implicitly. He could swear all he liked in Australia, thought their lordships in the Admiralty as they confirmed the appointment.

Every third Sunday, Henry went to preach in the Hawkesbury district, all of thirty miles from Sydney. There he used to stay overnight with Mr and Mrs Wright, free settlers who owned a large tract of land.

He went there shortly after Bligh's arrival, and before they had met, except for a formal introduction. Bligh had been meeting the society of Sydney and attending a succession of dull parties which he endured politely. He was accompanied by his daughter Mary and her husband Lieutenant Putland. Mrs Bligh had a horror of the sea and had remained in England with her other five daughters.

The new governor visited his chaplain's house on Saturday. Greatly to Samuel Marsden's annoyance, Bligh, bored and on his best behaviour, was captivated by the assistant chaplain's wife. Mrs Fulton, forty, small and decidedly stout, had such a sweet expression, such a happy nature. . . . He noticed her deeply curved mouth with its dimpled corners and had to transfer his thoughts quickly to Betsy at home in Devon. He remembered being introduced to Fulton, who seemed to be annoyed with Marsden at the time. An emancipist but obviously a gentleman, thought Bligh.

'Your husband is not here tonight. Not ill, I trust.'

'No, sir. He preaches at the Hawkesbury, and his horse is so slow that he has to stay overnight. He will be home on Monday.'

Bligh talked to Anne until Mrs Marsden removed him, and decided to attend Divine Service at the Hawkesbury the following day. This upset Mr Marsden who had prepared a suitably fawning sermon. Bligh, who always rose at dawn, was on the road at six o'clock, with a clutch of yawning soldiers, all with hangovers. Bligh, a ham-fisted but effective horseman, rode as if pursued by devils, but not fast enough. He reached the large barn which was used as a church as Henry gave the blessing.

Henry paused, his hand raised, as the new governor burst into the building, flanked by officers each a head taller than he and muttering, 'Late, devil take it.' Bligh's precipitate behaviour put everyone out, even the Wrights. Mrs Wright was honoured beyond words by the new governor's presence at the table, and fortunately he seemed to like boiled mutton, but what she could have done given warning. . . .

After the meal, Bligh instructed Henry to fetch his horse and ride back with him. Henry shouted to a servant who went away and returned with a sunken-eyed, hollow-backed white animal, over at the knees and with every rib showing.

Bligh exploded. 'You!' He roared at the nearest soldier. 'Give the parson your horse. On the double there, damn your eyes, you rum-guzzling villain.'

This was an exact description of Private Brown, and he handed his horse over without any sign of offence.

'What do I do with this, sir?' pointing to the mare.

'Shoot it.'

Henry intervened. 'No, don't do that. She's not much, but she's the only one I have. I can't walk out here.'

'Buy another, man. Keep that fellow's trooper until you find something suitable. Come along – can't hang about all day.' He kicked his horse in the ribs and trotted down the track. 'How long have you been in the colony?' Bligh hardly knew this lean-faced parson, but felt they might have something in common. A pity they could not talk about ships or the sea.

'Six and a half years, sir. Five of them on Norfolk Island.'

'What ship brought you from Ireland, Mr Fulton?'

'*Minerva*, sir. A ship of 558 tons, built in Bombay. She is owned by a Mr Charnock, and is usually chartered by the East India Bay Company. But for my circumstances, and for the poor souls in the prison, it would have been a great voyage.' Noticing Bligh's keenly interested expression, Henry continued, 'She logged 6,433 miles in thirty-three days, running down her easting, so Captain Salkeld told me.'

'By Christ, Mr Fulton, you are a strange parson – beg pardon, forgot myself – did you ever consider the sea as a career?'

'Indeed I did, sir, and I have travelled to India on my father's business on just such a ship as *Minerva*. I came late to the church.' Henry reined in his horse as they crossed a boggy place. 'My wife and I sailed to Norfolk Island in the ship that brought you here, and we returned on the *Nancy*, but neither compared with *Minerva*.'

'Of course not. *Nancy* is but a leaky old brig, and *Porpoise* is too wide for her length. An unhandy bitch is *Porpoise* – beg pardon . . .'

Henry and Anne now became regular visitors at Government House. Anne and Mrs Putland became friends, while Henry's admiration for Bligh was unbounded. Bligh managed to curb his tongue in front of Anne, and Henry had heard so much filthy language since his arrest that he hardly noticed it any more. In any case, Bligh's notorious swearing was confined to damning and blasting the eyes, blood and souls of those who annoyed him. By Botany Bay standards, this didn't count as swearing at all.

Henry became desperate for money as his social life demanded more spending. He was determined not to mention his problem to Bligh, who would only pass it on to Marsden. Marsden, still about, waiting for a ship, continued to turn off all his requests with threats to send him back to Norfolk Island.

At last, Henry wrote to Bishop Knox in Ireland. He told how he had started with five shillings a day, and how Marsden had refused him money, fobbing him off with a foundered horse. He explained that he had no commission as assistant chaplain, and that if Marsden chose, he could bring someone to supersede him, and send Henry back to Norfolk Island. He sent the letter with little expectation of a reply, and it didn't reach Knox, who had been promoted and was now Bishop of Derry, for ten months. When it did, Knox wrote to the Archbishop of Canterbury.

The Archbishop agreed to Henry's request for a commission and wrote to Lord Castlereagh, who passed on the message to Bligh. By then, another administration was in force and Henry had to wait until 1811 for his commission – five years.

William Bligh was autocratic, quick-tempered and a philistine. He was just, courageous and conscientious. He was well-informed, dogmatic and intolerant. Like most mortals, he was a mixture, but Bligh's ingredients were more diverse and explosive than most.

People saw in him what they wanted to see. To Henry Fulton, he was almost a hero.

Just as Henry had felt that Wolfe Tone would be the saving of Ireland, he was sure that Bligh would be the saving of Australia. The important difference was that Bligh could operate legally. He could hardly have been less like Tone, but Henry was often reminded by Bligh of his spoiled friendship with Ned Fitzmaurice. As a newly emancipated assistant chaplain, he didn't expect the governor's friendship – he didn't want it. He wanted somebody to respect.

Bligh had plenty to do. His instructions from London had been specific; he was to abolish harmful monopolies, and to limit the use of rum for trading.

Straight away, Bligh found he was up against men who had more power than Governor King, notably the rich settler John Macarthur. Macarthur had a monopoly in the meat trade, which brought him vast profits, and he was a clever, ruthless man. Previous rulers had preferred to let sleeping dogs lie. Bligh believed the best thing for a sleeping dog was a shrewd kick. He accused Macarthur of extortion, and made a dangerous enemy.

The meat monopoly was as nothing to the abuses in the rum trade. This was in the hands of the 'Rum Corps', who sold at huge prices to anyone who would pledge property or land in payment. Rum being as important as bread to a vast majority, this trade was a too valuable to be given up lightly. Bligh waded in, determined to stop profiteering and exploitation, regardless of the toes he was treading on.

Bligh wrote:

A sawyer will cut one hundred feet of timber for a bottle of spirits – value two shillings and sixpence – which he drinks in a few hours; when for the same labour he would charge two bushels of wheat, which would furnish bread for two months. Hence, those who have got no liquor to pay their labourers, are ruined by paying more than they can possibly afford for labour. A settler has been known to give an acre of wheat for two gallons of spirits, which (wheat) would maintain him for a year.

Before the year was over, Bligh had prohibited the exchange of rum for any commodity whatsoever, under threat of heavy penalties.

Henry and Anne met all the most powerful settlers at Bligh's table, as well as senior officers in the 'Rum Corps'. It was easy to see that Bligh's reforms were making him exceedingly unpopular, but impossible to tell him so. Only Mary Putland dared to do that.

'Papa dearest,' she said, 'those men hate you, Mr Macarthur especially. Should you not be more circumspect?'

'Circumspect? What woman's nonsense is this? I am here to make reforms, I am making them. You are a reformer, Mr Fulton, do you not agree?'

'I agree in principle, but – '

'You see, Mary, Mr Fulton agrees. I want to hear no more about the matter.'

As the year 1807 passed, the rumblings of mutiny in the colony were audible to everyone except Bligh, and of course the society ladies who closed their ears to them. Anne was reminded of Lady Prittie in Ireland, valiantly chatting to her dinner guests as if there had been no shots outside the window, and insisting that the coming rebellion was a storm in a teacup.

One day Anne, who was pregnant and uncomfortably over-weight, was sketching a group of aborigines with Sophie Tomson, a foolish, pretty woman with a real talent for drawing.

'My husband thinks there is a danger that the army will rise against the governor,' said Anne, sharpening pencils.

'Oh, Mrs Fulton, what an idea.' Mrs Tomson firmly changed the subject. 'These dark hunters make a truly romantic subject do they not? Let us leave politics to the men, shall we?'

Irritated, Anne said no more. Mrs Tomson insisted on the idea of the 'noble savage'. An aborigine, accompanied by a woman suckling her baby, was 'a child of nature, and his dusky mate, nourishing her offspring from nature's fount'. Mrs Tomson was ignorant of nature.

They worked in silence, and their subjects lazed in the sun. They liked being drawn, and would crowd round, exclaiming at the results. Mrs Tomson said suddenly, 'I wonder if they have souls.'

'Of course they have. Why not?'

'You may be right. Mrs Marsden says she would be more inclined to believe they had souls if they knew the use of a pocket handkerchief.'

Anne laughed. 'They haven't any pockets.'

'No. Such a pity. One has to draw them from the rear.' Mrs Tomson was carefully cross-hatching a black buttock. 'They seem scarcely human,' she said. 'They have no buildings, no money, no clothes, no art – '

'No art? They draw beautifully.'

'With a burnt stick.'

'You yourself use charcoal, Mrs Tomson. Your charming portrait of your husband. . . .' Anne, aware she had spoken sharply, tried to soften her remark. She watched the man she'd been drawing rise to his feet with a soundless movement and slide away into the shadows. A soul seemed too heavy and serious an appendage for such a creature.

Mrs Tomson gathered up her sketching materials huffily and went away. Anne sat on. From the direction of the barracks came the sound of a trumpet being learned by an inept pupil. She remembered a boating party on Lough Derg, picnicking on an island, then drifting peacefully. Mr Osborne, giver of the party, had hired an orchestra which fiddled away valiantly until the rain stopped them. Mr Osborne. Whenever Anne thought about Ireland, she came up against something or somebody she wanted to forget. When James died, the money Miss Eliza left him had reverted to Hetty. Anne was pleased for her sister, but worried sick about Henry's finances.

She sighed aloud. Just when their lives had been taking on some kind of order, there was going to be an uprising. Both she and Henry knew the signs too well. And she, with three young children and another due before Christmas, had to play the model parson's wife at Government House while daily expecting the bailiffs.

Chapter Thirty-One

When Marsden went to England, Henry Fulton was the only Anglican minister in the colony. He couldn't begin to cover the vast area allotted to him, so he appointed a number of lay readers. Even then, his Sundays left him tired out. He frequently took four services and rode sixty miles.

During the week, he visited the sick and gave bible lessons to children. He rode where no preacher had gone before, through swamp and bush to distant settlements. He was welcomed everywhere and felt needed. His life had changed course, and once more he had a sense of purpose. He sang to himself as he trotted along the overgrown tracks. He particularly liked preaching at the Hawkesbury, because the settlers there were totally loyal to Captain Bligh.

Unexpectedly summoned to Government House, Henry found Bligh pacing up and down in a towering rage. These rages had lost their power to alarm him long before. He stood waiting while the short, sturdy figure, with dark curly hair going grey and dark eyes in a pale face, strode to and fro, alternately swearing and begging Henry's pardon.

He had a document in his hand, and at last calmed himself enough to read it aloud. It was from Samuel Marsden, and concerned the payment of Henry's stipend in kind, by a horse, value £70 and ten wethers value £7 each. When the wethers were sold, in Marsden's absence, Henry was to receive a minimum of £50, to allow for losses.

'Now I know why you visit the moneylenders! Now I know why you agree to ride that stiff-legged old troop horse! I took you for an extravagant man – a gambler perhaps – I know you are moderate in drink. Only wait until that smooth-tongued canting bastard – begging your pardon – '

'There's no need to beg my pardon,' said Henry. 'I share your opinion and have cursed him myself often enough.'

'He told me you were greedy, never satisfied, always whining for this or that. Bloody hypocrite! And I can give you no government money – it isn't mine to give. I can grant you a piece of land which you may lease, but not within twenty miles. What is near at hand is spoken for. Marsden has five thousand acres and more sheep than he can count. He takes Our Lord's advice to feed his sheep literally, may he rot.' As he paced, Bligh's foot knocked against a footstool. He sent it crashing into a corner with a well-aimed kick.

'You will draw no rent until next year. All I can offer is a gift. You know your needs. What is it to be?'

'You have made me a member of the Civil Court, sir. That is better than any gift you could offer me. You have restored my self-respect.'

'Pah! An appointment is not a gift. It bears no relation to your clerical duties. Think again.'

'Thank you. May I keep that horse? I can't manage without it. My poor old mare died last week.'

'Oh, bugger the horse – beg pardon – it's yours. No, something better than that. Well? What would you like?'

'Captain Bligh, you are very good, but should you give us anything?' Henry spoke diffidently, fearing an explosion. 'I don't know if you realise it, but many people are finding fault with you for entrusting a parson who came to the colony in chains with such an appointment. Since you were obliged to send Mr Macarthur to prison, I have been worried by what I have heard. Perhaps if you were to give my wife a kid goat for Christmas it wouldn't be remarked. She kept several on Norfolk Island, and she and the children miss the milk.'

'God's teeth man, I can't give her a goat. What about a carriage and a pony to draw it?'

'I'm serious, sir. You mustn't give us anything of value. You will make trouble for yourself.'

The explosion came. 'Trouble?' The sudden yell made the glasses on the sideboard ring. 'I've fought on the high seas, faced typhoons, cannibals, mutineers and the Dutch fleet, and you talk to me about trouble? A parcel of petty officials and a few companies of drunken militia? Mr Fulton sir, you don't know what trouble is.'

Oh, don't I? thought Henry, but it was never wise to argue with

Bligh, and he went home not a penny richer, but knowing that technically, at least, he would soon be a landowner.

Anne, once she had grown accustomed to Bligh's temperament, enjoyed visiting Government House with Henry. A lack of social graces in her host failed to bother her. She preferred his company to that of the newly rich ladies of Sydney. Meals with Bligh could be stormy affairs, for Mary Putland had inherited her father's masterful nature as well as his dark eyes and curly hair. Her husband, a quiet, delicate man, picked at his food, while his wife and father-in-law wrangled. Her devotion to Bligh was evident with every look and word. He could do no wrong, but she couldn't agree with him.

Mary, who called on Anne often, bullied her in the kindest way – Anne seemed to comply while doing just as she wanted. One could not argue with Mary – it was too tiring. Sarah, a bright eight-year-old, had been learning from both her parents, and impressed Mary with her progress.

'You and Mr Fulton should start a school,' Mary said firmly, as she examined the neat sums on Sarah's slate.

'There's nothing we would like better,' Anne said. 'But Henry's work and our family forbid it.' She shifted her bulk on the settee with a sigh. 'I shall be glad when this baby is born,' she said. 'I have never felt the heat so much.'

They were sitting in the parsonage living room, because it was slightly cooler than the verandah. Sarah worked at her sums while John and Lydia played on the floor.

There were voices outside, then the housekeeper knocked and came in, a look of outrage on her face. 'There are some persons outside, ma'am. They wish to see you.' She withdrew, shutting the kitchen door with emphasis.

Mary giggled. 'Go on, Anne. A surprise for you.'

'Now what have you thought up? Mrs Brick wasn't impressed.' Anne went to the open door.

Outside were two soldiers leading a red and white cow on a halter. 'Governor's compliments ma'am, and he begs you will accept this cow.'

Mrs Fulton's cow was one of the subjects which John Macarthur's revolutionary committee discussed at their next meeting. True,

Macarthur was not present but in gaol. His place was taken by Major George Johnston, commander of the 'Rum Corps'.

The governor's impartial treatment of emancipists and settlers was a burning issue. It was conveniently forgotten that a man convicted of murder had been a frequent guest at Governor King's table.

Bligh had bought the cow from a farmer – as he was entitled to do – and had given it to Mrs Fulton, who had given birth to a son that week. 'Mrs Fulton is a free woman,' said Captain Kemp.

'No,' said Johnston, 'for she is a part of her husband's household, numbered among his possessions. The wife of a convict is as free as he is, no more, no less. She is an emancipist.'

There were murmurs of agreement, and Mrs Fulton's cow was just one of the factors which helped to damn Captain Bligh.

The housekeeper, Mrs Brick, had a son in the 'Rum Corps', and kept him informed of any supposed irregularities in the Fulton household. The worst of them, in her eyes, was Anne's distribution of herbal remedies to all and sundry, regardless of their social standing.

Ex-convict Mick Fry came to her, complaining of a recurring ulcer where his fetters had chafed him. She dressed it with a strong syrup of sugar and water, telling him that honey was even better. His wife, a game pullet if ever Mrs Brick had seen one, was actually invited into the parlour – they both were. Mrs Cait Fry, a dazzling redhead, wore a silk gown and carried a parasol, but Mrs Brick was not deceived. 'Not even a currency lass, but an Irish slut,' she muttered.

Henry, run off his feet at Christmas, was at home only to eat and sleep. Anne didn't mind. His whole manner had changed. He was like the man she had married – impetuous, confident, funny and tender. He wanted to name the baby William, after Bligh, but Anne wouldn't hear of it. 'No,' she said, 'it's high time we called a child after you. He must be Henry.'

'You refused flatly to call any of the girls Anne.'

'Next time,' said Anne, feeling fairly sure there wouldn't be a next time. She was beginning to feel that the last of her youth had gone, although it didn't worry her particularly.

Anne made full use of the cow. She milked it herself and as well as milk and cream, provided the family with butter, curds and whey and two sorts of cheese. It lived on waste ground, tethered on a long rope. Henry failed to master the art of milking. He was allowed to hold the rope and carry the bucket.

'Anne,' he said, 'have you heard any rumours about a military coup against Captain Bligh? I thought we were going to have a mutiny in court today, when Macarthur's case came up. If he had been refused bail, we would all have been in trouble.'

'I hear murmurs – nothing to alarm one. Mary Putland is sure trouble is coming, but I think she enjoys it. Poor Mary – her husband is very sick. She came to me for a tisane for him.'

'As to Mary,' Henry said, 'she would take on the defence of the residence single-handed. She is her father over again.' He swatted flies on the cow's neck, a deep crease between his brows. 'I hope I haven't helped to put the governor in danger by accepting a post in the Civil Court,' he said.

Anne stopped milking. 'No, love, you haven't, because you both work for justice. Surely all decent people want an end to monopolies? And sooner or later, this colony must use currency like anywhere else.'

'I think there is a shortage of decent people. Most of the settlers prefer to trade like explorers. They would barter beads and mirrors if there was no rum.'

Anne stood up, and Henry took the foaming pail from her. They walked back to their parsonage, his arm round her waist. 'Don't let's talk about mutiny,' Anne said. 'We are just becoming secure and happy here, after almost eight years of insecurity. Mary thinks we should start a school and so do I.'

'Why, that's a famous notion. I miss my Norfolk chickens. By the time we are old, this country should be a place our children can be proud of. It would be grand if we could help to make it so. Wait until there are more clergy to take some of my duties, then we will start our academy.'

As he set down the pail, a servant came running from Government House. 'Come at once, sir. Lieutenant Putland is dying.'

Henry grabbed his bag, with materials for Communion in it, and ran.

January 1808 was a momentous month for Captain Bligh. He found himself in a position where he could do nothing without vexing some powerful enemy. He had angered the settlers by curbing their monopolies; his only way of enforcing his will was by using the army. But he had angered the army by stopping their abuse of the rum trade. He had made two great and necessary reforms, and owing to his tactlessness and his habit of doing what he thought was right regardless of others, he seemed likely to lose his command – possibly even his life.

He talked freely to Henry, who had backed him in everything and whose ideas of reform were as arbitrary as Bligh's own. 'If this house is attacked,' Bligh said, 'I will burn my papers and escape to the Hawkesbury. There are enough loyal men there to return with me and retake Government House. I would rely on you to delay the attackers while I leave by the back of the building. I would gain nothing by remaining and allowing myself to be imprisoned.'

'How do you expect me to delay an army?' Henry asked with interest.

'Bar their way. Threaten them with hell fire. They won't lay hands on a man of God.'

'I hope you are right,' said Henry doubtfully. His experience had been the opposite.

The situation eased for a while, and was forgotten temporarily in Bligh's household when Lieutenant Putland died after a two weeks' illness. Henry took the burial service at George Street in Sydney, where he and Anne had erected a gravestone to James and Jane.

Then John Macarthur's case came up again, and he was freed on bail. It seemed likely that he made use of his freedom to stir up his followers, especially Major George Johnston, to depose Bligh. Meanwhile, Bligh had sent for Johnston, as head of the 'Rum Corps', to defuse any revolutionary action that might be brewing up. Johnston had fallen out of his carriage when he was drunk, and was suffering from a bruised arm and a hangover. He said he couldn't possibly come in such a state. It might kill him.

The next morning Macarthur was rearrested, and put in gaol. Macarthur's friends sent a message to Bligh, saying that he had been imprisoned on false evidence and demanding his release. Bligh ignored the letter, and a war of nerves continued all day. Late in the afternoon, Bligh decided that he must take some action. It was getting plainer all the time that the army was going to refuse to take orders from a sailor. He ordered the members of the magistrate's court to assemble at his residence.

Henry had just returned from Parramatta, and was looking forward to a quiet evening with Anne and the children. The atmosphere in Sydney was tense, and groups of people suddenly stopped talking when they saw him. At the barracks, almost half a mile from Bligh's residence, there was a hubbub of noise, and the greater part of the garrison seemed to be in the parade ground. Glad that Government House stood between his own home and the town, Henry obeyed the summons to wait on Captain Bligh immediately.

He found the other members of the court already there. One or two who lived close to the barracks had brought their wives. A meal was on the table, and Mary Putland, her face white with anger against her black mourning dress, was pouring wine. It was still very hot, and Bligh, also in mourning, had discarded his coat and neckcloth. He was not the man to baulk at dining in his shirtsleeves if it suited him.

It was now five o'clock on January 26th. Henry ate his meal uneasily, then he and Richard Atkins, the Judge Advocate, went to see what the 'Rum Corps' was doing. They were arming in the barrack square; fixing bayonets and priming their muskets. The two men ran back to report, elbowing through a rabble of country people, many of them drunk, who had gathered at the other end of town and were being harangued by one of their number.

Henry easily outdistanced Atkins and brought the news to Bligh, who forgot the ladies present with an oath which seemed to upset them more than the possibility of being murdered. Bligh begged pardon automatically. 'You don't think they mean to assassinate me, do you?' he asked.

'Hardly, but I wouldn't rule it out.' Henry was panting.

Bligh drained his glass of wine. 'The King, God bless him,' he said, and hurled the cut crystal goblet into the fireplace.

As the glass smashed, they all heard the drums beating to arms, and the notes of a bugle. The beat was as ragged as ever, and was accompanied by what might have been bellowed orders. Then screams and yells, male and female, broke out, and the dinner guests rushed to the front window.

Captain Bligh said to Henry, 'Take all the women into the parlour and keep them there.' They didn't need to be told twice, but picked up their skirts and ran – except for Mary Putland.

She went to Bligh and impulsively kissed him. 'Go and put on your dress uniform, Papa. Mr Fulton and I will deal with this drunken rabble.' She turned to Henry, her eyes sparkling with excitement. 'We will send them to the rightabout, won't we?'

The other men who had been dining found it necessary to go to the parlour to reassure the ladies, so Henry and Mary were alone in the hall as Bligh went to turn out the Government House guard. When they were paraded, and their commander had ordered them to prime their muskets, Bligh returned.

By now, the band could be heard rendering 'The British Grenadiers', a curious choice for mutineers. The leaders paused long enough to hand a letter to William Gore, the Provost Marshal. Bligh had started upstairs, shouting to his servant to get out his uniform and sword, when Gore called him. The letter was an order for Macarthur's release.

Bligh turned back, still in shirt and breeches, and snatched it from him. It was signed by 'Major George Johnston, Lieutenant Governor'. This was open rebellion.

Behind Gore strolled a small party of officers, elaborately casual, cold sober, watching every move.

'I am to ask you to sign this order, sir.' Gore spoke with habitual deference. 'It was written by Major Johnston.'

'I'll see him fry in hell first.' Bligh's voice was shaking, 'And Macarthur too, damn his soul. Tell him so.'

Gore left hastily, and Bligh dashed upstairs, roaring for his servant, John Dunn, and his secretary Edmund Griffin. Now the soldiers were surging across the lawn and the time had come for his escape to the Hawkesbury. Impressive at a distance, in their black shakos, scarlet tunics and white crossbelts, close to the soldiers made a less good impression. Some were roaring drunk, and they were at any time a badly drilled horde. Their faces were glistening with sweat and their gaitered legs kept time only spasmodically.

When they reached the two brass cannons in front of the great embellished cottage which was Government House, two soldiers turned them round so they were trained on the residence. This was only a gesture. Everyone knew they were not in working order.

Henry decided the time had come to bar the front door, as nobody seemed anxious to defend it with him. He put out his hand to lead Mary Putland inside, but she leaped forward, white with rage, and accosted the two leading officers who were advancing with drawn swords.

'You rebels,' she screamed. 'You traitors. You have marched over my husband's grave, are you now going to murder my father?'

Mrs Putland was only five feet tall, and slightly built. Her hair in its Grecian curls was escaping from a black ribbon. She carried a black silk parasol, rolled up; a pretty thing with ruffles round it. As Henry ran to prevent her from being hurt, she swung the parasol with both hands and brought it down on Captain Kemp's head. It snapped harmlessly and she lashed out at the other soldier with the broken remains. Henry caught her arm and dragged her back as she shouted furiously, 'Cowards. Stab me if you must, but spare my father.' As the men brushed her aside, Henry firmly hauled her across the lawn and through the front door which he closed behind them.

The house was not designed for a siege, or even for temporary defence. The upper half of the main door was glass, and Henry looked through it, keeping Mary Putland behind him with some difficulty. He was relieved to see that the soldiers weren't aiming their muskets; some of them, nonplussed by Mary's attack, were standing back, while the officers he recognised, Captain Kemp and Lieutenant Lawson, approached the shut glass door with their swords drawn.

'Open up!'

The bawled words would have carried half a mile. 'I will not,' shouted Henry, almost as loudly. Aside, he tried to persuade Mary to join the other women, but she refused indignantly.

'We mean to enter, whether you open the door or not.' Captain Kemp raised his sword as if to break the glass with the hilt.

'Over my dead body!' Henry knew he was sounding melodramatic, but he hadn't time to pick his words. He meant them literally, and the officers could see that he did. He sensed that these two men were not altogether happy about arresting the governor, although most of the army hated him. Perhaps it would seem an even less good idea when their blood had cooled. They were not, at any rate, prepared to kill a popular and respected clergyman. They changed their tone.

293

'We would be obliged if you would tell Captain Bligh that we want to speak to him,' said Lawson.

'The governor will see you when he is ready.' As Henry spoke, he was hoping devoutly that Bligh's stout body would not get jammed in a window-frame. How long would it take him to bundle his papers into a fireplace and set them alight, scramble out, get across the yard to the stables and saddle a horse? It was only a matter of seconds before the two officers would stop shuffling about looking embarrassed and force him to produce further delaying action. . . . But the necessity did not arise. Suddenly at his elbow Mary cried out, 'Our guard has deserted – the soldiers are in the house!' Her bedroom was on the ground floor, with a door into the garden: the soldiers had kicked the door down and were streaming through her room. Henry gave up trying to defend the front door as Mary broke away from him, grabbed a candlestick from a side-table and hurled it at a man who had paused to look at the trinkets on her dressing-table. Her aim was poor, and it crashed harmlessly to the floor. Henry caught her firmly by the wrists. 'Please, ma'am, do not anger them. You will make things worse for your father.'

The plea succeeded, as he knew it would. Mary had been known to throw a plate at Bligh during one of their quarrels, but she saw the sense of Henry's words and burst into furious tears.

The soldiers herded everyone into the parlour – everyone, that is, except Bligh. Henry's hopes rose – but were soon dashed again by the appearance of the governor himself, hot, dishevelled, bursting with rage, being shoved down the stairs by Lieutenant Minchin. Bligh was in his dress uniform. Had he abandoned the idea of flight to the Hawkesbury at the last minute and decided to confront the mutineers on the spot in the full dignity of his office, or had he changed into dress uniform to make his arrival at the Hawkesbury more impressive? An unimportant question, Henry concluded, as he had to watch his hero put under arrest, along with his secretary and some members of the Civil Court. After which, Henry was told contemptuously to go home and stay there.

Torn between worry about his family and loyalty to Bligh, he did as he was told. Two soldiers escorted him home. It was now quite dark, and he saw Anne outlined in their lighted doorway with little Harry in her arms. Sarah pushed past her when she saw Henry and ran and jumped into his arms. 'Papa, Papa. The soldiers took her cow. They said she wasn't ours ever. Oh please Papa, make them give us back our cow.'

'Hush, my poppet. The cow will be quite happy for a day or two, and I'll get her back if I can. Gracious, what a big heavy lass you are.' He set her down and took Anne indoors. 'Anne, love, have they frightened you? I have been thinking of you all day.'

'Thank God you are back. No, we were only frightened for you. We heard such a commotion, and the men who took the cow were most uncivil. Mrs Brick left at the first sound of the drums, but we won't miss her overmuch, will we? Tell me about Captain Bligh and Mary.'

Henry looked round at the two soldiers. 'Good evening gentlemen,' he said. Both saluted their prisoner and went out, closing the door.

Anne poured Henry a tot of rum, and he told her everything that had happened while she put the children to bed. Later, she and Henry lay in bed listening to bursting rockets and firecrackers and to drunken whoops and cheers. Henry held her close, wondering how much more ill fortune he would bring to the woman he loved so dearly.

Three days later, an officer came to the parsonage and told Henry that he was to see Major Johnston at the barracks. He went with his escort, but found no Johnston there. Instead, he was faced by a revolutionary court and roughly interrogated.

'Do you agree that the governor has behaved with impropriety?' The question was repeated over and over in different ways by different speakers. Henry replied obstinately that he did not. He added that mutineers had no right to speak of impropriety.

'Do you want to retain your position as principal chaplain? You shall if you admit that we were right to depose Bligh. If not, you will be suspended.'

'How dare you try to bribe me,' Henry said indignantly. 'My opinion is unchanged, but I argue your power to suspend me.'

'Will we be allowed to stay here?' asked Anne when he told her.

'Why not? There is no other parson to take my place. They would have to bring in one of the missionaries.' But that evening, Henry, Anne and the four children were turned into the street with what they could carry. They walked into the town and tried to find lodgings with social acquaintances. The ladies of Sydney, however, were waiting to discover which was the winning side before committing theselves. At nightfall, the family was taken in by a storekeeper and his wife, who had only a small attic to offer.

They settled down gratefully. To people who had spent ten months on the *Minerva*, any room was large enough.

Chapter Thirty-Two

Mr and Mrs Hogg were free settlers who sold cloth and light hardware. When they took in the Fulton family, they immediately lost the custom of the 'Rum Corps' and their women, as well as that of the better-off layer of Sydney society.

'No matter,' said Jethro Hogg, a staunch churchman and an admirer of Henry's sermons. 'We will come about when Governor Bligh is restored to power.'

Amabel, his wife, said, 'I trust it will be soon. We cannot afford to lose customers.'

'Hush, my dear. We have chosen the right road and we will reap our reward.' Jethro tied on his apron and went into the empty shop.

Anne, as usual, had only what money she needed for the next few days. She had to buy food for six, and the Hoggs sold no food. She went to another shop, with Sarah hanging on her arm and asking questions. 'Why are we living here? Why is Papa not taking service? What is happening to Captain Bligh? Why doesn't Mrs Putland come to see us any more? When will the soldiers bring back our cow? Where is Papa?'

Papa was visiting the moneylender. Officially suspended by the military cabal now in command, and deprived of the grant of land Bligh had earmarked for him, he was unemployed, homeless and penniless. He negotiated a loan at a high rate of interest, and bought a little wooden house with a shingled roof. It was sandwiched between two mansions, at the seaward end of the town, and wasn't unlike their first home there.

He had left his horse tied outside the moneylender's office. When he came out, it had gone. He often saw it after that, back with the 'Rum Corps'. There was nothing he could do – it would be argued that he had no right to the animal in the first place. Annoyingly, it was now the mount of Elijah Brick, son of his departed housekeeper.

The next day, the family moved out of Jethro Hogg's attic, and by dinnertime had settled themselves in their new cottage. Anne liked it. Although it was tiny, their few pieces of furniture looked less lost than in the parsonage, and there was no need for a Mrs Brick.

On Sunday, they went to the church, which Bligh had been rebuilding. He had sent workmen into it the day after his official appointment, and had put aside a large sum for the completion of the building. It still lacked a spire, but was fully enclosed, and the inside nearly finished. Henry had preached in it at every stage. He had stood within its walls when they were barely waist high, with a kitchen table which served as an altar, to pray for rain. He had knelt at a new priedieu within head-high walls, under a leaking, temporary roof, and prayed for deliverance from flood. Now he knelt at the back of the building with his wife and family, while a corporal watched to see that he made no attempt to go into the chancel. He had been given official notice of his suspension, for 'failing to own the impropriety of ex-Governor Bligh's behaviour, and for introducing a prayer for said Bligh into the Liturgy'.

Bligh's secretary had been arrested and taken to prison, but his servant, John Dunne, was allowed to stay with him at Government House. He was also allowed to run errands for the ex-governor, with a military escort. Mrs Putland, a lady feared by the rebels, was obliged to stay indoors with her father. John Dunne brought word to Henry that he was needed at Government House.

He found Bligh in full naval uniform but without his dress sword. He was seated at his desk, writing and talking to himself. He jumped to his feet and wrung Henry's hand, telling him to sit down. They had been left alone. Henry began to say something about the mutiny and was loudly interrupted.

'Never mind that. What's done is done. What could you expect from a horde of ignorant soldiers? Now, had I been given a few score of seamen, or even marines, all would have been different.' Bligh crossed his short legs in their silk stockings, and watched Henry's face. 'When I saw you first,' he went on, 'I thought to myself, well, here's a curst great maypole of a preacher – oddest looking fellow ever wore a cassock. Ah well, I suppose I must put up with him. But I find you are what is as rare as a repentant pirate – a completely honest man.'

'Come now, sir,' said Henry embarrassed, 'I may be honest, but so are the majority – '

'*If* you would let me finish. Thank you. I believe there are convicts here, working in chains, more honest than the majority. I hope there are. As for you, it is scandalous that you should be suspended and left homeless. I have written to the Colonial Secretary on the subject. In the meantime, I appoint you as my private chaplain.'

'I am honoured, sir. Many thanks.' Henry again shook the offered hand. 'I am delighted to accept the post on a voluntary basis, until you are reinstated. If you make this an official appointment during my suspension, I will probably be arrested as soon as I leave the house.'

Bligh's angry roar made his servant, whose ear was glued to the keyhole, back away hastily. 'How dare you, Mr Fulton, sir! Deposed as governor of this dunghill I may be, but I am still captain of my ship. Nobody but their lordships of the Admiralty can change that. Do you realise that I left a sixty-four gun warship to rule this godforsaken Sodom? I am a captain in his Majesty's navy, and entitled to a chaplain. Have you any further questions?'

'No, none,' said Henry faintly. 'Thank you, sir.'

'I regret that I cannot give houseroom to your family,' Bligh went on. 'I am allowed no guests. But you may come each morning to say prayers – ' he leaped suddenly to his feet and whipped the door open. 'Eavesdropping? I thought as much. Get below, God blast your squinting eyes.' He returned to the table, adjusted his coat tails and sat down. 'Now that we are not overheard, tell me what goes forth.'

'As far as I know,' said Henry, 'Major Johnston has no stomach for ruling here. He is at home, while Macarthur gives the orders. His friends chaired him round the town last night. They say that Johnston has written to Colonel Paterson in Van Diemen's Land to come and take over. There is nothing but confusion.'

'Paterson? Hasn't he drunk himself to death yet? Give him time – he will. As for Johnston, it is my firm belief that he is the bastard of some powerful nobleman. What other reason could there be for his preferment?' Bligh fetched a decanter of rum from the sideboard and poured two generous measures. 'To my new chaplain,' he said raising his glass.

'To my new ship,' said Henry, raising his.

★

299

Henry quickly settled in as a member of Bligh's household. He came and went pretty much as he pleased, spending more time with his family than since leaving Norfolk Island. Anne, most resilient of women, adapted to the change as she had adapted to all the others. Those who were loyal to Bligh, and there were many, were loyal to the Fultons too, and Anne didn't regret the others.

All the abuses of the rum trade returned, and Macarthur carried on his shady deals unchecked. Johnston, who had certainly bitten off more than he could chew, anxiously waited the arrival of Colonel Paterson, but Paterson stayed where he was. In July, a ship called at Sydney coming from London and on her way to Norfolk Island. On board was Major, now Lieutenant Colonel, Fouveaux, on his way back to his command. He agreed to take over until Paterson should rouse himself to come.

Although all Fouveaux's excesses had been condoned by London, he couldn't shake off his evil reputation in Australia. He assumed control without a soul to cheer him, unable to walk the streets without insults, gibes and snatches of bawdy verse being shouted from doorways.

Henry avoided meeting him, and refused an invitation to his house without troubling to give a reason. Fouveaux made a crafty proclamation, saying that the new administration was as bad as the old, and explaining that he was the man to mend the mistakes of both. He wound up with a long eulogy addressed to himself, having neatly avoided taking sides in the event of a counter-revolution.

He and Henry met face to face at Government House. Fouveaux was visiting Bligh officially, with the purpose of getting him to go to England. When Henry arrived, he heard Bligh shouting before he reached the door, and Mary Putland met him in the hall in a fine rage. Before she had time to explain, Bligh's door burst open, and Fouveaux came out in a hurry.

Fouveaux's devious mind quickly decided that Henry, as a friend of Bligh's, could be a useful ally. After the briefest of greetings, he tried to take him by the arm with an ingratiating smile. The smile was a mistake. Henry had last seen it when Cait was about to be flogged. He stepped out of reach, saying, 'Major Fouveaux, I believe we have nothing to say to each other.' With that, he went to Bligh's door and Mary opened it for him with a grateful smile. Then she told the servant to show Fouveaux out.

Fouveaux went home and wrote a letter to Colonel Paterson which he hoped would keep him away from Sydney. In it, he alleged that Captain Bligh, Henry Fulton and two others had 'monopolised the stores and revenues of the colony', and 'caused terror amongst all classes of people from the highest to the most obscure'. He accused Bligh of planning to ruin the settlers, and even of encouraging the barter of rum.

Meanwhile, Henry was writing to the Colonial Secretary with an eyewitness account of Fouveaux's brutality in Norfolk Island. He protested that Fouveaux was unfit to hold any position of trust. A letter from Fouveaux travelled on the same ship, complaining that Bligh was employing the 'renegade minister' who had plotted with him to despoil the inhabitants of Sydney.

In January, Colonel Paterson arrived from Van Diemen's Land to take over, and Henry sighed with relief. However, far from opposing Fouveaux, he at once retired to Parramatta and got on with the business of drinking himself to death. From there, he wrote to Bligh, demanding the use of the *Porpoise* to evacuate Norfolk Island.

This was a touchy subject. *Porpoise* was Bligh's ship, and he had already been enraged when he heard that her officers were taking orders from the rebels. He had complained long and bitterly to Henry about it, and about the insults he had received from Johnston and Fouveaux. When he heard that these officers had actually been granted land, he wrote violent letters to the rebel administration, not mincing his words. As a result, he was put under close arrest, and orders were given that nobody might visit him.

The next day was Sunday, and Henry talked his way past the guards with difficulty, but, as he wasn't allowed to speak to Bligh or Mary, he had no idea what was going on. He took the service, and as soon as he had given the blessing he was escorted out of the building and told not to return until the following week. 'I shall return tomorrow as usual,' Henry said.

'You'll be wasting your time,' said the corporal who was guarding the door.

That January was so hot that even seasoned immigrants died of heatstroke. Anne and the children wilted indoors.

Henry came charging in at lunchtime that Sunday, full of the governor's new problems. He had been touchy and irritable of late;

his suspension irked and angered him. When Joseph Holt's son married, the ceremony had to be performed by a magistrate.

The next day, Anne tried to keep Henry at home, but of course he took no notice. There was a chaise outside the residence, its single horse fidgeting in a cloud of flies, and a larger than usual contingent of men from the 'Rum Corps' on guard. He went in, and met Bligh being marched out by half a dozen soldiers. Bligh didn't see Henry until he stood in his way, demanding an explanation from the guard. The soldier shrugged and shook his head.

Bligh recognised Henry with a start and spoke through clenched teeth. 'That drunken imbecile Paterson wants to use my ship, damn him to eternity!' Henry had never seen him so angry, even when the mutineers had stormed his house. 'I will *not* release my ship. I will *not* go to England – ' Bligh's voice rose as he was bundled into the chaise. 'Therefore I must be confined in a barrack only fit for. . . .' The door was slammed and the horse plodded away.

Henry accosted Major Johnston, who was in the hall. 'This is infamous. How can you justify taking Captain Bligh away?' He would have said more, but was interrupted by a scream, 'After them!' It was Mary Putland, racing down the stairs in her usual hot weather outfit of a flimsy muslin dress worn over cotton trousers instead of petticoats. This fashion, considered the last word in modishness in the governor's daughter, was now condemned as wanton and disgusting. Mary raced after the chaise, holding up her skirt, in the glare of the noon-day sun. Henry, in his cassock, had to pick up his own skirts as he set off in pursuit. Two soldiers seized his arms but he tore himself free.

The chaise was hidden in a cloud of dust a hundred yards ahead, while Mary, running steadily, was catching up with every stride. As Henry raced after them, sweating in his formal clothes, people stopped to stare, open-mouthed.

They reached the barracks almost together. Bligh was pushed into one of the two small rooms provided, but turned back to catch Mary as she fainted at his feet.

Henry was forced back by the sentry and the door slammed in his face, so he hurried back to the residence to arrange for personal servants for both to be sent to the barrack. Major Johnston agreed that Bligh's servant should go – as a prisoner – but said that Mary Putland, there by her own choice, could do without.

'Major Johnston, I left her unconscious. She has only her father to care for her, and while he will do what he can, she must have a woman to see to – '

'I won't allow it,' Johnston said. 'She should have stayed behind, immodest creature that she is. No wonder she swooned – running about in this heat.'

Henry controlled his temper. 'I am going home to write some letters,' he said. 'I will be back tomorrow, and I expect to find Mrs Putland's maid with her.' He went away, knowing that Johnston, who was no hand with a pen, was nervous of his influence. He had already once been called to order by London, as a result of Henry's impassioned defence of Captain Bligh. Mary got her maid after two days.

On Friday, Henry called at the barrack, to find that the prisoners had gone. Bligh had set sail in his disputed ship, the *Porpoise*, having agreed to go to England. Henry was amazed that he had gone so quietly, and wasn't surprised to hear, some time later, that Bligh had sailed only as far as Tasmania.

With Bligh gone, the outlook for the Fultons was gloomy. Henry was again invited to resume his duties, but only if he denounced Bligh. He remained obstinately loyal, writing to everyone he could think of on the ex-governor's behalf, and sending violently worded articles to papers which circulated in the part of India where his father had worked. These gave Bligh's point of view and denounced Fouveaux's regime in the baldest terms. English editors refused his contributions without acknowledgment.

'Perhaps you should try to compromise with the rebels,' Anne said. 'I can't imagine how we are to keep ourselves if you do not.'

'I can't, my love. Don't you see? I'd be placing myself in Fouveaux's employment. I would sweep the streets before I'd be disloyal to Captain Bligh. Think how much he has done for us.'

'We have debts to repay, nothing in the larder and four hungry children,' said Anne.

'I haven't forgotten. Tomorrow, I will go to every house where there are children and see if I can arrange some classes in mathematics. What I would give for some books. . . .'

Henry's classes started two days later in a large empty house. He used the walls for a blackboard, and his calculations reached almost to the ceiling in places. He was paid in cash and kind, and his temper improved every day. Gradually, the scope of his classes widened to include English grammar, Latin and botany. His lack of books cramped his efforts, but bit by bit he managed to borrow some.

A missionary had been sent from a remote area to do Henry's work in Sydney. He was a mild, vague man with papery thin ears through which the light shone oddly, making the children giggle. Henry had the utmost difficulty in keeping his thoughts Christian and charitable when this man took the service. As he walked home, silent and rigid with rage, Anne told him that there wasn't a pin to choose between him and Captain Bligh.

It was August before a clergyman arrived, as a result of Marsden's efforts. The Reverend William Cowper – a brave man, since he had come expecting to find the country in open rebellion – got on well with Henry. Cowper pleaded with Fouveaux to reinstate Henry; Johnston and Macarthur having gone to face charges in England. He was astonished at Fouveaux's violent rejection of the proposal.

The new governor, Lachlan Maquarie, arrived in December. Like Cowper, he had been led to expect opposition and perhaps a fight before he could take over, so he came with two ships and a strong detachment of soldiers. These were commanded by Lieutenant Colonel O'Connell, and were intended to replace the mutinous 'Rum Corps'.

The members of the 'Rum Corps', knowing they were to be sent to England and probably charged, fell over one another to inform on their comrades to the new commander. Each man pleaded total ignorance of anything to do with the mutiny. None dared to own loyalty either to Bligh or Fouveaux, for fear of making the wrong choice. Henry was invited to Government House once again.

Maquarie, a stern-faced Scot, was a humane man, and Henry liked him at once. At last he was able to give an account of the mutiny and the events of the year that followed to someone who listened patiently until he had finished. Maquarie had heard so much against Bligh that this new version astounded him. 'You realise', he said, 'that your support of the ex-governor has kept you suspended?'

'I would rather remain so for the rest of my life than bow to Fouveaux and his henchmen,' Henry said hotly.

'I believe that you have had to remove to a cottage, and that you are obliged to teach children without books or equipment in order to eat. Is that correct?'

'I am deeply in debt. I have borrowed a few books, but they are quite inadequate. If I could lay my hands on some text-books, I could offer a better service. There is so much opportunity for a teacher here – so little for a child. If I were reinstated I would like to open a small school. I've been wanting to do that ever since I returned from Norfolk Island.'

Maquarie was studying a handful of letters. 'All these letters concern you, Mr Fulton. They are written by Governors Hunter, King and Bligh and by a variety of other influential men, including a bishop. Only Mr Marsden and Fouveaux speak ill of you, and I would discount Fouveaux. That leaves a ratio of fourteen to one. I have taken steps to restore your position, and you may conduct Divine Service from tomorrow. We will now retire to the drawing-room for a brief ceremony.'

The ceremony was anything but brief. Parson Cowper preached for an hour and a half and Henry didn't take in a single word. He repeated some sentences after Cowper and bowed his head in order that his stole might be placed round his neck. He had refused from the start to abandon his clerical dress, and was glad of it that evening. He thanked the governor, shook the hands of various people and, as soon as he decently could, went home.

It was quite dark as Henry dashed through the camp, and past the English soldiers' tents. There he was challenged by a sentry and warned to take his time if he didn't want a bullet in his back. He hastened up the street to his own door, and his hand shook so that he could hardly turn the key in the lock.

Anne was in bed asleep. Looking down at her face on the pillow, with the lines of worry smoothed out, Henry thought he should let his news keep until morning. He undressed quietly, stepped into bed and slipped an arm round her. She woke at once, half sitting up, her eyes wide. 'Henry, what has happened? What has upset you? Is it something dreadful?'

'No, it's something wonderful. The governor has reinstated me. Oh, my darling, I was never as happy.' He kissed her lips and her eyes and his hands went to the buttons of her nightgown.

She had been refusing him of late, saying that the change of life had started and she was too old for such things. Now, in her joy for him, she came to him like a young girl.

'We'll call this one Anne,' Henry said sleepily.

'Dear heart, I'm forty-four.'

'Are you? No one would think it. Anne after you, and perhaps Elizabeth after Aunt Eliza. You haven't gone to sleep, have you?'

'No, I was thinking. I have the strangest feeling that I have indeed conceived again. I feel sure of it. If it is a boy, he shall be William after Captain Bligh. He might even stand godfather.'

EPILOGUE

Anne was right – she had conceived her seventh child – but what looked like an end of their troubles was only an interlude.

Bligh returned to Sydney in January 1809 to the great embarrassment of the new governor. In May that year he at last went back to England because Major Johnston was to be court martialled, and Henry, who believed he had found his true vocation, to preach and teach in a place where his talents were sorely needed, was obliged to leave his work and his pregnant wife. He expected to be away for a year, but in fact it wasn't until May 1811 that he arrived back in Sydney. By that time, his youngest daughter, Anne Elizabeth, was twenty months old.

Henry had been an important witness at the court martial which took place in May 1810. Johnston was cashiered and Bligh promoted to Rear Admiral, although he never held another post on land.

Henry remained in Sydney for a while, and resumed his teaching on a more regular basis. Later, he was chaplain in Castlereagh and Penrith. He was made a magistrate, and promoted philanthropic societies. But his great interest was in education, and he amassed a large library over the years. He was a well informed man who had been a good scholar, and enjoyed teaching.

He opened a formal school when he moved to Castlereagh House, his new parsonage. This 'Seminary for Young Gentlemen' specialised in classics, modern languages and mathematics. Charles Tompson, the first Australian-born poet, was one of his pupils, and praised him as a teacher and pastor in his poem 'Retrospect'. The book in which it appears was dedicated to Henry.

Little has been written about Anne. She died on August 4th, 1836, and Henry followed her on November 17th, 1840.

Henry Fulton

The Historical Facts

Henry Fulton may have been born in Lisburn in Co Antrim, although this is by no means certain. His family's eagerness to cover his tracks after his arrest has led to a researcher's nightmare of evidence lost and papers destroyed. Australian sources give 1761 as his date of birth but, according to the age given in the *Minerva*'s convict list, Henry Fulton was born in 1765.

Henry entered Trinity College Dublin as a pensioner in January 1788, and got his BA degree in 1792. In January 1795, he married Anne Walker, a clergyman's daughter from Roscrea in Co Tipperary. Anne's uncle was the noted scholar, writer and churchman Dr Thomas Leland, for many years Professor of Oratory at Trinity. Doctor Leland, who was also Vicar of Bray and Prebendary of St Patrick's Cathedral, lived with his family at number 18 Clare Street Dublin. The house, which still stands, next door to the Oriel Gallery, was close to that of diarist Sir Jonah Barrington. Barrington took the rebel leader Wolfe Tone under his wing for a time during the period when Tone was practising law and Henry was at Trinity.

Henry probably joined the United Irish Society when the movement was still non-violent and respectable. He was encouraged in religious liberalism by Dr William Knox. Knox was Chaplain to the Houses of Parliament when Henry was at Trinity. There is no record of Henry studying divinity – he was interested in law and mathematics. Knox, the only Irishman known to have supported Henry after his transportation, ordained him in Killaloe in September 1792, shortly after becoming bishop of the diocese.

Probably because of his marriage to Anne Walker, Henry is said to have served as curate in Roscrea, but I have found no proof of this. One of my sources suggests that he served in the parish of Aughrim in east Galway and, as there seems to be no good reason for inventing this, I have assumed it to be correct in this book. In September 1796, Henry obtained the curacy of the Kilmore Union near Nenagh in Co Tipperary, and was also made vicar of Monsea. The living of Monsea belonged to the Crannagh estate which has always been my home.

At this time Henry's first child, James, was about four months old; the next child, Jane, was born in February 1798. The only source of dates here is provided by the gravestone erected to the two children in Sydney. Henry and Anne lived at Kilmore, and Henry was employed as a tutor by the local landlord, Sir Henry Prittie, later the first Lord Dunally.

Henry Fulton visited his parishioners on foot, carried out his work as a tutor and undertook to organise the defence of his patron's house in case of an attack. The seemingly harmless curate, although he would have been obliged to renounce the United Irish movement before taking orders, was more deeply involved than ever before. He and the Roman Catholic parish priest, Father William O'Meara, were swearing in United Irishmen in the priest's house (which still stands in Nenagh) and also at Templederry, not far from Henry's parish of Kilmore.

A source which draws on the Dunally papers, which have since been destroyed, says that Henry and Father O'Meara were discovered swearing in United Irishmen in Nenagh. However, it was in Co Limerick, about twenty miles away, that they were caught and imprisoned. The captain of the Nenagh garrison was Henry's contemporary and probably knew him socially; I have guessed that his divided loyalties may have been the reason why a company of dragoons failed to catch the two men. Henry had been informed on by Benjamin Tydd, one of Sir Henry Prittie's tenants. The so-called 'confession' which Tydd obliged Henry to sign is in Dublin Castle. Henry claimed that he signed under threat of flogging, 'pitch-capping' and reprisals against his family. He refused however to implicate anyone else.

Both priests were arrested in May 1798 and sent to Limerick gaol: Henry was tried by the Civil Court at Tipperary town in August, but Father O'Meara doesn't reappear until much later, when both men were being removed from Waterford to Cork. The story of the abortive mutiny is true.

While Henry was in prison, three hundred of his parishioners signed a petition for his release which was sent to the magistrate, Sir Henry Osborne. This came to the notice of Lord Claremont, who wrote to Osborne for an explanation. Sadly, his letter and the petition itself have disappeared, but Osborne's vitriolic reply is in Dublin Castle and much of it is included in this book.

Henry was transported to Botany Bay fourteen months after his arrest, accompanied by his wife and children. His career in Australia is comparatively well documented, although his five years on Norfolk Island are not. About the time of the 'Rum Rebellion', Henry wrote a number of letters which have survived, some of which include eye-witness accounts of the taking of Government House and the arrest of Governor Bligh.

The dates of Henry's conditional pardon, his full pardon and the births of his children are included in the book, while events after the last chapter may be found in the epilogue. As time passed, Henry became an influential man, a magistrate and schoolmaster, running his own school, as well as a clergyman with churches at Castlereagh and Penrith. Nine hundred acres of land were granted to him, and his eldest surviving daughter, Sarah Leland Fulton, was granted 1,200 acres on her marriage to a settler. She named the area 'Roscrea'.